Alex Berenson graduated ~~~~~~~~~~~~~~~~~~ ~~ 1994,
with degrees in history and economics. After working at
the *Denver Post* he joined the *New York Times* in 1999. In
2003 he spent three months reporting on the occupation in
Iraq. He lives in New York City. The first John Wells
novel, *The Faithful Spy*, was an international No. 1
bestseller and won the 2007 Edgar® Award for Best First
Novel By An American Author, it was also shortlisted for
the CWA Ian Fleming Steel Dagger.

'Heart-pumping adventure' *USA Today*

'Terrific and relentless suspense and action'
Kirkus Reviews

'A smart, economically written spy novel'
New York Times

'A fast-paced story of international intrigue and
espionage … John Wells is a fine character who will
likely propel Berenson's thrillers to success for some
time to come' *Chicago Sun Times*

'The authenticity Berenson brings to his ripped-from-
the-headlines stories makes them seem as vividly real
and scary as nonfiction or the nightly news' *Booklist*

'Pulse-pounding... The author's plausible scenario
distinguishes this from most spy thrillers'
Publishers Weekly

By the same author

The Faithful Spy

the ghost agent

ALEX BERENSON

arrow books

Published by Arrow Books in 2008

1 3 5 7 9 10 8 6 4 2

Published by arrangement with G.P. Putnam's Sons, a division of
The Penguin Group (USA) Inc., New York

First published in the United Kingdom by Hutchinson in 2008

Arrow Books
The Random House Group Limited
20 Vauxhall Bridge Road, London SW1V 2SA

www.randomhouse.co.uk

Addresses for companies within The Random House Group Limited can be found
at: www.randomhouse.co.uk/offices.htm

The Random House Group Limited Reg. No. 954009

A CIP catalogue record for this book
is available from the British Library

ISBN 9780099517573

The Random House Group Limited supports The Forest Stewardship
Council (FSC), the leading international forest certification organisation. All our
titles that are printed on Greenpeace approved FSC certified paper carry the FSC
logo. Our paper procurement policy can be found at www.rbooks.co.uk/environment

Mixed Sources
Product group from well-managed
forests and other controlled sources
www.fsc.org Cert no. TF-COC-2139
© 1996 Forest Stewardship Council
FSC

Typeset by SX Composing DTP, Rayleigh, Essex
Printed in the UK by CPI Bookmarque, Croydon, CR0 4TD

For Ellen and Harvey, my parents

*Let China sleep, for when she wakes,
she will shake the world.*
— NAPOLEON

*Be subtle. Use your spies for every
kind of business.*

— SUN TZU,

The Art of War

Part I

ONE

INCHEON, SOUTH KOREA

Ted Beck walked west down the rotting pier, squinting through his wraparound sunglasses into the late-afternoon haze. He was alone, and he moved without haste. He'd arrived early, and the boat he'd come to meet was nowhere in sight.

Finally he reached the end of the dock. Trash from three countries – China and the two Koreas – bobbed in the dank water, the eastern edge of the Yellow Sea. The air was heavy with smoke from the ships that docked at Incheon every day to load up on cars and televisions for the United States. The sun had baked the fumes into a brown smog that burned Beck's throat and made him want a cigarette.

He fished a packet of Camel Lights from his pocket and lit up. He'd tried to quit over the years. But if he was going to sign up for missions like this one, what was the point? He smoked slowly and when he was done flicked the butt away. It spun into the harbor, joining the empty beer cans and condom wrappers.

Then he heard the low rumble of a boat engine.

Incheon was an industrial port fifty miles west of

Seoul and a few miles south of the Demilitarized Zone, the strip that separated North and South Korea. During the Korean War, General Douglas MacArthur had landed here, cutting behind North Korean lines to stop the Communist advance.

A statue of him stood atop a hill not far from this pier. Binoculars in hand, the general looked out to the Yellow Sea, which separated China and the Korean Peninsula. This afternoon, Beck would head into those waters, on a mission smaller than MacArthur's assault but just as dangerous.

The rumble of the distant boat grew louder. Beck pulled his wallet out of his pocket, a battered piece of cowhide that had seen him through thirty-two countries and three counterinsurgencies. He wasn't carrying any identification or a passport, just money. About $3,000 in all. And three pictures: his wife and their two sons. He took out the pictures and kissed them.

Then he flicked his lighter to them and watched them burn, holding them as long as he could, until the flames singed his fingers and he had to let them go. Their remnants sank into the water and drifted away.

Beck carried out the same ritual before every mission, for reasons both practical and superstitious. If he was caught, the photographs would give his captors a psychological edge. More important, burning the pictures was his way of accepting the danger of the mission. When he came back, he'd put fresh copies in his wallet. Until the next time.

The message had come in twelve days before, to a signals-intelligence station at Camp Bonifas, on the edge of the Demilitarized Zone. The six hundred Americans and South Koreans who lived at Bonifas

4

stayed on alert twenty-four hours a day, knowing they would be the world's tripwire if the North Korean army came over the DMZ. As they waited, they monitored the North's airwaves, listening for messages from American spies across the border.

To the officers at the Bonifas station, the transmission was gibberish, a twenty-two-second series of 1s and 0s. But they knew it meant something, for it came in on a shortwave frequency reserved for the highest-priority messages. They forwarded it around the world to Fort Meade, Maryland, the headquarters of the National Security Agency. From Fort Meade, the message, now decoded, took a shorter trip, across the Potomac to a seventh-floor office at CIA headquarters.

There it caused Vinny Duto, the director of the CIA, to unleash a few uncoded curses of his own. For the message was short, simple – and unwelcome. The Drafter wanted out of the Democratic People's Republic of Korea, the country-sized prison commonly called North Korea. Immediately if not sooner.

The Drafter's real name was Sung Kwan. Dr. Sung Kwan. He was a scientist in North Korea's nuclear program, and by far the most important asset the United States had in North Korea. 'Asset' was a rather clinical way to describe Sung, who was after all a person, not a spy satellite or a well-placed bug. But the term was fitting. For Sung had told the United States exactly where the North Koreans held their nuclear weapons – information that was priceless.

Most analysts outside the CIA thought that North Korea hid its nukes in caves, hoping to keep them safe from an American airstrike. They were wrong. In fact, the nukes were kept in a warehouse in Pyongyang, North Korea's capital. The Dear Leader, Kim Jong Il, wanted them close by, protected by the same army regiment that provided his personal security.

Now the USS *Lake Champlain*, a guided missile cruiser in the Sea of Japan, had a dozen Tomahawk missiles targeted on the building. If the order came, the Tomahawks could turn the warehouse into rubble in minutes. All thanks to Sung. And now he wanted an emergency exfiltration. No wonder Vinny Duto was upset.

Sung was a careful spy. He had met American agents only three times, each time in Pakistan, outside the Orwellian gaze of the North Korean secret police. But now something had gone wrong. In his message, Sung said he was concerned for his safety and believed he needed to get out of North Korea. He didn't explain more.

At Langley, the officers on the North Korea desk struggled to make sense of Sung's message. How did he know he was about to be taken in? Had he been interrogated? Or had he been arrested already, strung up and left to rot? In that case, the pickup request was nothing more than bait, an SOS from a man who had already drowned, meant to lure would-be rescuers into an ambush.

The CIA responded to Sung with its own shortwave broadcasts, asking him for more detail. But as the days ticked by, the listening station at Bonifas remained quiet.

Finally Duto decided that the agency had to send in a team. Without proof that the message was a trap, Langley couldn't ignore Sung's plea. The agency always promised its moles to respond if they asked for help. The vow was both a moral obligation and a recruiting tool. Moles needed to believe that their agency handlers shared the risks they took.

Three men were going in. Beck, the leader, was a former Navy Seal, now a senior officer in the agency's Special Operations Group. He was accompanied by Seth Kang, a Korean-American operative who'd infiltrated North Korea before, and Choe Gu, a lieutenant in the South Korean navy. All knew the risks of this mission. But they couldn't say no, not once they understood the stakes.

The Phantom looked fast even when it wasn't moving. The boat was matte black, narrow and long, with an arrow-shaped hull that came to a razor-sharp tip. It was a cigarette boat, the kind favored by drug runners for quick trips in calm seas. But in place of an open deck, like most cigarette boats, the Phantom had a cabin covering its cockpit, topped by a small forest of microwave dishes. Its windows were two-inch-thick bullet-resistant glass. For extra range the Phantom carried three gas tanks that held six hundred gallons in all. For extra protection its hull was coated with Kevlar. And for extra speed it had twin Mercury engines that threw out 650 horsepower apiece. At full throttle, it ran at seventy knots.

Langley had given Beck carte blanche to decide how to pull off Sung's extraction. A helicopter was out. The North Koreans operated radar stations every few miles on the coast. Beck had considered using a fishing trawler before deciding on the Phantom. The boat was practically invisible on radar, and surprisingly quiet, thanks to the oversized mufflers on the Mercurys. Plus, if the North Koreans were waiting for them, a speedboat would give them a chance of getting away.

The Phantom was based in Miami, where the CIA and Drug Enforcement Administration used it to chase drug traffickers around the Caribbean. Three days before, the agency had chartered a cargo jet and flown the boat in, landing it at Osan Air Base outside Seoul to avoid pesky Korean customs agents.

Beck and his men had spent two nights jetting around the Yellow Sea to learn the Phantom's quirks. The boat seemed to want to fly. Jam the throttles and its nose lifted from the water as the engines opened up.

Beck hoped that tonight they wouldn't have to take it anywhere near its limits.

Right on time, 5:00 p.m., the Phantom curled up to the dock. Beck hopped on and stepped into the pilothouse, feeling the slight sway of the boat beneath his feet. Inside, the air was crisp, and the tinted windows provided relief from the sun. Beck slipped his sunglasses into his jacket pocket. As he did, his fingers brushed across the plastic bag he had picked up that morning from the chief of Seoul station.

Before they left this dock he would have to tell Choe and Kang about what he was carrying in the bag. They deserved to know. They deserved the choice.

Kang sat in the navigator's chair, scrolling through satellite photographs of Point D, the pickup site. North of the DMZ, the Korean Peninsula widened, jutting west into the Yellow Sea toward China. Point D was located on a sliver of land a hundred miles northwest of Incheon. The satellite photos showed unbroken forests on the hills around the inlet. Haeju, the nearest city of any size, was fifty miles east.

Beck and his men would arrive at the landing spot at 2330 and wait thirty minutes. If Sung didn't show, they would assume he had changed his mind – or been killed – and wait for a new message.

'Simple enough,' Kang had said two days before, when Beck explained. 'What could go wrong?'

Beck hardly needed to answer. For starters, North Korea claimed control of the Yellow Sea well past the twelve-mile limit of international law. The North Korean navy had been known to fire on fishing trawlers unlucky enough to cross their path. The Phantom would have to dodge them. Then there were the shore artillery batteries along the coast. And the minefields, some new, others left over from the Korean War.

Not to mention the possibility that the North Koreans already had arrested Sung and set them up. With the help of the NSA, Langley had done what it could to make sure that the Phantom wasn't heading into an ambush. For the last week, spy satellites had watched the waters around the pickup spot, looking for overflights by the North Korean air force or unusual activity by the navy. So far the satellites hadn't picked anything up.

Meanwhile, Chinook rescue helicopters and F-16 jets were on standby at Osan and the Navy had moved the USS *Decatur*, a destroyer, into the Yellow Sea.

But the helicopters had strict orders against violating North Korean territory. Pyongyang would view an American incursion into its airspace as an act of war. And now that the North had nuclear weapons, Washington couldn't antagonize it needlessly.

But the Phantom was expendable. It didn't carry American markings, or any markings at all. If North Korea captured it, the United States and South Korea would disavow knowledge of its existence. Beck and his men would have to be well outside the twelve-mile limit, fifty or more miles from the North Korean coast, to expect a rescue. Any closer, and they were on their own.

The good news was that they weren't going in blind. The Phantom carried the newest military and civilian mapping equipment, including a Global Positioning System receiver capable of pinpointing its location to one meter. The receiver was synched to software that plotted the topography of every major body of water in the world. The combination allowed Kang, the navigator, to track their course in real time.

Meanwhile, a satellite transceiver connected the boat to an encrypted radar feed from an E-2 Hawkeye circling above the Yellow Sea. Thanks to the Hawkeye, the Phantom could dodge enemy boats without risking detection by using its own radar. Beck wanted to do everything possible to stay out of sight. If they got caught in a firefight, they'd already lost. They couldn't outshoot the North Korean navy.

And so Beck had dumped the .50-caliber machine gun the Phantom had carried when it arrived at Osan. In its place, he had added a Zodiac, an inflatable flat-bottomed boat with a small outboard motor. The Zodiac was loaded with fresh water, a first-aid kit, even a spear gun, and hooked to the hull of the Phantom.

Aside from the raft, Beck, Kang, and Choe hadn't brought much survival gear. They each had a change of clothes, in case they wound up in the water. They had personal transceivers, a more powerful version of the ones used by backcountry skiers, which sent a signal that the Chinooks could track. But they hadn't bothered with body armor or even helmets. Instead Kang, who'd grown up in South Florida, was wearing a Miami Dolphins hat – for luck, he said. They weren't being

10

nonchalant or cynical, Beck thought. They knew they would get out quickly or not at all.

Beck sat beside Kang, who was tracking the radar link from the Hawkeye on a titanium-hulled laptop attached to the Phantom's dash.

'How's it look around the LZ?' The landing zone.

'Quiet.' Kang was thirty-eight, though he looked younger. A tattoo of the ace of spades covered his right forearm, near the elbow. Beck had wondered about the tat for weeks, but he hadn't wanted to ask.

Kang tapped on the laptop's keyboard and the screen lit up with white blips. 'That's Incheon. What a real port looks like.' He clicked on the keyboard again and the screen returned to the dark area farther west. 'And that's North Korea. Dead as a whatever.'

'The good citizens of the Democratic People's Republic don't need the corruptions of the outside world.'

'Yeah. Like food.'

'Well, they managed to come up with a nuke,' Beck said. 'How's the boat running?'

'Choe says it looks great,' Kang said. He said something in Korean to Choe, who nodded vigorously. Beck's Korean was weak, and Choe's English was worse, so Kang played translator. Choe tapped the throttles forward. The engines rumbled and the Phantom's cabin began to vibrate.

Beck looked at his watch. 1725. He wanted to reach the landing zone at exactly 2330. No reason to spend more time in North Korean waters than necessary. The Yellow Sea was flat in the summer. If they wanted, they could run safely at sixty knots. But Beck preferred to keep them in the high teens. The slower pace would save fuel and keep noise to a minimum. They would leave here in five minutes, give themselves plenty of time.

But before they went . . . Beck touched the plastic bag in his pocket. He didn't want to have this conversation, but he saw no other choice. He motioned to Choe to cut the engine. The Phantom sat beside the dock, bobbing on the low waves.

'Before we go –' Beck pulled out the bag. Inside were three glass capsules. 'L pills.'

'L pills?' Choe shook his head in confusion.

'L for lethal. Cyanide.' Choe still wasn't getting it, Beck saw. 'Poison. If they catch us. You bite down on the glass.' He took a capsule out of the bag and pretended to put it in his mouth.

Choe slammed a hand against the dash of the boat and stammered angrily in Korean. Kang put a hand on Choe's arm, but Choe shook him off.

'He says you're crazy,' Kang said. 'He says –'

'Never, never,' Choe said in English.

'He says it's a sin.'

'Yes, sin.'

'Fine,' Beck said. 'But tell him he knows as well as we do, if we get caught, no one's coming for us. No prisoner exchange. And the North Koreans, they'll make it hell. These pills, they're quick, and they work.'

Kang translated, rapid-fire.

'One more thing,' Beck said. 'Tell him, he should at least carry it. So he has the choice.'

Choe shook his head, fired back in Korean, and turned away.

'He says no,' Kang said. 'He says even talking about it is bad luck.'

Beck ran his tongue over his teeth. His mouth felt

dirty and he knew he'd smoked too many Camels this day. 'More for me, then. You want yours?'

Kang reached out. Beck shook the little capsule, hardly an inch long, into his palm.

'Remember to give it back to me when we're done,' Beck said. 'You don't want these lying around the house.'

'Roger that.'

Beck stuffed the baggie with the other two pills into his jacket. He checked the disposable cell phone he'd bought the day before. His station chief had the number. If Langley had decided to abort the mission, the call would have come to this phone. But Beck hadn't been expecting a call, and sure enough, none had come. He looked once more at his watch. 1730.

'Let's go,' he said. 'Go west, young man.' Koreans called the Yellow Sea the West Sea.

'Yes, skipper,' Kang said. 'A three-hour tour, right?'

'Something like that.' Beck hummed the famous theme song, hoping to clear the cabin of the bad karma the pills had brought. 'Just sit right back and you'll hear a tale, a tale of a fateful trip.'

'Think Ginger and Mary Ann will be waiting for us in Pyongyang?'

'Let's hope we never find out. Sing it with me now. "If not for the courage of the fearless crew, the *Minnow* would be lost."'

'"The *Minnow* would be lost."'

If Choe got the joke, he didn't smile. He looked away, out the front window. He pushed forward on the throttle and the Phantom slid away.

13

TWO

Drink this and you'll grow wings on your feet.

John Wells wound down the throttle with his gloved right hand. Beneath him the engine groaned and the tachometer rolled toward 8,000 rpm and the big black bike jumped forward. Wells leaned close to the bike's angular gas tank to lower his profile against the wind. Still he had to fight to keep upright. The Honda was a meaty motorcycle, heavier and wider than a true racing bike.

Wells lifted his head and peeked at the speedometer. Ninety. He'd imagined faster. Beside him the highway was a blur, the trees beside the road blending into a single leafy cipher. He was halfway between Washington and Baltimore, hardly a rural oasis, but at 3:00 a.m. even the interstate was empty. At this speed the road's curves disappeared in the dark. Interstates were built for bad drivers, Wells knew, grandmothers heading to the mall, truckers high on meth and anxious to get home. They were built with soft curves to forgive mistakes.

Even so, Wells was pushing the limits of this highway. Anything could take him out. A raccoon prospecting for garbage. A car changing lanes and forgetting to signal. A broken bottle blowing out his front tire, sending him over the handlebars and into eternity. A stupid, pointless way to go. Yet here he was in the dark, as he'd been the week before, and the week before that, on the nights when midnight and 1:00 a.m. came and went and sleep remained foreign territory.

Here the rich, smooth pavement soothed him. The speed made his mind vanish, leaving him with snatches of half-remembered songs, some old, some new. The words blended into a strange poetry he could never remember when the rides were done.

Wells relaxed the throttle and the tach and the speedometer dropped in unison. At seventy-five the wind dropped slightly and the Springsteen in his head faded.

From his earlier rides he knew he was approaching the sweet spot. He slowed to sixty as the road lifted him gently over a low hill. The trees disappeared. To his right, a shopping center parking lot glowed under over-sized lights. Behind a blue dumpster, two police cars nuzzled beside each other, windows down, the cops inside telling each other stories to make the night pass. Just a few hours to go. It was close to 5:00 a.m., and the sun would be up soon enough. Wells thought of Exley, alone now in their bed, wondering when he'd be back, and in how many pieces.

Jennifer Exley, his girlfriend. His boss at the Central Intelligence Agency, where he worked as a – as a what? Hard to say. Last year he and Exley had stopped a terrorist attack that would have dwarfed September 11. Now he was back in Washington, and – how to put this politely? – at loose ends. Osama bin Laden wasn't happy with him, that much was certain. In an hourlong communiqué that even Wells hadn't bothered to sit through, bin Laden had promised eternal glory to

15

anyone who killed him. 'Allah will smile on the martyr who sends this infidel to hell. . . .' Yadda yadda yadda. But as a practical matter, Qaeda couldn't touch him, at least in the United States. So Wells was waiting for a new mission. In truth, though, he couldn't imagine what that might be. He wasn't built for desk work.

Meanwhile, he burned his days with three-hour-long workouts, and his nights with these joyless joyrides. Exley hated them, and a week earlier, Wells had promised her they would end. He'd thought he was telling the truth. But this morning he hadn't been able to stop himself. Exley hadn't argued when he rolled out of bed and pulled on his jeans and grabbed his helmet. No, Exley hadn't argued, hadn't said a word, and Wells supposed he loved her for her silence.

But not enough to stay.

Now Wells flexed his shoulders and stared down the perfect three-lane void ahead. This time when he twisted the throttle he didn't hesitate but instead pulled back as far as he could. The bike surged, and suddenly Wells heard

Just don't play with me 'cause you're playing with fire. . . .

Not the confident strut of Mick Jagger but the bleak, reedy tones of Johnny Thunder.

The engine roared and the speedometer needle jumped from fifty-five to eighty-five and kept going. When it topped one hundred, Wells flattened himself on the gas tank and hung on. For dear life, he thought. Though anyone watching might wonder exactly what those words meant to him. And then everything faded but the wind and the road, the bike jolting off every crease, its wheels caressing the highway, and Springsteen's unmistakable voice in his ears:

Drink this and you'll grow wings on your feet.

Wells glimpsed the speedometer, its white needle past 120, its tip quivering. It maxed out at 125, with the tach in the red zone at 9,000 revolutions per minute. He had never pushed the bike so far. He laid off the throttle and watched himself come back to earth.

A few seconds later, he heard the siren screaming. The lights pulsed red-blue-red-blue in his mirrors, half a mile behind but gaining fast.

He flexed his hand around the throttle. Part of him wanted to wind it down and take off again. He doubted the trooper could match his speed. He could probably get to the next exit and disappear.

But Wells didn't want to tangle this cop in whatever game he was playing with God, or himself, or the patron saints of the interstate. Instead of taking off, he flicked on his turn signal – see, Officer, I'm careful – and eased the Honda to a stop in the breakdown lane. As he waited, he patted the bike's gas tank as if it were a horse that had just won the Kentucky Derby. Despite the trouble he was facing, an absurd pride filled him at the speed the machine had achieved.

The Crown Victoria screeched to a stop behind him, its headlights glaring.

'Turn off your vehicle, sir. Now!' Underneath the cruiser's scratchy speakers, Wells picked up a trace of nervousness. This trooper was probably just out of the academy, stuck on the overnight shift, jumpy about pulling over a triple-digit speeder with no backup. Wells pulled the little black key from the ignition and dropped it on the cracked pavement.

'Off the bike. Now.'

Wells wondered if Exley would appreciate the irony of his being shot in a traffic stop after getting the bike

17

to 125 without a scratch. Probably not. The statie crouched behind the door of his cruiser, hand on the butt of his pistol. He was young, Wells saw. Maybe twenty. He had a thick, square face, but even so he hadn't lost all his baby fat. 'Don't look at me, sir! Look straight ahead!'

Wells looked straight ahead, wondering why he always got sideways with the cops.

'Helmet on the ground.'

Wells pulled off his helmet. His eyes burned from the wind. Next time he'd wear goggles under the face plate. Next time?

'You have a wallet? Identification?'

'Yes, Officer.'

'In your pants or your jacket?'

'Pants.'

'Take it out. Slowly.' Wells pulled off his gloves and fished at his wallet. 'Put it on the ground and kick it to me with your foot.'

'Kick it with my foot? Not my hand?'

'You're talking back, asshole?' The trooper no longer sounded scared, just pissed. 'I have you on the gun at one eighteen.'

Wells dropped his wallet on the ground, and kicked it toward the trooper. The kid was about to get the surprise of his life, he thought.

'Lean forward and put your hands on the bike.'

The metal of the gas tank was cool under his fingers.

'Do not, don't, move.' The statie grabbed the wallet, flipped it open.

'Mr. Wick? James Wick? That your name?'

'Not exactly, no, Officer.' Might as well tell the kid. When he got brought in, the truth would come out anyway.

'You're telling me your license is fake?'

'There's an ID card inside.'

A few seconds later: 'Is this real? Is that you?'

'I'd be awful dumb to lie about it.'

'Turn towards me. Slowly.' The officer looked at the CIA identification card in his hand – the one with Wells's real name on it – then at Wells. 'You expect me to believe this crap?'

Then Wells heard the faint thump of a helicopter's blades. A few seconds later, the trooper heard it too. Together they looked up as the helicopter closed on them, dropping through the night, landing on the side of the highway, a black two-man bird with a long narrow cockpit. The passenger door opened and a man Wells had never seen before stepped out.

The trooper's mouth dropped open. Wells was just as shocked. The agency had been watching him? Watching these rides? Did he have no privacy left?

'Officer,' the man shouted over the whirr of the rotors, 'do you know who this man is?'

The trooper holstered his pistol. 'Well, he said – I mean, he said – but I wasn't sure –'

'You believe him now? Or do I have to get somebody with stars on his collar to talk to you?'

'Yes. I mean no. I mean yes, I believe him.'

Without another word, the man walked back to the helicopter. As it rose off the side of the highway, the trooper rubbed his eyes like a kid waking up from a dream.

'Damn.' The statie shoved the identification card into the wallet and tossed it back to Wells. 'I'm sorry, Mr. Wells.'

'You don't have to apologize. Pulling rank on you like that was a real jerk move.'

19

'No, no. If I'd known it was you, I never would have pulled you over. That's the absolute truth.' The officer stepped over to him and extended his hand. He didn't seem bothered at all by what had just happened.

Can't even get arrested, Wells thought. When did I turn into such a saint? But he knew exactly when. The moment he shot Omar Khadri in Times Square. Wells wasn't sorry for what he'd done. If he had a hundred more chances to kill Khadri, he'd take them all. But he was sick of being a hero. He shook the officer's hand, feeling the sweat on the young man's palm.

'Won't you get in trouble, letting me go?'

'Radar gun's been on the fritz all week. Says one eighteen when it means fifty-eight.' The trooper turned back to his car, then stopped. 'Be careful out there, Mr. Wells. We need you safe.'

'You too, Officer. Lot of crazy drivers out there.' Wells meant it ironically – crazy like me – but the trooper didn't laugh. Wells thought sometimes that no one except Exley would ever laugh at him to his face again, no matter how much he deserved it. No one laughed at heroes. How could he trust a world that took him so seriously?

The trooper returned to his sedan. Wells got back on his bike. At the next exit he turned back to Washington. He kept the Honda at an even sixty-five the whole way home.

When he got back to Logan Circle the black Lincoln sedans with tinted windows were waiting, one on Thirteenth and the other on N. Two men in each, their engines running. As always. Security guards from Langley, there to watch out for him. And watch him, evidently. Wells hadn't liked having them around

20

before tonight. He liked them even less now. But Vinny Duto had insisted. If nothing else, they would keep the other residents in the building safe, Duto said. He promised that the guards wouldn't follow Wells or Exley without their permission. Until tonight, they seemed to have kept their side of the bargain.

Wells parked his bike in the building's garage and went upstairs. As quietly as he could, he opened the door to Exley's apartment. Their apartment, he supposed, though he had trouble thinking of it that way. Down the narrow hall filled with black-and-white pictures of Exley's kids, past the little open kitchen. His boots smelled of grit and oil and the highway. He tugged them off. Exley's looked child-sized next to them.

'Jennifer?' he murmured. No answer. She was asleep, or more likely too angry with him to answer.

Exley's old Persian rug scratched his toes as he walked toward the bedroom. She'd picked up the carpet during her posting in Pakistan. It was one of the few possessions she really cared about, its reds faded but the weave still tight. The apartment had only three rooms – this living room, their bedroom, and a spare bedroom where Jessica, Exley's daughter, slept when the kids stayed over.

Exley and Wells had talked about finding something bigger, maybe a row house on Capitol Hill so her kids could have their own bedrooms. David, Exley's son, was ten, too old to sleep on the lumpy couch in the living room. Maybe someplace with a garden for Wells to weed and plant. Someplace they could keep a Lab, a big happy mutt that would slobber all over the house. They had even called a broker, gone to a few open houses. But everything they saw was too expensive, or too run-down, or too big, or small, or . . . The truth was that the house-hunting filled Wells with dread. He had run so long that he could hardly imagine being penned in by four walls and a roof.

Left unsaid was the possibility that the new house might be a place for him and Exley to have a baby of their own. Wells didn't know how he felt about becoming a father, though somehow it seemed less scary than buying a house. He didn't even know if Exley could get pregnant. She was on the wrong side of forty, but women that age had babies these days. Didn't they?

He stepped into her – their – bedroom. The lights were out, but an infomercial for an all-in-one barbecue grill played silently on the little television on her desk. Outside, the sky was just starting to lighten.

'Jenny? You awake? You won't believe what happened tonight.' Even as he said the words, he wondered if he should tell her. He didn't want to admit how fast he was going. Maybe he'd just have to take this up with Duto himself, though he hated visiting the seventh floor of the headquarters building, where Duto had his offices.

Exley stayed silent as he turned off the television, kissed her forehead, smelling the lemon scent of her face wash. He could tell from her uneven breathing that she was awake, but if she didn't want to talk he didn't plan to push. He put the helmet on the nightstand and pulled off his jacket.

In one quick move she rolled over, grabbed the helmet, and threw it at him. But Wells had played line-backer in college and still had a football player's reflexes. He caught it easily and put it on her desk.

'Jenny, I'm sorry. I know I said I wouldn't, but I really needed it tonight.'

'Where'd you go?'

'Up 95, towards Baltimore.'

'How fast?'

'I don't know, Seventy, seventy-five miles an hour. Nothing I can't handle.'

'John. Please. Shafer's had a helicopter on you the last couple weeks.' Ellis Shafer, their boss at the agency.

'Shafer *what*?' So that's who'd been watching him tonight. 'Did Duto put him up to it?'

'Haven't you figured out yet that Vinny Duto couldn't care less about you, John? Shafer did it because *I* asked him to. He said they clocked you at a hundred ten. I wasn't going to tell you, but that's why I asked you to stop.'

'Jenny –' He guessed he wouldn't be talking to Duto after all. A small consolation.

'I swear, John, I wish you were out drinking, screwing somebody else.' Her voice broke. 'Anything but this. Every time you leave I think you're not coming back.' He sat beside her on the bed and put his hand on her hip, but she pulled away. 'Do you even care if you live or die, John?'

'Of course.' Wells tried to ignore the fact that he'd asked himself the same question a few minutes before, with a less certain answer.

'Then why don't you act like it?' She searched his face with her fierce blue eyes. He looked away first, down to her breasts, their tops striated with tiny white stretch marks. Her milky white thighs. And the scar above the knee where the bullet had hit.

'Sometimes I forget how beautiful you are,' he said.

He heard a police siren whistling to the northeast, one of the precincts of Washington that hadn't gentrified. The siren wasn't as close as it sounded, he knew. Wells had spent a decade away from America, living undercover as an al Qaeda guerrilla, slowly ingratiating himself with the group. He'd picked up more than a few survival tricks along the way, including the knowledge that gunshots and sirens carried much farther at night than during the day. Just another bit of wisdom that no longer did him much good.

'Your hand,' she said. He looked down. His left hand was trembling on his jeans. She caressed it in hers until the shaking stopped.

'I don't know what I'm doing anymore,' he said. For a while they were silent. She squeezed his hand and he found his voice again. 'You know, I thought when I woke up in the hospital and saw you there that it would all be okay. That I was out on the other side. And now . . .' In the distance a second siren rang out, then a third. Trouble in the night.

'Even Utah isn't Utah,' Exley said. He looked at her questioningly. 'When I was a kid, I used to love to ski. Before everything went bad with my family.' She slipped a hand around his shoulder. 'Nothing scared me. Bumps, steeps, any of it. I didn't want to hit puberty because I thought having a chest would mess up my balance. And it did.'

She arched her back, jokingly thrusting out her breasts, and despite his gloom Wells felt himself stir. He imagined her, a narrow boyish body cutting down the mountain, her ponytail tucked away. 'They must have been surprised when they saw you were a girl.'

'Mainly we went to Tahoe. We did it on the cheap, stayed in motels, brought sandwiches to the mountain. The most fun I remember having as a kid.But I always

24

wanted to go to Utah.' She ran a hand down his arm. 'My dad didn't want to. Said we didn't have the money. But I pestered him and finally, when I was twelve, we flew to Salt Lake City. Me, my brother, my mom and dad. The whole happy family. My mom didn't ski much, but she always came.'

'She was afraid to leave him alone,' Wells said. 'Poor Exley.' He kissed her neck softly.

'Lots of people have alcoholic dads.'

Yeah, but you're the one I love, he thought. And didn't say, though he didn't know quite why.

Outside the sirens faded. Wells walked to the window, looked at the agency's guards in the Crown Victorias. He turned back to the bed. Exley had her legs folded under herself kittenishly now.

'You listening, John?'

He laid a hand on her knee.

'Anyway. It's snowing when we get to Utah. Snows all night. The next morning we drive up to Alta. I'm so excited. The best skiing in the world. And we get there, we buy our tickets. We get on the lift . . .'

He tried to slide his hand between her legs, but she squeezed them tight.

'We get to the top. And we ski down.'

'So you ski down? That's the story? How was it?'

'Great. But, you know. It was *skiing*, like Tahoe. Just skiing. And I kept thinking that it was costing money we didn't have, and I should have loved it, not just liked it. So somehow I was disappointed, even though I knew I shouldn't be. I didn't say anything. But my dad, he figured it out. Because at the end of the day, he said to me, "Even Utah isn't Utah, huh?"' She paused, then continued. 'There's no magic bullet. Nobody in the world will blame you for feeling like hell, needing time

25

to put yourself back together. But this – you're not being fair to yourself. Or me.'

He knew she was right. But he wanted to ask her, how long until I don't dream about tearing men apart, gutting them like fish? How long until I sleep eight hours at a stretch? Six? Four? Until I can talk about what I've seen without wanting to tear up a room?

'You're not crazy, John,' she said. 'You don't have to talk to me if you don't want to. People specialize in this stuff.'

'A shrink?'

'They're professionals.' The desperation in her voice disturbed Wells more than anything she'd said, gave him a clue how hard he'd made her life.

'I'll be okay. I just need to figure out what's next. I promise.' He felt himself close up again. Good.

'Or me. You can talk to me if you want.'

'I will. But not now.' Instead he reached for her. She pushed him away, but just for a moment. And for a little while they thought only of each other.

THREE

The North Korean shoreline was just a mile away, but Beck hardly would have known if not for the blue line on the laptop screen that marked the coast. Thick clouds blotted out the stars, and even through his night-vision binoculars Beck saw no buildings, roads, or cars. No signs of life at all. Just an inky darkness stretching to eternity.

The Phantom crept in at ten knots an hour, its twin engines rumbling quietly. Beck, Choe, and Kang had traveled 120 miles west, past the tip of the North Korean coast. Now they were swinging back east-northeast toward Point D. With any luck the Drafter, and not the North Korean army, would be waiting.

Beck's Timex glowed in the night, its blue numbers telling him they were right on time: 2320. The trip had been quiet so far, their biggest excitement coming in Incheon harbor a few minutes after they left. Choe cut too close to a containership, and the Phantom hit the boat's giant wake. It sprang out of the water like a forty-five-foot-long Jet-Ski and thudded down, sending Beck sprawling. He wasn't sure, but he thought Choe had hit the wave on purpose, revenge for Beck's offer of the cyanide pills.

They'd run at twenty knots most of the way, using the radar feed from the Hawkeye overhead to dodge the handful of ships along the coast. The dark sky had helped too. Beck had seen only two boats in the last hour, and neither had spotted the Phantom.

They closed on the coast, barely five hundred yards away now. Through his binoculars Beck saw a broken rock wall, its stones crumbling and scattered. But still no signs of life.

'Stop,' he said. The engines quieted and the boat rocked gently on the sea's dull waves. The lights mounted in the pilothouse filled the cabin with a dim blue-black glow.

'Depth?' Beck said to Kang.

'Twenty-four feet. Lucky we ride high. This thing's just a big lake.' Indeed, the Yellow Sea was exceptionally shallow. It got its name from China's Yellow River, which filled it with mountains of silt. Its average depth was less than 150 feet.

'Anything in our way?'

'Smooth the whole way in.'

From here, the Phantom could reach shore in thirty seconds, but Beck didn't want to move until he knew what awaited them. A couple of miles east, a cluster of lights, seemingly placed at random, glowed weakly. Through his night-vision binoculars, Beck looked west and east as far as he could, then tried again with his thermal scope. He saw nothing but the lights and the dying stone wall.

'Cut the engines,' he said.

The twin Mercurys stopped. In the hush that followed Beck heard only the breathing of the men around him, the listless slap of the waves, the faint beeping of the Phantom's radar. There were birds and animals and people too in the hills up ahead. Had to be. But they were silent as ghosts.

'Must be what the moon is like,' Kang said.

'Imagine living here.'

A whistle sounded to the north, eerie and distant. Choe said something in Korean.

'He says it's a steam train,' Kang said. 'The North Koreans still run coal locomotives.'

The whistle faded. Beck signaled to Choe to turn the engines back on and a moment later heard their reassuring rumble.

'Bet you can pick up waterfront property cheap around here.'

'Seth, was it this dark when you came over here before?'

'Once yes, once no. You're figuring –'

'Not figuring anything yet.'

An alarm on Kang's laptop beeped. He tapped a few keys and the monitor opened up. 'Well, this isn't good. Two boats, coming around Kudol' – a spit of land about ten miles southeast. 'They were hanging close to the coast before, so the Hawkeye didn't pick them up.'

'How fast?'

'Twenty, maybe twenty-five knots.'

'Aiming for us.'

'Looks that way.' The laptop beeped again. 'More bad news.' Kang pointed to the screen. Another white blip was moving toward the Phantom, this one from the southwest. 'He was stopped in open water, maybe twenty-five miles out. I had him figured for a fishing trawler. Now he's moving our way.' The screen beeped again. 'This one too, straight in from the west.'

'They're setting up a cordon?'

'Looks that way.'

29

'Can we outrun it?'

'Shouldn't be a problem. For a few minutes.'

Beck checked his watch. 2330. No way was he waiting a half-hour. He would give the Drafter ten minutes, no more. He had been in tight spots before. During the first Gulf War, his SEAL team had landed in Kuwait City to sabotage a Republican Guard tank brigade. In the Philippines, he'd helped fight an ugly counterinsurgency against the Muslim guerrillas of the Jemaah Islamiyah.

But this mission felt different, not like a fight at all, more like they were bait dangled before a hungry animal. He was sure they'd been set up. Though all this activity could still be a coincidence, North Koreans out on pleasure cruises in the middle of the night.

Yeah, right.

Point D was a small inlet formed by a creek that flowed into the Yellow Sea from the northeast. A good spot for a pickup, easy to find in satellite photographs. And with the tide high, the Phantom could ride in nearly all the way to the beach.

'Ted,' Kang said urgently, 'these just popped.' He pointed at two yellow blips on the radar screen. 'Jets,' Kang said. 'At three thousand feet. Just under the cloud cover. Running at three hundred fifty knots.'

'How far?'

'Sixty kilometers. Six, seven minutes, give or take.'

Choe sputtered in Korean and pointed at the shore. A man in a baggy nylon jacket had stepped out of the woods, walking strangely, almost limping. He raised a pair of binoculars and slowly scanned the water. As he spotted the Phantom, he waved slowly, metronomically. A backpack was slung across his shoulders.

30

'Well, hello, soldier,' Kang said.

Beck stared at the man through his own binoculars, trying to decide if he was looking at Sung Kwan, the Drafter. The CIA had secretly taken long-lens photographs of Sung at its meetings with him. Twelve hours before, in a secure room in the American embassy in Seoul, Beck had stared at those pictures, trying to memorize Sung's face.

But Sung had few distinguishing characteristics. He was short and squat, like many Koreans, and wore the oversized glasses that Korean and Chinese men favored. His most notable feature was a birthmark on his left cheek. Beck peered through his own binoculars, looking for the birthmark. He thought he saw a smudge on the man's cheek, but couldn't be sure. Too bad Sung wasn't seven feet tall or missing an arm.

'Bring us in,' Beck said to Choe. 'But slow. And be ready to take off.'

'Slow,' Choe said. He eased the throttle forward. They were two hundred yards from shore, then one hundred, and through his binoculars Beck could clearly see the birthmark.

'That's him,' Beck said. He waited for the trap to spring, for North Korean soldiers to pour out of the trees. But the woods stayed silent. Sixty yards out, the depth finder beeped.

'Any closer and we beach,' Kang said. Choe was already swinging the Phantom around. Beck stepped out the back of the pilothouse and waved for Sung to swim out to the boat. The North Korean limped into the sea. Halfway out, with the water at his shoulders, he began to yell.

'He can't swim,' Kang said.

'*He can't swim?* Maybe he should have thought of

that before he chose this godforsaken beach for his pickup.' Beck took one more look at the shore. Still silent. 'I guess this is why I get the big bucks.'

Beck pulled off his clothes and his pistol and put them in a pile and dove off the Phantom into the cool salty water. He swam underwater as long as he could, coming up for air a few feet from Sung. He reached Sung and wrapped his arms under Sung's shoulders, the grip lifeguards used to save drowning swimmers. Sung's body was flabby in his hands.

Panic filled Sung's face and he struggled, from fear or surprise or both, his arms swinging wildly. But Beck overcame his thrashing and dragged him back to the Phantom, where Kang pulled him up.

'Go,' Beck yelled as soon as he'd hoisted himself out.

Choe pushed the throttle forward and the boat took off, swinging hard right, throwing Beck against the pilothouse wall.

'Dammit, Choe.'

Choe let up on the throttle and the Phantom straightened out. They headed southwest, skimming the waves at fifty-five knots.

'You all right?' Kang said.

'Fine.' Beck's forehead was throbbing, but he counted himself lucky. They were halfway home. Sung chittered at them in Korean.

'He says he's sorry he doesn't know how to swim,' Kang said.

'Me too.' Beck flipped on the pilothouse lights. The birthmark was unmistakable.

'Calm down,' he said to Sung in Korean. 'You're safe.' He pushed Sung onto a bench at the back of the cabin. 'Just sit.'

Beck grabbed dry clothes from his bag, pulled them on, tucked his pistol into his pants. He had a lot of questions for Sung, but they would have to wait until the Phantom got into international waters. 'Run a simulation,' he said to Kang.

Kang tapped on his keyboard, projecting the Phantom's position and those of the enemy boats for the next half-hour, assuming both sides stayed on their current tracks.

'On this heading, the boat to the west is our biggest problem,' he said. 'We'll make contact in roughly five minutes.'

'How about the jets?'

'One's heading straight for us. The other west in case we run for the open sea. And there's this.' Kang pointed at two more yellow blips moving toward them. 'Those are airborne, less than a thousand feet, a hundred fifty knots.'

'Helicopters,' Beck said. 'They're pulling out all the stops.'

'Anxious to make our acquaintance.'

Beck examined the screen. None of the enemy boats or planes were headed directly for the Phantom. 'Doesn't look like they have a fix on us, though.'

'They need visual contact. Radar's their big weakness.'

'So we hope,' Beck said. The helicopters were the real problem, he thought. The boats couldn't catch them, and the jets couldn't fly low or slow enough to spot them. But helicopters could. Which meant that –

'Tell Choe not to follow the coast,' Beck said. 'I want him to run southwest. Two hundred fifteen degrees.' Into the open water of the Yellow Sea. They'd

33

still have to get by at least one boat, but at least they'd be separating from the helicopters.

The North Koreans had obviously chased Sung toward the pickup point. But they hadn't expected a speedboat, Beck thought. Without a radar fix, they were tightening the net methodically, coming from all directions, hoping to get a visual fix on the Phantom and blast it out of the water.

But the North Koreans didn't know how fast the Phantom could run. The speedboat had geometry on its side. Only one enemy cutter stood between it and the open sea. And with each mile the Phantom ran, the search area widened, making it harder to find. In forty-five minutes they'd be in international waters, with F-16s, the world's best babysitters, watching over them.

'And tell him to stay straight, max us out,' Beck said to Kang. Best to get out of danger as fast as possible. Their speed would save them. Kang said something to Choe, and suddenly the Phantom was flying across the flat sea at seventy-five knots, kicking up long, low waves of foam. Despite the danger, Beck couldn't help but be amazed by the boat. Under other circumstances he would have liked to sit beside Choe and watch the ocean roll by, Corona in hand.

But not tonight. Even before it reached the enemy cutter, the Phantom had to run another obstacle: two small islands five miles off the coast, separated by a three-mile-wide channel. Both islands had naval stations, according to the satellite photos.

Overhead, the clouds were lifting slightly and the night sky was brightening, showing a sliver of moon, not what Beck wanted. He scanned the islands. Changnin, to the east, was silent, and for a moment he wondered if the satellites were wrong. Then, to the west, a stream of red tracers lit the night. The bullets landed far short of the Phantom, but they meant trouble nonetheless. Whoever was on that island had seen the boat pass.

As Changnin disappeared behind them, Beck heard the faint whine of jet engines. 'How close?' he said to Kang.

'At least five minutes out.'

'And the cutter?'

'We'll cross him in three minutes.'

'Range?'

'A thousand meters, give or take.'

Beck could have adjusted their heading to give them more room around the enemy boat. But running straight ahead meant that the two boats would cross each other for only a few seconds, giving the enemy ship little chance to fix its guns on the Phantom.

In the corner, Sung huddled in his chair, arms folded, clothes soaked, thin black hair matted against his skull. Beck wondered what was wrong with him. He didn't look like a man who had just escaped the world's most repressive regime. Maybe he was afraid of what would happen to his family. According to his dossier, he was married and had two teenage sons.

'You're safe now,' Beck said in his halting Korean.

Sung just groaned and shook his head. Beck turned to Kang. 'We've got to find out what's wrong with him.'

'Right now we've got bigger problems,' Kang said. 'That fighter's closing.'

Through the cabin's tinted windows Beck saw the North Korean jet, its running lights blinking in the night. The fighter was moving south-southwest, a couple of miles behind them but closing, the screech of its engines intensifying by the second.

35

'Either he's got X-ray vision or they bought new radar when we weren't looking,' Beck said. The jet banked steeply, looking for an angle to fire.

'He's under two thousand meters,' Kang said. 'Fifteen hundred . . . one thousand . . .'

The fighter had stubby wings high on its fuselage and eight rocket pods under its wings. A Russian-made Su-25, a single-seat jet introduced in the 1980s. Obsolete by Western standards but still plenty lethal.

The Phantom shook as the Su-25 screamed by and unleashed a pair of rockets. The surfboard-sized missiles crashed into the water behind the boat, the force of their explosions sending five-foot-high waves across the sea. The Phantom jumped out of the water and crashed down, jumped and crashed, *slap-slap-slap,* until the waves finally subsided. Beck put a hand against the cabin wall and stayed upright this time.

The noise of the jet faded as the fighter prepared to swing around for another pass. Then the North Korean cutter appeared out of the darkness, a gray-black boat with heavy machine guns mounted behind the cabin. The cutter's twin spotlights swung left and right, searching for the Phantom, finding it and for a moment filling the pilothouse with a white light, implacable and all-knowing. As if God himself were watching.

In the sudden brightness, Beck saw Sung trembling in his chair. The cutter's machine guns opened up, their rounds thunking into the Phantom's hull and the glass of the pilothouse. The windows shook and began to crack, long white scars cutting through the clear plastic. So much for running straight at the enemy, Beck thought. Time for Plan B.

'Choe! Hard right! Heading two-seventy! Now!'

Beck threw Sung down and lay on top of him and

waited for the Phantom's twin engines to get them out of trouble. Choe swung the boat west, easing off the throttle as he did, just enough that the boat wouldn't tip. Beck closed his eyes and heard windows shatter as shards of fiberglass cut into his neck.

The guns faded as the Phantom pulled away. Beck stood and shook plastic shards off his clothes. The windows at the back of the cabin had been partly shot through. Even supposedly bulletproof glass couldn't hold up to close-in machine-gun fire. The roar of the engines filled the pilothouse.

Boom! Sparks flew from the engines. The cabin shook and the boat's nose lifted out of the water. The Phantom slowed and dragged right. Choe laid off the throttle. 'Engine! Engine!' he yelled in English, before switching to Korean.

'He says we lost one of the Mercurys and the other one is light on oil,' Kang told Beck a few seconds later. 'We can't do better than thirty-three knots and we'll be better off at twenty-five.'

Under other circumstances, thirty-three knots, or even twenty-five, would have been fine. Not tonight, Beck thought.

'How come they're finding us so easily?' Kang looked at Sung.

'I was wondering that too.' Beck grabbed Sung's backpack. Sung tried to stop him, but Beck lashed him, a hard flat chop that snapped the North Korean's head sideways and sent him sprawling. Beck flipped over the pack. A pair of threadbare nylon pants, a thin cotton shirt, cheap black shoes, all drenched –

And, inside a waterproof bag, a plastic box, twelve inches by eight by four, three lights blinking red and green on its top. A transponder, broadcasting the Phantom's location to every North Korean ship and jet within twenty miles. The man they'd come to rescue had betrayed them.

FOUR

TYSONS CORNER, VIRGINIA

The Elevator's dingy steel doors groaned open. Exley stepped onto a threadbare brown carpet that probably hadn't been vacuumed since Saddam Hussein was alive. At the end of the corridor a discreet brass nameplate reading 'Okay Enterprises' marked a black door. Exley touched her thumb to a security reader, and a deadbolt lock slid back with a heavy thunk.

The welcome scent of fresh coffee filled her nostrils as the door closed behind her. The office that greeted her was as absurdly ordinary as a dentist's waiting room. Motivational posters and Thomas Kinkade lithographs covered the walls. Narrow wooden chairs sat next to a table of old magazines for visitors to thumb through. But no one ever read the magazines. No one ever visited Okay Enterprises.

'Mornin', Ms. Exley.'

'Mornin', Tim.' Tim was a solidly built man in his late forties. Today, as every day, he wore pressed khakis and a sport coat to hide his shoulder holster. He rarely spoke. Shafer, Exley's boss, swore by him. Beside his desk, the coffeemaker burbled happily.

'Guess I got here just in time.'

'Brewed it figuring you were coming.' Tim's accent was unplaceable, sometimes vaguely Southern, sometimes flatter, more Midwestern. He was already tipping steaming coffee into a plastic mug, camouflage print with 'Operation Iraqi Freedom' stamped in white on the side. Shafer had bought the mugs at an Army-Navy surplus store. They'd originally cost $9.99 each but were marked down to a dollar. 'Pretty good deal,' Shafer had said. 'I wanted some with Rumsfeld's face on the side, but I guess those got pulped a long time ago.'

Exley took the mug gratefully. 'Thanks. Have a nice weekend?'

'Mmm-hmm.' He turned back to the *Post* on his desk.

I'll take that as a yes, Exley thought. She and Wells had wondered about Tim's personal life ever since Shafer brought him in. Was he married, divorced, a bigamist, gay? Did he live near the office? Did he spend weekends on Jupiter and come to Earth via warp drive every Monday morning? She'd never know. She wasn't even sure that 'Tim' was Tim's real name. Shafer, who did, wasn't telling.

'Tim's a very private person,' Shafer said when she asked. 'I'm sure you and John can respect that.' And he'd smiled his Cheshire Cat smile. But Shafer had given her one crumb. Tim had never worked for the agency.

Tim's pedigree, or lack thereof, was no accident. These scruffy offices reflected the unique and uneasy position that Wells, Exley, and Shafer occupied at the CIA. They still spent about half their time at the Langley campus, a few miles down the road. But Shafer intentionally kept this space as far outside the agency's orbit as he could.

The agency paid for the suite, and CIA electronics countermeasures teams swept it for bugs every month. What Shafer didn't tell them was that he had his own contractors sweeping the place as well, looking for devices that the agency might have missed – or planted. And instead of having the agency's guards provide security, Shafer depended on Tim.

Naturally, Vinny Duto hated the arrangement. He had every right to be unhappy, Exley thought. Shafer was breaking agency regulations, and a dozen laws besides. But after what had happened in New York the year before, Wells, Exley, and Shafer were untouchable.

Of course, the aftermath of the mayhem in Times Square had been messy. Both Wells and Exley had been shot along the way and needed months to recover. And Wells faced another burden. The agency had never disclosed Exley's identity, but Wells's name had come out, though not his picture or biographical details. The agency had offered to announce to the world that Wells had died, and even give him a fake funeral. But Wells had rejected that idea, telling Exley that he didn't want to have to explain to Evan, his son from his first marriage, that he was alive but pretending to be dead. Anyway the plan wouldn't work, he said. Too many people, both inside and outside the agency, knew he'd survived. Instead he had to cope with moments like the one with the trooper.

For everyday life, the agency had given Wells a new identity, complete with driver's license, passport, and credit cards. To confuse anyone who was looking for him, Langley had created fake websites that claimed to have the truth about him but were filled with disinformation. A few said Wells had died and was buried under a fake name at Arlington. Others claimed that 'John Wells' didn't exist at all and that the attack he'd stopped was a CIA plot to make the War on Terror seem relevant. Still others said he'd retired from the agency and was living under a CIA protection program.

Fortunately, Wells couldn't be easily traced. Thousands of men shared his name, and the only pictures of him in circulation were twenty years old. But he couldn't be completely disguised either. Too many officers at Langley knew him. So did his buddies from the Army and friends from high school and college. Enough fragments about his life were floating around the Internet that a steady stream of tourists now visited his childhood home in Montana.

Meanwhile, Duto and Wells circled each other warily. They'd never gotten along, and even the fact that Wells had stopped the New York attack didn't end that hostility. Wells was uncontrollable, the anti-bureaucrat. What he'd done in Times Square made the rest of the agency look incompetent, almost irrelevant. But Duto, no fool, knew that he couldn't attack Wells directly. So he'd gone the other way, giving Wells, Exley, and Shafer free rein. They had Top Secret/SCI/All Access clearances, the same as Duto's own. They could crash any meeting, read any analysis, get the details of any operation they wanted.

At the same time, Duto had put them outside the agency's usual chain of command. They reported directly to him, and he'd made clear that he didn't plan to take responsibility for their mistakes. In a way, they'd become an agency within an agency, a mini-CIA. Exley and Shafer had been in a somewhat similar position years earlier, but now they were a lot more powerful.

Exley wasn't sure how to use the carte blanche they'd been given, and she didn't think Shafer did either. As for Wells . . . Wells spent his time these days working out, riding his motorcycle, and watching westerns. He was in great shape physically, if not mentally. Exley wished she could figure out how to get him out of his funk – a polite word for clinical depression. But she knew better than anyone that pushing on him would only backfire.

She tapped on Shafer's door.

'Enter.' Shafer was stretched on his couch, poking at his laptop. He was legendary among longtime CIA employees for his fashion sense, and not in a good way. At various times Exley had seen him in red pants, a brown suit – something only Ronald Reagan could pull off – and her personal favorite, black leather boots more appropriate for a transvestite hooker. Shafer had worn those on one of Washington's rare snowy days. When she asked Shafer where he'd found them, he told her that he couldn't find his winter boots and had stopped at Nordstrom's for replacements.

'These were on sale,' he said.

'I'll bet.'

Sometimes Exley thought Shafer intentionally dressed badly to buttress his reputation as an absent-minded genius. Then he'd show up in something like today's ensemble – a canary-yellow polo shirt coupled with jeans that ended two inches above his skinny ankles – and she'd reconsider. No one would know-ingly look so ridiculous.

'Flood at home?' she asked him. He looked blankly at her. She decided not to explain.

43

'Check this out.' Shafer pointed at his computer, its browser set to a page from eBay. 'A Dartmouth yearbook, Wells's year. It's being advertised as having a picture of "The Real John Wells." A headshot.'

Exley looked, then looked again to be sure. 'Someone's bidding eight hundred dollars? For a yearbook? Got to be a joke.'

'You should take some candids.'

'Funny,' Exley said.

'Where is your better half, by the way?'

'He was up late riding. As you know.'

'Someone needs to steal that bike.' Shafer closed the laptop. 'How is our problem child?'

'Please don't call him that.' Shafer was infuriating, but she trusted him more than anyone else at the agency, including Wells. She sat beside the window, which was coated with a layer of Teflon that damped the vibrations of the glass, making eavesdropping from outside impossible.

'It's easier for me,' she said. 'I still have David and Jess to take care of. I have my friends. He doesn't have friends, Ellis. The people he knows die at an unusually high rate.'

'He ought to stop killing them.' Shafer vigorously rubbed his nose. She looked away in case he decided to poke a pinky inside, as she'd caught him doing over the years. 'He could write a book. A memoir. At least it would give him something to do.'

She couldn't help but laugh. 'A memoir? "How I got shot saving the world." By John Wells. Then he could go on *Oprah* and talk about it. Jump on her couch.'

'Good. Let him quit, then. He wants to be someplace nobody cares who he is, let him run an orphanage in Africa. You too. The agency'll make sure you never have to worry about money. Duto will write the check himself just to be rid of you.'

She had considered something similar herself. And yet she couldn't imagine it working, not now. 'I don't think he's ready for that.' She paused, trying to find the words. 'Ellis, nobody else in the world could have stopped Khadri.'

'You don't believe that.'

'I do. And you do too. Without him Manhattan would be a toxic waste dump. Nobody's paying for your college yearbook. Or mine.'

'I wish you were my girlfriend,' Shafer said. 'You're good for the ego. Saving a few kids in Africa would be a waste of his talents, you're saying.'

'Don't pretend you don't agree.'

'I agree he's earned the right to do what makes him happy. You too. If the two of you can figure out what on God's green earth that might be.'

'It's not just that. I think he has post-traumatic stress disorder. He doesn't sleep. Sometimes he's not there at all. I wake up in the morning, he's on my laptop, playing solitaire, like he's been there all night.'

'It would be the least surprising thing in the world if he had PTSD. Have you ever talked to him about what it was like over there?'

Exley felt her eyes well up. She turned away so Shafer couldn't see. She'd failed. By failing to challenge Wells, she'd failed him. 'He needs an op, Ellis. We need to get him an op.'

'Killing more guys isn't gonna get him over PTSD.'

'It'll get him off that damned bike. If he's going to take these chances, let it be for a good cause.'

'You think what we do is for a good cause?'

45

'Please stop proving how smart you are, Ellis.' She was tired of this conversation. 'There's something else I wanted to ask you about. Unrelated. I think.' She walked out.

In a few minutes she was back, carrying a sheaf of papers from her safe.

'After-action reports from Afghanistan, ours and the Army's, raw field files. The Pentagon didn't want to send them, but I gave them my clearance and told them they didn't have a choice.'

'Membership has its privileges,' Shafer said. Exley handed Shafer some papers. 'This is a summary of reports from SF units' – Special Forces. 'Basically, the Taliban tactics are steadily improving. Their body counts are down, ours are up.'

'So we took out the dumb ones.'

'It's more than that. This report mentions "company-level coordination typically seen among professionally trained armies." And this one.' She opened another file. ' "Enemy command-and-control has improved. . . . A combination of suppressing fire and point-to-point movement not seen before." It's all over the place.'

'Fine. The Talibs are learning how to fight. Good for them, bad for us. So?'

Exley pulled out another report. 'Two months ago, in Kandahar' – the city in southern Afghanistan where the Taliban had been headquartered. 'A Colonel Hamar in the Afghan army tells us that the Taliban are getting "professional training" – his words – from "foreign fighters." '

'The only foreign fighters in Afghanistan are bin Laden's boys. They're hardly professionals. Unless

46

you think blowing yourself to bits is a hallmark of professionalism.'

'Let me finish, Ellis. By the way, the good lieutenant colonel died shortly after passing this rumor along.'

'I'm going to guess it wasn't natural causes.'

'Throat cut in half.'

'In Kandahar that's practically natural.'

Exley passed Shafer a photograph of a blood-drenched corpse rolled up in a rug. 'His body was left in front of the local police HQ.'

'I guess that's what's known as sending a message.'

'Anyway. So the Special Forces say the Talibs are fighting better. Kandahar reports foreign fighters. Then this from the Tenth Mountain Division.' She handed him another file.

'More foreign fighters?'

'In eastern Afghanistan near the Pak border.'

'Nowhere near Kandahar,' Shafer said.

'I looked for more reports from the Tenth Mountain, but there weren't any. They just rotated in. So I checked back to the old reports from the 101st.' The 101st Airborne Division.

'More foreigners.'

'Gold star, Ellis. Two reports. But no one linked them to the new ones. You know once a division leaves, its intel goes with it. These were also in eastern Afghanistan.'

'Okay. I'll play.' Shafer began to read again, not skimming this time. Exley waited. One of Shafer's strengths was his willingness to reconsider his preconceptions when he got new evidence. She wished more people at the agency – and across the river in the White House – shared that trait.

Finally Shafer looked up. 'Are you saying what I

think you're saying? The Taliban is getting outside help? Some foreign power is sending its own soldiers to give the Talibs tactical support?'

'I seem to remember we did something similar.' During the 1980s, America had aided Afghan guerrillas against the Soviet Army. Some of those same guerrillas had now turned against the United States.

'Supporting the Talibs would be an act of war against the United States. All of NATO too.'

'Proxy war.'

'Let's say you're right. Who's doing it? The Russians would never help the Talibs. No matter how badly they wanted to hurt us. They haven't forgotten they lost a hundred thousand soldiers fighting in Afghanistan.'

'Someone else, then.'

'Who? Nobody in NATO. They're on our side. Iran and Pakistan would hardly count as foreign. North Korea? China? Anyone say anything about Asians?'

'No. The fighters are specifically identified as white. Mercenaries maybe?'

'Maybe. But it's a seller's market these days for mercenaries.'

Shafer was right, Exley knew. Former Special Forces soldiers could make $5,000 a week providing security in Iraq. South African and Russian soldiers made less, but even so they could take home $10,000 a month. They would want even more money to help the Taliban against the United States. Not for moral reasons either. Simply because of the risk.

'The Talibs couldn't afford these guys,' Shafer said. 'Who would pay them?'

'I think it's time to find out.' She handed him the last report in her file. 'Also from the Tenth Mountain

48

Division. Two days ago. A fairly big camp in eastern Afghanistan, at least fifty Talibs. And several white fighters.'

'And they're going after it?'

'Not at the moment. They have other priorities. And it's in a very difficult location. Way up in the mountains. I think we should get a satellite up to take a look at it.'

'Sounds reasonable. And then?'

'I don't know. Depends on what we see. Maybe we can convince the SF to go after it.'

'Okay. Talk to Greg Levine at NSA.' Shafer scribbled a number for her and handed back the files. 'If he gives you any lip, tell him to call me. And Jennifer – do you want me to say anything to John?'

She walked out without answering. Let somebody else deal with Wells for once.

Three hours later, Exley walked into Shafer's office at Langley. Wells was already there. A nice surprise. She'd called and asked him to show up, but she hadn't been sure he would.

'We got them already?' Shafer said. 'This must be a record.'

'Levine said they had a satellite right there and it would be no problem as long as I had a cost center for him,' Exley said. 'I told him to put it on your tab.' As part of the government's internal accounting procedures, the National Security Agency dunned the CIA whenever Langley asked for photographs that required the NSA to alter the orbit of its satellites. The agencies had teams of auditors to squabble over the accounts, though in the end the American taxpayer footed the bill for everything. The system was either a necessary check on spending or a cosmic joke, depending on who was explaining it.

'There it is. Your tax dollars at work.' Shafer clicked on a folder on the workstation in the corner, which was linked to a fiber-optic network that transferred encrypted images between Langley, the Pentagon, and NSA headquarters. The agency refused to extend the network to the offices at Tysons Corner, so they had to come to Langley to see photographs like these.

The folder popped open, revealing dozens of graphical files. Shafer clicked one and turned to the fifty-inch flat-panel screen that hung on one wall of his office. But the screen stayed dark.

'Wow, the Eiffel Tower,' Exley said.

'No, it's the rain forest,' Wells said. He was lounging on the couch, his long legs stretched on Shafer's coffee table. He showed no ill effects from his ride the night before. Exley noticed that he'd even shaved.

'Everybody's a critic,' Shafer said. He fiddled with the back of his workstation and clicked again. This time a remarkably clear image of the Afghan mountains filled the flat panel. At the end of the Cold War, American spy satellites had been celebrated for their ability to read license plates from space. Now they could read not just license plates but newspaper headlines.

Shafer focused on a patch of flat ground several hundred yards long, the most likely spot for a camp. Wells lifted himself off the couch and stared. The mountains had woken him up, Exley thought. She hadn't seen him so alert in months.

'It's a camp for sure,' Wells said. 'A big one.'

'Then where is everybody?' Exley said. Only two men were visible in the photograph. They sat against the side of the mountain, rifles slung over their shoulders. 'These were taken a couple of hours ago. Near dusk over there. Dinnertime. Shouldn't they be lining up?'

'They'll be back soon. Look, there's two campfires going. You don't do that unless you've got a lot of guys to feed. And over here –' Wells stepped close to the screen and pointed to the southern part of the camp, where holes were dug behind a makeshift rock wall. 'Those are privies. At least five of them. Another sign they've been there awhile, and they're decently organized.'

'The report says forty to fifty men.'

'At least that. Ellis, pull it back. Give me the widest view you can.' Wells ran his finger over the screen, tracing a line from the ridge, south, into the valley. 'See this?'

Shafer got it first. 'A trail, down the side of the mountain.'

'Follow it south, south –' Shafer scrolled down the screen, leaving the plateau and moving into the valley.

'No wonder the evil American infidels always knew where we were, back in the day,' Wells said. 'If we'd had one of these, it would have been a fairer fight.' He grinned at Shafer. His confusion of 'we' and 'they' was no accident, as Shafer and Exley well knew.

'Want to switch sides again?' Shafer said.

'I'm not so sure they'd have me, Ellis.'

'Anyway, where would you ride your bike?' Exley said.

'Children,' Shafer said. 'Focus, please.'

'Fair enough,' Wells said. He stepped closer to the screen. 'Can you scroll farther down?'

'This set doesn't run any farther south. We get another pass tomorrow.'

51

'Magnify it. The southern edge.' Wells looked at Exley. 'See what they did at the base of the valley? Just left of where the trail ends.'

'Those branches?'

'See how they're arranged? They look like they're part of the forest, but they're not. They're thicker.'

Slowly, Exley recognized the hidden shapes under the branches. 'Trucks?'

'Pickups, at least four. Toyotas most likely. All with fifty-cals. When I was with them, they never would have bothered to hide them.'

'Which means –'

'It doesn't prove anything,' Wells said. 'But yeah, it's evidence they're getting lessons.' He looked at Exley. 'Well done, Jenny. Though I have to admit I don't get it. Who would be crazy enough to help the Taliban right now?'

'What do you think we should tell Bagram?' Bagram Air Base, north of Kabul, the headquarters of the American military command in Afghanistan.

'They've got to hit it,' Wells said. 'Find out if it's real. Though it's gonna be tough. Whoever's up there can enfilade anyone coming up that trail something vicious. And I'll bet they've got heavy stuff in those caves. Mortars, RPGs, some SAMs' – rocket-propelled grenades and surface-to-air missiles.

'You want to go? Summer vacation in Afghanistan? For old times' sake?'

Shafer had asked the question, but Wells looked at Exley instead. She hated to see the eagerness in Wells's face. He looked like a hound that had just sniffed out a fox. Did killing thrill him so much? She wasn't sure she wanted to know the answer. Anyway this mission was what she'd told Shafer she wanted for Wells. Something that would test him, get him out of his funk.

'Go for it, John.' Anything beats the bike, she thought.

'If the guys at Bagram will have me, I'll think about it.'

'It may take a few days to put together, but you're right,' Shafer said. 'We have to hit it. And they'll have you.'

Shafer's phone trilled. Shafer held a finger to his lips, warning Exley and Wells to stay quiet, and picked up. 'Hello, Mr Tyson.' George Tyson was deputy director for counterintelligence, the man in charge of making sure that foreign intelligence services didn't infiltrate the CIA.

'When? Where? Tomorrow would be better . . . No . . . if it's urgent, okay. We'll see you there. Yes. We. Me and the two musketeers.'

He cradled the phone. 'Strange. Tyson wants to talk to us tonight. Not here. Says something's happening in Korea.'

FIVE

Betrayed. The word rang in Beck's mind as he opened the Phantom's hatch and hurled the transponder as far as he could into the foaming water. *Betrayed.* He threw Sung against the side of the cabin. *Betrayed.* He drove his right fist into Sung's soft belly until the North Korean's mouth flopped open and his legs went flaccid. Sung slid to the floor, gasping, wordlessly begging for oxygen.

'Ask him,' Beck said to Kang. 'Ask him why he's killing us.' Beck was even more furious with himself than with Sung. He should have checked the bag as soon as Sung got on board. But he simply hadn't imagined that Sung would destroy his own chance for escape.

'If he doesn't start talking, I'll put a bullet in him.' Beck drew his pistol. 'I will, too. Tell him.'

Kang finished translating. The cabin was silent. Then Sung spoke, the words coming in broken spurts.

'He says the security services have his family. Wife, parents, children, cousins. They'll all die if he doesn't follow orders.'

'How did he blow his cover?' When Sung heard Kang's translation, he shook his head before muttering a response.

'He didn't. He's sure. It must have been someone on our side. One day the police came. Nothing he said mattered. They knew.'

'Why didn't they just arrest us, sink the boat, when we landed?'

This time Sung said nothing at all. Beck put aside his pistol and kneeled on Sung's chest and hit him in the face, twice. He got his shoulder behind the second punch and felt Sung's flat nose break under his fist. 'There's no time for this.'

Sung spoke, the words so quiet that Kang had to lean in to hear. 'He doesn't know. He thinks they wanted to see where we were going, who would meet us.'

'Why didn't you warn us?' Beck asked Sung directly in Korean. The North Koreans had forced Sung to ask CIA for the pickup, of course. But he could have flashed a different code, one that told them that he'd been compromised.

'No choice.'

'Of course you had a choice,' Beck said.

Sung murmured to Kang. 'He wants to show us something. Says you have to get up,' Kang said.

Beck stood. The North Korean shrugged off his nylon sweatpants. He wasn't wearing underwear, just some surgical gauze over his crotch, stained black-red with blood.

Sung lifted the patch.

'Jesus,' Beck said.

Sung's penis and testicles had been removed, leaving a raw hole in his crotch that had been pulled together with crude black stitches. A plastic catheter poked from the wound, spilling drops of reddish-tinted urine.

'Fuck. Animals.'

Tears ran down Sung's cheeks, mixing with the

blood still streaming from his nose, the combination a ghastly purple under the cabin's blue running lights. More than ever, Beck was glad for the little glass capsules in his pocket. He pulled up Sung's sweatpants as gently as he could. Sung was talking again, his shoulders shaking.

'He says, he says they told him he would die no matter what,' Kang said. 'For betraying Kim Jong Il. But they said if he warned us, they'd hurt his sons and his father also, the same way they hurt him.'

'Tell him he's not gonna die. We're not letting him die. Even if he wants to.'

Now that Beck had dumped the transceiver, the North Koreans had lost them, at least temporarily. The radar feed from the Hawkeye showed that the Su-25 and the helicopters had made two loops around the transceiver. Soon enough they'd realize their mistake and widen the search.

Meanwhile, Choe had changed the Phantom's course, turning the boat to 165 degrees, south-south-east, angling slightly toward South Korea. If they had both engines running, they could have gotten to international waters in twenty minutes. Instead they had an hourlong ride. Still, Beck wanted to believe the worst was over. With every minute that passed, they were closer to getting out.

Sung lay curled against the wall, a hand covering his crotch, his body shaking. Beck wanted to ask more questions, but this obviously wasn't the time. Beck reached for his emergency first-aid kit. He grabbed a bottle of forty-milligram OxyContin and shook one and then another of the yellow pills into Sung's hand. The North Korean popped them into his mouth with a hopeless shrug and choked them down. Whatever you're giving me, his eyes said, whatever it does, I'll take it.

Five minutes passed, and another five. Sung sighed and closed his eyes, and Beck hoped the Oxy had knocked him out, or at least dulled his pain. The feed from the Hawkeye showed that the helicopters and the Su-25 had split up, circling south and west as they searched for the Phantom. Through the blown-out windows at the back of the cabin, Beck saw one of the helicopters making long diagonals to the north, its spotlight shining down on the empty black waves. We might get out of this, Beck thought. Busted engine and all. We really might.

Then –

Ping! Ping! Ping!

The pilothouse vibrated as the sonar waves bounced off the Phantom's hull, three in a row in quick succession. Beck had never felt sonar so strong. The boat's sonar-detection system began to sound its automatic alarm, the whine of its horn filling the cabin, telling them what they already knew: a submarine had targeted them. From very, very close. Just like that, they were in worse trouble than ever.

'Where is he?' Beck said.

'Six hundred yards east. Periscope depth. Want me to ping him back?'

'No.' What was the point? They had no torpedoes or depth charges, and on the one-in-a-million chance that the sub had missed them, they might as well stay quiet.

'Choe,' Beck said. 'Heading two-one-five.' Southwest again.

'Two-one-five.' Choe began to turn the helm.

'Tell him to push that engine as fast as he can,' Beck said to Kang.

'I think he figured that out all on his own.' But Kang said something in Korean to Choe nonetheless. Without looking up, Choe said in English, 'Thirty-three knots.' He spat a stream of Korean, a language that had never sounded uglier to Beck than at this moment. Beck knew enough of what Choe was saying to understand that Choe was cursing him for leading them on a mission doomed to failure even before it began. Nonetheless, Choe pushed the throttle forward and the Phantom picked up speed.

Ping!

Again the cabin rattled. The sub was double-checking its range. Its skipper couldn't believe how close he was either. But Beck didn't think the sub would fire without being certain it wasn't accidentally targeting a fishing trawler.

He looked east but couldn't see the periscope. He wondered if the sub had tracked them all the way from the rendezvous point. Probably not. The North Koreans had ordered it here in case the Phantom somehow escaped their cordon. Running across the sub was nothing more than bad luck. The kind of bad luck that would kill them all.

Still, as long as it could move, the Phantom had a chance, Beck knew. North Korean subs were badly made copies of Russian Romeo-class subs, whose basic design was fifty years old. Thus the telltale active sonar pings. Unlike modern subs, the Romeos needed active sonar to lock on their targets, even at close range.

The North Korean torpedoes were equally dated, copies of old Russian 53-61 Alligators, with a top speed of forty knots and a range under ten miles. With both engines, the Phantom could easily have outrun the torpedo. Instead, the boat's fate would depend on how quickly the North Koreans could load and fire, how badly the years of famine had degraded their readiness.

Beck's watch read 00:00:30. A new day. He hoped he'd see the end of it.

Thirty seconds later, Kang looked up from his screen. 'They've launched,' he said.

'Range?'

'Twelve hundred yards.'

Now it's just math, Beck thought. Either that Alligator runs out of juice before it gets to us, or it tears us up. The torpedo was running 1,200 yards a minute, give or take. With its blown engine, the Phantom was limited to about 1,000 yards a minute. The torpedo had started 1,200 yards behind, but it was picking up roughly 200 yards a minute, maybe a little less. Unless it ran out of fuel, it would be making their acquaintance in six minutes, seven at most.

For a moment, Beck thought about ordering Choe to stop the Phantom so they could try to launch the Zodiac raft. But they probably couldn't get to it before the torpedo hit, and even if they could, they'd have to leave Sung behind. Beck wasn't willing to abandon the North Korean, even though his treachery had put them in this jam. He'd suffered more than any of them.

The seconds ticked by miserably. 00:03:40 . . . 00:03:41 . . . 'Range?'

'Seven hundred fifty yards and closing.'

Beck wished they could do something more. Take evasive action. Drop chaff. Fire their own torpedo. Call in air support to blast that damned sub out of the water. But they could only run, and hope.

00:05:56 . . . 'Range?'

59

'Three hundred fifty yards. Still on us.'

'Is he slowing?' The torpedo wouldn't stop all at once. It would sputter to a halt as it exhausted its stores of kerosene and hydrogen peroxide.

'Not yet.' Kang turned the Dolphins hat around. 'Time for a rally cap.'

00:07:03 . . . 'Range?'

'Under two hundred . . . a hundred fifty now.' Kang's tone was steady. 'Wait . . . he's slowing.' Hope crept into his voice. 'He's at thirty-eight knots. Thirty-seven.' The hope faded. 'He's still coming. A hundred yards now.'

Even so, the torpedo was now hardly gaining ground on the Phantom − and it was near the end of its effective range. If they could just stay ahead for a minute longer, they might get free.

'Sixty-five yards . . . Sixty . . . but he's lost another two knots. Down to thirty-four. He's hardly catching us now. Fifty yards.'

And now Beck could see the wake of the torpedo, cutting through the flat waves, chasing them, trying to destroy them. It was just a mindless piece of steel, but Beck hated it more than he'd ever hated anything.

'Only forty yards,' Kang said. Then his voice lifted. 'He's down to thirty-three.' At thirty-three knots the torpedo wasn't closing anymore.

'That's right,' Beck said to the thing behind them. 'Die. Get lost and die.'

'Thirty-two.' Kang didn't try to hide his joy. 'We're outrunning him!'

In their excitement neither Beck nor Kang noticed that a red warning light had flared on the dashboard. 'Oil!' Choe yelled. 'Oil!'

'What?'

Choe pointed at the light, the engine oil-pressure warning light. They'd run the damaged Mercury too hot for too long. Minute by minute, the oil leak had worsened. They'd dripped oil like blood across the sea. Now the engine had no oil left at all, and –

With a loud *thunk*, it seized up, leaving the Phantom without power.

And no power meant the Phantom was a floating paperweight.

With only its momentum to carry it along.

But the torpedo hadn't forgotten them.

And even as Beck put all this together, the Alligator slammed into the Phantom's keel. The torpedo's firing pin smashed backward. Electricity flowed into the firing cap, setting off the charge. A fraction of a second later, the Alligator's warhead exploded, blasting the boat with 670 pounds of explosive.

The Russians had designed the Alligator to sink destroyers and cruisers, big ships with thick steel hulls. The Phantom didn't stand a chance.

The explosion threw the speedboat twenty feet in the air. The blast wave tore through the cabin in a fraction of a second, splitting the four men inside into unrecognizable bits. They had no time for last words or even last thoughts, just a bright flash of pain followed by the unknown and unknowable. By the time the blasted hull of the Phantom crashed into the sea, they were dead.

The boat itself lasted longer. It burned for ninety seconds, a floating funeral pyre visible in the night for miles. Then water filled its hull and it sank, taking its crew of corpses to the bottom of the sea.

SIX

Even before the Phantom disappeared beneath the waves, word of its destruction was spreading.

The North Koreans knew first, of course. The sonar operators on the *Nampo*, the submarine that had launched the torpedo, picked up the explosion immediately. After radioing its commanders, the *Nampo* chugged toward the wreckage, seeking survivors. It found no life, just an oil slick and pieces of the Phantom's hull.

The torpedo had blown apart the Phantom at 12:08 a.m. By 12:25, word of its sinking had reached North Korea's military headquarters in Pyongyang, a crumbling concrete building ringed with antiaircraft guns and missile batteries. Five minutes later, Kim Jong Il, the chubby gnome who ruled North Korea, received a report of the Phantom's sinking at his palace in Pyongyang. He celebrated with a glass of Johnnie Walker Blue, his favorite scotch. He had taken the Drafter's betrayal personally. He knew only too well that his survival depended on the nuclear arsenal he had so carefully assembled. Kim had personally ordered Sung's arrest and castration, an object lesson to anyone else who might betray him. Kim had no regrets about what he'd done. Regret had no place in his vocabulary. Loyalty, on the other hand, was a word he understood. The fact that a boat had come for Sung proved the man's treachery beyond any doubt. His death was fitting punishment.

Now Kim had a call to make – to the man who had informed him of the Drafter's treachery. He didn't like depending on the Chinese. They used him and his people as pawns against the United States. But he couldn't deny that this time, they'd proven valuable.

Washington learned of the Phantom's sinking not long afterward. At 00:08:02 local time, the boat disappeared from the screens of the E-2 Hawkeye. The plane immediately passed a message to the sonar operators on the USS *Decatur* – the destroyer in the Yellow Sea – advising them to listen for shock waves that might signal an explosion.

The *Decatur* didn't have long to wait. The blast from the Alligator created a pressure wave that passed through the water at a mile a second, reaching the destroyer in under a minute. The sonar operators aboard the *Decatur* were used to tracking quiet Soviet submarines. To their trained ears, the blast wave sounded like a scream.

The *Decatur* reported the explosion to the combat information center at the USS *Ronald Reagan*, an aircraft carrier steaming in the Korea Strait. The *Reagan* sent the news to Osan Air Base. From there it went to CIA station in Seoul. A few minutes later, the South Korean coast guard station at Incheon passed word that two containerships were reporting a fire in the Yellow Sea.

At this point, Bob Harbarg, the chief of Seoul station,

decided he had to tell Langley. He fired off a Critic-coded message, the highest priority, reporting that the Phantom was missing and presumed lost. The agency hadn't saved the Phantom, but it had done a fine job watching the boat sink.

The only question left was whether Ted Beck and his men had somehow escaped the boat. Four Chinooks scrambled from Osan Air Base to search for signals from the transponders that Beck, Kang, and Choe carried. A Predator drone was launched to photograph the site of the explosion. But the Chinooks and Predator found nothing. As the hours ticked by, the sailors on the *Decatur*, the crews on the Chinooks, and the spies in Virginia had to accept the truth. The men aboard the Phantom were lost.

On the *Decatur* and at Osan, the mission ended there. But at Langley, the Phantom's sinking brought new urgency to a different set of questions.

That night, Wells and Exley walked down the Mall under a cloudless sky. The moon hung behind them, the Washington Monument rising toward it like a needle poised to pop a balloon. Aside from the joggers and Frisbee players sweating in the night air, they had the open green field to themselves. The hard-packed Mall path crunched under their feet, a sound Exley found oddly satisfying. She reached for Wells's hand, squeezed it. He squeezed back.

'Jenny.' His voice was hardly above a whisper. 'I won't go if you don't want me to.' She knew what he meant. Afghanistan.

'Shh.' She put her arm over his broad back, rubbing the scar tissue left over from his run-in with the police in Times Square. 'Does it still hurt?'

'It's fine.'

Would you tell me if it did, she wondered. Not a chance.

About thirty yards away a fat man in a gray suit sat reading the *Post*. He waved to them and pushed himself up, grunting like a loaded semi heading up a mountain pass. He was at least three hundred pounds, a coronary waiting to happen. He pulled a white handkerchief from his pocket and mopped his head.

'George Tyson. You must be the famous John Wells.' He put the handkerchief away and extended his hand. Wells let it dangle.

'Right. You don't like being called famous, Mr. Wells. And you don't like counterintelligence.' Tyson's accent was humid and southern.

'Any reason I should?'

'I want to tell you that Vinny Duto didn't ask my opinion of you. Back in the day, I mean. He had strong ideas about you. Still does.'

'And if he had asked? What would you have said?'

'A fair question, Mr. Wells. But try to remember how you looked to us back then. With your Quran and your disappearing act. Accept my apologies, then, and shake an old man's hand.'

Wells reached out for Tyson's big paw – and found himself gripping a joy buzzer. He grunted, more from surprise than pain, as the electricity rattled his palm. Tyson smirked. Wells vaguely remembered hearing about his practical jokes, his way of keeping alive the CIA's traditions from the 1950s, before the agency turned into a bureaucratic monster.

'Cute, Mr. Tyson.'

'So now you're wondering if I'm a fool, or merely

pretending,' Tyson said. 'Hard to say, I reckon. Maybe both.'

'Actually I was wondering how many punches I would need to break your jaw.'

'I'd rather we didn't find out. It's interesting, though, the way you responded to an unanswerable question with one that has a definite answer.'

'Double as a shrink in your spare time?'

'I'll bet you don't like them either, Mr. Wells.' Tyson turned to Exley. 'And you must be Jennifer Exley. Where's Ellis?'

'Waiting in the car, like you asked,' Wells said. To Exley: 'Whatever you do, don't shake his hand.'

'I'd never mistreat a lady.'

They walked on, heading toward the Capitol. Then Tyson turned back toward the Monument, craning his neck like a curious tourist. 'Mr. Wells? Would you say there's anyone on us at the moment?'

'I'd say no. Why? You have some genius tracker following us? Somebody who can smell bear scat at fifty paces?'

'As a matter of fact, I don't. As far as I'm concerned, the fewer people who know about this meeting, the better.'

'So we're on the Mall? I see why you're a master of counterintel.'

'Come now, Mr. Wells. You know there's nothing better than a nice open space where we can see anybody who wants to see us. I'm not concerned about these joggers.'

'Yeah, you don't strike me as the type to care much about exercise.'

'John,' Exley said. She turned to Tyson. 'Ignore him, George. He's been acting out recently.'

66

'So I hear.'

'So *you* hear?' Wells said.

'Mr. Wells. I heard only from Ellis. He's concerned about you.'

'Is that why you're here? An intervention? To convince me to behave?'

'Mr. Wells. Believe it or not, I've got a few other problems.' Tyson's syrupy accent faded notably. He stuffed the joy buzzer into his pocket and leaned in close to Wells, putting his hands on Wells's shoulders. 'I said that Mr. Shafer is concerned about you. Not that I am. Others across the river may think that you're some kind of superspy. *You* may think so, for all I know.'

'No, I don't –'

'Please let me finish. Me, I'm not a fan of the great-man theory of history. The Confederacy had all the best generals and we still lost the war. I think you got lucky in Times Square. We all got lucky. You are here tonight because Mr. Shafer wants you to be. Not me. Are we clear?'

Wells's face tensed and he stood rigid under Tyson's heavy hands. He stepped back, shook Tyson's hands off his shoulders. For a moment Exley thought Wells might actually hit Tyson. Then Wells's face softened.

'We're clear. Thank you.' He stuck out his hand, and after a moment Tyson put out his own. They shook for a long time before Wells finally let go.

'Thank me?'

'Somebody needed to say it. Thank you for not treating me like I'm something special. Or some wounded animal. Even if I am.'

*

Baseball practice had ended hours earlier, but fluorescent lights still shined over the field at Cardozo High School, just up Thirteenth from Exley's apartment. In fact the lights never went dark, possibly because of Washington's legendary municipal incompetence, possibly to make the stands by the field less inviting for midnight trysts. Now Exley, Shafer, and Tyson sat in the stands, waiting for Wells. They'd driven around Washington for fifteen minutes, confirming that no one was following them, before Wells dropped them off and promised to find parking.

Wells trotted up, holding a plastic bag and handing out paper bags.

'Beer?' Tyson peered into the bag distastefully.

'For our cover,' Wells said. 'Picked them up at that package store on U Street.'

'For our cover?' Exley couldn't help but laugh. Wells's mood had certainly improved, with the promise of a mission and his dressing-down from Tyson, she thought. Even if he hadn't said a word she would have known. He was watching the world in a way that he hadn't in months.

Wells popped open his beer and took a swig. Tyson looked at him. 'What kind of Muslim are you, anyway, John?'

'Don't spend much time at the mosque these days,' Wells said.

'I might feel the same if my co-religionists spent their days thinking of new and exciting ways to kill me.' Tyson poked the can out of the bag. 'Budweiser?'

'Budweiser, George. Put hair on your chest.'

'Is she going to drink one too, then?' Tyson looked at Exley. 'I've never had a Budweiser in my life. It's Yankee beer.'

'Budweiser's from St. Louis,' Exley said.

'All beer is Yankee beer,' Tyson said. 'Real Southerners drink whiskey.'

'George, why can I picture you overseeing a plantation, whip in hand?'

'That's your overactive imagination. Now, this is turning into a real fun evening, but I'd like to tell you why we're here.' Over the next half-hour, Tyson filled them in on the Phantom's mission, and its failure.

'And we had no hint of trouble before our guy, the Drafter, asked for the extraction?' Exley said when Tyson was finished.

'No. We saw him eight months ago in Pakistan, offered to get him out then. He refused. They'd just promoted him. Which is another reason I think it was from our side. Kim Jong Il doesn't have enough good scientists to turn on them for no reason.'

'And counterintelligence investigations always leave a trail,' Shafer said. 'No matter how hard you try, you can't watch the suspect without him knowing.'

'He sees someone's been poking in his office,' Tyson said. 'Or we dangle something and he wonders why all of a sudden he's got new access. Moles have this spooky sense of when we're watching.'

'Tell me about it,' Wells said, remembering the years he'd spent in the mountains. Every day he had wondered if al Qaeda and the Taliban would recognize him as an American agent.

'So I suspect Sung would have known if they were after him,' Tyson said. 'Instead he was as snug as a termite in a lumberyard until the day he told us to get him.'

'Could you repeat that last bit?' Wells said. 'In English?'

'Ignore the Dixie twang and you have the facts,'

Shafer said. 'Odds are the North Koreans were tipped from the outside.'

'Maybe they caught him holding something classified,' Exley said.

'He was too careful for that,' Tyson said. 'His stuff all came shortwave or face-to-face.'

'How important was he, this guy?' Wells said.

'Our most important human source.'

'In North Korea?'

Tyson sighed. 'Anywhere. He told us where they hid their nukes.'

'Then maybe it wasn't the North Koreans.' Wells raised the Budweiser to his lips, filling his mouth with the cool tart liquid.

'How do you mean?'

'Maybe they got tipped by some other hostile service, somebody who wanted to hurt us bad and knew this would do it.'

'Makes perfect sense,' Shafer said. 'Somebody gets this, banks it, takes it out now, gives it to the North Koreans when it can really mess us up.'

'I understand, Ellis,' Tyson said irritably. Tyson raised the beer to his mouth, took a tiny sip.

'Not bad, is it, Mr. Tyson?' Wells said.

'I wish I could say yes. Please give it a good home.' Tyson handed the bag to Wells.

'So why are you telling us this?' Exley said.

'For the moment I'm taking the usual steps,' Tyson said. 'My staff is examining who had access to the Drafter's identity or the information he provided. Looking for unusual travel patterns for the officers in the North Korean unit.'

'You're going to have a lot of people to look at,' Shafer said.

'And it's no secret that our record in these investigations has been less than stellar.'

'Counterintel doesn't get the cream of the crop,' Wells said. 'Present company excepted.'

'I can't disagree. It's far more exciting to be chief of station in Tokyo than stuck in Langley poring over bank records. And anyone with half a brain knows that questioning the loyalty of one's fellow employees won't win friends when it comes time for the promotion boards to meet. But you –'

'Have no friends anyway,' Exley said.

'I was going to say that you have shown the ability to work outside the agency's institutional confines.'

'In other words, no friends,' Wells said.

'I was hoping you might run your own informal inquiry. You'll have access to everything that the official investigation turns up. If you need subpoenas or extra eyes, I'll get them for you. In return I ask only that you let me know what you find.'

'Like who got our boat blown to bits twelve hours ago. More black stars.' Every time a CIA employee died on a mission, the agency added a black star to the north wall of the lobby at its original headquarters building. There were now more than eighty stars.

'Exactly, Mr. Wells.'

'You never told us – who was on that boat?'

'Lead agent was named Ted Beck.'

Wells pounded a fist into his open palm. 'Dammit.'

'You knew him?' Tyson said.

'He was one of the good guys.' Beck had been one of Wells's instructors at the Farm – officially called Camp Peary, the CIA's training center for new recruits – back in the mid-1990s. Beck wasn't much past thirty, but even then he was bald as a cue ball, tough and strong.

He and Wells had shared a love for Pierce's Pitt Bar-B-Que, a restaurant off Highway 64 where a full rack of ribs cost just $9.95.

Suddenly Wells was irritated at himself for the self-pity he'd indulged in over the last months. He'd sacrificed some, for sure. But Ted Beck – and lots of others – had sacrificed far more.

'You're the only one who will know what we're doing?' Exley said.

'Yes. I can give you something in writing. If you feel you need that protection.'

'Not necessary,' Shafer said.

'I'm in,' Exley said.

'Mr. Wells?'

'I'd love to. Especially now that I know who got hit. But I've got my own business to take care of. In Afghanistan.'

'Well.' The stands creaked as Tyson stood up. 'Good luck with that.'

Part 2

SEVEN

TEHRAN, IRAN

The tarmac at Menrabad Airport, outside Tehran, was a living graveyard of aviation. Baggage carts and tanker trucks jostled for space with planes that had long ago become extinct at more modern airports: 727s, DC-10s, even Russian Tu-154s cast off by Aeroflot. At the end of the terminal sat a four-engine 707, the original Boeing passenger jet, introduced in 1954 and a favorite of aviation buffs. In America, the plane would have been a museum piece. Here it was transportation.

In the midst of this muddle, three Iranian Army jeeps and two Mercedes limousines sped along, horns honking, headlights flashing. The convoy was led by a black Toyota Land Cruiser with tinted windows, a distinctive rising siren, and a single red light on its roof, like a 1960s police cruiser.

The light and siren identified the Toyota as belonging to Vevak, Iran's fearsome secret police force. As the Toyota approached, baggage handlers jumped back and the Tata tanker trucks made way, their drivers ducking their heads. Avoiding Vevak's attention was critical to a long and healthy life in Iran.

75

The Land Cruiser pulled up beside an Airbus A340 painted in the distinctive white-and-gold of Air China, the state-owned Chinese national airline. Four Chinese men stepped out of the first limo and positioned themselves around the second. Only then did the doors of the second Mercedes open. Five men emerged, two bodyguards in suits and three older men wearing the uniforms of the People's Liberation Army.

The last man to step out was taller than the rest, broad-shouldered, deep into middle age, with short black hair and shining golden sideboards on his green uniform. He was General Li Ping, chief of the People's Liberation Army and one of the nine members of China's Politburo Standing Committee, the group that ruled the world's most populous nation.

Li and his bodyguards strode up the jetway as the Land Cruiser and limousines rolled away. A few minutes later, the Airbus accelerated down the runway, its engines purring, and lifted into the cloudless night.

From the outside, this Airbus looked like the usual Air China A340 widebody that flew the 5,000-mile route from Beijing to Tehran three times a week, down to the stylized red phoenix painted on its tail. But inside, this jet was very different. In place of the usual complement of three hundred seats, it held twenty lie-flat recliners. Near the front of the plane were two staterooms, with king-sized beds, bathrooms, and showers. The jet also came equipped with its own full-time crew from the Chinese air force, as well as three armed guards who lived in a suite at the back and never left the plane unattended.

For despite its markings, this Airbus was far from an ordinary commercial jet. Only the nine men on the Standing Committee had the right to use it. Naturally,

China had official state aircraft as well, painted with the country's five-starred red-and-yellow flag. But the A340 offered advantages for those times when Politburo members wanted to keep their travel plans secret. American spy satellites watched over all the major airports in Iran. But they weren't looking for an Air China widebody. The jet gave General Li a way to travel invisibly to his meetings in Tehran, meetings he'd been having more and more often.

In some ways, China and Iran had every reason to get close. Both nations had long and proud histories. Both had suffered during the twentieth century from invasions and internal strife. Both were now powerful once again, though for different reasons. China's strength was built on two decades of spectacular economic growth. Iran's gains were based on oil and the failure of American policy in the Middle East. The Islamic Republic now dominated the Persian Gulf and had the ability to choke off half the world's oil.

Any serious threat of war between Iran and the United States would take the price of crude to $100 a barrel. An actual American attack on Iran would move oil closer to $200 and put the world into recession. If Iran retaliated by destroying the giant fields to its west in Saudi Arabia, the world would have to ration oil for the first time since the original wells had been drilled in Pennsylvania 140 years before.

And despite what environmentalists liked to pretend, the modern world could hardly exist without oil. Airplanes would be grounded. Electricity and fertilizer would double or triple in price. Middle-class Americans and Europeans would be squeezed, and the lives of the poor everywhere would grow more desperate. So Iran was not just another third-world country that got the world's attention only for plane crashes and earthquakes. When its leaders spoke, London and Washington had to listen. But America didn't enjoy being at Iran's mercy, a fact that the leaders of the Islamic Republic knew only too well. To make sure that the United States never tried 'regime change' in Iran as it had in Iraq, they wanted a nuclear arsenal.

Li understood the Iranian desire for nukes. It was no coincidence that the five permanent members of the United Nations Security Council – China, America, Russia, Britain, and France – were the five countries with the largest nuclear stockpiles. Because of their unique destructive power, nukes guaranteed national security like no other weapon. No country that openly possessed a nuclear stockpile had ever been invaded. With nuclear weapons to give it cover, Iran could push its neighbors around even more aggressively.

For that reason, Washington and Jerusalem had vowed to stop Tehran from getting even one bomb. In response, Iran had turned to China for support.

And China? China had reasons to help Iran. Li had reasons too, his own reasons, ones that not even his fellow ministers on the Politburo Standing Committee could imagine.

Thus Li had made the trip to Tehran three times in the last year, each time in secret on this Airbus 340, for talks with Mahmoud Ahmadinejad, the Iranian president.

The trips hadn't been easy. China and Iran might need each other, but they didn't necessarily trust each other. Li found the atmosphere in Tehran as suffocating as the long black robes the women wore, and the national obsession with Islam as bewildering as the calls to prayer that rang through the presidential palace.

Before Li's first visit to Iran, his staff had prepared a thick book for him about Islam. He had skimmed a few pages and then tossed the binder aside. Prophets, angels, devils, an all-knowing God . . . Islam was just like Judaism and Christianity. Li didn't believe in any of them. Like many Chinese, he wasn't very religious, though every so often he burned fake money to honor his father and mother, both long dead. He wanted to make his mark in this world, not wait for another life. Meanwhile he had a question for his hosts, one he didn't plan to ask: If the Iranians had such faith in Allah, why were they so desperate for nuclear bombs?

The A340 reached 38,000 feet and leveled off. Li touched a button on his leather recliner. Sun Wei, the Airbus's steward, appeared in seconds. 'General.'

'Please ask the pilots if we can expect a smooth flight.' Chinese men his age rarely exercised – at most they contented themselves with tai chi – but Li took his workout regimen very seriously. He always brought an elliptical trainer with him on the Airbus.

Wei disappeared. A minute later he was back, holding a gym bag packed with Li's exercise clothes. 'The winds are with us, General. A smooth flight.'

In the main stateroom, Li changed in silence and alone. Some other members of the Standing Committee had valets to help them dress. Li hadn't fallen so far into bourgeois decadence, not yet anyway. Though he had to admit that he'd grown used to great luxury. He had chauffeurs, guards, housekeepers. Still, he always tried to remember that he served the people, not the other way around. Unlike other leaders, he hadn't used his position to make a fortune from bribes or corrupt business deals. He had no hidden bank accounts, no villas in Hong Kong.

For the next hour Li forgot himself on the trainer. When he was finished, he stretched and showered and returned to his chair. A glass of freshly squeezed orange juice awaited him. Sun Wei knew the favorite drinks of everyone lucky enough to be a regular passenger on this plane.

Li sipped his juice and tried to relax. As always, he was glad to be free of Ahmadinejad, the Iranian president, a scrawny man with hard black eyes. At their first meeting, a year earlier, Ahmadinejad had begun by haranguing Li about the United States and Israel, the eternal enemies of Muslims everywhere. The words spilled from Ahmadinejad's mouth so quickly that Li's translator could hardly keep up. Though the Iranians kept the presidential palace frigid, sweat rolled down Ahmadinejad's face as his voice rose.

For half an hour, Li had sat across from Ahmadinejad, hands folded patiently in his lap, waiting for the man to exhaust himself. He was used to sitting through boring speeches, though usually they came in his own language. The Iranian poured out words, a river of nonsense. He seemed to be preaching at an audience of thousands, an audience that only he could see. Finally Li broke in.

'Mr. President,' he'd said, first in Chinese, then in English. 'Mr. President.

'The Chinese people appreciate your grievances with the global hegemon, the United States. We agree that every state has the right to rule itself.'

'Yes, yes. But the problem is deeper. The Zionists –'

Li had no intention of sitting through another rant. 'And I thank you for your hospitality. But I must return to Beijing tomorrow, and we have much to discuss.'

Ahmadinejad seemed to have forgotten that Li was an emissary from a country more powerful than his own, not a rival to be bullied. 'General, before we can continue, you must understand –' But Li never found out what he had to understand. Before Ahmadinejad could go on, the clean-shaven man beside him whispered into his ear.

The man was Said Mousavi, the head of Iran's secret police, and whatever he had said, his words were effective. Ahmadinejad ran his hand through his coarse black beard and whispered back to the security minister. From then on, his conversations with Li had been mostly businesslike, though Ahmadinejad still blustered occasionally about Zionist conspiracies. Yet by the end of their second meeting, Li realized that the Iranian was more subtle than he appeared. As much as anything, his windy speeches were intended to distract, to hide Iran's real ambitions.

If outsiders had known of these meetings, they would have assumed China had the upper hand. Yet it was Li who flew to Tehran, not Ahmadinejad to Beijing. The men who ran Iran took such eagerness as a sign of China's weakness. Li didn't try to change their minds. He had his own reason for wanting these meetings in Tehran instead of Beijing. This way, only he and his closest aides knew exactly what he was telling Ahmadinejad. Of course, he reported back to his fellow ministers on the Standing Committee after each meeting. But he didn't report *everything*.

As they tried to build a bomb, the Iranians needed engineering help, lots of it. Even for a sovereign country with a multibillion-dollar budget, building a nuclear weapon was harder than it looked.

Nuclear weapons are both complicated and very simple. Conventional explosives get energy from breaking chemical bonds between atoms. Nuclear bombs release the energy bound up inside individual atoms, a far bigger source of power. The difference in power is staggering. Fat Man, the bomb that the United States dropped on Nagasaki in 1945, used fourteen pounds of plutonium to produce a blast with the energy produced by 42 million pounds of conventional explosive. The bomb killed 70,000 people immediately and tens of thousands more over the next generation. Yet by modern standards, the Fat Man bomb is puny.

Fortunately for humanity's survival, most types of atoms can't be used in nuclear weapons. The exceptions are plutonium and a certain kind of uranium, called U-235, so-called fissile materials. The United States and other major nuclear powers prefer plutonium for their bombs, because plutonium is even more potent than uranium. But plutonium is also harder to handle, and it doesn't exist naturally. Making it requires nuclear reactors, big buildings that are prime targets for guided missiles or bombs. So uranium is the nuclear material of choice for countries like Iran, which need to make bombs in secret.

Still, uranium can't simply be pulled out of the ground and plugged into a nuclear weapon. In its natural state, uranium ore consists of two different isotopes, U-235 and U-238. They look the same, a heavy dull yellow metal. But they have different atomic structures. U-235 can be used to make a bomb. U-238 can't.

In its natural state, uranium is made up of 97 percent U-238, the useless kind, with just 3 percent U-235 mixed in. When the United States began the Manhattan Project to develop nuclear weapons, its scientists had to find a way to separate the valuable U-235 from U-238. They found the answer in centrifuges, enclosed chambers that spin very fast, and enabled them to pull the lighter U-235 out of the U-238.

In theory, the centrifuge procedure is relatively straightforward. But as the Iranians had found out, bridging the gap between theory and reality could be difficult. Even under the best of circumstances, it required a small army of well-trained engineers and physicists. The Iranians had an added challenge. Because of the threat of the Israeli air force, they were working in labs buried seventy feet underground.

Until this meeting, Ahmadinejad hadn't told Li exactly what problems the Iranians were having. In part, his reticence was a matter of national pride. The Iranians hated to admit that they had failed where North Korea had succeeded. At the same time, Tehran worried that Beijing might be cozying up to them just to betray them to the United States.

To overcome that suspicion, Li had gone to great lengths. Not even the other members of the Politburo Standing Committee knew the steps he had taken. Now, finally, his efforts were paying off. This time around, Ahmadinejad and his scientific advisers had made very specific requests, asking if China could lend Iran electrical engineers, metallurgists, and physicists – a hiveful of highly trained worker bees to build a very large stinger. In return, Ahmadinejad offered to name China as Iran's preferred partner for oil and natural gas development, and to give China first call on Iranian crude in case of a worldwide shortage.

Li hadn't tried to hide his excitement at the offer. An alliance between China and Iran would be a giant shift in world politics. For the first time since the end of the Cold War, major nations would align in open defiance of America.

Naturally, Li agreed. The approval of the Standing Committee would be a formality, he said. And why would the Iranians doubt him? He'd given them reason to believe that China hated the United States as much as they did.

Li knew this alliance was risky. He didn't fully trust the Iranians. But he needed their help, needed it now. He was setting China on a collision course with the United States. Without Iran's support, his plan couldn't succeed. And despite what he'd told the Iranians, the plan was *his,* his alone. The other eight members on the Politburo Committee didn't know what he was doing. They would never have supported him.

Li believed he had sound reasons for taking this path. The others on the committee were cowards and thieves. He needed to act, and quickly. One day, the full truth would came out, and the world would judge his actions. By then he'd be dead, though not forgotten. Never forgotten. In the meantime, though, he needed to keep his scheme secret. For if the Standing Committee learned exactly what he'd done, his future would be short and bleak.

Li turned his chair to face Cao Se. Technically, Cao was only the seventh-ranking officer in the PLA, but in reality he was closer to Li than anyone else. Li and Cao had served together in China's three-week war in Vietnam in 1979. Li had come out unscathed, but not Cao. A mine had taken off his left leg below the knee.

Sometimes Li wondered whether Cao was marked to take the misfortune for both of them. Perhaps in a previous life he had served Cao. Now the roles were reversed. Where Li was tall and handsome, Cao was small, his face pockmarked. His wife had died in childbirth in 1986 at a Shanghai hospital, and he had never remarried.

A few years before, Li had caught Cao staring at him. The look wasn't sexual, more like the devotion that a child lavished on a distant father. Sometimes Li wondered if a more independent adviser would have served him better. Yet loyalty like Cao's was rare, and Li needed at least one man he could trust completely.

Cao knew more about Li's plan than anyone else. Even so, Li hadn't told Cao exactly what he was doing. As much as he trusted Cao, he couldn't take that chance. Not yet.

'General.' Cao was drawing intently in a spiral notebook, his lips pursed tight, his face rapt. At the sound of Li's voice, Cao snapped the notebook shut.

'Keeping secrets, Cao?'

'You know I have no secrets.'

'Let's see.' Li reached out for the notebook.

'It's nothing to do with anything, General.' Nonetheless, Cao handed it over.

The book's pages were filled with sketches of buildings in thick black ink, skyscrapers and highways and apartment complexes. Long flowing strokes that caught the motion and vitality of city life. Li recognized the giant Jin Mao Tower in Shanghai, the Empire State Building. Other buildings seemed to be of Cao's own creation, narrow towers that stretched to the sky, stadiums with cantilevered roofs.

'Cao. These are excellent.'

'A way to pass the time.'

'No. Truly. You could have been an architect. You have a talent.' At this, Cao smiled. 'Why didn't you tell me?'

'I didn't think you'd be interested, General.'

Li handed back the book. And wondered, What other secrets have you been keeping from me all these years, little Cao?

'So what did you think of Ahmadinejad today?' This conversation would necessarily be limited. Li and Cao knew that the A340 had a dozen bugs scattered through its cabin. As defense minister, Li controlled most of them. But not all.

'These Iranians are strange people,' Cao said. 'In a way, they're like the Red Guards' – the young revolutionaries who had tormented China in the late 1960s. 'They don't mind tearing everything down. They take a certain pleasure in it. If they got the special weapon, they might actually use it.'

'They think the world could end tomorrow. It gives them freedom.'

'At first I didn't think we could trust them. But now . . . Our interests are aligned. We help them, they help us. We're in different beds but we have the same dream.'

Li smiled. Cao had reversed the Chinese proverb of 'different dreams in the same bed.' The implication of the saying was that no two people could fully trust each other. Even a husband and wife who'd slept beside each other for fifty years had different dreams.

In this case, though, Li and Ahmadinejad knew that they were in a marriage of convenience. Their opposition to the United States had brought them together.

They didn't need to trust each other, as long as their interests were aligned.

'Different beds, same dream,' Li said. 'It's enough for a partnership.'

'For now.'

'It won't have to be forever, Cao.'

EIGHT

ANNANDALE, VIRGINIA

The golden retriever lunged after a fat gray squirrel, dragging the man in the green windbreaker forward. He fell on the muddy ground, banging his knee against a bulbous stone, his curses echoing through the empty woods. The dog ran off, chasing the squirrel until it darted up a birch tree and disappeared.

'*Lenny!* You moron! Come here.'

The dog stared stupidly at him, then trotted back, his leash trailing on the muddy ground. The man could only shake his head. For months Janice had told him to get that dog-training video with the Mexican guy. He would have bought it already if she hadn't nagged him so much. Even when she was right, she was wrong.

'Lenny. You dope.'

He patted the dog's flank. Lenny licked his hand by way of apology before flopping onto the ground. Rain had fallen all night, leaving the earth soaked. The dog rolled from side to side on his back, ecstatic at the chance to cover himself in dirt.

No wonder this stupid animal was his favorite creature in the world, the man thought. This simple sense of joy that he had lost long ago. If he'd ever had it. Certainly he preferred Lenny to his wife. If their house were burning and he could save only one, he'd probably grab the dog.

'Enough. You're making a mess.'

He took Lenny's leash and stood, trying not to lean too hard on his knee. The rain had let up before dawn, but a drizzle continued, spotting his forehead. He breathed in deeply, hoping the cool damp air would soothe his lungs.

The man looked around the leafy woods to be sure he was alone. Wakefield Park lay in suburban Virginia, just west of the Beltway. But it seemed to belong somewhere more rural. Sparrows darted through beech trees, and foxes regularly made their way to the creek in the center of the park. In the early mornings, the place was deserted aside from a few mountain bikers – and the man in the green windbreaker.

It was the perfect spot for dead drops.

The man checked the gold Rolex he wore only outside the office: 6:07. Time to move, before the bikers showed up. He tugged on Lenny's leash and off they went, Lenny's head twisting from side to side as the idiot dog looked for more squirrels to chase.

Ten minutes later the man stopped near a granite out-cropping beside a burned-out tree stump. He was alone, though he could hear the morning's first biker yodeling gleefully over a rise to the east.

From his jeans the man pulled a little black plastic case that looked like the control for a car alarm. The case had two buttons, one black, one red. He pushed the black button.

To the west, up a slight hill, he heard two chirps.

Maybe 150 feet away. He walked up the hill and pushed the black button again. This time the beeps were closer, thirty feet. He paced closer, one careful step at a time. He looked around, making sure he was still alone. He was. Once more he pushed the button. The beeps came again –

There. It lay by a tree, a broken oak branch like any other. Only it wasn't. It was the dead drop to end all dead drops. The branch was genuine, and originally from this park. But at a lab outside Beijing it had been hollowed out, its center replaced with a waterproof plastic compartment big enough to hold two thin sheets of paper – or a flash memory drive. Big enough to betray the CIA's most important secrets.

The Chinese had installed a receiver in the branch that responded to a signal in the plastic case the man held. The technology was simple, basically a car alarm with better encryption, but foolproof. He and his handlers could make drops just about anywhere. For the last three years, they had used Wakefield, a perfect spot, a fifteen-minute walk from his house.

He reached down for the branch –

And a squirrel ran by and Lenny tugged on his leash. Stupid dog.

'Go. You deserve each other.' He dropped the leash. The retriever took off.

'Alone at last,' the man said. He picked up the branch, rubbing his fingers over its bark, feeling for the hidden pressure points at each end. If they were pressed simultaneously – and only if they were pressed simultaneously – they would release an electromagnetic lock and pop open the center compartment.

There. He found the first pressure point. Now where

was the other? He probed the bark. There. No, there –

'Hey! Buddy!'

Dammit. He turned to see a mountain biker pedaling toward him. The guy was wearing the ridiculous gear they loved, a neon-yellow reflective jacket and tight Lycra shorts.

'This your dog?' Lenny trailed after the bike.

The man in the green windbreaker felt his heart thump crazily. 'Yeah. His name's Lenny. He thinks one day he's gonna catch himself a squirrel. Thanks for bringing him back –' Stop talking, he thought. You're just a guy out walking your dog.

He snapped his mouth closed. He dropped the branch and reached for Lenny. 'You dummy,' he said to the retriever. 'You're gonna get lost.'

'Ought to keep an eye on him. I almost hit him.'

'You're right. My mistake.'

The biker rolled closer. The man felt oddly light-headed. *He knows. I'm not sure how, but he knows.* Why had he left his Smith & Wesson in his basement?

'Well?'

'Well what?'

'Shouldn't you put him back on the leash?'

'Sure. Of course.' He reattached the leash. 'Thanks for bringing him back.'

'No prob, man.' The biker nodded victoriously and turned down the hill. The man in the windbreaker sat down and waited for his pulse to return to normal. After all his years of tradecraft, he couldn't believe that a jackass on a souped-up twelve-speed had almost busted him.

'Lenny. You almost caused me big trouble.'

Instead of answering, the dog squatted to relieve himself. Or maybe that was his answer, the man in the

91

green windbreaker thought. He let Lenny take his time, waiting until he could no longer see the biker, until he could no longer feel his heart thumping sideways in his chest. When he was sure he was alone, he turned back to retrieve the branch – and the instructions inside.

NINE

Wells walked down a white sand beach, dipping his feet into the waves lapping along the shore. The water was the clearest blue imaginable, so bright it almost seemed neon. Exley lay on the beach under an umbrella, wearing a modest bikini that changed color as he looked at it, now red, now yellow, now green with camouflage stripes. That's wrong, he told her. War isn't sex. But she didn't hear.

He turned back to the ocean. Instead of sand, the water covered a bank of fluorescent lights. Off, he said to Exley. Turn them off. She ignored him, and when he looked for her, she was gone. He tried to run for her, but the waves ripped him away from the beach, away from her –

'Mr. Brown.'

Wells woke, muzzy-headed, to a hand shaking his shoulder. Instead of a beach, he was on a C-17. The cabin stank of sweat and stale unwashed bodies. They'd been airborne for twenty hours.

'You okay, sir? Look a little green.'

'Fine, Lieutenant.' Wells rolled his head, futilely trying to unlock the scar tissue in his back. Instead of standard seats, the military plane had plastic benches screwed to its walls. They seemed designed to torture the spine.

'Lieutenant, how long was I out for?'

'Five hours, give or take,' the lieutenant said. 'We'll be down in forty-five. Pilot just turned on the lights.'

The lights. That accounted for his dream, Wells thought. All around him, men in fatigues were slapping themselves awake, swigging mouthwash, stretching, anything to shake off the boredom of an 11,000-mile journey. Wells had hitched a ride to Bagram Air Base in Afghanistan with the 504th Parachute Infantry Regiment of the 82nd Airborne, which was being sent overseas for the third time in five years. Macho chatter filled the cabin, soldiers psyching themselves up for the grueling days to come:

'Ready to land?'

'Heck no, Sergeant. Let's spend another day in this tin can.'

'Ramirez, is that my toothbrush?'

'Nuh-uh, moron. Check your ass – it's probably stuck there.'

'Think this is what it's like to be an astronaut? When I was a kid, I always wanted to be an astronaut.'

'You can't even find Uranus, Roberts – get it? Uranus. Like –'

'I get it.'

'All right, who farted?'

'Who didn't?'

Then, from the back of the cabin, the all-purpose Army cheer: 'Hoo-ah!'

'Hoo-ah!'

'Those Talibs ain't gonna know what hit 'em! They going down like Chinatown!'

'Hoo-ah!'

'Like your sister on prom night!'

'Hoo-*ah!*'

'We're sending Osama straight to hell!'

'Hoo-ah! Hoo-ah!' At first out of sync, but then melding into one giant 'HOO-AH!' so loud the cabin rattled.

Hoo-ah: short for 'Heard, Understood, Acknowledged.' 'I get it,' 'yes sir,' and 'rock on,' all in one. Not just following an order but being *proud* to follow it. Nothing like *hoo-ah*, the word or the spirit, existed in civilian life. Wells couldn't help but smile. He felt privileged to be with these guys. After all these years of war in the desert and the mountains, the United States Army was still the world's finest fighting force. Though the Marines might disagree.

Now, the men in charge, they were another story. They – their kids, at least – ought to do some time over here, and not on the guided two-day tours the Army gave them so they could tell the talk shows how they'd been to the front lines. Let them spend months dodging mortars and roadside bombs, feel for themselves how a base could turn into a prison after a while.

Enough, Wells thought. No more thinking. He'd volunteered to come back here. He had a job to do. 'Hoo-ah!' he said to himself. He chugged half a bottle of water in one gulp, soothing his raspy throat, then poured the rest over his head, smiling in satisfaction as the lukewarm liquid ran down his face. He pulled a towel from the pack under his feet and wiped himself dry.

'Love those whores' showers,' Lieutenant Gower said with a smirk. He was a sturdily built black man, twenty-six or so. Wells liked him, mainly because Gower, despite his obvious curiosity, hadn't asked

Wells anything about who he was. For twenty hours they'd talked about sports, played chess – Gower had beaten him handily – and otherwise ignored the question of how Wells had found his way onto this particular plane.

'Got that right,' Wells said. He decided to pull Gower's chain. 'Reminds me of 'Nam.'

Gower's eyes widened. 'You served in Vietnam? For real?'

'Tet, Khe Sanh, all of it. I got a wall full of ears at home. Now, that was a war.'

'Serious?' Gower looked at Wells. 'You're messing with me.'

'Yeah, I am. Do I really look that old? I'd be sixty.'

'We all look sixty right about now. Tell you what, though. You got some juice. Not just anyone can get on a fully loaded C-17 on two hours' notice.'

'I thought this was a Hooters charter to Bangkok.'

'Understood, sir,' Gower said. 'Figured I'd give it a shot.'

The cabin's speakers clicked on. 'From the cockpit. We know you love it up here, but it's my duty to inform you we'll be on the ground in Bagram in about thirty minutes.'

The inevitable '*Hoo-ah!*' passed through the cabin. 'Those of you who have visited fabulous Afghanistan before know that we like you to saddle up at this point in your trip. This is not optional.'

Throughout the cabin, soldiers pulled on their body armor and helmets. Wells reached down for his bulletproof vest, standard police-issue protective gear, far thinner than the flak jackets everyone else wore.

'That all you got?' Gower said, looking at the vest. 'It'll hardly stop a nine.' A pistol-fired, low-velocity 9-millimeter round. The plates in the Army's flak jackets were designed to handle high-velocity 5.56-millimeter AK-47 rounds, which would shred Wells's vest.

'I like to travel light.' Wells pulled on his helmet.

The intercom clicked on again: 'For your safety, this will also be a red-light landing. We know you Army boys get friendly in the dark, but please try to keep your hands to yourself.'

The overhead lights flicked off, replaced by the eerie glow of red lights mounted in the cabin walls. 'We will be coming in tactically, so strap in tight and enjoy the ride.'

Around the cabin, men buckled themselves into the harnesses attached to the walls of the C-17. 'Anyway, we hope you've enjoyed your trip,' the pilot said. 'Thanks for flying this Globemaster III. We know you have a choice of airlines, and we appreciate – Oh, no you don't. Forget it.'

'Funny man,' Gower said.

'Wishes he was flying an F-16.' Wells tightened his harness around his shoulders. The C-17 swung hard right and tipped forward into a dive.

'He best not go all JFK Jr. on us,' Gower said. He laughed, but Wells could hear the tension in his voice.

'Don't like flying, Lieutenant?'

'I know what you're thinking. Why'd I sign up for the Airborne? Wife says the same thing.'

'And you tell her a man's got to face his fears.'

'That's right. So what are you afraid of, Mr. Brown?'

The question stopped Wells. 'I'm not sure.'

'Gotta be something. Everybody's afraid of something.'

'Failure, maybe.'

'Good answer. Gives nothing away.' Gower sounded disappointed.

But Wells knew there was another answer, one he would never share with Gower: *Myself. I'm afraid of myself.*

Pop! Pop! Chaff flares exploded off the C-17's stubby wings. Then the jet swung into a corkscrew. Gower's fists were clenched in his lap. The plane leveled out suddenly. Seconds later it touched the ground, bounced, then touched down again, rocketing along the 10,000-foot runway.

And then they were done. The brakes and thrust reversers kicked in, and the C-17 stopped in one long, smooth motion. 'Welcome to Bagram Air Force Base, thirty miles north of beautiful Kabul, Afghanistan. Local time is 0200 hours,' the pilot said. No cheer this time. The abrupt landing had reminded the soldiers of the danger they were about to face, Wells thought. He scanned the tense faces around him. Many of the men in this cabin had never seen combat. Their commanders would have to help them channel their adrenaline, turning it from fear into the vigilance that might save their lives.

The Pentagon liked to think of training soldiers as a science. It was really alchemy, an unquantifiable process. Some of these men would freeze under pressure, make bad decisions, get themselves or their buddies killed. Others would find calm in the heat of battle, out-think the enemy, save themselves in seemingly impossible situations. And no test could tell them apart. Only live ammunition could.

Of course, even the best-equipped, most able soldiers didn't always survive. Sometimes every choice was wrong. Wells had never seen Ted Beck in action, but he knew Beck's skills. *If I'd been on that boat, would I have survived? Would I have seen something he missed?* Wells couldn't say for sure, but the odds were against it.

'Ever been in combat, Lieutenant?' he said to Gower.

'Not yet, sir,' Gower said. 'Anything I should know?'

'Just stay calm. You'll be good. I can tell.' Wells hoped he was right.

The overhead lights flicked on, replacing the spectral red glow of the landing lights. Wells blinked against the white glare, remembering his dream.

'Good luck, Lieutenant.' He offered Gower his hand.

'Luck, Mr. Brown. If the 504th can be of service, lemme know.'

Wells looked at the portable chess set in Gower's pack. 'Next time, you have to teach me some openings so I can give you a game.' He felt oddly disappointed as he turned away from Gower. Another good soldier he would never see again.

But when he stepped onto the tarmac, a pleasant surprise awaited him. Glen Holmes stood outside the C-17, a bit thicker than he'd been when Wells had met him in 2001, but otherwise instantly recognizable.

'Mr. Wells. It's been a long time. The Special Forces welcomes you to Bagram.'

Wells looked at the eagle on Brown's shoulderboards. '*Colonel* Holmes. You've moved up in the world.'

'Yeah, I'm a real trailer queen these days. Hardly leave the base.'

'Trailer queen?' Wells had to smile. 'Never heard that before.'

'You've done all right yourself since we last met, John.' Holmes grinned. 'That might be the biggest understatement of my life. You need a nap, or can I interest you in a cup of coffee?'

'Coffee sounds great.'

A few minutes later they sat in Holmes's B-hut as a lieutenant carried in two oversized plastic tankards. 'Starbucks,' Holmes said. 'My wife sends it every month.' The lieutenant lingered by the door. 'Thank you, Carlo,' Holmes said. 'Dismissed.'

'Yes, sir.' He saluted smartly and was gone.

'Funny,' Holmes said. 'He never hangs around when it's just me.'

'Everybody here know who I am?'

'Not the regular units. But SF is too small to keep secrets. Only a few hundred of us in the whole country. Anyway, you must be used to it by now.' Holmes grinned at Wells.

'Langley seems to wish I would disappear.'

'Well, you're among friends here.'

'You sure? Vinny Duto never shot me. More than I can say for you.' Wells tugged up his sleeve to show Holmes the scar on his biceps, left over from the night in 2001 when he'd first met Holmes.

'If I recall, you asked me to. The most surreal night of my life,' Holmes said. 'I sure didn't expect to see you again.'

100

'All these years –'

'And look how far we've come.'

Wells smiled. 'Yeah, about thirty miles. So how is it these days?'

'Had to spoil the trip down memory lane,' Holmes said. 'Still mostly okay. Afghanistan isn't Iraq. Not yet, anyway. But the Talibs are getting tougher. They've got new tactics this year. Their snipers are more accurate. And there are these rumors they've got professional help.'

'Why I'm here.' Plus I'm driving the woman I love crazy, Wells didn't say.

'If we had another division, even a couple brigades, things would be different.'

'But we don't.'

'No, we don't. They're busy you know where.'

'They'd do a lot more good here.'

'We just do what we're told.' From a file cabinet, Holmes pulled out a silver flask and two smudged glasses stamped with the Army's 'Black Knight' football logo.

'Would you be offended if I offered you a drink?'

'Not at all.'

'Glad to hear it.' Holmes poured them both a healthy shot. 'Macallan, eighteen-year-old. Been saving it for the right visitor.'

'To the men you lead,' Wells said, thinking of the soldiers on the C-17.

They raised their glasses. The scotch hit Wells immediately. He wanted nothing more than to lie on the wooden floor of Holmes's hut and sleep.

'You must be beat, John,' Holmes said. 'Carlo will find you a rack. Check it before you bunk down. A scorpion stung one of my guys last week. On the ass.'

'Ouch.'

'Yeah. Got his share of shit for it too. Swing by at 1300. I'll fill you in on what we're planning. Your office did great work on these foreign guys. Caught something we should have figured out a while ago. It's time for us to hit them where they live.'

'Sounds like a plan to me.'

TEN

'Eddie! Dinner!'

Even in the basement, through the locked door, her voice grated on his ears.

'In a minute,' he mumbled. He tapped a Marlboro from the box on the cluttered coffee table, touched lighter to cigarette with practiced hand. He closed his eyes in satisfaction as smoke filled his lungs. A nasty habit, but so what? Everybody died sometime. He exhaled through his nose, feeling his nostrils tingle.

He was stocky but solidly built. A touch under six feet, with thinning gray hair and a forgettable face, jowly and middle-aged. The face of a manager who'd never make vice president. The smoking and the Dewar's didn't help. His eyes were his only memorable feature: the right brown, the left green, with a striking black stripe that cut through the iris. The flaw was purely cosmetic and didn't affect his vision.

He was a mole, a double agent. For seven years, he had sold secrets to China. An act of treason. Punishable by life in prison. Or death.

He looked around the windowless room. A dirty white shag rug covered the floor. The walls were paneled with cheap imitation wood and decorated with framed pictures he'd taken in Hong Kong decades before. His only overseas assignment. A softball trophy from the Reston summer league sat on his desk.

He kept the trophy as an ironic joke. But what good was a joke that no one got? Everyone he knew – coworkers, neighbors, even the Mexicans who cleaned his Acura – pegged him as a capital-L loser. On pain of death, he had to hide the only interesting part of his life. Tragic. He was tragic. He puffed on the cigarette, and a kind of pride filled him with the smoke. Tragic, but heroic. He broke society's rules, lived apart from the common mass of men. He knew the chances he took, and he –

'Eddie!'

Where had his wife learned to howl like that? He ignored her and reached for the envelope inside his green windbreaker, the letter he had picked up that morning. The paper inside was neatly folded, a single sheet printed in the oversized Arial font the Chinese always used.

'Dear Mr. T.' – he always smiled at that, a cultural reference his handlers probably didn't get – 'As always, we most appreciate your work. You are truly our most valued asset. A bonus pay of three months has been received in your account for your service. Also please accept this gift.'

The English wasn't perfect, but he got the point. They were happy. A gold Krugerrand had been taped to the paper. Nice touch, the mole thought. They'd never given him gold before. He flicked open his Swiss Army knife and cut the coin off the letter. The springbok stamped across its back gleamed even in the smoky basement air. It felt dense enough to stop a bullet. He flipped the coin in the air and caught it neatly. And a three-month bonus? That was an extra seventy-five grand.

'Eddie! The roast will be cold!'

Janice. Always spoiling his rush.

'For the love of God, shut up!' he yelled upstairs.

He slipped the coin into his pocket and returned to the letter. The rest was routine, until the end: 'In light of the most recent events prudence dictates that we Discontinue' – he wasn't sure why they'd capitalized the word – 'Marco Trap immediately.'

Marco Trap was a mailbox on Moncure Avenue, just off the Columbia Pike, that he and the Chinese used as a signaling station. A vertical chalk stripe meant he'd left documents or a flash drive at the dead drop in Wakefield. Two horizontal stripes meant they'd picked up the papers. A diagonal yellow stripe meant he or they needed an urgent face-to-face meeting. A red stripe meant an emergency, a same-day meeting.

'Please begin use Tango Trap,' the letter continued. 'All other procedures remain. We regret any inconvenience but you are too worthy to take chances. Most gratefully, your friend, George.'

George, aka Colonel Gao Xi. Officially, George was a cultural liaison at the Chinese embassy, responsible for bringing pandas and acrobats to America. In reality, he ran the Washington branch of the Second Department of the Chinese army – the main intelligence service of the People's Republic. Put another way, George was China's top spy in America. For three years, he had served as Eddie's personal handler. There was no greater proof of the value of the secrets Eddie delivered.

The mole skimmed the letter again, wondering why the Chinese had changed the mailbox. He couldn't imagine their signals had been noticed. Maybe they were nervous because of what had happened in the Yellow Sea. The North Koreans hadn't exactly been subtle. But the mole didn't think anyone had connected the Drafter with him.

Anyway, the CIA lost sources all the time. It was part of the game. Sure, the Drafter was more valuable than most, and the fact that the agency had lost its own men trying to rescue him guaranteed that the incident would get attention. But the CIA had been in perpetual crisis in the years since September 11. The mole didn't figure the loss of one agent would be at the top of anyone's agenda. The East Asia desk would wind up issuing a report about the dangers of emergency exfiltrations that no one would read. By the time anyone put together what had happened in North Korea with the agency's continuing problems recruiting in China, the mole would have retired.

The Chinese were just being paranoid, the mole decided. They'd used Marco for eighteen months. Time for someplace new. Fine with him. He got the information. George kept him safe. They were partners.

The mole took a final drag of the Marlboro, then touched its burning ember to the letter until flames swallowed up the paper and smoke filled the basement.

'*Eddie!* Is something burning?'

The mole picked up the .357 Smith & Wesson snub-nose on the coffee table and pointed the gun at the ceiling. The thought of killing his wife was oddly comforting, but he knew he would never follow through.

He popped open the revolver's cylinder and dropped five of the six rounds into the ashtray on the table. He pushed the cylinder shut and gave it a long spin, watching life and death click through the revolver. Life

– life – life – life – life – death. Life – life – life – life – life – death. Smooth as a traffic light turning green to red and back again.

'Round and round she goes, where she stops, nobody knows,' he said.

The cylinder stopped. The mole pointed the gun at his eye and looked down the barrel at infinity. Or, more likely, at an empty chamber. He didn't plan to kill himself anyway. Why give the world the satisfaction? He slipped the bullets back into the cylinder, unlocked a file cabinet, and dropped the Smith & Wesson and the Krugerrand inside. He poured a healthy shot from the bottle of Dewar's that was a fixture on the coffee table and downed the scotch in one burning swallow.

'Be right up, dear,' he yelled up the stairs.

The kitchen smelled of pot roast and string beans. Janice might be the only woman alive who still cooked pot roast. The room was dark, lit only by a brass lamp in the corner. Janice didn't like bright lights. They hurt her eyes, she said. She sat at the table, chewing steadily, eyes down. Lenny lay under the table, tongue hanging wetly out of his mouth as he waited for scraps. The world was in the twenty-first century and this house was stuck in 1958, down to the fresh-cut daisies on the kitchen table.

But the mole couldn't deny that he'd built his own prison. He'd met Janice playing softball on the Mall in 1996, back from Hong Kong after his humiliation there. She was an Alabama girl, a kindergarten teacher in Reston who hung out with the Langley admins. She was the prettiest woman he'd ever dated. But even at the beginning she'd been high-strung, a thoroughbred prone to anger and depression. And drinking, though he hadn't realized how much until after they married. Of course, he drank more these days too.

Still, they would probably have been okay if not for their son. Janice had had a difficult pregnancy. They had needed two years, and four cycles of in vitro, before they finally conceived, and Janice had spent most of her last trimester in bed. But Mark, their baby, came out of her healthy and strong. He stayed that way for almost two years. Then one day he had a stomachache and diarrhea and a touch of fever. Dr. Ramsey, their pediatrician, took his temperature and sent them home. The second night his fever spiked to 103. Ramsey told them to put a cool towel on Mark's head, put the boy to bed, and bring him in first thing in the morning.

At 3:00 a.m. Mark woke up, screaming, a thin red gruel dripping out of his mouth. Janice held him in her arms as they drove to the hospital, the mole running red lights on Arlington Boulevard, using his emergency driving training from the Farm for the first and only time. Even now he could remember the fear in the young emergency room doctor who examined his son. Janice wouldn't agree, but for him that moment was the worst of all. He'd never seen a doctor look frightened before.

The rest came as inevitably as an avalanche rolling downhill: intravenous antibiotics, oxygen mask, organ failure, last rites. He would always believe that Mark knew he was dying. Even at the end, even after the boy had stopped moving, his eyes never closed, trying to grab as much of this lousy world as he could. He was dead four days after that first stomachache. A freak bacterial infection, the doctors said. Nothing anyone could have done.

Sometimes the mole thought Janice had died along with their son. She wouldn't even try to get pregnant again. After a few months, he asked her to stop taking her birth control. She said she would. But a new tray of twenty-eight foil-wrapped pills kept appearing in their bathroom each month. Eventually the mole stopped asking.

She stopped working too. Teaching kindergarten was too stressful. All those little ones running around. Instead she stayed home. To catch up on her reading, she said. Two years later, they moved. She said she didn't care, but he insisted, figuring a new house would be a new start. He pushed her to find a new job, work at the mall in Tysons Corner, anything to get her out of the house. And she did, part-time. But something in her was broken. About then he approached the Chinese.

Janice wasn't quite an alcoholic, but when her moods turned black she sat on the couch, watching soaps and sipping the afternoon away. The mole knew he ought to divorce her, but he felt bound to her. She was the price he paid for letting his son die, the price he paid for spying. And she could be sweet. Every so often she reminded him of the woman she'd been, the beautiful girl who took him to the National Gallery and showed him her favorite paintings. But his loyalty didn't stop him from spending nights at the Gold Club. And his narcissism was so complete that he never wondered if she might be happier without him.

He poured himself a glass of wine from the half-empty bottle and regarded his wife. She gave him a sweet, cockeyed smile. This was sloshed, happy Janice, infinitely preferable to drunk, sad Janice. He sipped his wine, feeling its mellow glow smooth the burn of the Dewar's, and sliced off a piece of the roast, slipping it under the table for Lenny. He was suddenly ashamed of his joke downstairs with the Smith & Wesson.

'This is great.' He chewed the meat heartily and sucked down his wine, then retopped her glass and his until the bottle was empty. Why not? They had cases more in the basement. Jan didn't like the idea of running short, and he supposed he didn't either.

'Not overcooked?'

'Not a bit. And you look great today, honey.' He tried not to think about the fact that she'd look even better if she lost the forty pounds she'd gained since Mark died. Her stomach had turned as soft as her mind. They still had sex every so often, mainly for old times' sake.

'How was work?'

'Great,' he said sincerely, thinking of the $75,000 the Chinese had thrown him. There was more where that came from, for sure. The Chinks had money to burn from selling all those toys and computer chips. The Chinese were the future. The good ol' U.S.A. was over. Always best to bet on the come. In his own way he was helping the trade deficit.

Anyway, he'd played them just right, not giving up too much at once, always leaving them wanting more. Doling out secrets slowly wasn't just greed – it was self-protection. In the mid-1980s, Aldrich Ames, the worst traitor in the CIA's history, had almost overnight given nearly all of the agency's top Soviet spies to the KGB. Then he'd watched in agony as the Soviets arrested them all.

'You're going to get me arrested!' Ames had complained to his handlers. 'Why not just put up a big neon sign over the agency with the word *mole* written on it?' Eddie hadn't made the same mistake, and he didn't intend to.

110

He sipped his wine and smiled at his wife. 'Yeah, Gleeson' – his khaki-wearing, infinitely stupid boss – 'hinted I might be up for a promotion.' Unlike much of what he told Janice, this was true.

'Well . . . that's great. I don't suppose you can tell me the details.' She smiled like a girl hoping against hope for a pony on her birthday.

'It would be a transfer within East Asia. More responsibility, more counterintelligence work.'

In fact Joe Gleeson probably just wanted to get rid of him. But the mole didn't care. If the move went through, he'd be the senior counterintel officer for all of East Asia, with access to every operation from Tokyo to Tibet. More details for the Chinese, more bonuses for him.

'Counterintelligence.'

'You know, Spy versus Spy, all that stuff. Find their guys before they find yours.'

'Would we be traveling?' Janice clung to the ridiculous hope that he would get another foreign post. Ridiculous both because she could barely function even in suburban Virginia and because the agency would send him to Mars before it gave him another front-line job.

'Maybe a little, but it would be based at Langley.'

'Well, that sounds nice.' She finished her wine and poured herself another glass from a new bottle.

'How about you?'

'It was such a busy day.'

He tried not to smile.

'I took the car in this morning. You know how the brakes have been squeaking.' Janice brought in her Volvo to be serviced about once a week. The mole sometimes wondered if she was screwing a mechanic at the dealership. He hoped so. 'Then this afternoon there was a sale at Macy's – I found this great dress I want you to see.'

'Just buy it, honey.'

'Really? It's not on sale.'

'Do I ever say no?'

'Umm . . .' He'd meant the question rhetorically. Janice's requests were usually modest, and his second career meant that he never had to turn her down. He even surprised her with the occasional diamond bracelet, though nothing too extravagant. He didn't want her showing off to the Knausses or their other so-called friends in the neighborhood.

Her face cleared as she arrived at an answer. 'No, sugarplum. I don't guess you do.' She stood, tottered over to him, leaned down to give him a sloppy kiss, running her tongue down his cheek until she found his mouth. 'You're the best.'

Lying beside Janice that night, the mole wondered what to do with his bonus. Maybe he should give Evie a present, that diamond tennis bracelet she wanted. But he was sick of Evie. When he'd met her at the club, she'd entranced him. Those fine long legs. And she'd seemed smart, at least compared with the other girls. He'd spent months tipping her extravagantly for her lame lap dances, until finally she agreed to have dinner.

Six months later they were still seeing each other. But her charm had worn off. She never shut up, and she was no genius, though she sure thought she was. Like she was the only stripper ever to go to college. If he had to listen to her talk about Occupied Palestine, as she called it, one more time . . . And the yoga. He didn't mind that she liked it. It kept her flexible, that was for

112

sure. But she took it so seriously. For a year she'd been training to be an instructor. A year? How much preparation could a yoga instructor possibly need? It was *stretching*, with a little bit of chanting, for God's sake. He'd thought she was joking when she told him the classes cost $1,500 a month. He'd laughed out loud and she'd stamped off. He hadn't even gotten laid that night.

Okay, forget the tennis bracelet. Forget Evie. Time for a new stripper, one who didn't have any illusions about being a rocket scientist.

Somewhere in the night a dog barked. The mole folded his hands behind his head, feeling the rough skin of his scalp. He imagined God looking down on all the honest souls asleep in their beds. And him, awake, his house a tumor glowing red in the night. Could the neighbors feel it? The mole made sure his lawn was mowed, his gutters cleaned. He and Janice brought apple pie and beer to the neighborhood barbecues. But the neighbors *knew*, he was sure. They knew something was wrong, though they would never guess what.

Damn. He'd felt so good a minute before, thinking about the bonus. Now the glow was gone. People thought they understood him when they didn't understand anything at all. Until the Chinese, no one had respected his talents. The agency had always pigeon-holed him as a back-office loser.

It had started with Dick Abrams, the old Hong Kong station chief. That snotty Yalie, with his fake half-British accent. 'We think you belong back at Langley,' Abrams had said. 'You're too cerebral to be in operations. Take it as a compliment.'

Too cerebral. The words were almost twenty years

old, but the mole heard them so clearly that he half-expected to see Abrams beside him tonight instead of Janice. He flushed at the memory. They'd been in Abrams's immaculate office, sitting on the couch that Abrams used for his quote-unquote informal chats. No matter where the mole looked, he couldn't avoid the photograph of Abrams and Bill Casey, the old director, a legend in the Directorate of Operations. Abrams hadn't bothered with a picture of William Webster, Casey's replacement – his way of letting visitors know that he would be around long after Webster was gone.

The mole sneaked a peek at his watch: 3:15. He was suddenly thirsty. Knowing that this meeting was coming, he had skipped his usual lunchtime scotch-and-soda. Now he wished he'd had a double instead.

'Is this about the incident?' the mole said.

'The incident?' Abrams had said, icy and smooth. The mole focused on meeting Abrams's eyes. As a kid, he'd found eye contact difficult. Over and over, his mother had told him, 'Look me in the eye. Don't be weak.' Her words only made the task harder. But he knew she was right. He practiced, staring at teachers, his friends, even strangers at bars. He pretended they weren't real, that he was watching television. Now he could look the devil himself in the eye. He raised his head and stared at Abrams.

'The incident?' Abrams said. 'You mean when you got drunk and propositioned the Italian ambassador's wife?'

'His daughter, you mean.' Even as the mole blurted out the words, he realized that Abrams had intentionally misspoken to trap him.

'Right,' Abrams said, drawing out the word. 'His

daughter. She was sixteen, right?' She didn't look sixteen, the mole thought. Not in that dress. And maybe I'd had a few too many Dewar's, but so what? The CIA, especially the Directorate of Operations, was filled with hard drinkers. In stations like Rome or Hong Kong, where not a lot was happening, getting sloshed at lunch was practically a necessity.

But trying to justify what had happened would only make matters worse, the mole knew. Abrams didn't care. He was enjoying himself, enjoying the chance to make sure the mole knew what a flop he'd been. The mole wished he could lean over and lock his fingers around Abrams's neck.

'Anyway, we think you'd be better off back at Langley,' Abrams said in that maddening voice of his. 'Not in a front-line operational role.'

So back he'd gone to Langley, where he could never outrun what had happened in Hong Kong. Other officers padded their expense accounts, stole petty cash, screwed secretaries. But the comic value of what he'd done ensured it would never be forgotten. He'd become a walking punch line, an object lesson for a generation of case officers. *Whatever you do, don't put the moves on the ambassador's daughter.* He'd made matters worse by refusing to bend to drones like Joe Gleeson. He'd never learned how to kiss the right asses. How to play golf. Silly him. He'd figured that intelligence counted for something at the Central Intelligence Agency.

The mole felt his mood changing again. So what? Forget golf. Without wasting a single Sunday chasing a little white ball around, he'd beaten them all. Today alone, he'd made $75,000. That was a year's pay, after taxes, for Joe Gleeson. For him it was walking-around money.

Suddenly he knew how he would spend his bonus. The Corvette. He smiled in the dark. A '67 Sting Ray convertible, silver. The eBay listing said the car was in Tampa. He could pick it up there, drive it to Miami, garage it with his M5, another beautiful piece of steel. Too bad nobody at Langley would ever see it. The mole could imagine jaws dropping as he cruised through the parking lot with the top down.

Of course he wouldn't keep the 'Vette in his name. Ditto the M5, or the condo in Miami he'd bought a few years back. A Florida company, London Two, owned everything. In turn, London Two's shares were held by a shell company based in the Caymans.

From there the trail went to Rycol Ltd, a shell corporation in Singapore that got $25,000 every month from the Fung Long Jack Co. Fung Long was a real business, a shipping company owned by a Chinese businessman in Singapore. If anyone asked, and no one ever would, the monthly payments were commissions that Fung Long paid Rycol for buying fuel for its fleet. Even Fung Long's owner didn't know what the money was really for. He just knew that his cousin, a senior Chinese general, had asked him to make the payments, and that $25,000 a month was a small price to keep his cousin happy.

Originally, the mole's handlers had paid him the old-fashioned way, leaving cash at dead drops. But the mole quickly learned that using cash for big trans-actions was risky. Strange but true: banks hated handling cash. Especially after September 11, they strictly enforced the rules requiring them to report deposits of more than $10,000 to the Treasury

Department. So he'd set up this system, which so far had been foolproof.

The mole had decided even before he approached the Chinese that he wouldn't spy unless he could enjoy his money, and that meant finding ways to use it legally. He had no interest in stashing a million bucks in his basement. Of course, the paper trail would provide ironclad confirmation of his spying if he was ever caught.

But he didn't expect to get caught. The agency had a dismal record of finding double agents. Both Ames and Robert Hanssen, an FBI agent who became a mole in the mid-1980s, worked with impunity until their Soviet handlers betrayed them – and Ames and Hanssen had been far less cautious than he was.

Over the years, the mole had realized that stealing secrets was easier than it looked. Case officers in China, and everywhere else, sent in torrents of reports to justify their existence. They filed *everything*: contacts with Communist officials, requests for authorization to approach potential agents, gossip about new programs the government was considering. The briefings piled up on his desk. The mole read them all,

one reason his superiors valued him, despite his occasional outbursts of temper. His biggest problem was deciding which documents were important enough to steal. For the mole had realized something else since he'd switched sides: The most vital information was the simplest – the names of the agency's operatives in China and Taiwan, and the spies they'd recruited. If actual names were unavailable, specific information about where the agents worked. The locations of drop points. The objectives of active operations. The agency's assessment of China's military capabilities.

No, the hardest part of being a double agent wasn't the actual spying. It was resisting the temptation to brag. Destroying the letters George sent him instead of saving them. Never encouraging Janice to wonder why he spent so much time in the basement.

All these years, he'd kept his mouth shut. It wasn't always easy, especially at the Gold Club after he'd had too many scotches. He comforted himself with the knowledge that the strippers wouldn't believe him anyway. The scene was only too easy to imagine: 'Want another dance?' Candy, or whoever was working him that night, would ask, after slipping his twenty dollars into her garter. She'd go through the motions of dancing, not even pretending to be interested, as some horrendously predictable song ticked away: *Don't you wish your girlfriend was a freak like me? Don'tcha, don'tcha?*

'Hey, Candy, ever wonder where I work?'

'Not really.' Pause, as she figured out he wanted her to ask. 'Where?'

'Over at Langley.'

A genuinely puzzled look from Candy. 'Langley? That a hospital?'

He'd be flattered. 'Do I look like a doctor?'

'Not exactly, no.' By now she would have used the conversation as an excuse to stop dancing.

'Langley. You know, the CIA.'

'You work for the CIA. Kidding, right?' She'd be leaning in, looking at his eyes, drunk herself, unable to see him as anything more than a middle-aged groper.

'Uh-uh. Dead serious.'

'Serious, huh?' A big stripper smile, then a finger pointed at him in imitation of a pistol. She'd put her hand on his leg. 'Well, let's see your gun, big boy.'

'Wanna know something else? I'm a double agent.'

'You go both ways? I thought you might. That's cool. I got a couple friends –'

'No!'

'Sorry, baby. Didn't mean to hurt your feelings.'

'I mean, not like that. I spy for the Chinese government. Treason.'

'Treason? What's that?'

And the song would end.

Ugh. Forget it. One day, after he'd retired and Janice had died of cirrhosis and he was living someplace with no extradition treaty, he'd write his memoirs and name every name he could remember. Until then, he would keep his mouth shut. He closed his eyes and imagined Corvettes, a flotilla of shiny convertibles, until sleep took him.

ELEVEN

The Black Hawk's rotors began to spin, first slowly, then faster and faster. At rest, the twenty-six-foot blades drooped under their own bulk. But they stiffened as they accelerated. In seconds they disappeared into a relentless blur. Wells felt himself instinctively pull his head back, though he stood fifty feet from the helicopter. Those rotors could liquefy a skull.

Wells checked his watch. 1655. Five minutes to takeoff. Then the rotors slowed. Inside the cockpit, the pilots hunched over the Black Hawk's instrument panel.

The blades dribbled to a stop, and the helicopter's crew chief hopped onto the tarmac. With his green flight helmet and black goggles, he looked like the love child of a palmetto bug and a Green Bay Packers punter. 'Warning light on the hydraulics,' he yelled. 'Take a few minutes to check.' He scrambled back inside the cabin.

Any delay was bad news, Wells thought. They needed to be in the air soon to hit the campsite at dusk. Sweat prickled his chest, though he wore only a faded green T-shirt under his bulletproof vest. He reached for a bottle of water from the cooler at his feet and sucked it down in one long gulp.

Around him, men in Kevlar vests squatted over topo maps and double-checked their radios. A and B Companies of the 3rd Battalion. Twenty Special Forces soldiers in all. Two squads of the best-trained fighting men anywhere, about to head into the Hindu Kush.

Wells unholstered his pistol, checking that its slide was smooth and its magazine full. As he finished, he noticed Greg Hackett staring at the 9-millimeter Makarov. Hackett was the youngest member of B Company, a short man whose head seemed to rise directly out of his massive shoulders. He had a heavy brow and a thick nose, the face of a half-finished marble bust that a sculptor had decided not to finish.

'Mr. Wells, sir. Permission to ask a question.'

'If you promise to stop calling me sir, Hackett.'

'Yes, sir – I mean John.' Hackett looked at the pistol. 'Is that the one you used?' Wells didn't know what Hackett meant, and then he did. 'On Khadri, you mean.'

Hackett nodded. He couldn't keep his eyes off the weapon.

'Since you ask. Yeah.' Wells handed the Makarov to Hackett. The sergeant cradled the pistol like a newborn.

'No need to fetishize it, Sergeant. It's just a gun.'

Hackett handed the pistol back. 'Can I ask one more question, sir? How does it feel to be back here?'

'Sergeant, don't you have something to do?'

Wells had come to Afghanistan years before September 11, when most Americans had never heard of Osama bin Laden. He'd fought alongside Qaeda and Taliban guerrillas for almost a decade. He had even become a Muslim during those years. Eventually, the guerrillas had accepted him as a believer.

But Wells was happy to hunt his former allies today. He didn't count himself as Muslim anymore. He couldn't honestly say whether he believed in God after everything he'd seen. And even during the years when he had accepted Islam as the one true faith and prostrated himself to Allah five times daily, he had hated bin Laden's nihilistic vision of the religion. The Taliban and Qaeda gloried in encouraging teenagers to become suicide bombers. They were unworthy of Islam.

And they were unworthy of Afghanistan. Afghans were tribal to a fault, splintered into narrow sects whose hatreds dated back centuries. The Taliban had taken advantage of Afghanistan's internal fractures to impose a vicious dictatorship in the 1990s. Seemingly out of spite, they had undone what little progress Afghanistan had made during the twentieth century, destroying the country's hospitals and schools. During the American invasion after September 11, the planners at the Pentagon joked that the United States would bomb Afghanistan *up* to the Stone Age.

The American attack had forced the Talibs out of power. Now Afghanistan was stumbling toward modernity and democracy. But the Taliban hadn't gone away. The guerrillas were trying to turn tribal leaders against the United States and its allies. They had a real chance of succeeding, because in any crisis Afghans turned inward. Wells understood why they depended on themselves. For hundreds of years, outsiders had come and gone, most often leaving the country in worse shape than they found it in. But –

A hand on his shoulder interrupted his thoughts.

'Goggles!' Captain Steve Hughley, the commander of B Company, yelled.

Wells had been so busy figuring out Afghanistan's future that he'd missed the Black Hawk starting up again. He tucked in his earplugs and pulled down his goggles as the helicopter's rotors reached full speed, kicking up dust and pebbles from the tarmac.

'Ready?' Hughley yelled.

'Yeah!' Wells screamed back. His enthusiasm was real. He hadn't flown in a Black Hawk since his days as a Ranger in the mid-nineties. He'd forgotten how magnificent these helicopters were up close. And how loud. Even with his earplugs in, he was nearly overwhelmed by the screech of the Black Hawk's 1,800-horsepower turbines.

The ten-ton helicopter bounced slightly off the runway in its eagerness to take flight. The crew chief waved B Company forward. Down the tarmac, A Company was boarding its own bird. Wells pulled a windbreaker over his vest and grabbed his pack. Inside the cabin, he settled into his seat – designed to collapse to the floor of the cabin if the Black Hawk crashed – and clicked on his harness.

'Comfy?' The crew chief tugged the six-point harness tight and offered Wells headphones. Wells took them gratefully. Insulation was wasted weight for combat helicopters, so the Black Hawk wasn't soundproofed. Inside the cabin, the roar of the turbines was overwhelming, a scrum of white noise that made conversation or even thinking nearly impossible.

The crew chief hooked in. When he and the gunner on the other side were set, the helicopter's frame began to rattle as the turbines spun at peak power for takeoff. The Black Hawk burned three gallons of fuel a minute, so pilots didn't waste time once the crew strapped in.

The copilot pulled back the Black Hawk's yoke and

the helicopter rose effortlessly off the tarmac. Wells knew that the Black Hawk had the aerodynamics of a brick and would plummet if its engines failed. Yet the copter seemed to belong in the air. As soon as it took off, its frame stopped shaking and the scream of the turbines lessened. It banked right and kept climbing, leaving Bagram's stubby huts behind.

Wells looked around the Black Hawk's cabin at B Company, an impressive group, even by Special Forces standards. Three of the soldiers spoke Pashto, a fourth Dari. Their sniper team had finished third in the Army's shooting competition two years back. Hughley, the company captain, was one of the few black commanders in the Special Forces. He was six-three, with arms that seemed to be carved from oak. At West Point, he'd played defensive tackle. And somewhere along the way, he had picked up fluent Arabic. A few Saudis still lingered in the mountains, fighting alongside the Taliban, and at dinner the night before, Brett Gaffan, the company radioman and unofficial comedian, had told Wells how one Saudi they'd captured had refused to believe that Hughley spoke his language:

'So Abdullah – he's sitting on the ground, see – he's peeking over his shoulder, looking all scared. Captain's like, "Calm down, dude. You're not getting whacked." How do you say "whack" in Arabic, Cap?'

'You don't.' Hughley's tone was deadpan.

'How 'bout "dude"? They gotta have a word for "dude," right?'

'You believe the crap I have to listen to every day?' Hughley said to Wells.

'Anyway, this camel jockey, 'scuse my French, starts looking around harder than Jeff Gordon on turn four, trying to see who's really talking to him.' Here, Gaffan craned his neck from side to side, imitating the Saudi, before jamming a forkful of mashed potatoes into his mouth. 'So Cap gives him some more mumbo-jumbo.'

'Finish your dinner, Gaffan.' Hughley turned to Wells. 'I told him it was no trick, I was the one talking.'

Gaffan dribbed a glass of lemonade into his mouth and swallowed mightily. 'Then Abdullah says something back, and Cap nods at him and tells us to stand him up. Then it gets weird, 'cause Abdullah gets real close to the captain, like he's getting ready to give him a kiss.'

'He wasn't that close.'

'All due respect, sir, he was. Wasn't he?'

Nods around the table.

'And we're all confused, wondering if we're gonna be whacking Abdullah after all. And you know we try not to kill our captures, even though damn sure the other side ain't showing us the same courtesy.'

More nods.

'But then we're thinking, maybe Cap *wants* a kiss. Since he hasn't seen his wife in six months, and the dude was kinda cute.'

'Now you're scaring me,' Hughley said.

'Nah, he was cute. Wasn't he?' Gaffan looked around the silent table. 'I know y'all thought so too, so don't deny it . . . anybody?' Pause. 'Okay, then. Let's make like I never said that.'

'Too late,' said Danny Gonzalez, the company's medic.

'Moving on. Then Cap starts singing –'

'Praying.' Hughley looked at Wells. 'The first sura.'

'And Abdullah leans in close, making sure Cap's

really the one talking – How was his breath, by the way, sir?'

'Lemme put it this way, Sergeant. I wouldn't have kissed him even if I did play on your team.'

'Sir. Uncalled for and untrue. I believe that's harassment, sir. Anyway, he gets in real close.' Gaffan stood up and leaned so close that Wells could count his pores. 'Looking up, because Cap's maybe a foot taller than he is.'

'Sergeant, did you put Tabasco on your burger?' Wells said, getting a laugh from the table. ''Cause it sure smells that way.'

Gaffan sat down. 'Guess I'll be brushing my teeth when dinner's done,' he said sheepishly. 'Anyway. Abdullah gets this scared look on his face, like, "Damn. It's no joke. This black dude talks my language. Not only that, he talks it better than me." Looked like somebody stole his pet camel.' Gaffan stuck out his lower lip in an exaggerated expression of sadness. Everyone at the table laughed now, Wells too, harder and harder, some pent-up emotion in him pouring out.

'The kicker is, 'bout ten minutes later, old Abdullah starts blabbing to Cap and won't shut up. True?'

Hughley nodded. 'He was our best source last year.'

Joined by two Apache attack helicopters, the Black Hawks turned east, diving as they left the base. When they leveled off, they were just two hundred feet above the ground, low enough that Wells could see the dust kicked up by a rusty jalopy as it rolled down the two-lane road that angled away from the base. Staying low made them harder to hit with rocket-propelled grenades or surface-to-air missiles.

To the south, a road dead-ended at a massive garbage

126

pile, a hundred-foot-tall monument to Afghanistan's poverty. No fires were visible on the pile, but a haze of black smoke drifted from the trash. The stench of sewage filled the cabin as the Black Hawk flew through the smoke's inky tendrils. Women and children trudged over the smoldering debris, looking for rags or scrap metal, anything they might trade for dinner.

In a field nearby, scrawny boys played soccer with a makeshift ball. Wells could see a breakaway develop even before the players did. A kid in a raggedy blue T-shirt cut past his defender, awaiting a pass from the midfield –

But before Wells could see what happened next, the game faded behind him. These Black Hawks cruised at 150 miles an hour. Wells decided to imagine that the kid had scored, in keeping with his newly optimistic outlook. Maybe he should write a self-help book. The power of positive thinking. And shooting first.

The fearsome mountains of the Hindu Kush jutted ahead of the helicopter. The peaks, capped with snow even in summer, stretched hundreds of miles to the northeast. Near Afghanistan's border with China, they rose above 20,000 feet. Around here they were closer to 15,000 feet, still higher than any in the continental United States. The CIA and the Pentagon believed that bin Laden was hiding in the Kush or just south, in Pakistan's Peshawar Province. But without solid intelligence, finding anyone in the Kush was impossible. The range was an endless maze of valleys and caves, among the most difficult places on earth to search. Snow fell by October. By December the dirt tracks that the Afghans optimistically called roads were impassable. The guerrillas holed up in tiny villages and waited for spring, knowing that even the best-equipped

American units could not touch them. In the summer, the Talibs moved between the mountains and Kabul, planting bombs, hijacking supply trucks, and generally wreaking havoc.

And they were getting more dangerous. A month before, fifty Taliban had attacked a police station east of Kabul. When a rapid-reaction team from Bagram responded, a second band of guerrillas ambushed it. Eight American soldiers died.

Then mortar fire hit the 10th Mountain Division at Camp Blessing, an outpost near the Pakistani border. Six men died. Mortar attacks weren't uncommon in Afghanistan, but attacks this accurate were. So two squads from camp had hiked into the mountains to talk to the villagers who lived north of the base. Everywhere they went, the soldiers offered gifts: medical supplies, pens and paper, and candy – Afghans loved Tic Tacs, for reasons no one could figure. The idea was to keep the locals friendly, or at least neutral, and get information about the source of the mortars. In most villages, the squads were met with tea, suspicious looks, and little else.

But in a nameless village twenty miles north of Camp Blessing, the soldiers got a surprise. Bashir Jan, the village's headman, told them about a guerrilla outpost to the west. Besides fifty Taliban, the camp contained several 'white fighters,' he said. And why had he given up this precious information? The guerrillas were stealing the village's goats and refusing to pay, he said.

'The guys said he was furious,' Holmes told Wells. 'Couldn't have been madder if they'd taken one of his wives.'

'Never look a gift goat in the mouth,' Wells said.

Bashir's report was the one that had spurred Exley to get the satellite photographs. Now the mercenaries, whoever they were, were about to get a call from Companies A and B. Two companies from the 10th Mountain Division, including the unit that had first discovered the camp, would provide tactical support. The plan didn't make the 10th Mountain happy. Their guys were the ones who'd died in the mortar attack, and they had developed the original intel. As far as they were concerned, they deserved the kill.

But the terrain demanded an air attack, as Wells had realized immediately when he'd seen the satellite photographs. Armored vehicles couldn't get through, and an assault on foot was impossible. The campground was hundreds of feet above the valley. Guerrilla snipers would devastate attacking infantry. Plus the mountains in this part of the Kush were riddled with tunnel networks. If they got advance warning, the guerrillas would disappear into their underground labyrinth before they could be destroyed.

Thus the 10th Mountain had been pulled back like a rottweiler on a choke chain, and the Special Forces ordered in. The helicopters would strike at dusk, destroying the camp before the Talibs could respond. Speed would be key. If the operation worked as planned, the guerrillas would panic. The Special Forces would cut off the caves. With that route blocked, the guerrillas would flee down the mountain, into the unfriendly arms of the 10th Mountain, whose men would wait at the base of the valley.

A high-risk operation, Wells thought. But the soldiers in these helicopters had the best chance in the world of pulling it off. And they had a secret weapon.

*

The sun was low as the four-helicopter convoy reached Jalalabad, one hundred miles east of Kabul. From here, they would fly northeast along the Pech River and into the mountains. One of the Apaches had briefly flown over the valley two days before, the only live visual recon of the campsite. More overflights might have spooked the guerrillas.

Wells looked at his watch. 1840. They should be at Chonesh in less than an hour, assuming nothing went wrong. An hour after that, they'd know where they stood. If they hadn't broken the camp by then, they would probably be stuck in a firefight, with little chance for reinforcements until the morning.

Afghanistan was eight and a half hours ahead of Washington, so Exley was probably at work right now, Wells thought. He pictured her in their suite in Tysons Corner, sipping coffee from the ridiculous mugs that Shafer had bought. She knew this mission was happening tonight, and though she hadn't asked for details, she had to know it wouldn't be easy. Yet she'd given him her blessing to go, encouraged him even. Because she'd known he needed the action, needed to feel useful.

In truth, the Special Forces were doing him a favor by letting him participate in this mission. Technically, Wells was replacing B Company's second medic, who had been shot in the leg two weeks earlier and was recovering in a military hospital in Germany. But Special Forces units were often short a soldier or two. Initially, Wells had worried he might distract the other men in the unit, who'd fought together long enough that they knew one another's moves instinctively.

The night before, he'd told Holmes he'd sit out the attack if Holmes thought he didn't belong. 'No hard feelings if you don't want me, Glen,' Wells said.

'You kidding?'

'What do you mean?'

'You gonna make me say it out loud? These guys love you. You're better for morale than the Cowboys cheerleaders.'

'Really?' Despite himself Wells had felt a flush of pride.

'John, look, we've got some history. I don't pretend to know you all that well, but it's obvious, what happened in New York is all twisted in your head. Put aside the politics for a minute and think on what you did. The people you saved. That's what these guys see. Believe me. Hughley wants you out there tomorrow. I do too.'

1910. The Pech River flowed shallow and fast beneath the Black Hawk, its clear water reflecting the gold of the sun's dying rays. Two children stood beside the river, waving their thin brown arms metronomically as the helicopter roared by.

The Black Hawk banked left, turning north into a narrow valley, hidden from the sun by a crumbling rock ridge. In the sudden darkness, the helicopter's gunners hunched intently over their .50-caliber machine guns.

In these valleys, the ride got dangerous. Fly too high, you opened yourself to a lucky shot with an RPG or a SAM. Fly too low, especially at night, you could get taken out by a canyon wall. The topo charts for these valleys were notoriously sketchy. The pilots usually stayed low, figuring they could dodge a mountain more easily than a missile.

The helicopter pulled up steeply as the valley tightened. Ahead, a trickle of water coursed down a near-vertical rock face. The Black Hawk banked right and cut through a gap in the rocks, its skids skimming the tops of the stubbly oak trees that speckled the mountain. The helo topped the ridgeline, and a new valley opened beneath. The Black Hawk followed the contours of the mountain downward, changing pitch and direction like a supercharged roller coaster.

'In my next life I want to be a helicopter pilot,' Wells yelled to Hughley.

'I know what you mean.'

Suddenly, Wells was cold. A few minutes before, they'd been in the sun at 6,000 feet. Now they were in shadows at 10,000, and the temperature had fallen twenty degrees. He was glad he'd followed Hughley's advice and thrown thermals in his pack. Even if the mission went perfectly, they'd be out all night.

1930. The Black Hawks slowed while the Apaches raced ahead. Part of the plan. The Apaches didn't carry soldiers, but without them the operation had little chance of success. The Apaches – AH-64 helicopters, each carrying a crew of two – were the secret weapon that would enable twenty-two American soldiers to take on fifty guerrillas. In the Army's dry jargon, the Apaches would 'prepare the battlespace for the insertion.'

In the cabin of Wells's Black Hawk, the crew chief held up five fingers, silently signaling that the helicopter would reach the landing zone in five minutes. The soldiers nodded, their faces expressionless. The silence was anticipation, not fear, Wells thought. These men wanted to get on the field and play.

1933. The Black Hawks swung over a ridge and hovered at the southern end of the Chonesh Valley.

Two hundred yards ahead, the Apaches were preparing the battlespace. Their preparation consisted of firing AGM-114N Hellfire missiles at the guerrilla camp.

The Army had developed Hellfires at the height of the Cold War to defeat the armor of Soviet T-80s. A generation later, the missiles were re-engineered to take out an enemy that preferred caves to tanks. In place of shaped charges to cut through steel, these Hellfires held a fine aluminum powder wrapped around high explosive. The twenty-pound warheads sprayed molten shrapnel in every direction, killing anyone in a twenty-five-foot radius.

As Wells watched, the forward Apache fired two missiles. The Hellfires glowed in the dusk, trailing brilliant white exhaust as they screamed toward the plateau and exploded in orange fireballs. Seconds later the sounds of their impact reached the Black Hawks, echoing off the valley's rock walls and into the night.

Whoomp! Whoomp! The trailing Apache fired two more missiles. For the first time, the guerrillas responded. A small white burst flared toward the helicopters, a rocket-propelled grenade fired blindly into the night. At this distance, the RPG was as harmless as a baby's fist. It ran out of propellant short of the Apaches and crashed to the valley floor.

The Apaches fired their last Hellfires, then pulled up to make way for the Black Hawks. Time to go in. Wait too long, and the guerrillas would regroup, or just disappear into the caves. The Black Hawks accelerated toward the plateau. Wells pulled on his night-vision goggles for a closer look. Already the guerrillas were reorganizing. Two men ran out of a cave holding an RPG launcher. They twisted toward the Black Hawk and fired. Again they missed, but not as badly as before.

'No white flag,' Wells yelled to Hughley.

'You were expecting one?'

'Surrender's not part of their playbook. They'd rather die.'

'Let's help 'em, then.'

1935. The Black Hawks reached the landing zone. The men in the cabin leaned forward, poised to unhook their harnesses and rappel down. Side by side, the Black Hawks descended – a hundred feet, ninety, eighty –

Whoosh! An RPG sailed between the helicopters, exploding against the side of the mountain. On the plateau below, guerrillas fired AK-47s, the rounds clattering off the Kevlar floor mats that protected the Black Hawk's cabin. The Black Hawk's gunners perched over the .50-calibers, firing back in controlled bursts. The brass jackets from spent machine-gun rounds poured out of the guns and into the night. The helicopter lurched downward, leveling out fifty feet above the ground. The lead gunner raised his left fist, the signal to drop.

'Now!' Hughley screamed above the turbines. '*Now!*'

TWELVE

BEIJING, CHINA

The banquet had begun hours before, but the tables remained spotless, the linens pressed, the buckets of champagne chilled just so. Tuxedoed waiters changed plates and filled glasses with perfect efficiency.

From the outside, the banquet hall looked as drab as every other building in Zhongnanhai, the walled compound in Beijing where China's leaders lived and worked. But inside, the hall – officially called Huairentang, the Palace Steeped in Compassion – seemed to have been transported directly from Versailles. Mirrors gilded with twenty-four-karat gold lined the walls. Orchids and lilies flowed out of a red ceramic pot, a priceless fourteenth-century treasure. Behind a screen a pianist played Chopin on a Steinway grand. Oversized crystal chandeliers dangled from the ceiling, beaming soft light on the hard faces of the men who sat at the table.

The food, too, was superb: moist dumplings of sweet potatoes and ginger; fresh steamed lobsters, their meat basted with a sweet-spicy chili; the choicest cuts of lamb, sizzled in a slightly bitter soy sauce;

shark-fin soup, a Chinese delicacy, the fins succulent and chewy.

Yet the nine men at the table, China's supreme leaders, had manners more suited to an all-you-can-eat buffet. They ate greedily, lifting slabs of foie gras into their mouths, sucking loudly on giant Alaskan king crab legs. At first glance, the nine could hardly be distinguished. Oversized wire-rim glasses and helmets of black hair framed their faces. They wore black suits and white shirts and red ties knotted tightly around their throats. All but one smoked, sucking deeply on Marlboros and Hongtashans, stubbing out their cigarettes on the sterling silver ashtrays around the table.

They could have been a family of undertakers, very successful undertakers. They were the nine members of the Politburo Standing Committee. And only history could explain their frenzied eating. Even the youngest of them remembered the Cultural Revolution, the decade beginning in 1966 when Mao and the Red Guards upended China. Four of these men had spent their twenties in reeducation camps, brutal places where they spent their days dragging hoes through rocky soil and their nights confessing their sins at 'struggle sessions.' All nine had known family members and friends who didn't escape the camps, who died from pneumonia or famine or beatings by the Red Guards.

No one in this room ever talked openly about those years. But they remembered. And all nine had learned the same lesson that the Cultural Revolution taught everyone in China – though the lesson wasn't the one that Mao had hoped to teach. Or maybe it was. Take what you can, while you can. Because no matter how secure you think you are, you'll lose everything if the Party turns on you.

Among the look-alikes at the table, Li Ping, the defense minister, stood out. Unlike the rest, he didn't smoke. He couldn't avoid drinking. To have skipped the toasts would have been impolite. But he sipped his wine while the others guzzled.

And where the other eight were paunchy, Li was trim, thanks to his workouts. Li wasn't modest about his physique. He challenged army officers half his age to work out beside him and smirked when he left them behind. 'It's the fat pig that feels the butcher's knife,' he told them.

The others on the committee called him 'The Old Bull,' emphasizing the 'old,' not-so-subtly implying that he ought to act his age. Li didn't care. Exercise kept him strong. He wanted to distinguish himself from the men around him, whose bodies and minds were equally corrupt.

To the world outside Zhongnanhai, Li was a 'conservative,' a 'hardliner.' He knew his reputation. He couldn't read English, but each morning his deputies gave him translations of CNN and foreign newspapers. The foreigners didn't understand him or China, he thought. He wasn't conservative. He didn't want to undo the progress of the last two decades. But unlike the 'liberals' who ran the Party, he didn't care about getting rich. His ambitions ran deeper.

China's elite was composed mainly of technocrats, engineers, and economists who spent their lives doing the Party's bidding. They rose slowly, running villages, cities, then provinces. Along the way they proved their loyalty to their bosses while building power bases of their own. Li had followed a different path. He'd come up through the Army, the only real soldier in the Party's top ranks.

Li had served with distinction in China's last major war, its invasion of Vietnam in February 1979. As a young captain, he'd commanded a company that was among the first units over the border. The war was not even an asterisk in the twentieth century's bloody history, but Li had never forgotten it.

The Vietnamese had known the Chinese were coming. Their soldiers and militiamen were battle-hardened from a decade of war with the United States. China sent in a huge army, hundreds of thousands of soldiers. But its men were underequipped and unready, peasants who'd received only a few weeks of training before being sent to the border. Some could barely load their rifles.

Li's company was in the vanguard of a division attacking Lao Cai, a town just south of the border. His unit came under constant fire from the Vietnamese militias. The ground was soft and spongy and the mines were everywhere. The Vietnamese especially liked simple explosives that the Americans called 'toe poppers,' pressure mines with just enough power to blow off a man's foot. Making matters worse, Li's only medic was killed by a sniper in the battle's first hours. After that he'd had to leave injured men where they lay. Taking care of the wounded was a luxury the Chinese army couldn't afford.

In the first two days of fighting, he'd lost fifty men, a third of his soldiers. But somehow he and Cao Se, his first lieutenant, kept his company together even as the units around them collapsed. Finally, facing the prospect of a devastating defeat, the People's Liberation

Army brought up heavy artillery. The big guns surprised the Vietnamese and turned towns near the border into rubble. By the time Li's unit limped into Lao Cai, only dogs and amputees were left.

Three weeks later the Chinese pulled back across the border, proclaiming the invasion successful. They'd taught Vietnam a lesson, they said. Li had learned a few lessons himself. At first the suffering of his men had stunned him. But over the years, he reconsidered. Strategically, the war had put the Vietnamese in their place. Afterward they treated China with more respect. War ought to be avoided, but sometimes it was necessary, he thought.

For him, too, the war had been a success. The near-disaster in Vietnam frightened the People's Liberation Army into professionalizing its officer corps. For the first time in decades, fighting skill, not ideological purity, became the most important factor behind promotions. The change helped Li. His abilities had been obvious from the first days of the Vietnam invasion. He intuitively knew how to position his soldiers, when to concentrate fire and when to disperse. He thumped other commanders in the war games at the National Defense University. He rose quickly. By 2004, he'd become chief of staff. Two years later, he was named defense minister and commander of the army.

Of course, skill only went so far. Li would never have become a minister if the others on the Standing Committee had doubted his loyalty. But they didn't. To them, Li was the ultimate soldier, always following orders. In truth, as long as Li mouthed the right words, the Party's leaders didn't care if he believed in 'socialism with a human face.' They certainly didn't. Being rich and powerful in China meant being part of the Party. So the Party's leaders faithfully recited the 'Eight Dos and Don'ts' – 'Know plain living and hard struggle, do not wallow in luxuries' – and then rode limousines home to their mansions. The sayings were the equivalent of a fraternity's secret handshake. By themselves, they meant nothing. But knowing them got you in.

Li preferred to be underestimated. Even when he joined the Standing Committee, the others didn't view him as a political threat. After all, he hadn't even succeeded in getting rich from his position. Besides 'Old Bull,' the liberals – those members of the elite who had profited the most from the new China – had another name for Li. They called him 'Guard Dog,' though never to his face.

But the liberals misunderstood Li. He was greedier than any of them, though not for money. Li wanted to prove himself the greatest of leaders, the savior of the Chinese nation, remembered eternally for his courage. In his dreams, he lay beside Mao in the massive crypt in Tiananmen Square. Every day thousands of Chinese lined up to glimpse his body. They shuffled by in awe, wishing they could bring him back. The lines grew until the crowds filled Tiananmen and poured into the streets of Beijing. But the people were so eager to see him that no one complained.

When he woke, Li never remembered his dreams. He never consciously realized how deeply he thirsted for glory. He didn't understand his motives, and that made him dangerous indeed.

Sitting in his usual spot, two seats from the head of the table, Li lifted his crystal wineglass and studied the burgundy liquid inside. A Château Lafitte '92, 10,000 yuan a bottle, $1,300 US. The men around him had gone through a half-case of the stuff tonight. They surely believed they'd earned it.

In May 1989, hundreds of thousands of students had filled Tiananmen – the great open square less than a mile from here, the spiritual heart of all China – to demand democracy. The Western reporters who covered the protests called that time the Beijing Spring. For a few weeks it seemed that China might move from dictatorship to freedom. After all, on the other side of the world, Communist regimes were falling peacefully.

But China wasn't East Germany or Poland. China had gone through a century of upheaval so terrible that even World War II seemed mild. An invasion by Japan. A long, bloody civil war. The disastrous Great Leap Forward, which led to a famine that killed tens of millions of Chinese. The Cultural Revolution. The Chinese weren't ready for more turmoil, not so soon. They hardly protested on June 4, 1989, when the men of Zhongnanhai brought in tanks to clear Tiananmen. Hundreds of protesters were killed that day in Beijing. The People's Liberation Army? On June 4, only the last word was true.

The leaders of the Chinese Communist Party never admitted what they'd done in Tiananmen. Instead they offered their people an unspoken bargain. Don't challenge us. In return we'll let you drop the farce of socialism. 'To get rich is glorious,' Deng Xiaoping, at the time China's paramount leader, famously said. 'It doesn't matter if the cat is black or white as long as it catches mice.' Some people said now that those words had never actually crossed Deng's lips. But the sentiment was real enough.

For two decades, rulers and ruled had stuck to the

141

deal, and China had produced the greatest economic miracle in history. In the 1980s, China was a third-world country, poorer than India. Now it had the third-largest economy in the world, behind only the United States and Japan.

And yet . . . and yet. Under its glittery surface China's economy had reached a dangerous tipping point, Li thought. The boom had given hundreds of millions of Chinese a decent standard of living. But it had left hundreds of millions more in the dust.

Li sipped his wine, the smoothest he'd ever tasted – 10,000 yuan a bottle. His father Hu had worked at a tire factory until his heart gave out on his fifty-second birthday. Hu hadn't made 10,000 yuan in his entire life. He'd never owned a television or refrigerator or even a telephone. He'd saved for years to buy his most prized possession, a Flying Pigeon bicycle, a single-geared steel beast that weighed almost fifty pounds.

Yet Li never remembered his parents complaining. They'd never felt poor, since no one they knew was any better off. And they hardly needed money. The tire factory gave them a two-room apartment with a communal bathroom. They didn't have much, but their lives were secure. They never had to worry that Hu would be fired or the factory would close. Such things simply didn't happen.

Now, though, factories closed all the time. Real estate developers tore down the cluttered Beijing neighbor-hoods called hutongs, to build apartment buildings across the giant city. The apartment towers were cleaner than the hutongs. But the hutong families didn't get to live in the new buildings. They were shipped to hovels on the outskirts of the city, beyond the Fifth Ring Road, where the capital's wealthy wouldn't see them.

Today, men like Li's father knew they were poor. They couldn't imagine the opulence of this room, or the private clubs in Beijing where the wealthy gathered. But they knew China had left them behind. Fewer and fewer of them were willing to accept their fate. All over China the pot was boiling up. In southwest China, farmers had attacked police stations over land seizures. In north China, coal miners had rioted to demand safety equipment after an explosion at a mine in Hebei killed 180 men.

Even worse, the economy wasn't booming anymore. So far, the government had hidden the slowdown from the outside world. But Li knew the real numbers. Growth had slowed month after month, from ten percent to eight to five and now to three. And no one, not the economic minister or the governor of the Central Bank, could explain what was happening, not in words that made sense to Li. They said the economy needed more reform, not less.

But Li spent more time outside Zhongnanhai than the other senior leaders combined. He might not be an economist, but he had eyes. He saw old women with bowed heads begging for help, their clothes dirty, empty bowls between their hands. He saw the peasants lined up in Tiananmen to plead for work, even though the police beat them just for being there.

The poet Du Fu had written, 1,250 years earlier, 'Within red gates, wine and meat rot, while on the street outside people starve.' Dynasties crumbled when emperors forgot their subjects. Inside Zhongnanhai, life was sweeter than ever. The men around him imagined they could call in the tanks again if they needed to. But this time the rebels wouldn't be students. They would be miners and peasants and factory workers. They would be men, not boys, and this time they would fight.

Li wouldn't let that happen. He wouldn't use the People's Liberation Army, his army, against civilians. He would take control of the situation, not for his own glory, of course, but to save the nation from the greed of its rulers.

But taking control wouldn't be easy. Li couldn't openly challenge Zhang Fenshang, the economic minister and the most powerful man on the Standing Committee. Zhang was supposedly second-in-command, ranking behind the general secretary, Xu Xilan. In reality, Zhang was the most powerful man in China. Xu was eighty-two and feeble, a figurehead who 'consulted' Zhang before any important decision.

Together, Zhang and the other liberals – Li gritted his teeth to think of the word – held six seats on the nine-member committee. To defeat them, Li needed to outmaneuver them. If he could take control of the committee, the people would rally around him. The rich businessmen might protest. But eventually even they would understand that Li didn't want to destroy them, just make them share some of their wealth.

Li knew he would have only one chance to take power. If he failed, he wouldn't just lose his spot on the Standing Committee. At best, he would spend the rest of his years under house arrest. At worst, he would suffer a tragic accident, and his death would be announced to the people in somber tones.

No, he couldn't fail. And he needed to move quickly, before the people grew so angry that even he couldn't calm them. In the last few months, he'd put a plan together. And now, after his visit to Iran, he believed he'd found the key to making it work.

'*All warfare is based on deception*,' Sun Tzu, China's most famous military strategist, had written 2,500 years earlier. Under normal circumstances, Zhang could easily defeat Li. But what if Zhang suddenly faced a threat beyond his control, a threat not from inside China but from outside?

Li knew his plan was dangerous. But not acting would be even more dangerous.

Dessert – a rich pear cake with ginger ice cream – was served, and the plates cleared. The waiters poured cognac. Then they disappeared, leaving the nine men at the table to the country's business.

Zhang, sitting beside Xu, the general secretary, raised his glass. 'To the glory of the new China.'

'And to the people,' Xu said. 'To the wisdom of the Chinese people.'

'Of course, Comrade Xu,' Zhang said. 'We must always serve the people.'

Li sipped from his snifter, feeling the glow of the golden liquid in his mouth. Cognac was one of his indulgences. A glass before bed made his sleep pleasant.

The Standing Committee met for the banquets once a month. The dinners always followed the same script. Only when the waiters had left the hall did business begin. Of course, the committee met in regular sessions several times a week, but the truly important decisions were made at this table – with no aides to overhear or record the sessions. Even in here, even speaking only to one another, committee members chose their words as carefully as Mafia dons on a phone line tapped by the

145

FBI. Speaking too clearly signaled weakness, not strength.

'Comrade Zhang,' Xu said. 'Please begin.'

'The economic situation has not changed,' Zhang said. 'The transition period' – what the liberals called the economy's slowdown – 'is continuing. But there's no reason for concern. The will of the people is excellent. Business conditions are good.'

Zhang had said the same thing the month before, and the month before that. How much had Zhang stolen from the national treasury and hidden in banks in Singapore? Li wondered. How many bribes had he taken? Five hundred million yuan – $60 million? A billion yuan? Two billion? *With money you are a dragon, with no money, a worm.*

'Then what is the problem?' Xu said.

'General Secretary,' Zhang said, 'just as a farmer must let a field lie fallow from time to time, the economy must slow occasionally before it grows again.' Though he'd lived most of his life in Shanghai, Zhang liked to use farming metaphors with Xu, whose parents had been peasants. 'We're pruning the deadwood so saplings can prosper. If the young trees aren't rising fast enough, we must prune more vigorously.'

To the men at the table, Zhang's meaning was clear. The government should close more state-owned factories, like the tire plant where Li's father had worked. Li couldn't believe that Zhang had the audacity to propose more layoffs with so many people already jobless. But arguing openly with Zhang would be futile.

'Yes,' Xu said. 'I see.'

'I'll propose a plan for the Congress next month' –

the annual Communist Party Congress, which would officially ratify the decisions these nine men made.

'Does anyone else have thoughts on Comrade Zhang's view?' Xu said. Li held his tongue. Then Xu turned toward him.

'Comrade General Li. How was your visit to Tehran?'

Now or never, Li thought. 'Very productive, General Secretary.' He outlined the oil-for-nuclear-help deal he'd discussed with the Iranian president. Li could see that he'd caught Zhang by surprise, as he'd intended.

'Zhang, what do you think?' Xu asked.

Zhang sipped his cognac, trying to buy time. Li could imagine his calculation. An open alliance against the United States would have enormous risks. On the other hand, a confrontation with America would buy time to right the economy. And Zhang didn't want to appear as though he feared the United States.

Zhang looked at Li. 'What's your view, Comrade General?'

Zhang was hoping to force the responsibility for the decision back on Li. In doing so, Zhang had slipped into Li's trap. Zhang had never before given up control on an important issue. He would find retaking it more difficult than he expected, Li thought.

'My view, Comrade Zhang?' he said. 'Let's seize this opportunity. The Iranians can give us leverage against the hegemonists' – the Americans. 'Our industries will benefit from a guaranteed supply of oil. And the Persians will be a new market for us. They see all that we've done. They can help us through the transition period. Anyway, why should we let the Americans decide what nations have certain weapons?' – nuclear bombs. 'The Persians don't threaten us.'

'And the Americans? What will they say?'

'Let them talk,' Li said. 'Talk does not cook rice.'

'It isn't their talk that concerns me,' Zhang said. 'What if they misunderstand our peaceful intent?'

Li had to admit that Zhang could turn a phrase. Of course the United States would 'misunderstand' if China allied with Iran, America's biggest enemy.

'The hegemonists aren't interested in any more wars.'

'You're certain.'

'Nothing is certain, Comrade Zhang. But they are distracted now, and our army and navy are valiant.'

The table was silent when Li finished speaking, and he knew he'd won. They'd send him back to Tehran to finalize an agreement with Iran. For the first time since the end of the Cold War, the United States would face a challenge to its global dominance.

The Americans would want to respond. But they had their own problems, Li knew. The death of their North Korean spy had cost them their best intelligence on Pyongyang. The war in Iraq had sapped their army. They were on the defensive – and the public announcement of the Chinese/Iranian alliance would irritate them further. Like a wounded bear, they would lash out but with words, not actions. The American president would speak against the agreement, and that would irritate the men around him. No one in this room wanted advice from the United States on how China should conduct its affairs.

But neither Washington nor Beijing would expect the war of words to go any further. What no one at this table realized was that Li intended the agreement with Iran to be only the start of China's confrontation with America.

'It's agreed, then?' Li said. 'We'll accept the Iranian proposal?'

Nods around the table. By springing the deal on them this way, Li had given them little choice. Turning down the offer would have made them look weak, and none of these men wanted to look weak, least of all Zhang. If they'd known what he planned next, they would have been more cautious, but they didn't.

Li raised his glass to his lips. Another step toward the power he'd been chasing for so long. He took a deep sip of cognac, filling his mouth with its sweetness.

THIRTEEN

'Now!' Hughley yelled. *'Now!'*

Holding the frame of the juddering Black Hawk, Wells tugged on his pack: sixty-three pounds of ammunition, grenades, energy bars, water, bandages, and the other essentials of close combat.

A Kevlar cable was coiled on the floor, its end knotted to the helicopter's frame. Wells threw it out the side. He shimmied down, hand over hand, feeling the cable's rough fibers under his gloved fingers. AK-47 rounds whistled by, and he wondered if he should have chosen heavier armor. Five feet from the ground, he jumped, landing lightly despite his gear.

The sun was gone now. But the quarter-moon and stars shined on the open plateau, making Wells's night-vision goggles a distraction. Wells pulled up the goggles and took stock. The plateau was a half-mile long and five hundred feet wide. Boulders and stunted trees littered the ground, offering decent cover.

Around the drop zone, the Hellfire missiles had done their job. Burned men were strewn across the plateau like trees tossed by a category 5 hurricane, the stench of their barbecued flesh heavy in the air.

A guerrilla in a long white robe twitched and moaned beside a rock seventy-five feet away.

As planned, the attack had caught the guerrillas building campfires for dinner. Sheep and goats were tethered near the caves, maybe the same animals that had provoked Bashir Jan, the village headman, to reveal the existence of the camp. Somehow, the animals had survived the missiles. Their desperate bleats cut through the night over the crackle of the automatic rifles and the roar of the Black Hawks. The goats, the fires, the dead men: the scene was a waking dream, a twenty-first-century Goya painting, Wells thought.

The satellite photos had shown three encampments across the plateau. The Apaches had targeted most of their Hellfires at the northern and center camps, trying to drive the guerrillas south, toward the 10th Mountain. But either the southern camp had been the biggest, or the plateau as a whole had held more men than they'd been told. Thirty or more men were scattered behind rocks and trees to the south. A smaller group was half-hidden behind boulders that obstructed the entrance to a cave west of the loading point.

Wells unstrapped his carbine and dropped to the ground. The plateau was cold, more stone than dirt; a rock poked at his groin. The men by the cave were the immediate threat, he thought. They had already almost taken out a Black Hawk with their RPGs. He opened up at them with three-shot bursts, hoping to distract them from the helicopter.

Thump! Thump! Hughley landed beside him, followed by the rest of B Company, as A Company hit the plateau two hundred feet to the southeast. When the last soldier touched the ground, the Black Hawks pulled away.

'We're in it now,' Wells yelled to Hughley.

'Yeah, and we ain't getting out till the sun comes up.'

The men of B Company fanned out in a two-hundred-foot arc. Wells and Hughley lay nearest the caves. A Company had set itself similarly. The position looked more solid than it was, Wells thought. Already the Talibs to the south were spreading out, enlarging the battlefield, giving themselves new angles to fire on the SF soldiers. Guerrillas – like civilians – usually clustered when they came under fire, hoping for safety in numbers. The fact that these men had done the opposite offered more evidence that they were getting professional help.

'Shit!'

Even without looking, Wells recognized Hackett's voice. The stocky sergeant hopped on his right leg toward Hughley and Wells. Ten yards away, he fell. Wells ran for him, picked him up, and threw his shoulder under Hackett's arm. Together they struggled toward Hughley like kids in a three-legged race.

'Sir, I took one.' Hackett spoke evenly – he could have been talking about someone else – but the pain in his voice was unmistakable. 'Left leg. Bad, I think.'

Wells put Hackett down and shined a penlight on his leg. The bullet had hit low on the thigh, just above the knee. Blood pumped steadily out from the wound, shining under the light. The popliteal artery. Hackett grunted as Wells palpated the area around the wound. Hughley put a flashlight to the sergeant's face. He was pale, his massive jaw gritted against the pain.

Get a tourniquet on him, Wells thought. Cutting off the artery might cost Hackett his leg, but the alternative was worse. A trauma surgeon could sew up the wound, but the nearest surgeon was in Bagram, so the tourniquet would have to do.

'Take off your pack, Sergeant. I'm gonna wrap it tight.'

'A tourniquet?' Hackett's voice lifted slightly.

Hackett knew what a tourniquet meant, Wells thought. He wanted to give Hackett a hit of Demerol, but the sergeant had already lost too much blood. An opiate would put him in shock. 'It's gonna sting a little. Bite on this.' Wells found a mouthguard in his pack and pressed it into Hackett's hand. Beside them Hughley fired short bursts at the cave.

'How we doing?' Wells said to Hughley.

'Worry about my soldier.'

Wells grabbed a combat tourniquet – a black plastic band big enough to fit over a man's leg, with a sturdy plastic handle attached. He pulled on latex gloves and tugged the band above the spurting wound. The sergeant groaned and bit hard on the mouthguard. Wells pulled the loop of plastic tight around Hackett's thigh.

'Just a few seconds more.'

'*Down!*' Hughley yelled as a guerrilla popped up from behind a boulder beside the cave to fire an RPG. It exploded behind them, lighting the night.

'That the best you can do?' Hughley said. He fired a burst at a guerrilla who'd foolishly stood to watch the RPG. The Talib screamed, his hands rising to his throat. He fell hard and didn't move.

'Hold tight, Sergeant,' Wells said. He turned the handle of the tourniquet, tightening it around the meat of Hackett's thigh. Hackett's shoulders trembled. He moaned softly, a low sound hardly recognizable as human.

The blood slowed to a trickle but didn't stop. Wells wiped down the wound and taped a thick, clean bandage around the sergeant's leg. He pulled off his gloves, slick with blood. 'Sergeant. It's over. You're gonna be okay. Just get comfortable. Keep your leg up.'

'Yessir. I'm cold, sir.'

Wells pulled an aluminum blanket from his pack and wrapped it over Hackett's shoulders, then grabbed a water bottle and dumped in a pouch of Gatorade powder. 'Drink this.'

'He gonna make it?' Hughley whispered.

'If I knew, I'd say.'

'All right.' Hughley nodded at the boulders where the men with the RPGs were hiding. 'Gotta take them out, protect our flank. Can you handle it with Gaffan? Gonzalez can give you some support while he watches Hackett.'

Two guys against five, maybe more, Wells thought. Not great odds. But he saw Hughley's problem. B Company was already down two men, since Gonzalez, the medic, would have to take care of Hackett. That left the squad at nine soldiers, including Wells. A Company had ten more. Facing at least thirty guerrillas to the south, Hughley couldn't spare a third guy on the flank.

'Sure,' Wells said. Through his tactical radio, Hughley ordered Gaffan and Gonzalez to their position. As the men reached Hughley and Wells, another RPG flared out from the boulders.

'*Shit!*' Gaffan and Gonzalez threw themselves down as the grenade exploded behind them.

Hughley pointed toward the rocks. 'Gaffan, you and Wells are taking out that position. Danny, you're staying with Hackett. I'll link the rest of the squad up with Alpha.'

154

'Yessir.'

Hughley sprinted off. They had a long night ahead, Wells thought. Instead of fifty guerrillas, the camp had held a hundred or more before the attack. Even now the bad guys outnumbered the Special Forces two to one. They should have had at least one more squad to even up the odds. But second-guessing the plan now would be a waste of time, and they couldn't afford to waste time. They had to move fast, get control of the battle-space. The Talibs surely knew of trails that led up the mountain and would give them angles to shoot down on the plateau. If they put snipers above the battlefield, the SF soldiers would be exposed, sitting ducks. Before that happened, Hughley had to drive the guerrillas off the southern end of the plateau and into the valley.

Meanwhile Wells had his own problems to solve. Hackett lay on his back, breathing in fluttery bursts. He would be lucky to get through the night, Wells thought. 'Gaffan.' Wells pointed to the rock seventy-five feet away where the guerrilla in the white robe lay. 'Let's move.'

Wells laid out a covering burst as Gaffan sprinted for the rock and slid in. Five seconds later they switched roles, Gaffan firing as Wells ran to the rock. Up close, Wells saw that the wounded guerrilla was in terrible shape, the left side of his face gone. His right eye opened wide as he registered their presence. He twisted away, his hands scratching at the dirt.

'I'll do it,' Wells said. 'Watch the cave.'

'But –'

'Watch the cave, Sergeant.'

Wells leaned close to the man and said in Arabic, *'Dear Lord, pour patience upon us and make us die as Muslims.'* The Quran, verse 7, line 126.

155

He unholstered his Makarov, shoved it into the man's mouth, and pulled the trigger. The single shot echoed into the darkness. The guerrilla's skull exploded, spewing a devil's volcano of blood and brains. Another thousand sleepless nights, Wells thought. He pushed the corpse away, furious that the man hadn't had the decency to die on his own. The body flopped over, arms askew. No one who died tonight would get a proper burial.

'Maybe I'm just projecting, but I swear he looked relieved,' Gaffan said.

You're just projecting, Wells didn't say. Warned you not to watch. He put the man's cracked skull out of his mind. He'd save the nightmares for later. 'Let's do this, get close enough to lay a forty in that cave.' A high-explosive 40-millimeter grenade, fired from the M203 launchers attached to the carbines he and Gaffan carried.

Wells pulled open the barrel of his 203, popped in the grenade – a cylinder that looked like a shotgun shell – and cocked the barrel. He pointed to a stunted tree a hundred feet to their right. 'Ready?'

Gaffan nodded.

Wells popped up, fired, and dropped down. His grenade blasted into the mountainside, a red-white explosion that faded fast. He'd missed, but not by much. Now let them fire back. The Talibs were loose with their ammo. Let them shoot until their magazines ran dry. Then Wells and Gaffan would break for the tree, where they'd be close enough to do some damage.

But the Talibs refused to play along. Instead of random AK-47 fire, they fired only a few well-aimed shots. Two rounds hit the dead Talib, making the corpse jump, a caricature of resurrection. Gaffan had no chance to move from the shelter of the rock.

'Somebody's been teaching these guys to shoot,' Wells said.

'I'm thinking that too, sir.'

Now Wells and Gaffan were pinned. The guerrillas had them targeted and would cut them down the next time they poked their heads up. They watched helplessly as two guerrillas emerged from the boulders by the cave and ran left, diving behind a mound of dirt kicked up by a Hellfire missile. From their new position, the Talibs had an angle on Gonzalez and Hackett, who were stuck because of Hackett's leg. Sure enough, rounds began smashing into the low, flat rocks that sheltered Gonzalez and Hackett.

'Pinned here, sir,' Gonzalez yelled through the night. Then: '¡Maricón! ¡Puta! Bitch got my Kevlar.' He fired back ineffectually.

Not good.

'Now what, sir?'

Wells thought for a few seconds. Could he aim a grenade well enough to drop it over the boulders that hid the guerrillas? Doubtful. But –

'Load up with CS.' CS was a powerful chemical irritant that left its victims temporarily blind and gasping for breath. All SF soldiers carried CS grenades in addition to the traditional high-explosive variety. Wells popped a gray-and-green aluminum CS grenade in the 203.

'But sir –' Gaffan said.

'Sergeant. Stop calling me sir. Call me John, Wells, dogface, whatever. Not sir. Makes me feel like I'm two hundred years old.'

'Yes, Mr. Wells.'

'*Mr.* Wells? All right, it'll do. Now stop arguing and

load up.' Lying on his stomach, Wells crooked his arms at the elbow so that the barrel of his carbine pointed up like a mortar. He imagined the gas grenade arcing out of the M4 and landing behind the rocks like a perfectly thrown football. He squeezed the trigger. The carbine jerked back as the grenade soared out.

A few seconds later, white smoke drifted down the side of the mountain, a hundred yards above the entrance to the cave. Not close enough. Wells stayed on his stomach, keeping his arms still.

'Gimme your M4 and reload mine,' Wells said. Gaffan put his own carbine in Wells's hands. Wells tilted his arms back slightly, calculating, again imagining the gas canister landing behind the boulders. He fired. The grenade landed thirty yards short. Better, but not good enough.

AK fire rattled at Wells and Gaffan as the white CS smoke dispersed across the plateau. A rocket-propelled grenade flared out from a gap in the boulders, sailing over their heads. Good. The men behind the boulder were getting anxious.

'Again,' Wells said. Again Gaffan traded carbines with him. Wells lowered the barrel slightly and squeezed the trigger. *Pop!* This time the canister landed on the rocks where the guerrillas had hidden. Smoke poured out in all directions, as Wells had hoped. He had chosen to use the CS grenades instead of standard high-explosive grenades because with the CS he didn't have to have perfect aim. If he could get reasonably close, the gas would disperse over the boulders, doing his work for him.

Men yelled in Arabic. Seconds later the coughing began, a vicious hacking as if the men behind the boulder were trying to spit up their poisoned lungs.

'Again.' Again Gaffan handed him a reloaded carbine. Wells adjusted his aim infinitesimally and fired again. This time the shot went slightly long, landing on the mountainside a few yards above the cave. But the smoke seeped down into the area where the guerrillas were hiding. The coughing grew louder.

'Get your mask on,' Wells said. 'One more, then we go in.'

Wells fired the fifth canister, then pulled on a gas mask. The mask made breathing a conscious decision rather than an automatic fact. Inhale. Fill your lungs. Exhale. Hear air rattle through the activated charcoal filters. Inhale again.

Wells pulled his helmet back on and popped a fresh grenade – standard high-explosive, not CS – into the 203. Two men in brown robes crawled from behind the boulders, their bodies shaking, clots of white phlegm dripping down their faces.

Gaffan took aim. 'Wait,' Wells said. But no more men joined the two.

'Okay. Drop 'em.'

Gaffan squeezed the trigger of his carbine. The first guerrilla twitched spasmodically and collapsed face-first. The second man stood and turned toward them, raising his arms blindly, in defiance, or surrender. Gaffan didn't wait to find out. He fired again. The man pressed a hand to his robe, twisted, and fell.

'Looks like we got the dumb ones,' Gaffan said. Behind the boulder, the desperate coughing continued. At least two men left back there, Wells thought. No point in waiting any longer. CS was nasty, but its effects wore off fast. 'Cover me,' he said to Gaffan. 'On three.'

'I'll go, John.' Gaffan started to stand.

Wells shoved him down. 'You cover.' Wells

crouched in the shadow of the rock. It was 250 feet to the boulders in a straight line, though he would be zigzagging to keep the guerrillas from getting a clean shot. He wasn't as fast as he'd once been, but he was fast enough. He held up three fingers to Gaffan, two, one. He took off.

And as his legs pumped over the plateau's broken rocks, the mania of hand-to-hand combat filled him. He knew he would survive. God, Allah – whatever He was called, whatever He *was* – wouldn't let him die out here. He was invincible. Indestructible.

Wells sprinted, the M4 cradled across his chest, hurdling a low rock, always moving, cutting over the field like a running back who'd made the safety miss and knew the end zone wasn't far off. When he was a hundred feet away, a man stepped from the shadows of the boulders, white, holding an AK in both hands, wearing a jean jacket –

And a gas mask like Wells.

A gas mask. Choose now or never choose anything again. No point in trying to shoot. He was running too fast to have a chance of hitting the guy. Instead Wells pulled the second trigger on the carbine, launching his high-explosive grenade. Maybe he'd be close enough at least to rattle the man in the mask –

Thata-thata-thata. The guerrilla's AK exploded with a staccato burst.

Wells dove to his right. He landed hard on his shoulder and rolled, reaching for his carbine.

The grenade blew in an enormous white flash. Wells ducked his head as shrapnel rained around him. When he looked up, the man in the jean jacket no longer existed.

Wells sat up. He didn't think he'd been hit, but his

right arm hung out of its socket and his shoulder felt as though it were on fire. Wells reached across his body and cradled the shoulder in his left hand. He grabbed his right biceps and tugged his arm forward, trying to pop the joint into place. The pain was the worst he'd ever felt. A river of agony flooded through his chest. Tears flooded his eyes and filled his gas mask. Wells dropped his arm.

He caught his breath and again wrapped his left hand around the top of his right biceps. In one convulsive movement he jerked his arm forward. The world spun. He pulled even harder. He could feel the joint give. The stars merged and the sky glowed a chunky white. Wells didn't stop pulling. Then the joint popped back into place and the pain lessened. Wells tried to lift his arm and was amazed to find he could. Then he picked himself up and ran for the rocks, to see if anyone else was still back there.

But when Wells finally ended his 250-foot marathon and reached the mouth of the cave, he didn't find anyone. Anyone alive, anyway. The grenade had slammed into the chest of the man in the jean jacket, a one-in-a-million shot that had blown him apart. His headless torso lay in a thick pool of blood. The head, still covered with the gas mask, lay ten feet from his body. Through the clear plastic mask its eyes watched Wells, promising to visit him while he slept. 'Asshole,' Wells said aloud, unsure if he was talking to himself or the man he had killed.

And he wasn't finished yet. There was another one. Somewhere in that cave, there was another one.

FOURTEEN

Shafer walked into Exley's office in Langley, folder in hand. 'Mis-ter Mole. Oh Mis-ter Mole. Where are you?'

Exley looked up from the papers she was pretending to read. 'Cute, Ellis.'

'How's the hunt? We any closer to whack-whack-whacking this mole?' Shafer stood in front of Exley's desk and battered imaginary moles with an imaginary mallet. 'Never was any good at that game.'

'Ellis, are you stupid? Did you forget what's happening *right now*? While you stand in my office with your tongue hanging out like an escapee from *Sesame Street*?'

'Of course I know. He's gonna be fine, Jennifer. You said it yourself. He was born for this.'

'He's in trouble. I know it.' She did, too. She didn't believe in extrasensory perception or astrology or any of that voodoo. But she knew Wells was in trouble, bad trouble, at this moment.

'You're just nervous.'

'And you're just a bureaucrat whose idea of living on the edge is extra-spicy taco sauce. You don't get what it's like, having a gun in your hand, killing them before they kill you.' And I do, Exley didn't say. I've only done it once, but once was enough.

'Jennifer –'

'So don't patronize me, Ellis. Yeah I'm nervous. Until I hear from him, that's not going to change. Now, can we do some work?'

Without another word, Shafer pulled up a chair. Together they looked at the list Exley had been trying to focus on all morning:

TOP SECRET/SCI/EPSILON
RED – ACCESS Work Group – Update 2B

> Abellin, Paul
> Balmour, Victoria
> Baluchi, Hala
> Bright, Jerry
>
> . . .

The list consisted of everyone who knew the Drafter's name or enough details about his identity to compromise him. Already it was fifty-three names long, and despite its length, it still wasn't finished. Tyson had told Exley and Shafer to expect several more names before the updates stopped.

The length of the list testified to Langley's screwed-up priorities, Exley thought. The agency jealously guarded the information the Drafter provided, while treating his name with a carelessness bordering on negligence. The data was valuable, the source worthless.

After just a couple of weeks working this case, Exley had gained new respect for Tyson's job. Even under ideal circumstances, when the agency had been tipped

163

to the exact identity of a spy in its ranks, counter-espionage was tough. Just showing that a CIA employee had hidden income or had failed a polygraph wasn't enough. To build ironclad cases, Tyson's teams needed to catch moles in the act of turning over classified information to their handlers.

Meanwhile, as they investigated, they had to be sure they weren't following false leads from foreign spy agencies. During the Cold War, the KGB had more than once sent Langley down dead-end paths. The sad truth was that without a tip, discovering who had betrayed the Drafter would be incredibly difficult, Exley thought. At this point they had no suspects. And the North Koreans had made sure that the Drafter wouldn't be able to help.

For now, Tyson's work group had put together basic bureaucratic details for each of the fifty-three people on the list: Date of Hire, Pay, Career History/ Evaluations, Marital and Family Status, and – maybe most important – Date of Last Polygraph.

No bank records. They would need subpoenas for those. Tyson's group had run the names through the FBI's criminal records database, checked for felony arrests or convictions. No one had any, though Virginia and D.C. police records showed two misdemeanors. Edmund Cerys, a case officer who'd spent time in Hong Kong in the 1990s, had been caught urinating in public after a Redskins game. And Herb Dubroff, deputy director for the East Asia Division, had gotten himself busted for setting off fireworks on the Fourth of July. Neither arrest exactly screamed double agent.

Shafer extracted his own copy of the list from his file folder. The names were covered with doodles, evidence

164

of his untidy mind. 'Anything jump out?'

'Way too many people had his name. Especially on the DI side.' The DO, or Directorate of Operations, was home to the case officers who managed spies like the Drafter. The DI, or Directorate of Intelligence, had the analysts responsible for thrashing out the reports that the agency sent to the White House. 'There's no excuse for it. Those guys should all get code words only.'

'When you're an asset that long, your name leaks. It's inevitable. Both sides of the house, the analysts and the case officers, they all think they deserve to know details about the assets. They say it's crucial for judging the information.'

'But they're really just trying to prove what big swinging dicks they have.'

'Now, why would you say something like that?'

'Anyway. There are five on this list who haven't taken their polys on schedule. Two others showed signs of quote-unquote minor deception on their last test but haven't been reexamined. All seven now have tests scheduled for next month.'

Any CIA employee with access to sensitive information was supposed to take a polygraph every five years as a routine precaution. In practice the agency was short on polygraph testers. Some mid-level officers went a decade between tests.

'Next month. Glad to see they're taking this so seriously,' Shafer said. 'I'll call Tyson, ask them to move it up.' He dropped the sheet of names on her desk, stood up, and started to pace. She recognized the signs. He was about to have a 'Shafer moment.' In half an hour they'd have a new way of looking for the mole. Maybe it would make sense, maybe not. But at least they'd have some leads to chase.

'Forget the list for a second,' Shafer said. 'Who are we looking for? Who is this guy? What kind of man betrays his country?'

'Betrays his country? Isn't that a little theatrical, Ellis?'

'What would you call it, then?'

'Fine. Betraying his country it is.'

'But in a way you're right. He's not betraying his country. He's betraying *us*. The agency. He's been passed over for promotions. His career hasn't gone how he wanted.'

'That fits half of Langley,' Exley said.

'He's on his second marriage, or his third.'

'Hanssen was on his first marriage.' Robert Hanssen, the FBI double agent.

'That's the exception, but okay. Strike the second marriage. He's a loner for sure. Not many friends at the agency. Middle-aged, forty to fifty-five. Scores well on tests but terrible interpersonal skills. Always sure he's the smartest guy in the room.'

'I didn't know you were spying for North Korea, Ellis.'

'I'll remind you I'm on my first wife.'

'Like Hanssen. Why are you so sure it's a he?'

'It's a he, Jennifer. Women aren't double agents.'

'Because we're such nurturing souls. Like Paris Hilton.'

'Because women don't have the stomach for this kind of risk.'

'That's crap and you're an MCP.'

'A *what*?'

'A male chauvinist pig.'

'Wow. Haven't heard that since Gloria Steinem stopped burning bras. Anyway, I'm right.'

'What about Mata Hari?'

'An exception.'

Exley didn't bother to argue. 'So does he have kids?'

'Possibly. Ames didn't, but Hanssen did.'

'Go on. What else?'

'I don't know, but there's something. Some sexual tic, maybe.'

'He's in the closet, cruising Dupont.' Dupont Circle, the center of Washington's gay population, a few blocks west of Exley's apartment. 'Could you be any more predictable, Ellis?' Exley was enjoying this back-and-forth now. 'Maybe he's just a happy suburban dad, likes it missionary once a week.'

'You don't do this if you're happy.'

'Right you are. Does he do drugs?'

'More likely he gets his kicks legally. Gambling. Drinking, maybe.'

'We can track that,' Exley said. 'A DUI.'

'With a good lawyer he could get a DUI knocked down to a misdemeanor speeding ticket. And traffic records are a nightmare. Even if we just do Maryland and Virginia, it'll take weeks. But we can try.'

'And we can send NSLs to Vegas, ask the casinos if anyone on the list is a major player.' NSLs were national security letters. The agency sent them to companies when it was looking for information to aid espionage or terrorism investigations.

'Thought you believed in the Bill of Rights,' Shafer said.

'They're voluntary. Nobody has to answer.'

'Of course,' Shafer said. With very limited exceptions, the CIA couldn't operate on American soil, so compliance with the letters was voluntary. They were requests, not warrants. But in the post-9/11 era, big companies didn't want to get sideways with Langley, so they usually found ways to give the agency the information it asked for.

'Anyway, this is a totally legitimate use,' Exley said. Shafer's comment stung. She didn't usually think of herself as the type to trample the Fourth Amendment.

'We're fishing, Jennifer. We have zero evidence on any of these people. No judge on earth would give us a warrant.' Shafer pointed at the list. 'Even if it turns out that Jerry Bright, whoever he is, loses ten grand a week in Vegas, it proves nothing.'

'So you don't think we should send the letters?'

'I didn't say that. If Jerry Bright is losing ten grand a week, I want to know where the money's coming from. When you have no clues, you've got to fish.'

'But maybe you're wrong. Maybe our mole's not a gambler or drinker or any of it. Maybe he's a true believer.'

'In the cult of Kim Jong Il? He wants to move North Korea toward its glorious future?'

'Point taken,' Exley said. 'He's not doing it for love. But what if he's in Seoul? In that case, none of this will get us anywhere.'

'You know what, Jennifer? You're right. Let's forget the whole thing, take the afternoon off.'

'That's not what I mean –'

'Seoul's been a well-run station for a long time. I think he's here, not there. And I think that John had it right that night we met Tyson. I think our mole is working for somebody else, not North Korea.'

Exley flinched as Shafer mentioned Wells. For a few minutes, she'd let herself forget the raid. Now she thought of him, wearing the bulletproof vest he insisted on in lieu of the Kevlar plates he said were too heavy.

'So this mole is in it for the money? You think he needs money, Ellis?'

'Not exactly. The money's how he keeps score.'

'If he's spending it, it'll leave a trail.'

'He can hide it. He can put it in his wife's name, his parents, set up a trust.'

'Whatever name he puts it in, if he's spending, then we can see it. He'll have something. A vacation house on the Chesapeake.'

'If you say so.' Shafer sighed, the sound he made when he thought Exley had missed an obvious point. Exley hated that sigh. 'Suppose he got a million bucks over the last decade. That would be a big haul, as much as Ames. But over ten years, it's only a hundred grand a year.'

'Maybe you don't think so, but a hundred grand a year is a lot of money, Ellis. Especially tax-free.'

'If wifey's a lobbyist, say, she's making more than that. A lot more. And he'll have the nice car and the house on the Chesapeake anyway.'

'What if his wife doesn't work?'

'Then it would be more obvious, sure.'

'She doesn't, Ellis. I'm sure of it. He's divorced or his wife doesn't work.'

'Or maybe she works eighty hours a week and the marriage is dead and he's blowing the money on hookers. He feels emasculated, so he's getting her back.'

'I don't think so. The marriage is broken, but they're not divorced.'

'A completely unfounded, wild-ass guess.'

'As opposed to everything you've just said?' Exley looked at her list. 'Okay. We're looking for a man forty to fifty-five, maybe divorced, maybe in an unhappy

169

marriage. He may have a DUI or a public intoxication on his record, but that's not a requirement. Money that he can't explain is a bonus.'

'Also a high IQ, but at least one spotty personnel evaluation. That's the pattern. Doesn't mean it's right in this case, but it's worked in the past. And put in the two guys who failed their polys. That's an automatic red flag.'

'Minor deception doesn't mean you failed.'

'It does to me.'

Exley checked off names. 'I'm going to count peeing in public as intoxication –'

'Good call.'

'Looks like at least ten guys make the cut. Edmund Cerys, Laurence Condon –'

'I know Condon,' Shafer said. 'It's not him.'

'Now we're not even sticking with our own made-up rules?'

'Fine. Leave Condon on. But it's not him.'

'Edmund Cerys. Laurence Condon. Tobias Eyen. Robert Ford. Joe Leonhardt. Danny Minaya. Keith Robinson. James Russo. Phil Waterton. Brad Zonick. Besides Condon, anybody ring a bell?'

Shafer shook his head.

'So I guess . . .' Exley fell silent. 'Now what? Let me guess. Continuing this highly scientific process, we throw darts to decide which of our suspects did it.'

'Try again.'

'Property records, financial disclosure forms, divorce records. We ask around, try to figure out who has a bad marriage, who's a closet drinker. We get Tyson to authorize the national security letters for them and everyone else on the list.'

'Correct. Toodle-oo.' Shafer grabbed his file and

walked out, looking altogether too pleased with himself for Exley's taste.

'Toodle-oo yourself, you ass.'

'And say hi to John for me,' Shafer called from the corridor. 'He's fine, you know.'

She decided not to rise to the bait. In his own childish way, Shafer was trying to make her feel better. She looked down again at the names. She wasn't sure Shafer's theories made sense. Maybe the mole was highly successful, a genius who spied just for the thrill. But at least they were moving. And almost certainly they were coming at the search from a different angle than Tyson's people.

She picked up the phone and dialed Tyson's office.

'George? It's Jennifer Exley. I need help with some names. . . . Yes. Ten in all.'

FIFTEEN

The cave entrance was a black mouth in the side of the mountain, seven feet wide, nearly as tall. Handmade bricks lined the opening, evidence that guerrillas had turned the space inside into a semipermanent refuge. Wells wondered when the bricks had been laid. The Afghans had been defending these mountains for a long, long time. Some of their underground networks had been built not after the Soviet occupation in 1979 but the British invasion of 1838.

Until he went in, Wells couldn't know if the cave was a cul-de-sac used for weapons storage or a deeper link to a tunnel network. Either way he'd be blindly chasing an armed and desperate guerrilla. Prudence dictated that Wells lob in a couple canisters of CS and hope that whoever was inside came out on his own.

Then Wells thought of Greg Hackett, his life dribbling away through the tourniquet on his leg. The soldier in the cave might be the one who'd taken Hackett down. Prudence was another word for fear.

Wells set his M4 neatly against a rock. Inside the cave's narrow passages, the rifle would be a hindrance. He would depend instead on his Makarov and his knives. He grabbed his headlamp from his belt, clicked it to be sure it was working, strapped it to his helmet. He stepped toward the cave – then stopped as he heard someone yelling his name. Gaffan.

'John! You all right?' Gaffan said. 'Looked like you went down hard.'

As if in answer, Wells's right shoulder began to ache, a dull pain that Wells knew would worsen. But he could still use the arm, and that was enough.

'Keep watch here. Clean up anyone who sticks his head out. I'm going in.'

'I'm coming with you.'

'We'll be in each other's way. You cover me on the way in. Then stay here.'

'You're the boss, sir.'

Wells didn't bother to wonder if Gaffan was being sarcastic. He darted across the mouth of the cave and flattened himself against the jagged rocks beside it. As Gaffan positioned himself on the other side of the entrance, Wells peeked inside. He reached for his headlamp, then reconsidered. Not yet. Light would give away his position. Instead he stared into the darkness. Slowly his eyes adjusted enough for him to understand what he was seeing.

The guerrillas had shaped the cave into a tunnel that sloped into the mountain. Rough brick covered parts of its walls, but the ceiling was untouched stone. Wells half-expected to see flint-tipped arrows on the ground, charcoal drawings of men hunting woolly mammoths on the walls.

But this cave had no drawings, and no arrows. A thousand generations of human cleverness had replaced them with deadlier tools. AK-47 rifles lay beside used RPG launch tubes. Aside from the weapons, the space

173

was empty as far as Wells could see. The darkness took over about thirty yards in.

An acrid whiff of the CS gas Wells had fired floated out of the cave, faint but enough to make his nostrils burn. Wells had never thought he'd wish for a faceful of CS. But now he did. The fact that the gas had dispersed so quickly meant that the passage ran deep into the mountain. Not what he wanted.

Across the entrance, Gaffan stood ready. Wells held up three fingers, two, one –

And stepped inside. If someone was watching the entrance Wells was most vulnerable at this moment, his silhouette visible against the sky. He took two steps forward, dove behind an empty crate, and waited. But no shots came. He pushed the crate aside and crawled into the mountain.

Inch by inch the rock womb darkened. Soon Wells couldn't tell if his eyes were open or closed. He straightened up slowly. Before he could stand, his helmet bumped the ceiling, sending a jolt down his neck and into his damaged shoulder. The passageway had shrunk. The ceiling here was lower, no more than five feet. Wells wondered how much smaller it would get.

He leaned back against the wall and tried to orient himself. When he looked back the way he'd come, he could see a pinprick of light – or more accurately, a slightly paler shade of black. The outside world was at most a hundred yards off, but it seemed much farther away. Wells's pulse quickened. Twice in college he'd gone spelunking. But those had been afternoon trips into the White Mountains with a half-dozen friends and a guide, not excursions into the heart of darkness.

Don't be dramatic, Wells told himself. If he needed

light, he had his headlamp, and a flashlight too, a tiny Maglite hooked to his belt. He closed his eyes and thought back to his days playing linebacker in college, watching the quarterback's eyes, knowing where the ball was going even before the receivers did, stepping in front of the errant pass and in a few seconds turning the game inside out, the big men on the other team trying to reverse course, all that momentum heading the wrong way as Wells cruised down the sideline to the end zone. Six times in four years he'd returned interceptions for touchdowns. Wells opened his eyes and found that his heart had slowed to its usual pace, forty-eight beats a minute. His fear was gone and he knew he'd be calm for as long as he needed.

The good news was this cave ought to be easy to navigate. The men who used it wanted shelter, not excitement. Its most dangerous passages should be walled off. And knowing that he might have to fight underground, Wells had come prepared with two special pens. One marked rocks with a fluorescence visible in the dark from hundreds of feet. The other gave off a glow visible under a special ultraviolet light he carried. If the tunnel got complicated, Wells would use the pens to mark his return path.

Besides the pens, Wells carried glowsticks and two high-intensity flash-bang grenades, concussive bombs designed to stun rather than kill. The flash-bangs, a more powerful version of the ones that police carried, had two big advantages over standard high-explosive grenades. They kicked up less shrapnel, and they wouldn't collapse the roof of the tunnel and trap Wells inside the mountain.

Wells also carried an expandable rubber-coated titanium baton, the caver's equivalent of a blind man's cane. But he hadn't bothered with more traditional spelunking equipment, like climbing gear or rope. He had already decided he would turn back if he reached a passage he couldn't navigate with his hands.

The air in the cave was cool, almost clammy, but surprisingly fresh. The tear gas was gone. Ventilation shafts must connect the cave to the surface, Wells thought. In the distance, water trickled faintly, an underground spring. Air, water . . . if they had food down here, guerrillas could hide in these tunnels indefinitely. As long as they didn't go crazy.

Then, somewhere in the distance, Wells heard a hacking cough that started and stopped like a sputtering engine. The sound of a man who was torn between the need for silence and the even more powerful instinct to force out every molecule of tear gas inside him. The coughing went on a few seconds more, then stopped for good. But Wells had heard enough to know he was on the right track.

Baton in hand, Wells edged forward, deeper into the darkness. Rushing would only hurt him now. Either this passage led to a much larger network of tunnels, in which case he couldn't possibly catch the man ahead of him, or it dead-ended and his enemy was waiting. In that case, silence, not speed, was his most important ally.

Meanwhile, Wells would keep his headlamp dark and hope to sense changes in the layout of the tunnel without seeing them. He would trust his balance, try to handle the curves of the tunnel the same way he felt I-95 under his bike at 125 miles an hour. Of course, he might wind up crawling into a crevasse. But if the man ahead of him was preparing a trap, silence and darkness would be Wells's best hope.

The passage twisted right. Wells touched the baton against its walls and ceiling to be sure it hadn't forked somehow, then edged forward again. A few yards farther on, the tunnel tightened and dropped steeply. Wells tucked his knife sideways into his mouth, his teeth clenched around the rubber handle, and crawled forward inch by inch. He was glad he'd chosen the thin bulletproof vest. A flak jacket would have been uncomfortably tight. The passage here was four feet wide, not quite as high, just big enough to give him space to turn around and crawl back out if he needed to. But if it became much tighter, he would no longer have that option. Had he missed a fork somehow? Was he lost already?

Wells reached for his headlamp – and again pulled his hand away. The ceiling and walls here were still smooth, proof they'd been bored out over the years. He had to trust he was on course. He began to crawl again. He'd never been anywhere so dark. Unmoored from light, his eyes made their own world. White flashes and red streaks darted through the blackness like fish. Wells took a chance and lit up his watch, cupping his hand over the glowing dial. 2130. He'd been in here barely twenty minutes. He would have guessed hours.

Already the T-shirt under his bulletproof vest was damp with sweat. A maddening rivulet of sweat trickled down his nose. He wiped it off twice and then gave up. The burn in his right shoulder worsened steadily. Wells wondered whether the injury would betray him in close combat.

Every couple of minutes, Wells stopped to listen. But he heard only a distant trickle of water. Then he lost even that comfort. Silence and darkness entombed him.

Crawl. Wait. Listen. Nothing.

Crawl. Wait. Listen. Nothing.

Crawl. Wait. Listen. Something.

A scraping in the distance, the sound of a man moving. After a few moments, the noise stopped. Wells crawled on, faster now, but doubly careful to move in silence. At last the tunnel flattened. When Wells stopped again, he felt that the air had changed, freshened somehow. Which meant that ahead of him this tunnel opened up into some kind of cave. And there he'd find his quarry.

Wells moved forward, confident now. His adrenaline surged, a natural high stronger than any drug, strengthening and focusing him. The burn in his shoulder faded. Far better to be the hunter than the hunted.

Yard by yard, the tunnel widened out. Again Wells heard scraping. He unholstered his Makarov.

Then he saw the light – a hundred yards ahead, maybe less. Wells raised a hand to shield his eyes, which had grown used to the darkness. A flashlight, shining down the tunnel toward him, though the beam didn't reach him directly because of the curve of the tunnel. Wells flattened himself against the rocks and waited. If he'd been seen, the shooting would start soon enough.

But instead of shots, he heard a voice. No, voices. Two men, speaking a language Wells didn't immediately recognize. Not Arabic or Pashto. Certainly not English. The words were muffled, but the men seemed to be arguing. The light snapped off, on again, off again. Then a word rang clearly through the darkness. '*Pogibshiy.*' Russian for 'lost.'

Wells realized he'd caught an incredible break. These men weren't Taliban guerrillas. They were

Russian, hard as that was to believe. And they were confused. They'd reached a junction, and they didn't know which path to take. One probably wanted to give up, crawl out and take his chances with the Special Forces. The other wanted to push on and risk getting lost forever. Or maybe just sit tight, wait, and come out in a day or two. But the first man feared that the SF would dynamite the cave entrance and again they'd be stuck.

Because they couldn't agree, they'd given away their position with their fighting. A stupid mistake, born of fear.

Now that he knew that he faced two men, prudence – that word again – dictated that Wells turn around, crawl out, and wait. In a space as confined as this, they could easily overpower him even if he surprised them. But what if they didn't come out? What if they went deeper into the cave? They would either find another path out or die in here. Either way Wells would lose the chance to interrogate them.

And Wells wasn't willing to lose that chance. He needed to know who'd sent them. The Talibs, brutal as they were, were fighting for their God and their country. These Russians were nothing more than mercenaries, killing American soldiers for money.

Forget prudence.

Wells crawled forward, Makarov in his hand, flashbang grenades on his hip. He'd left the baton behind. It was useless to him. He moved fast now, as fast as he could. Which wasn't all that fast. The tightness of the tunnel restricted him to a crablike scuttle. But he figured he'd reach the end of the passage in less than a minute, and then –

Then he tripped.

He banged down hard. Hard and loud. Wells heard the Russians scrambling. A flashlight beamed at him, no more than twenty yards away.

Seconds later, the shooting started.

SIXTEEN

GUANGZHOU, CHINA

The three elevated highways came together in a jumble of ramps that soared above the warehouses of northern Guangzhou. Once called Canton, the city had been a commercial center in China for centuries. Now Guangzhou was a metropolis of eight million people, the manufacturing heart of southeastern China. The trucks and buses on its highways never stopped, even on damp nights like this one, when rain pounded down and the air seemed too humid to breathe.

Beneath the highway junction lay a darker world. The concrete pillars that supported the roads formed a kind of room, noisy with the thrum of big engines in low gear. The space had no lights, but it was illuminated secondhand by cars passing on the nearby surface roads. Their headlights gave the space the unsteady glow of an after-hours club, offering glimpses of the rats that dodged through the pylons. The place wasn't exactly a five-star hotel.

But it was dry, Jordan Weiging thought. He had walked for hours, looking for a place to escape the rain, ever since those cops had chased him from Huangshi

Boulevard. Damned cops. Jordan had learned to hate the police since he came to Guangzhou six months before. They seemed to be everywhere, and they were quick to use their sticks.

Jordan hadn't been looking for trouble on Huangshi, only a doorway where he could sleep in the shadows of the street's skyscrapers. He hadn't thought anyone would care. Huangshi was Guangzhou's version of the Las Vegas Strip, giant hotels beside low-rent two-story bars. Even in the rain, whores walked the avenue, smiling and blowing kisses at the men who surveyed them. They wore thigh-high skirts and tight tank tops and were barely in their teens. Even the ugliest ignored Jordan, though. In their own way, they were showing him mercy. He was so obviously broke that tempting him would have been unkind.

But the police hadn't been so polite. Tonight they had pulled up as he rested in the shadow of the Guangdong International Hotel and told him to move on. He pleaded with them for mercy, told them he meant no harm, and one seemed ready to let him stay. But the other, a skinny man with dirty yellow teeth, spat at his feet.

'Damned migrant,' the cop said. 'We have too many of you rats already.'

'What about them?' Jordan pointed to four street-walkers. The girls cocked their hips and cooed like pigeons at the cops.

'The hotels don't mind them. Anyway, they pay us in ways you can't.' The cop tapped his wooden nightstick against his hand. 'Now move.'

So Jordan moved. The rain cut through his jacket and sweatpants and soaked his feet until he couldn't feel

182

them. He wanted to lie down on the cracked sidewalk and let the water wash him away. Let the cops find him and do their worst. Then he stumbled onto the space under the junction, where the North Ring Highway met the Airport Toll Road.

The McDonald's wrappers and dirty blankets showed him he wasn't the first to find the space. Jordan wondered why anyone who could afford the luxury of eating at McDonald's would sleep here. Probably the wrapper had come from the road above.

At least he was out of the rain. He pulled off his jacket and folded it neatly, then slumped against a pylon on the cleanest patch of ground he could find. Whoever had been here before had a taste for Red Star Erguotou – cheap, strong sorghum liquor. Empty bottles of the stuff littered the place. Jordan reached for one, hoping for a few drops. He was amazed when he heard liquid sloshing inside, almost half a bottle. He took a tiny sip, coughed as the liquor burned his mouth.

He waited a moment to be sure the bottle wasn't contaminated, then took a longer swig. His stomach was empty – he hadn't eaten all day – and the liquor hit him quickly. He rubbed his eyes. He wanted to believe that this bottle proved that his fate had changed. One day, when he was rich, he'd hold it up and explain to his children how he'd come to Guangzhou and built a fortune from nothing.

He looked at the Red Star bottle, still a quarter full. He ought to save it, he knew, but he couldn't help himself. Tonight he would drink like a rich man. He tipped up the bottle and gave himself another slug.

Jordan's real name was Jiang. Jiang Weiging, in the traditional Chinese style, family name first and given

183

name last. But he thought of himself as Jordan, hoping that some of the luck of Michael Jordan's name would rub off. In his pack, he carried a dirty Chicago Bulls cap, black with a snorting, red-faced bull over the brim. His most prized possession.

He had loved basketball as long as he could remember. During the good years, before his father got sick, his family had enough money for a television and a VCD player – a cheap Chinese version of a DVD. Jordan's father liked basketball too. Together they'd watch highlights from the NBA that had been copied onto video disks and sold for two yuan, barely a quarter, at the market in Hanyuan.

In his heart, Jiang knew he wasn't much of a player. He was strong but small, barely five feet. When he was seven, he'd lost his left pinkie and ring fingers to the spokes of his father's bicycle. So he'd never play in the NBA, the *National Basketball Association* – he felt a chill at the mere thought of the words, and he wondered whether the rain and the Red Star were making him sick – but he loved the game anyway.

Americans thought the Chinese liked basketball because China was jealous of America, Jordan thought. But he didn't want to be American. He couldn't even imagine what it would be like to be American. He didn't care about other American sports. But the flow of basketball, the mix of grace and power in the game, felt natural to him.

Jordan reached into his pack and pulled out his Bulls cap. He rubbed its logo and a genuine smile creased his face. Even now he could see his namesake jumping high, slamming home a dunk.

Jordan had come to Guangzhou from Chenhe, a village in Sichuan Province. Ziyang, his father, had died of AIDS three years before, after getting HIV from a contaminated needle. He'd been infected while selling plasma to raise money for Jordan's school fees. To save money, the plasma collection stations reused needles, a horribly efficient way to spread the virus. Whole villages were infected before Beijing outlawed the practice.

After Ziyang got sick, Jordan took his father's place in the fields. He couldn't afford more school anyway. 'Without money you can't expect a miracle,' his mother told him. Jordan had gotten seven years of school, and he figured that was enough. He could add, subtract, multiply, and divide. He read well enough to get by, though the complicated characters confused him. For two years, he and his mother muddled along.

Then she took sick, losing weight, coughing furiously, clots of phlegm and blood. Jordan brought her to the hospital in Hanyuan. The doctors looked her over and said they couldn't do anything, even if she could have afforded treatment. She died a few months later, leaving Jordan alone. His nearest relatives were his second cousins, who lived in a village a few miles away and could hardly feed their own children.

He collected a few yuan by selling off his mother's clothes and the little television, and set off for Guangzhou, the heart of the Chinese manufacturing miracle. He'd just turned sixteen. Everyone knew there was work to be had in Guangzhou and Shenzen, the twin boomtowns of Guangdong Province. Boys not much older than Jordan had come back from Guangzhou with motorcycles and computers. Some had even built houses for their families. He would find a job too.

But he didn't.

What Jordan didn't know, what he couldn't be expected to understand, was that China was a victim of its own success. The factories that made toys and shoes and cheap furniture, the low-skill products that had provided jobs for tens of millions of migrants like Jordan, were themselves migrating to other Asian countries. In Indonesia and Vietnam, land was cheaper, construction costs lower, the workers equally diligent. In higher-end manufacturing for laptops and televisions and cars, China was still growing. But no chip company would hire a sixteen-year-old boy with eight fingers and a seventh-grade education. For the low-end jobs that were left, in construction and basic laboring, Jordan was competing with men who were older and stronger than he. The cop who'd rousted him was right. Guangzhou had too many migrants.

So Jordan joined the endless stream of workers who trudged between construction sites and run-down factories, offering their labor for a few yuan a day. Some days he found work, and on those nights he slept with his belly full. But even in the last few weeks the jobs had gotten scarcer, the crowds outside the factories bigger. He'd worked only three times in the last week. He'd spent his money as carefully as he could. He hadn't permitted himself a bottle of Coke, his favorite treat, in months. Even so, he was down to his last twenty yuan – less than three dollars – hidden in the brim of his Bulls hat. He didn't want to spend those two crumpled ten-yuan bills, didn't want to be left with nothing. So he was holding on to them, even though he felt faint with hunger and had begun to hear the voice of his father in his head telling him to eat.

Maybe tomorrow he could convince a restaurant to let him wash dishes in return for some spoiled vegetables or day-old fish. Yes, tomorrow he'd try the restaurants. He closed his eyes and thought of steaming hot soup, thick with dumplings, as his mother had made during the good years. He took another sip of the Red Star and drifted off to sleep.

He opened his eyes to see two men looking curiously at him. He scrambled up, keeping his back to the pylon. He had a knife in his bag, a cheap switchblade that had once been his dad's.

But the men didn't seem threatening. They were much older than he was, and their faces were weary. One was the thinnest man Jordan had ever seen. The other was fat and held a bottle of Red Star. As Jordan looked at him, he sat down slowly. Jordan couldn't tell if he had meant to sit or just given up on standing.

'So you've found the Hotel Guangzhou,' the thin man said. He laughed, a rasping laugh that became a hacking cough that shook his body. Jordan's mother had coughed that way a few months before she died. When the cough stopped, the man pulled a crumpled pack of cigarettes from his pocket. He put one in his mouth. 'Want a cigarette, boy?'

'I don't smoke.'

'May as well start. You'll die faster. Less time to suffer.' The man laughed and tossed him the pack and the lighter. Jordan looked at the cigarettes. Basketball players didn't smoke, he was sure.

'Try one,' the man said. 'You'll feel less hungry.'

At that, Jordan put the cigarette to his lips. His hand trembled as he lit it. The sour smoke filled his mouth and he coughed.

'Easy, boy. A little at a time to start.'

Jordan took a small puff and choked the smoke into

his lungs. His brain seemed to come alive. The feeling wasn't entirely pleasant, but he hadn't felt so awake in weeks. He took a longer drag.

'Not so much, boy, or you'll regret it.'

Too late. Nausea filled him. He slumped against the pylon. But he held on to the cigarette, and when the feeling passed he took another, more tentative puff. This time he felt better. And the man was right. His hunger was gone. 'It works.'

The thin man rubbed his hands together. 'Yu, I've gotten him hooked. My good deed for the day.' He laughed his awful hacking laugh. A moment later, Yu giggled drunkenly back, a high-pitched sound that didn't fit his heavy body.

The thin man sat beside Jordan, who flinched. 'Don't worry,' he said. 'I'm not one of those. My name's Song. What's yours?'

'Jiang,' Jordan said.

'Where do you come from, Jiang?'

'Sichuan Province. I came here to work.'

'Of course you did. If only you'd come last year, or the year before that – Well, anyway.' Song braced a hand on the ground and stood, slowly unfolding his skinny limbs. Watching him made Jordan smile. Song moved like a puppet whose strings had gotten tangled.

'Do you like basketball?' Jordan said. He suddenly very much wanted Song to stay and talk. The skinny old man was the first person who'd treated him with any kindness in months.

'Sure. Why?'

'I don't know.'

'If you like, we can look for work together tomorrow,' Song said. 'We may not find any, but at least Yu and I can show you the city. You see what a success we've made here.' He kicked ineffectually at Yu, who lay on his side with his eyes closed. 'Don't you want your blanket, fat pig?' But Yu simply rolled away.

'Good night, Jiang.'

'Good night, Master Song.'

And Song laughed again, so hard that he had to lean against a concrete pylon to stay upright. 'Master . . . master . . .'

Jordan closed his eyes and listened to Song's hacking. Life had to get better, he thought. It could hardly get worse. He sipped his bottle of Red Star until sleep took him. And as he finally drifted off, he had no way of imagining that soon enough he would provoke a crisis whose repercussions would echo around the world.

SEVENTEEN

The flashlight flicked off and in the dark the shots ricocheted past Wells like a jackhammer gone mad. Wells pressed his head down, brushing his lips against the stone and dirt, as shards of rock rained down on him.

The pace of firing slowed and Wells lifted his head. 'Stop!' he yelled in his perfect Arabic. 'Stop! It's Mohammed! Don't shoot!'

Silence. Then another fusillade of shots. For now the darkness and the tunnel were protecting him, making it hard for the Russians to get a bead on him. Only his head and shoulders were visible, making him a very narrow target. They would need a perfect lucky shot to get him. But if they kept shooting from twenty yards out, they'd get that shot eventually. Or they might roll a grenade his way – though blowing up the tunnel would block their only sure escape route.

The shooting stopped. 'Mohammed?' a man shouted.

'Mohammed, brother of Ahmed.'

'Brother of Ahmed?' The Arabic was rusty, Russian-accented.

'Brother of Ahmed!' Wells yelled. He only needed

to distract them for a few seconds. 'I know these tunnels. I can save us.' Wells braced his right hand, the one holding his Makarov, against the tunnel. A surge of pain ripped through his damaged shoulder and he gritted his teeth.

With his left hand, Wells reached for his flash-bang grenades. He still intended to take at least one of these men alive. He unhooked the flash-bangs and wriggled his left arm forward until the grenades were in front of him. He braced his right hand, the one holding the Makarov, against the side of the tunnel.

'Yes, my Russian brothers. I know these tunnels. The path to the left leads –'

'Wait – speak slowly –' the man at the other end called in his broken Arabic.

'*Topko ubeyte ego!*' the second man yelled.

Wells had heard enough Russian during his days in Chechnya to know what that meant. *Just kill him.* 'Grenade,' the man added, a word that needed no translation.

'*Nyet*,' the other man said. Wells relaxed a little. *Nyet* on the grenade, *da* on the flashlight, which would make an excellent target.

He chattered in Arabic down the tunnel. 'You must know Ahmed. He wears his robe loose but his shorts tight. Men love him, though sheep fear him –' For the second time in an hour, the thrill of combat filled Wells. Crackheads must feel this elation when they put flame to pipe. *Zeus. I am Zeus.*

'*Topko ubeyte ego*,' the man said again. The unmistakable *click* of a magazine being jammed into an AK-47 echoed down the tunnel.

At the end of the tunnel, the flashlight clicked on. This time the Russians wouldn't fire blindly. They started shooting in short bursts. A rock fragment cut Wells's cheek, under his eye, and blood flowed warm down his face.

But now Wells could aim too. He squeezed off two shots from the Makarov. He heard a yelp in Russian and the flashlight dropped to the ground. Now they might be desperate enough to send a grenade at him. Before they could, he tumbled the flash-bangs down the tunnel. As the grenades rolled away, he buried his head in his hands, closed his eyes, and counted to himself like a kid playing touch football at recess: 'One Mississippi, two Mississippi, three Missi –'

The name flash-bang didn't begin to do justice to these grenades. Through his squeezed-tight eyelids, Wells saw a pure white light. The noise from the explosions was louder than anything he had ever heard, something more than sound. A shock wave pummeled his ears. He knew he wasn't moving, couldn't be inside the narrow tunnel, yet he seemed to be spinning in two directions at once. The men howled in Russian, their voices barely audible over the noise in Wells's head.

Wells opened his eyes and breathed in deeply. The heavy thermite smell of the grenades brought him back to reality. He needed to move fast, before the Russians regained their bearings. On hands and knees, Wells crawled forward in the dark. The tunnel spun around him. He concentrated on the blood flowing down his cheek and didn't stop moving. His stomach tightened and a surge of nausea overcame him. Before he could hold back, Gatorade and soda crackers burned his throat and poured out of his mouth. He ate lightly before missions and this was why.

Wells grabbed the side of the tunnel. Somehow he

kept moving, pumping his legs forward. Hours passed, or seconds, and then the walls opened up around him. He lost his balance and fell, landing on one of the Russians. The man was twisting sideways, moaning, hands wrapped around his ears. The grenades had blown out his eardrums, Wells thought. The man grabbed feebly at him, but Wells jammed the Makarov into his mouth and pulled the trigger. The Russian's arm trembled and fell, a last hopeless flutter.

Wells rolled off the corpse and waited, listening in the dark. He was guessing that the man he'd killed had taken the worst of the flash-bangs. The second one might be able to move, or at least to crawl. He waited, listened, and –

There.

In the blackness, Wells heard the Russian's breath, as close and quiet as a seashell in his ear, no more than ten feet away. *Where?* Wells couldn't turn on his flashlight without giving away his own position. The Russian must have the same dilemma. Wells crab-scuttled left, silently, silently, his back to the wall of the cave, holding the Makarov in his right hand.

Step. Step.

Then a burst of AK fire.

But Wells was untouched. The Russian was hitting only the corpse of his partner. Wells threw himself off the cavern wall. The Russian spun toward him, but Wells knocked the barrel of his rifle up and away. With a low arcing kick, he swept the other man's legs out. The Russian fell back, landing hard. Wells jumped him, and with a knee astride his chest landed a clean left to his chin and another to his nose. The fight went out of the Russian fast. As Wells punched him a third and fourth and fifth time, he hardly resisted. Wells didn't know if he was disoriented or just resigned to his fate.

Wells flipped the Russian onto his stomach and looped flexcuffs – the temporary plastic handcuffs that police sometimes used in place of regular metal cuffs – tight around the man's wrists and ankles. Then he snapped open a yellow glowstick.

The cavern was small, no more than eight feet high and twenty-five feet around. On one wall, a guerrilla had spray-painted the Arabic phrase '*Allahu akbar*' – God is great – in black on the grayish-green stone. Small stalactites hung from the ceiling. The walls and floor bulged as if the mountain were laced with tumors.

Three rusty oil drums sat near the far wall, next to a child-sized BMX bicycle. Bizarre. Maybe the guerrillas had been practicing a circus act in their downtime. Aside from those odd relics, the cavern seemed empty. Beside the oil drums two passages led deeper into the mountain. They were just three feet high, narrower than the tunnel that connected the cave with the surface. Wells understood why the Russians had hesitated to take them. If they dead-ended, they'd be little more than traps.

Wells tossed the glowstick aside. 'Speak English?' he said to the Russian.

'Sure.'

'Is anyone else here?'

The man spat on the ground. 'See anyone?'

'If I do, I'll kill you first. Understand?'

'I understand. No, we are alone.'

Wells drew his knife. The Russian's eyes widened. He rolled onto his back and tried to squirm away. 'I just want to be sure you're not hiding anything,' Wells said. He put a knee on the Russian's chest and slashed at the man's sweater and T-shirt, pulling them off. Then he hacked away the man's camouflage pants until the Russian was naked except for ill-fitting cotton briefs. But the guy didn't seem to have any extra weapons. A surprise. Every decent commando carried an extra knife, just in case.

'Now the boots.' Wells sliced at the man's boots. The Russian kicked wildly.

'Boots? *Nyet.* My feet.'

'*Nyet?*' Wells turned the Russian onto his stomach, grabbed the man's little fingers, and pulled them sideways until he could feel the tendons about to snap. '*Nyet nyet*, Vladimir. If I didn't need you, I'd leave you down here for the spiders. Got it?'

'Okay, okay.'

Wells wondered if he'd meant his threat. He'd killed many men, but never an unarmed prisoner. In New York, he'd spared the life of a Saudi terrorist he'd captured. Treating captives with decency was one way the United States separated itself from its enemies. At least it had been once. Now America seemed to have lost its moorings. Wells wondered if he had too.

Wells flipped the Russian on his back and sliced into the black leather of his boots. He tore them off. The stench of the Russian's feet filled the cavern. 'Time for a bath, Vladimir.'

'I told you leave them on.'

Wells peeled down the man's socks. As he did, a sharp metal point, warm with body heat, pricked his left palm. A knife was taped to the back of the man's right leg.

Wells stepped on the Russian's chest, leaned in with his steel-toed boots until he felt the man's sternum compress. A slow groan escaped the prisoner's lips.

Wells lifted the Russian's leg and ripped off the knife. The tape tore, taking a chunk of skin with it. 'Now you're ready for beach season, Vlad.'

'Name is Sergei.'

'Congratulations.' Wells tossed the knife into the darkness. He ran his flashlight over the Russian, looking for other hidden knives or guns, but saw nothing.

'Any other surprises?'

The Russian said nothing.

'I'll take that as a no.' Wells cut open the flexcuffs binding the Russian's feet but left his hands tight. 'Now. You're going in there.' Wells pointed to the tunnel that led to the surface. 'When you're in, I'll cut your hands free so you can drag your ass out of this cave. Understand?'

'What about you?'

'I'll be right behind you. Please be smart. I'm guessing getting shot in the colon is an unpleasant way to die.'

'Colon? I don't understand.'

Wells grabbed the Russian's arms and dragged him toward the entrance to the tunnel. Allowing the prisoner to lead was dangerous, Wells knew. If he had to kill the man in the narrowest part of the tunnel, he might end up stuck behind the corpse. But if he led, he risked the Russian's jumping him from behind. This way he could easily watch the man. Anyway, he didn't think this guy wanted to die underground.

At the entrance to the passage, Wells flicked on his headlamp and pushed the Russian to the floor of the cavern. 'Lift your arms behind your back.' The Russian obeyed.

Wells put a knee on the man's back. With his left hand, Wells pressed the man's head down. With his

196

right, he cut the cuffs. This was the moment of maximum danger, the last chance for the prisoner to lock him up in hand-to-hand combat. When the Russian's hands were free, Wells stepped back.

'Now crawl.'

'Naked?' His accent lengthened the word – *naaaked* – so it sounded vaguely pornographic.

Wells kicked him in the ribs. 'Not my problem. Anyway, you're not naked. Crawl.'

Twenty minutes later, Wells saw the dim light of the entrance. The Russian hadn't tried anything. As the tunnel widened out, Wells flexcuffed his hands and legs again and dragged him out.

A flashlight stunned his eyes.

'Halt!' Gaffan yelled.

'It's Wells. Got a hostile with me.'

'Yessir. Step slowly, now.' Wells stepped forward. 'You okay? You've got blood all over you.' Wells had forgotten the cut on his cheek. 'Nothing, Sergeant. Looks worse than it is.'

The ground shook with the rumble of a fighter jet. Gaffan quickly filled Wells in. While he was underground, the Special Forces had gotten air support in the form of a pair of F-16s from Bagram. 'Those Air Force boys don't like flying in the mountains at night, but once we told 'em we could lose two squads if they didn't get off their asses, they came through all right.'

Because of the tightness of the terrain and the fact that the Special Forces were so close to the Talibs, the jets hadn't eliminated all the enemy positions. But their presence had given the Americans a chance to regroup. Now the SF had killed at least a dozen Talibs. The rest were trying to escape into the caves or down the mountain. Still, this fight had been anything but a cakewalk. The Special Forces had taken three dead and three more seriously wounded, including Hackett, who probably wouldn't last the night.

'We shoulda come in with another squad,' Gaffan said. He looked at the prisoner, who sat hog-tied against the side of the mountain. 'So who's he?'

'Good question.' Wells nudged the Russian. 'Who are you?' The prisoner strained against the flexcuffs.

'Take these off and I will show you who I am.'

'He went soft in the cave and it looks like he's not too happy about it,' Wells said. 'All I know is his name isn't Vladimir. It's Sergei. Who are you, Sergei? Tell us about yourself.'

Part 3

EIGHTEEN

The stewpot bubbled and burped above a low fire, filling the hut with the rich aroma of chicken and carrots and potatoes melting together. Jordan reached for the pot, but his mother swiped his arm away. No, she said. First your father eats. She sat above him on a wooden throne, reaching an impossibly long arm down to stir the pot. Saliva filled Jordan's mouth and the hole in his stomach swelled to the size of a basketball. He looked around but didn't see his father.

A scoop, its thin aluminum handle twisted from years of use, lay by the pot. Jordan grabbed it. *Wait,* his mother said. He's come back. He's right behind you. Jordan turned and saw his father, a blush of purple tumors crawling across his face. The old man reached out with a skeletal hand. And though he knew he shouldn't, Jordan wanted to keep this wrecked, dying man from dirtying the stew. He blocked his father from the pot and reached in with the scoop. But the pot was empty, aside from a tiny chicken wing. As Jordan watched, the wing fluttered out of the pot, a final insult.

'No,' he said aloud.

Jordan opened his eyes and looked around. The stew – along with his poor dead parents – vanished as he woke. Nothing had changed. On the concrete highway above him, trucks rumbled. The morning air was hot and humid. Song and Yu slept under a thin woolen blanket, Yu clutching an empty bottle of Red Star.

The stew was gone, but Jordan's hunger stayed with him as he pushed himself to his feet. Nothing metaphorical about this feeling. Jordan didn't want love or hugs or a pony. He wanted food. All day, every day, his stomach ached.

In the mornings, if he managed to earn a half-loaf of stale bread and a cup of tea sweeping the sidewalk for a friendly storekeeper, his cravings faded to a low growl, background noise. But in the afternoons, the emptiness in his belly overwhelmed him. He drank water then, ate vegetables that were more brown than green, anything to fill his stomach. The cigarettes helped too, though he knew he couldn't afford them. A pack of cigarettes cost as much as a bag of potatoes.

Worst of all were the hours before bed. Then his belly ached so badly that he wanted to cry, though he never did. To keep him smiling, Song and Yu told tales about girls they'd known, peasant girls who sneaked off in the dark to lie with them.

'Once this missus and I, you know, we were ready to –' Song leered, his mouth opening in a gap-toothed smile. 'I pulled up her dress and put her on the ground and she yelped.' Song moaned, a passable imitation of a teenage girl. 'Turned out her bum had ended up in a chunk of horse dung. I would have gone ahead straightaway – she was none too clean even before that – but she made me take her home. Silly girl. We could have had a bit of pleasure, and that's too rare in this world.'

Song and Yu howled with laughter and even Jordan found himself smiling. He didn't know if the stories

202

were true, and he didn't care. The words distracted him. Song and Yu gave him food too, when they had any. If not for them he didn't know what he would have done. Yet he wasn't even sure why they liked him. Maybe because neither had a son, or even a daughter, and they saw him as a substitute.

Each morning, Jordan fought through his daily routine of a hundred sit-ups and push-ups. Even with his belly empty, he never skipped his workout – and it never failed to amuse Song and Yu. 'Arnud Schwarzenga,' they called him. More seriously, they told him to conserve his strength, that the exercises wasted energy he couldn't spare.

He knew they were right, but he refused to quit. He had once heard his hero Michael Jordan say that he worked out even if he could hardly move. 'Every day,' Michael had said, with that famous grin. So Jordan stuck to his exercises. Despite his troubles, he had somehow managed to stay optimistic. He never stopped to think about why. Unlike most sixteen-year-olds in America or Europe, he had seen enough death to know that just being alive was a privilege, one everyone lost eventually. While he had it, he would do his best to honor his father and mother.

'Ninety-nine . . . a hundred.' Jordan finished his last push-up and stood.

'Arnud . . . Arnud . . .' Song smirked. 'One day you have big muscles too, Jiang.' They didn't call him Jordan. He'd kept that name to himself, for himself.

'Come on, Master Song,' Jordan said. 'Let's go.'

Song dragged himself up and pulled the blanket off Yu. 'Up, fatty. No work means no Red Star tonight.'

Yu grumbled and tossed the blanket aside. He was filthy, his sweatshirt stained and his pants frayed.

Jordan tried not to imagine what his mother would think of the way he lived. Poor as they'd been, she'd always kept their home clean. She swept every day and made him wash himself every morning, even in the winter when the cold water stung him and made his privates shrivel so he could hardly see them. Jordan brushed the dirt off his clothes as best he could. If he found work today, he would buy soap, even a little bottle of shampoo. He couldn't believe he wanted anything more than food, but he did. He wanted to be clean.

In the meantime he pulled his lucky Bulls hat over his greasy black hair and away they went. Song had heard of a new job site, an apartment building being demolished downtown, with plenty of work.

The sun was just visible when they reached the entrance to the Guangzhou subway. With no money for the fare, they skipped over the electronic turnstiles instead of buying a ticket. In theory the cops could arrest them, but in reality they'd just be shoved off the train at the next stop if they were caught; the police didn't want anything to do with them.

Fifteen minutes later they reached their stop. Jordan felt himself sag as he walked up the steps to the street. The world went gray and he stumbled backward. Song wrapped an arm around him and gently set him down.

'Jiang?'

'I just need a cigarette.'

'A roast pig too, by the looks of it,' Yu said. He dug into his pocket for a coin. 'Come on, Song, let's get the boy some bread at least.'

They found a vendor and bought Jordan a small ripe orange. He wanted to force the whole sphere into his mouth at once. Instead he peeled it slowly, offering slices to Song and Yu. Though he knew he ought to share – they'd bought it for him, after all – he felt a pang with each piece he gave up. The vendor watched him eat and when he was finished handed him another orange and a pear too. He waved aside Song's fumbling effort to pay. Usually Jordan didn't like taking charity, but today he didn't mind. The fruit filled his belly and gave him a jolt of energy.

'Feeling better?'

Jordan nodded.

'Now let's win this job.' They cut through a narrow pedestrian mall hemmed in on both sides by concrete apartment buildings. Some stores were already open. Inside a butcher shop, men in dirty aprons shooed flies away from slabs of meat strung from ceiling hooks. Next door, in a store filled with glass jars that brimmed with crumbly green tea, two old men haggled over a plastic bag of leaves. Farther down, the aroma of honey-filled dumplings wafted from a pastry store. Jordan forced himself to look away from the pastries before he spent the last of his money, the emergency money in his Bulls hat.

Two blocks down, they turned left onto a crowded avenue. Song looked at the signs. 'This way,' he said. A dozen or so equally dirty men were walking in the same direction. They made a right, and after a short block, turned onto a street blocked by police sawhorses.

'Dammit,' Song said. Scores of men, a hundred or more in all, milled around. So much for finding easy work.

'You woke me for this?' Yu spat onto the pavement. On their right, the steel skeleton of a half-finished skyscraper rose, the construction site blocked by barbed wire, its gates locked. The other side of the street held the apartment building slated for demolition. Two giant cranes stood beside it, wrecking balls poised to tuck into the eight-story brick building like hungry men slicing up a steak.

But the building wasn't empty, Jordan saw. On the fifth floor an old woman leaned out, shouting to the street. 'Don't do the capitalist roader's work! We poor people must stay together!'

Yu laughed. 'Capitalist roader? That old missus probably thinks Mao's still alive. Didn't anyone tell her we're all on our own these days?'

'See, Jiang?' Song asked. 'They want us to clean everyone out so the cranes can knock down the building. It's dirty work, but we'll eat tonight.'

'Dirty work,' Yu said. 'Yes, it is.'

A Mercedes sedan and two police cars rolled past the sawhorses and onto the street, forcing the men to make way. A stocky young man in a black T-shirt and slacks stepped out of the Mercedes and raised a bullhorn.

'Ten yuan' – hardly more than a dollar – 'for every man who rids the building of these squatters,' he yelled.

'Ten yuan?' Song said. 'He must think we're desperate.'

'He's right,' Yu said.

'You snake!' the old woman yelled down. 'We're not squatters. I've lived here longer than you've been alive.'

'And now it's time for you to go.'

The woman disappeared. When she came back, she held a metal pot.

'Swine!' she yelled. She lobbed the pot at the Mercedes. The men scattered as the pot shattered the sedan's windshield.

'Crazy old bitch!' the man yelled. Another pot flew out of the window and smacked the hood of the Mercedes, denting the shiny black metal. Two police officers stepped out of their cars and ran into the building.

A low rumble passed through the crowd. 'Dirty work,' a couple of men said. 'Dirty work.' More faces appeared in the building's windows. 'You can't throw us out,' voices shouted. Sirens screeched, at first distantly, but growing louder.

'Twenty yuan!' the man in the black T-shirt yelled. 'I'll pay twenty!'

'It's blood money,' Song said. Jordan felt light-headed at his words. Blood money. His father had died for blood money. 'Don't be afraid,' his father's spirit said to him, not in his head but for real on the street. He looked around, but the spirit was gone.

'Are you all right?' Song said to him.

'Fine, Master Song.'

'You should leave. You don't need to be involved in this.'

'Not unless you come too.'

'Then let's all stay and see what happens. We've been pushed around too long.' Song's eyes were hard and shiny as pebbles. 'Dirty work!' he yelled at the Mercedes.

'It's honest work,' the man yelled back. 'If you don't like it, starve.'

For a few minutes, not much happened. The man in the black T-shirt raised his offer to thirty yuan, and a couple of the laborers stepped toward the building. But the other men on the street blocked them from going inside and they gave up. Then three more police cars appeared, sirens screaming. A dozen cops stepped out, tapping nightsticks against their thighs. A paddy wagon blocked off the street from the other direction. More migrants had shown up, and the street was thick with men now, milling around the police cars.

From the fifth floor the old woman yelled, 'Leave me! Leave me!' as a policeman dragged her from the window.

'Leave her!' a laborer yelled.

Holding bricks and rebar rods, trash from the construction site, the migrants surged toward the police. A police officer grabbed the bullhorn from the man in the black T-shirt.

'Get out now or we'll arrest all of you roaches.'

Song stepped forward. 'We've done nothing wrong.'

'Not another word from you.' The officer raised his truncheon.

'Let him alone,' Jordan said.

The officer smirked. 'And who are you? Skinny little migrant.' The cop shoved Jordan and grabbed his Bulls cap. *All I have*, Jordan thought. The hat was everything, his money, his luck, his connection to his father –

'Officer –' Song put a hand on the cop's shoulder. Without a word, the cop swung his nightstick, catching Song in the ribs. As Song doubled over, the cop brought the stick down on Song's skull. Song's eyes rolled up and he dropped like a sack of potatoes.

'Murderer!' an old man shouted from the apartment building. 'You killed him!' A clay pot flew out of the building and smashed on the roof of a police car.

'Murderers! Murderers!' The chant rumbled through the crowd, wavering like a fire trying to catch. For five seconds, then ten, the police and the migrants stared at each other, no one quite ready for more violence.

208

'Order!' the officer with the bullhorn said, and the crowd took a half-step back. 'Go on now.' On the ground, Song groaned.

Jordan reached down and at his feet, as if his father had put it there, he found a beer bottle, a big one, broken in half, its glass edges sharp as a steak knife. In one motion, he picked it up and stepped forward and swung at the cop's neck.

Even before the blood began to spurt, the cops were on Jordan. He fought as hard as he could, though after the first dozen blows he stopped caring. Yu stepped up and the police jumped him too. 'Murderers!' the laborers shouted. 'Murderers!'

And then nothing could stop the riot.

Swinging crowbars and bricks, the migrants overwhelmed the police and smashed stores and cars across Guangzhou's city center. Someone – the police never discovered who – set fire to the apartment building that had been the flash point for the riot. With firefighters unable to get to the building, twenty-four people inside died.

By mid-afternoon, the fighting had spread to the giant factories on the outskirts of Guangzhou, where migrants worked for wages that barely covered their meals and rent. More riots broke out in Shenzen, a city of 8 million between Guangzhou and Hong Kong, and Shaoguan, to the north. In all, 142 rioters, 139 civilians, and twenty-three police officers died during two days of fighting, which ended only after the People's Liberation Army rolled through Guangdong to enforce a province-wide curfew.

The government tried to impose a news blackout on Guangdong, arresting reporters who wrote about the riot.

But word spread quickly, carried by cell-phone cameras and Internet postings that popped up as quickly as the censors could pull them down. Beijing downplayed the violence, but the videos were ugly: factories burning, police firing tear gas and rubber bullets, tanks rumbling through Guangzhou's crowded streets.

As news of the violence spread, China's other metropolises saw scattered riots. The police in Shanghai arrested 125 people. In Beijing, the party declared a nighttime curfew and closed Tiananmen Square for a week. China hadn't seen such widespread unrest since the Tiananmen shootings in 1989.

Jordan never knew what he and Song and Yu had begun. He died the first day, his body battered beyond recognition by nightstick blows, not that he had anyone to claim him anyway. He was cremated in the city morgue, and the wind carried his ashes to the ocean.

As the riots entered their second day, the Standing Committee called an emergency meeting in Beijing. Li expected that the liberals on the committee would at least be willing to discuss whether their economic policies had fueled the violence. He was wrong.

'These troublemakers, can the Army deal with them?' Zhang asked him.

'Of course the PLA can overcome the rioters,' Li said. 'But shouldn't we consider the reasons for the violence? The economic slowdown?'

'The slowdown is over, Minister Li. Our economy is growing again.' Indeed, Zhang had just presented new statistics that seemed to say that the economy had finally begun to turn. Li didn't know what to make of the numbers. If the economy was getting better, why was Guangzhou burning?

'Don't the protests concern you?'

'There are always troublemakers. That's why we have your men. As long as you do your job, I haven't any concerns.' Zhang shuffled through his papers. 'Do you remember when the Americans had their riots? In California?'

'Of course, Minister.'

'Then you remember that the Americans didn't change their policies after those criminals tried to burn down Los Angeles. They sent in their army, and in a few weeks everyone had forgotten.'

Whatever doubts Li had about his plan disappeared that day. Zhang and the liberals would never see reason. He needed to take control, and soon, whatever the risks.

Fortunately, his next step was already in place.

NINETEEN

LANGLEY, VIRGINIA

On the big flat-panel television, the man rubbed his short black hair. His face showed no emotion but his hands betrayed his nervousness, moving constantly, drumming aimless patterns on the table in front of him. A cigarette smoldered in an ashtray before him. He picked it up and dragged deeply, then looked up as an unseen door opened.

'I'm sorry for the delay. We're ready to begin if you are.'

'I'm ready.'

'The questions may seem obvious, but please answer all of them.'

'Of course.'

'Let's begin with your name.' The woman asking the questions had a smooth English accent, a voice that reminded Exley of a life she would never have, with hunting dogs, and high tea on a silver caddy. Of course, in reality the woman probably had a farting husband and screaming twins. She probably lived in an undersized two-bedroom apartment in the wrong part of London and rode the Tube to work. Still, she had that voice.

'My name is Wen Shubai,' the man said.

'Age and nationality?'

'Fifty-two.' The man stubbed out his cigarette. The butt joined a half-dozen others in the ashtray. 'I'm Chinese. Born in Hubei Province. The People's Republic.'

'Where do you live now, Mr. Wen?'

'London.' He spoke English carefully, the words proper but heavily accented, the voice of a concierge at a five-star Beijing hotel.

'And where do you work?'

'Until today, the Chinese embassy.'

'What's your title?'

'Officially, director for trade between China and the United Kingdom.'

'What did you actually do at the embassy?'

'Head of Chinese intelligence service for Western Europe.'

'You were a spy.'

The man extracted a fresh cigarette from a flat red Dunhill box. A manicured woman's hand, as elegant as the voice asking the questions, held out a silver lighter.

'Senior officer. I oversaw operations all over Europe.'

Tyson paused the interview there, catching Wen with a Dunhill between his lips. 'This was filmed about thirty-six hours ago at a safe house just west of London. And yes, Mr. Wen Shubai is who he says he is. He shucked his bodyguards late Saturday night at a rest stop on the M1. The Brits were happy to have him.'

'A rest stop on the M1?' This from Shafer.

'Defecting during a state dinner at Buckingham Palace would have been more elegant, but so be it.

213

Anyway, he has a lot to tell us, which is why I've asked you to my happy home. I'm sure you'll agree it's worth your while.'

Exley, Shafer, and Tyson were in a windowless conference room on the seventh floor of the New Headquarters Building at Langley, next to Tyson's office and just a few doors down from Duto's. Wells – who'd gotten back from Afghanistan a few days before, his shoulder banged up but otherwise basically intact – had begged off Tyson's invitiation, telling Exley only that the mission had been a success, that they'd caught a Russian commando, and that he had to go to New York to 'take care of something.' Exley found his coyness irritating, but she was trying to give him the benefit of the doubt. He was used to operating alone, after all.

'So this guy Wen came over the day before yester-day?' Shafer said.

'Correct. The Brits have been debriefing him more or less nonstop ever since. You know the drill, check what he says against the available evidence. Treat him with respect but not too much, make sure he knows we're doing him a favor and not the other way around. Get everything out of him while he's still fresh off the boat, so to speak.'

'We have anyone in the room?'

'Not yet. Wen's been making noise about wanting to talk to us, but the Brits say he's on their soil. Their country, their case. Et cetera. We'll get a crack at him eventually, under their watchful eyes, of course. But I've asked Duto not to press the Brits too hard on this. It may actually be to our advantage to leave Shubai with them.'

'Why?' Exley said.

'I promise all will become clear. Let's get to more of Mr. Wen's greatest hits.'

Tyson fast-forwarded the DVD. Exley watched, fascinated, as cigarettes magically appeared in Wen's hands, shrank to nothing, and then reappeared fresh. She hadn't wanted to smoke this much in months.

'Ahh – here.'

'Why did you defect?' the interviewer was saying.

For the first time, Wen appeared flummoxed. 'When I came from Beijing two weeks ago, I decided.' He took a drag on his cigarette and said nothing more.

'But why now? After all these many years.'

'I wanted to speak freely. In China, that's impossible.'

'Come now, Mr. Wen. We're not making a publicity video for Taiwan. You don't expect us to believe that you defected so you could hold up placards in the streets. You're a fifty-two-year-old man, not a college student. How much freedom do you need?'

Wen squeezed his hands together. 'You already know, so must I answer?'

'Please.'

'I am due to return to China. I don't want to go. I love a lady here. And now I find out my wife, who lives in Beijing, has relations with my superior officer there.'

'Relations?'

Wen shook his head tiredly. 'Sexual relations.'

Tyson paused the DVD again. '"How much freedom do you need?" I love that. The Brits.'

'Best friends to your Confederate forebears,' Shafer said.

'True enough. Neither we nor the Brits can confirm the bit about his wife. But he has been sleeping with a

215

woman here, a lawyer at a British export-import company. Monica Cheng's her name. He met her a few months back at a trade show to promote Chinese exporters. The Brits found her yesterday, asked her, and she confirmed. She's under twenty-four-hour watch.' Tyson passed around pictures of the woman. She was Chinese, in her early thirties and pretty.

'Is it possible she's fake?'

'Possible, sure. But she was born in London. She looks genuine and she says they were serious. He was, at least. And there's something else.'

Tyson pressed play and the DVD spun.

'Are there any other reasons you decided to defect?'

Wen reached for another Dunhill. Only after accepting a light did he speak.

'There are no penalties to me for what I say?'

'Mr. Wen. You are a guest of the British government. An invited guest. How you treated your former employer is of no concern to us. Honesty is the best policy.'

'May I speak to a solicitor?'

A pause. 'I'm afraid that wouldn't be practical at this time.'

Wen appeared unsurprised. 'Let me say, then, that the PLA checks –' Wen broke off. Looking left, offscreen, he said a word in Chinese. 'Audits,' a voice replied in English. Wen nodded. 'The Army audits my spending. One of the people, the auditors, raised a question.'

'You were accused of theft?'

'There was a certain account in my name. For operational purposes.'

*

216

Tyson stopped the DVD again.

'This part he absolutely refused to put on camera. Mr. Wen Shubai seems to have been stealing from the PLA with both hands. He's got an account with two million dollars at UBS. Says it was to fund covert operations inside Europe.'

'Sounds like it was funding Operation Move My Girlfriend Monica to Barcelona,' Shafer said.

'He says the PLA's auditors refused to accept his perfectly legitimate answers about the account. So he did what any of us would do.'

'He fled into the arms of a foreign power.'

'Precisely, Mr. Shafer.'

'Did you two practice this routine?' Exley said. 'You could take it on the road. Big bucks. Shafer and Tyson, CIA vaudeville.'

Shafer and Tyson looked at each other in mock befuddlement. 'I don't know what she's talking about, Ellis,' Tyson said. 'Anyway, it would have to be Tyson and Shafer.'

'So do we believe Mr. Wen?'

Tyson folded his hands together, raised his index fingers to his lips. 'Well. Here's the thing. We do.'

'We think he's the genuine article, not a fish thrown our way by the Chinese to confuse us, as our old friends at the KGB used to do.'

'We and the Brits both. Reasons –' Tyson counted them out on his fingers.

'One: If he's a fish, he's a very big fish. He's extremely senior. That's a lot to give up, and we don't know why they would. Two: Monica's real. Three: The money in his UBS account is real and he's been putting it there for a while. Four: The Chinese government is conducting, shall we say, urgent inquiries as to his whereabouts. And five: The Chinese have never liked those KGB-style counterespionage ops.'

'They love to spy.'

'Not the chess match kind of spying. The simple kind. The pay-the-engineer-get-the-blueprints-for-the-fighter-jet kind.'

'The kind that works,' Shafer said.

Again Tyson fast-forwarded through the DVD. 'And then there's this,' Tyson said. 'You can watch the whole tape if you like, of course, but I promise these are the highlights.' He clicked the DVD.

'Does China have agents within the Central Intelligence Agency?'

'Yes. Until last year, two. Then one was dismissed.'

'What happened to him?'

'I don't know precisely. He hardly showed up on my' – again Wen said something in Chinese and the unseen voice translated – 'on my radar screen. He was in what the Americans call the division of intelligence.'

'The Directorate of Intelligence.'

'Yes. The analysts. He translated Chinese news-papers and similar things. He was not very senior.'

'What about the other agent?'

'He was in the other division – directorate. Operations.'

'Was he also low-level?'

'Not at all.' Wen sat up in his chair as he said this, Exley noticed. Though he was now betraying China, he was still unconsciously proud that his service had infiltrated Langley. 'He had access to many operations. Not just in China. All over Asia.'

'How long did he work for you?'

'Several years.'

'And did you recruit him?'

'I never met him.'

'Let me ask it another way. Did the Second Directorate recruit him or did he approach you?'

'Ahh. No, he approached us. He was white. We prefer ethnic Chinese.'

Exley was transfixed. Soon there'd be arrests, a criminal case, an accounting of the secrets this mole had betrayed, the lives he'd destroyed. But for now there was only this video, the first flake in the blizzard. History unspooling in this office.

'Do you know how he approached you?'

'Unfortunately, no. But I am sure we didn't trust him at first.'

'Because he was white?'

'Also because he had come to us. We didn't understand that.'

'But you learned?'

Wen smiled. 'He wanted money. Lots of money.'

'And you gave it to him.'

'His information was valuable.'

'Very valuable?'

'He could have asked for ten times as much.'

Again Tyson paused the DVD.

'Based on what Wen says next, it seems safe to say that our entire China network is blown. Has been for years. We've lost five agents there since 2004. This explains why. The ones who are left have probably been doubled by the Chinese and are feeding us disinformation.'

'It's as bad as Ames,' Exley said.

'Worse,' Shafer said. 'The Soviets were on the way

out when Ames betrayed us. He got some people killed, but he didn't change the Cold War. But this –'

Shafer broke off. He didn't need to say anything more, Exley thought. The struggle for dominance between the United States and China had only just begun. Now this CIA mole, whoever he was, had given China an enormous advantage. His treachery had opened a window on America's most secret intelligence programs and military capabilities while giving China the chance to conceal its own.

'How many agents do we have in China?' Exley said.

'Even before this, we were incredibly thin over there. A half-dozen PLA officers, a couple of mid-level politicians. But no one really senior. With one exception. Maybe.'

'Maybe?' Shafer said. 'Mind if I ask what you're talking about?'

Tyson looked at Shafer. He seemed to consider his next words carefully, though perhaps the hesitation was as much an act as everything else he did, Exley thought.

'I've said too much already. The ramblings of an old man.'

Exley saw the pit bull hiding in Tyson's basset hound face and decided to drop the subject. Still, what he'd said didn't make much sense. Why would one agent have escaped if the mole had given up everyone else?

'George,' Shafer said, 'I have to ask again. How do we know that this fine gentleman isn't just messing with us?'

'Watch and learn, Ellis.' Tyson clicked the DVD one more time.

*

'How much did you pay this spy?' the English woman said.

'I don't know exactly, but millions.'

'What did he give you?'

'Everything the Americans did in China. If they recruited someone, planned an operation, everything.'

'Were you worried that the CIA had planted him? That he was a source of disinformation?'

'Disinformation?' The off-screen translator said something in Chinese. Wen nodded vigorously, almost angrily. 'Yes. Of course, we considered he might be trying to fool us. You think we don't understand these situations?'

'Of course, of course,' the woman said soothingly.

'At first we test him, use him only to check information we already know. But everything he gives us is correct. Very specific, and always correct. So we know he must be real.'

'Mr. Wen, what was the most valuable information this agent provided?'

'Easy,' Wen said. 'He told us the Americans had an agent in North Korea. A nuclear scientist. The Americans called him Drafter.'

Exley heard a gasp. She needed a moment to realize she'd made the sound. The Chinese had given the Drafter to the North Koreans?

'When was that?'

'Two years ago, maybe.'

'When did you tell the North Koreans what you'd learned?'

'Not until this year. A few weeks ago.'

'Why did you wait?'

'I don't know. How do the Americans say it? "Above my pay grade."'

221

'Do you have any idea?'

'I think some people think China should stand up to America. United States has many problems right now. Time for China to show its power. If America doesn't answer, then China knows it is winning.'

'People in Zhongnanhai, you mean?'

'Yes. Ministers. The Standing Committee. But not everyone.'

'We'll return to that later. Let's focus on this scientist – the Drafter, as you call him. What did you tell the North Koreans about him? His name?'

'We didn't know his real name. But enough so that they could identify him.'

'And how did you find out about this? It wasn't to do with Europe.'

'Of course I find out.' Wen looked irritated. 'I was home in Beijing when the North Koreans sank the boat that the Americans sent to rescue him. I am eighth-ranking officer in the Second Directorate. Of course I hear.'

Tyson paused the DVD.

'Not the seventh-ranking, and not the ninth-ranking. The eighth-ranking. Ellis, you believe him now?'

Shafer nodded. 'Obviously he's telling the truth. The Chinese have somebody inside. Otherwise they wouldn't have known the Drafter's code name.'

'And the Chinese wouldn't give up the mole,' Tyson said. 'He's too valuable. So Wen's defection is real. He did it on his own, not on orders from Beijing. Maybe for Ms. Monica Cheng. Maybe because of those pesky audits.'

Shafer looked at Exley. 'You agree?'

Exley considered. 'I'm not sure. We already knew

we had a mole. Even if we haven't made much progress finding him.' The traffic and property records they'd searched hadn't offered any clues, and they were still waiting for new polygraph results. 'The real test is whether he helps us find the mole.'

Tyson grinned. 'Ms. Exley. You are the brains of the operation, I see now.'

Exley was tired of playing the good student to the two masters. 'And you're a smug, patronizing jerk.'

Tyson's smile didn't disappear. 'You sound just like my wife. The strange part is that I really was trying to pay you a compliment. You're two hundred proof spot-on.'

He clicked the DVD.

'Can we stop for tonight?' Wen's suit jacket was off, sweat stains widening under his arms.

'A few more questions. And then I promise you can rest. Now. This mole within the CIA. Did you know his name?'

'No.'

'Department?'

'Told you already, he was in the Division of Operations.'

'Where in the Directorate of Operations? On the China desk?'

'Not sure. Asia, but maybe not China. Also he spent time in what the Americans call counterintelligence. Don't know where he is now.'

'Can you tell us anything else about him?'

Wen closed his eyes. 'Something happened to him. Something bad. Personal. A few years ago.'

'Like he was in an accident?'

Wen shook his head. 'Not exactly. Something else.

A big problem. He didn't tell us. We found it ourselves when we were checking him.'

'Anything else? I promise, this is the last question tonight.'

'He served in Asia. A long time ago.'

'Do you know where?'

'No. And you said last question.' At that Wen stubbed out his cigarette, folded his hands on the table, and closed his eyes.

Tyson clicked off the DVD, leaving the screen black.

'So, Ms. Exley, you see I wasn't trying to be smug and patronizing, though perhaps I can't help myself. You asked the right question.'

'And the answer is yes,' Exley said. She felt slightly mollified. 'Wen gave us enough to find our mole. He's spent most of his career on the Asia desk. He's worked in counterintelligence. He was in Asia briefly and had "a family problem."'

'I'm guessing it wasn't an argument with his mother-in-law,' Shafer said. 'There can't be too many case officers who match all those criteria. If we check that against your seventy names, we should get him, or get very close.'

'Soon, please,' Tyson said. 'Because the Brits told our China desk about Wen's defection yesterday. The mole will be wondering if Wen has tipped us to him already.'

'That's why you'd rather have the Brits hold on to Wen?'

'Exactly. Until we know who the mole is, we're better off with Wen as far from Langley as possible. Meanwhile, based on what he said about the mole having some connection to counterintel, I have to assume that we don't have much time before he runs. If this guy's been around as long as Wen says, he'll know he's in trouble.'

'Not just from us,' Shafer said. 'The Chinese might try to clean this up themselves.'

Exley needed a second to understand what Shafer meant. Would the Chinese be cold-blooded enough to kill their own mole if they believed the agency was about to arrest him?

'Doubtful,' Tyson said. 'It wouldn't help their recruiting any.'

'I agree,' Exley said.

'You two have an optimistic view of human nature,' Shafer said. He stood to go. 'Anyway, we have some work to do.'

TWENTY

VIENNA, VIRGINIA

The glint of Exley's wedding band caught her by surprise as she drove. She'd pulled it out of storage for today's job.

After meeting with Tyson, Exley and Shafer had spent the rest of the day going over the list of agency employees who'd known enough about the Drafter to betray him. Of the eighty-two names on the final list, twelve matched at least the broad outlines that Wen had given for the mole's career history, or had suffered a serious accident or illness five to ten years ago. Unfortunately, none of the twelve men fit in both categories. That would have been too easy, Exley thought.

'The dirty dozen,' Shafer said. Separately, thirteen men now matched the soft criteria that she and Shafer had devised earlier. Five employees were on both lists.

'So now what? Do we talk to them?' Exley said.

'Not yet, I think. Tyson will have his people looking for hard evidence on the twelve who meet the criteria that Wen mentioned. Suspicious travel patterns, hidden accounts, the usual. Let's be a little less formal. I'm going to poke around Langley, play doctor, see what I can pick up.'

'And me?'

'Why don't you talk to the wives?'

And so this morning Exley had pulled on her wedding band and prepared to make a tour of suburban Virginia and Maryland. She was aiming first at the five names on both lists. She didn't know how many wives would be home, but she figured at least a couple. And she knew claiming she was on a house-hunt would get her inside their houses. Amazing how freely bored women would talk to a friendly stranger.

No one had been home at her first stop, in Fairfax. But this time she'd scored, if the Jetta in the driveway was any indication. She parked her green Caravan by the edge of the road and hopped out.

A flagstone path cut through the neatly manicured lawn. Rosebushes added a touch of color to the front of the yellow house. She stepped over a battered Big Wheel and pressed the doorbell. Inside the house she heard a toddler crying.

'Coming.' A woman opened the door a notch and peeked out. She was pretty, late thirties, carrying a baby on her hip. 'Mom mom mom!' a boy squalled from upstairs.

'Hi,' she said, friendly but wary, the classic suburban combination, trying to figure out if Exley was a Jehovah's Witness or an Avon saleswoman or just a neighbor. People moved to Vienna so they wouldn't have to worry about strangers knocking on their doors.

'Sorry to bother you,' Exley said. 'My name's Joanne.' She was going with an alias, in case the woman mentioned this visit to her husband. 'I was

227

looking at the Colonial up the block and I'm hoping to find out about the neighborhood and I saw your car in the driveway.'

The woman looked uncertain. 'I thought they'd accepted an offer.'

'They're still showing it.'

'Mommy, come here!' the invisible boy yelled.

'Well . . . if you don't mind watching me change a diaper, I'll give you the rundown. My name's Kellie, by the way.' She extended a hand. She was glad to have some company, Exley thought.

'Nice to meet you.'

'He's beautiful,' Exley said of the blue-eyed, red-faced little boy holding on to the safety gate that blocked the stairs.

'Isn't he? Name's Jonah. But he's got a temper.' She picked him up. 'Come on, J. No more crying. We'll get you fixed up.'

'They all cry at that age,' Exley said. 'I've got two of my own. Trust me, they grow out of it.'

In Jonah's bedroom, Exley watched as Kellie changed the diaper with one hand while soothing the baby with the other. Already, Exley knew that this woman had mastered the chores of parenting in a way Exley never had. She couldn't explain why she needed ten minutes to change a diaper, but she did. She never doubted that she would take a bullet for her kids. But she had to admit that she hadn't been cut out for the daily grind of chasing them around, wiping up their snot, making them paper bag lunches for school.

Lots of women loved that part of being moms, or at least said they did. Maybe they were right. Maybe those chores were essential to building a lifelong relationship

228

with kids. But Exley couldn't lie to herself. She'd been desperate to get back to work after four months of maternity leave.

Now as she watched Kellie wipe off Jonah's butt and pull on a clean diaper, she wondered: If she had another chance, could she be different? She and Wells? She didn't know if she could imagine Wells as a father, though of course he was one already. He'd had a son with Heather, his ex-wife, just before he went to Afghanistan to infiltrate al Qaeda. But Wells saw the boy – Evan – only a couple of times a year. Not that he had much say in the matter. Heather, who had sole custody of Evan, was remarried and lived in Montana. She said that Evan had accepted his stepfather as his real dad and she didn't want to confuse the boy by giving him too much time with Wells.

Maybe having another child would settle Wells, Exley thought. Or maybe not. He had so many days when he didn't get along with the world, when he reminded Exley of a barely domesticated guard dog, half German shepherd, half wolf. But even at his angriest, Wells was sweet to her kids, sweet to kids in general. And kids loved him for his size and strength. What kind of father would he be with a boy of his own? Somehow Exley knew that she and Wells would have a boy. Though the truth was that the odds were against her getting pregnant at all.

Kellie finished putting on Jonah's clean white diaper and ran a soothing hand over his face. 'Pretty soon you'll be a big boy and no more diapers.'

'No diapers!' Jonah yelled happily.

Kellie looked sidelong at Exley. 'So what do you do, Joanne?'

'Me? I'm a consultant.' The word *consultant* was

vague enough to mean anything, and boring enough that no one cared anyway.

'I used to be a lawyer,' Kellie said. 'Then one day I woke up and I was *this*.'

'You're great at it, though.'

'When the little one gets to preschool, I'm going back to work. Of course, Eddie – that's my husband – wants one more, but I told him unless he figures out a way to get himself pregnant, that's not happening. Come on downstairs and let's have coffee.'

'I wish I could have stayed at home for a while,' Exley lied. 'We couldn't figure out a way to afford it, though. Is your husband a lawyer too?'

'No. He works for the government. But we saved up when I was working and we're pretty careful. How about yours?'

'My husband? He works for the government too. Not too far from here. Maybe they're in the same business.'

'Sounds that way.' CIA wives liked to hint that their husbands worked at Langley. Proof that the agency hadn't completely lost its mystique, Exley supposed.

Kellie pulled up Jonah's pants. Now that he didn't have a full diaper, he was pretty well behaved, Exley thought. Cute too. 'You sweetie,' she said to him. 'What's your favorite thing to do in the world?'

'Hockey! Play hockey!' Jonah grabbed a miniature hockey stick and swiped the floor. 'Play hockey.'

'Eddie's got him on skates already.'

'He can skate?' Exley's surprise was genuine.

'Play hockey play hockey –'

'You'd be amazed.' Kellie grabbed the boy's hand. 'Jonah, come on downstairs to the kitchen with us. You can play down there.'

'Can I have juice?'

'Of course, sweetie.'

They walked back to the downstairs, which was festooned with pictures of Kellie and Edmund on their honeymoon in Hawaii, Kellie and Edmund and Jonah at the rink, the kid cute as anything with his helmet and stick and skates . . . Edmund Cerys wasn't the mole, Exley thought. Not even an Oscar-winning actor could fake the way he looked at his wife in these pictures. He'd gotten drunk at a Redskins game and picked up a misdemeanor for pissing in the parking lot, but he wasn't spying for the Chinese or anyone else. Zero for one.

She settled into the kitchen and prepared to let Kellie tell her about the neighborhood. Then her cell phone trilled in her purse. Wells.

'Hi,' he said. 'I have a favor to ask. Can you come up to New York? Today?'

TWENTY-ONE

EAST HAMPTON, NEW YORK

Even at 2:50 a.m. on a Wednsday morning, East
Hampton glowed with wealth. Wall Street skyscrapers, Hollywood back lots, Siberian oil fields –
wherever the money came from, it ended up here,
waves of cash crashing in like the Atlantic Ocean's
low breakers. Under the streetlamps, the town's long
main street shined empty and clean. The mannequins
in the Polo store cradled their tennis racquets, poised
to play in their $300 nylon windbreakers. To the
north, toward the bay, the houses cost a mere seven
figures. South, in the golden half-mile strip between
the main street and the ocean, the mansions ran $10
million and up.

Wells and Exley were heading south.

Wells cruised at twenty-five miles an hour on his big
black bike, its engine running smooth and quiet. Before
him, the traffic light at the corner of Main Street and
Newtown Lane turned red. He eased to a stop and
patted the CB1000's metal flank. The bike was his, but
the license plate wasn't. He'd liberated it from a Vespa
scooter a few hours earlier. He'd also removed all the

identifying decals on the bike, making it as anonymous as a motorcycle could be.

Exley stopped beside him at the wheel of a gray Toyota Sienna minivan that Wells had hot-wired from a parking lot at a bar in Southampton ninety minutes before. The minivan's owner – the 'World's Hottest Single Aunt,' at least according to the sticker on the van's back bumper – was presumably still getting liquored up inside. By the time she discovered the Sienna was gone, it would have served its purpose. Wells hoped she had insurance.

The light dropped green. Wells eased past the forty-foot-high wooden windmill that marked the end of the town center. A half-mile later, he turned off Route 27 and onto Amity Lane. Besides his standard riding gear of black leather jacket, black helmet, black gloves, and black boots, Wells had on black jeans and a black long-sleeve cotton shirt. He wished he had a pair of black skivvies to complete the package. Tucked in a shoulder holster, he carried a pistol, a Glock this time instead of the Makarov. It was black, naturally, with a silencer threaded to the barrel. He hoped he wouldn't even have to draw it. His black backpack held two other weapons, the ones he planned to use.

The afternoon before, Wells had for the first time found a way to take advantage of the fame he didn't want. He walked into the East Hampton village police station, an unassuming brick building on Cedar Street, just behind the center of town.

'Can I help you?' the cop behind the counter said.

'I'd like to speak to the chief.'

'He's busy. What can I do for you?'

Wells extracted his CIA identification card, the one

with his real name, and passed it across the counter.

'Hold on.' The officer disappeared behind a steel door, popping out a minute later to wave Wells in.

The chief was a trim man in his early fifties with tight no-nonsense eyes. Even in East Hampton the cops looked like cops. 'Ed Graften,' he said, extending his hand. 'It's an honor, Mr. Wells. Please sit.'

'Please call me John.' Wells was beginning to feel foolish. Did he really expect this man to help him?

'What can I do you for? Don't suppose you locked your keys in your Ferrari or the brats in the mansion next door are making too much noise. The usual nonsense.'

'Chief – I have a favor to ask. The name Pierre Kowalski ring a bell?'

'Course. His daughter Anna set a record this year for a summer rental. If the papers were right, it was a million and a half bucks for the house.' Wells had seen the same stories. Anna had spent $1.5 million on a seven-bedroom mansion on Two Mile Hollow Road, just off the ocean. Not to buy the place. To rent it. For three months.

'Nice to have the world's biggest arms dealer for your dad,' Wells said. 'I have it on good authority' – in fact, Wells had seen the report in two gossip columns – 'that he is in town this week. I'd like to talk to him. Alone.'

Graften was no longer smiling. 'Mr. Wells. Are you sure you are who you say you are? If not, now would be a good time to leave.'

'I am, and I can prove it.'

'Then . . . I guess I could put a patrol car out front of his gate. I'm sure his driver speeds. They all do. We could stop him, bring him in here. But his lawyers would be on us in two minutes and we'd have to cut him loose –'

'I don't want to get you in trouble. All I need is –' Wells paused, then plunged on. 'If you pick up an alarm from his house tonight, take your time getting there. I won't hurt him, I promise. Or take anything.' Except information, Wells didn't say.

'What about his guards?'

'I can take care of them. But I'd rather keep your men out of it.' Wells didn't mention Exley's role in his plan.

'Don't suppose you can tell me what you want from him.'

'Let's just say I don't expect him to file a complaint with you about my visit.'

'You can't do this officially, Mr. Wells?'

'I wish I could.' The CIA couldn't legally operate in the United States. Wells would have to ask the FBI to try to get a warrant for Kowalski. And Wells doubted that any federal judge would sign a warrant based on the secret testimony of a single Russian special forces commando now in prison in Afghanistan. Even if they could find a friendly judge, Kowalski's lawyers would fight them for months. They'd never even get him in for an interview.

Trying to move against Kowalski in Monte Carlo or Zurich, where he spent most of his time, would be equally impossible. His homes there were fortresses, much better protected than this vacation house, and the local police would hardly look kindly on a request like this from Wells. No, tonight was his best shot. Maybe his only shot. In any case, Wells didn't care about arresting Kowalski. He just wanted to know where the trail led.

Graften sighed. 'How long do you need?'

'Half an hour maybe.'

'You won't hurt him.'

'I'll do my best.'

Graften looked at the ceiling. 'All right. If you can prove you are who you say you are, I'll get you a half-hour. No more. At three a.m., let's say.'

'Then let me do that.'

It was 2:55 a.m. Wells rolled down Further Lane, Exley following. Heavy green hedges hemmed in the road on both sides. The hedges weren't ornamental. Twenty feet tall and too thick for anyone to see past, much less walk through, they served as walls protecting the mansions behind them. Every couple of hundred feet, the hedges parted for gated driveways. The homes behind the gates were lit up in the night like cathedrals in the Church of Wealth.

Wells had reconnoitered the Kowalski house four times, once the previous night on his motorcycle and three times during the day on a mountain bike he'd bought at a garage sale in Sag Harbor. He had also examined town maps and satellite photos, so he knew the mansion's exterior layout and the land around it. Beyond that he would have to rely on instinct.

He hadn't wanted to involve Exley. But unlike most of his neighbors, Kowalski had his property protected with more than hedges and alarms. Instead of a gate, his driveway was permanently blocked by a black Cadillac Escalade, lights on and engine running. Two unsmiling men watched the road from its front seats. When Anna or her friends came or went, the men rolled the Escalade back to unblock the entrance to the property. As soon as the driveway was clear, they moved back into place. They couldn't be avoided.

The good news was that Wells hadn't seen closed-circuit cameras around the property. Cameras were rare in the Hamptons. Billionaires didn't like being watched, even by their own guards. But cameras or not, unless Wells could get the men out of the Escalade, he'd have to shoot them where they sat. He wanted to avoid killing anyone, for both practical and personal reasons. Kowalski was a powerful man with powerful friends. Shooting his men would cause inquiries that Wells would rather avoid. And though Kowalski was in a worse-than-ugly business, Wells didn't want to play judge, jury, and executioner tonight.

Wells figured if he could solve the problem of the front gate he'd be okay. This late in the night, only a couple of guards would be awake inside the mansion. They'd be bored, drinking coffee, trying to keep their eyes open. No matter how much they tried to stay alert, they would hardly be able to avoid slacking off. East Hampton wasn't exactly Baghdad. And if anything really went wrong, they could normally expect backup from the village police. But Wells had taken the cops out of the picture.

Just before the corner of Further Lane and Two Mile Hollow, Wells pulled over and dropped the CB1000's kickstand, placing a flattened Coke can under the base so the stand wouldn't sink into the earth and tip the Honda over.

From the minivan, he pulled out the mountain bike he'd bought two days before. Next to the CB1000, the bicycle looked almost toylike. But the bike had one great advantage over the motorcycle. It was silent. Wells took off his helmet and pulled a black mask over his face.

'You still want to do this?' he said. 'Because we don't have to –'

'Please. It's easy for the world's hottest single aunt to get lost in East Hampton after she's had a few.'

Exley popped open a peach wine cooler and took a swallow, then poured a couple drops onto her blouse, which was open two buttons, enough to reveal a black lace bra that left little about her breasts to the imagination.

'That ought to distract them,' she said. 'Just another overaged drunk chick looking for love.'

'Jennifer. Be careful. If something goes wrong, I want you to go, ditch me –'

But she'd already rolled off.

He didn't fully understand Exley. He supposed he never would. She loved her kids terribly, he was sure. Yet here she was again, risking her life to help him. Was she doing this for him? For the adventure? Both? Wells wished he could ask.

Exley turned right, down Two Mile Hollow, toward the ocean. On the train from Washington the afternoon before, she'd wondered if she should have said no to Wells. Then she remembered the day Wells had attacked the Taliban camp. The afternoon came and went with no word. She felt sure that something terrible had happened, a sniper's bullet, a helicopter crash. Then she started to believe that her premonition had actually caused Wells's death, that he would have been fine if only she'd shown more faith.

That night she'd found herself at the multiplex at Union Station, sneaking between theaters, not even pretending to watch the movies, willing the minutes to pass, waiting for her cell to ring. Finally, at 2:00 a.m., it did. She expected the caller would be Shafer, asking her to come down to Langley so he could give her the news in person.

Instead the voice on the other end belonged to Wells, cool as ever, telling her that she'd been right about the foreign fighters and that he'd be back soon. After they hung up, she'd promised herself she wouldn't doubt him again. So when he'd asked for her help for this mission, she couldn't say no. She knew her thinking was illogical, but so be it. Everyone was entitled to a bit of magical thinking.

She approached Kowalski's mansion, swerving a bit from side to side. In her rearview mirror, she saw Wells at the corner, a couple of hundred feet behind her. Then he was gone and she was alone.

As he waited, Wells unzipped his backpack and pulled out the gun he'd picked up at Langley, a Telinject Vario air pistol. The Telinject was loaded with a syringe filled with ketamine – the drug that club kids and other fun-seekers called Special K – and Versed, a liquid sedative closely related to Valium. Veterinarians and ranchers used these guns to sedate unruly animals. The CIA kept a handful for its own purposes. Wells had borrowed two, after getting an afternoon's training from a specialist in nonlethal weapons in the agency's Directorate of Science and Technology, the unit that handled fake passports, wiretaps, special weapons, and the rest of the trickery that accounted for one percent of the agency's work but ninety-nine percent of its mystique.

'Planning to break into the D.C. Zoo, liberate the chimps?' the specialist – an attractive forty-something redhead with the thoroughly Irish name of Winnie

239

O'Kelly – asked him. 'You know they bite.' Wells merely smiled. She handed over the pistols. 'Try not to lose them. They're not particularly traceable, but you never know.'

Clubgoers took ketamine because at low doses the drug produced what doctors called a 'dissociative reaction,' almost an out-of-body experience, giving users the feeling they were in two places at once, watching themselves from a distance. At higher doses, ketamine caused unconsciousness in seconds. Further, ketamine wasn't an opiate derivative, so it wouldn't suffocate the guards if Wells accidentally overdosed them. At worst they would wake up stiff and headachy. The Versed in the mix would put the guards to sleep even faster.

Of course, the syringes couldn't work their magic unless Exley got the guards out of the Escalade.

Exley drove past the mansion's driveway. The Escalade was on the left, three tons of steel deliberately designed to be ugly. Its hood stared out at the street, a gas-guzzling fake tank driven by rich men who liked acting tough while knowing that other, poorer men would do the real fighting for them. Exley passed by slowly, making sure the men in the Escalade saw she was alone.

A hundred yards farther on, the road dead-ended at the empty parking lot for Two Mile Hollow Beach. Signs warned that any car without a town beach pass would be towed. 'So much for free public beach access,' Exley said to herself. But of course anyone paying ten million bucks for a house didn't want to share the sand.

She turned the Sienna around, double-checked the

240

syringe in her purse. The reality of what she was about to do filled her. Then she turned the radio up, loud, and drove back down Two Mile Road toward the Escalade, now on her right. Just outside the driveway of the mansion, she stopped and parked in the road, making sure the Sienna was angled toward the Escalade. She stumbled out of the van and walked to the open gate.

The Escalade's windows stayed shut as she approached. She rapped hard on the driver's-side window. In the background the van's radio blared.

Finally the window slid down. 'Can I help you?' The man inside sounded distinctly unhelpful. He was big and muscular, and his T-shirt didn't hide the holster on his hip. Exley noticed a dog in the back seat, a big German shepherd that looked up eagerly at her, its red tongue lapping its teeth.

'I'm so lost. This guy I met, he told me about this party in Amagansett. This is Amagansett, right?'

'Lady. If you're looking for Amagansett, go back to that road up there and make a right. Good luck. This is private property.'

Exley turned away. 'Drunk skank,' one of the men in the Escalade said, deliberately loud enough for her to hear, and the other laughed. 'Headed for the drunk tank.' The window slid up.

Exley got back in the Sienna, buckled her seat belt. *Don't think too much*, she told herself. She put the van in gear, floored the gas, and –

The crash with the Escalade whipped her toward the steering wheel. Her belt tightened and the exploding air bag caught her, knocking her back. Even though she'd known the collision was coming, its force surprised her, and she heard herself scream.

She gathered herself. She'd wrenched her neck and

had a cut on her arm, but she hadn't broken any bones. The Sienna had taken the brunt of the impact, its hood crumpled, radiator leaking, windshield starred. The Escalade, taller and heavier, had little visible damage, though Exley saw its air bags had inflated. The bottle of wine cooler had broken and the minivan stank of peach. She reached into her bag and grabbed the syringe.

She unbuckled herself as the doors of the Escalade opened and the men inside stepped out. They didn't look happy.

From his spot on the corner, Wells watched Exley park. When she stepped out of the van to talk to the men, he began to pedal the mountain bike beside the hedge on the east side of the road, the same side the Escalade was on. He stayed hidden in the shadow of the hedge. Unless the men looked directly his way, they wouldn't see him.

Wells took his time, not wanting to get close too soon. The grass under his wheels was wet with dew, and this close to the ocean Wells could smell the clean salt air. Under other circumstances, Two Mile Hollow would make a perfect lovers' lane.

Now Exley turned around, walked back to the Sienna, her shoulders slumped, her little ass wobbling slightly as she walked. She surely had the undivided attention of the men in the Escalade, Wells thought. Which was exactly what he needed. He was about fifty yards away, close enough that the men would see him if they looked his way.

They didn't.

Bang! The Sienna smashed into the Escalade so hard that the bigger vehicle rocked back and its front end lifted before thunking back down. Wells took advantage of the distraction to throw himself and the bike onto the grass. He was less than twenty-five yards from the Escalade now, on its passenger side. Exley had rammed the Sienna into the left front of the SUV, the driver's side.

The Escalade's doors opened and the men stepped out. Inside the Cadillac, a dog barked madly, its rapid-fire woofing echoing through the night.

'My door won't open,' Exley yelled through the night. 'Help me.'

'Dumb cootch,' the Escalade driver said. 'Fred, radio Hank, tell him what happened.' He yelled to the minivan. 'You know whose car you just hit?'

Fred the guard turned back to the Escalade. Wells aimed the air pistol, bracing it in both hands. He squeezed the trigger. Propelled by compressed carbon dioxide, the inch-long dart took off with a soft hiss and hit the guard in the center of his back. He yelped, then sighed dully as the syringe pumped anesthetic into him. He raised a hand to the sill of the Escalade to steady himself and slumped into the front passenger seat.

'You are one dumb drunk slut,' the driver of the Escalade said as he reached into it for Exley. She slumped across the passenger seat.

'I'm sorry, I'm so stupid, please help me,' she said. He grabbed her harshly and tugged her out, making sure to grope her breasts. As he pulled at her, she jabbed the syringe hidden in her hand through his khakis and into his thigh.

'Goddamn,' he said. 'Wha –' But even as he cursed, Exley felt his grip loosen. He crumpled, the deadweight of his arms dragging her down. She freed herself and looked at him, fighting the urge to kick him in the

243

balls. His breathing was slow, but he seemed fine otherwise.

'Sweet dreams,' she said.

'You all right?' Wells said from across the Escalade.

'Never better. Do what you have to do.'

TWENTY-TWO

It was 3:05 a.m. Wednesday. The radio's bright green LCD lights told the mole what he already knew. He was awake.

For the last few weeks, he'd found sleep harder and harder to come by. He lay in bed, eyes blinking slowly as a toad's, twisting the thin cotton sheets Janice liked. Two bottles of wine at dinner and a hefty snort of whiskey afterward hadn't been enough to knock him out. Worse, he didn't seem to sleep even when he *was* asleep. He had the odd sensation of his mind nudging itself toward consciousness. Sometimes he couldn't tell if he was awake or asleep, if his eyes were open or closed, until he tapped on the radio and heard a late-night commercial: 'We need truckers. Best rates per mile!'

So he made his way to the spare bedroom to watch reruns of *Road Rules* and *Laguna Beach* as Janice snored away obliviously in their bedroom. The mole had a weakness for the bikinied bodies that filled MTV's version of reality, though he had to mute the sound to spare himself the nonsense that poured from the mouths of the kids on screen.

Something was wrong. They were after him. Not the

indefinable impossible *they* who plagued the suckers who heard voices in their heads. Not aliens or Jesus. A very real they, probably in the form of a joint agency-FBI task force. He couldn't say how he knew, but he did. He'd never been nervous like this before. And he was damn sure he wasn't having an attack of conscience over what had happened to the Drafter. He'd traded in his conscience when his baby boy died. As far as the mole was concerned, God had no conscience, and if God didn't need one, he didn't either. No, this churning in his stomach wasn't guilt. It was fear, fear that he might be caught.

Yet when the mole stopped to consider the facts, as he did a hundred times a day, he had no evidence to support his fears. Almost no evidence. Except for the polygraph. A couple weeks before the North Koreans blew up the Phantom, he'd failed a poly. Not even failed, really. He hadn't muffed the big questions, the ones that he knew were coming. They were no secret, part of a routine as established as the Lord's Prayer. *Have you ever been approached by a foreign intelligence service? Have you ever accepted money from a foreign intelligence service?* And the granddaddy of 'em all, the Rose Bowl of polygraph questions: *Have you ever committed an act of espionage against the United States?*

The mole's exam had been scheduled months in advance, standard operating procedure. He'd hardly worried about it. In his basement lair, he practiced his answers until they bored him. When he walked into the musty offices in the basement of the Old Headquarters Building where the polygraph examiners worked their magic, he'd been relaxed and confident. In retrospect, maybe too confident.

The session was supposed to last an hour. For forty-five minutes, he breezed through. When the trouble hit, he was already looking forward to being done. Maybe he'd cut out of work early, head over to the Gold Club, celebrate getting this chore out of the way for the next five years. They had two-for-one drink specials before 7:00 p.m, and sometimes the girls went two-for-one on dances too, just to stay loose.

Then, apropos of nothing, the damned examiner had asked him if he had any hidden bank accounts. For some reason, the question had surprised him. He tensed up, actually felt his heart skip, and knew he was in trouble.

'Of course not,' he said. 'I have a brokerage account where I day-trade sometimes. Blow my retirement money. At Fidelity. That kind of thing, you mean?'

The tester, a chubby middle-aged man with a heavy English accent, looked curiously at the computer screen where the mole's blood pressure, heart and breathing rate, and perspiration levels were displayed in real time.

'I mean accounts you haven't reported to the Internal Revenue Service or on your financial disclosure forms. Might you have any accounts like that?' For the first time all session, the examiner looked directly at the mole while asking his question.

'Of course not.'

'What about offshore accounts?'

The mole pretended to consider. 'Can't say I do.'

'How about other valuable assets?'

'I don't get what you're going on about.'

'Cars, boats, houses? Collectible automobiles, for example. A second home?'

Collectible automobiles? Was that a shot in the dark

247

or did this guy somehow know about the M5? 'Nothing like that.'

The tester looked at the computer screen, then at the mole.

'Are you certain? Because I'm showing evidence of deception in your last several answers. I don't mean to imply you're doing anything illegal. People have many reasons to keep offshore bank accounts, as an example.'

This prissy English asshole with his singsong voice. As an example. The mole wanted to gouge out his eyes, as an example.

'I don't know what you think you're seeing, but I don't have any hidden assets. I wish.'

'All right. Let us move on, then.'

And they had moved on. But three weeks later, not long after the North Koreans sank the Drafter, the mole had gotten a call from Gleeson, his boss, asking him to schedule a second polygraph.

'Nothing serious. They have a few questions. Seem to think you have a bank account in the Caymans or something.' Gleeson had snickered a bit, as if nothing could be more ludicrous. 'Do me a favor and call them.'

The same day he'd received the official request in his in-box, sounding considerably less friendly. *Failure to comply with this notice may result in loss of security clearance, termination from the Central Intelligence Agency, and other penalties, including criminal prosecution . . .*

By the time the mole finished reading the letter, his hand was trembling. Until this moment he had never truly considered what would happen if the agency caught him. Of course, he'd known before he started spying that he could go to prison. But jail had always seemed like a vague abstraction. He was a white guy from Michigan. He didn't know anyone in prison. Prison was a building he drove by on the interstate with razor-wire fences and signs warning 'Do Not Pick Up Hitchhikers.'

Now he found himself thinking about prison as something more than theoretical. The vision was not comforting. At best, he would spend decades locked up. More likely the rest of his life, at someplace like the Supermax Penitentiary in Colorado, where the government housed Theodore Kaczynski, the Unabomber.

He'd be held in solitary confinement, caged twenty-three hours a day in a concrete cell with a window too narrow to see the sun. He'd get an hour of exercise in a steel mesh box, watched by guards who would never talk, no matter how much he begged them for the simple kindness of conversation. And he would beg. He was sure of it. Maybe the Unabomber liked his privacy. But the mole knew he couldn't spend that much time alone, without a computer or a television or even a radio for company. He would go insane, cut himself just for something to do. His mind would gnaw itself up until nothing was left. Even the thought of being locked up that way made his heart flutter like he'd just run a marathon, made him want to go down to his basement and put his .357 in his mouth with a round in every chamber, so that no matter how many times he spun the cylinder the result would be the same –

He breathed deep and pulled himself together. He was freaking out, and over what? Over a *form letter*. The agency didn't think he was spying for the Chinese or anybody else. They thought maybe he had a bank account he hadn't told them about. This letter was the

Langley bureaucracy in action, nothing more. He'd call them back, practice harder for the poly, and be done with it. One day, when he was writing his memoirs, he'd be sure to include this incident, letter and all. That way everyone would see that the agency had muffed its big chance to stop him.

Sure enough, when he called the polygraph office, a tired-sounding secretary told him that the examiners were backed up and that they couldn't schedule him for a month at the earliest. She sounded like she thought she was doing him a favor, like she handled reservations for some fancy restaurant in New York. 'So Thursday the seventeenth at noon?'

'That's the earliest availability. Do you want it or not?'

'Sure.'

'See you then.' *Click.*

With that he'd put the incident out of his mind, or at least to the side, a fly buzzing in another room. Even after the Drafter died, the mole figured he was safe. Then the rumors started.

'Did you hear?' Gleeson asked him one morning. 'They're running a full-scale review of how the DPRK' – North Korea – 'discovered the Drafter. Looking for leaks.'

'I thought the working theory was that it had nothing to do with us.'

'Maybe,' Gleeson said. 'Or maybe we have another Ames. Anyway, I need that report on my desk by two.'

'No problem,' the mole said as Gleeson walked off.

For a week, he heard nothing more. Then he got a call from the same secretary in the polygraph office who had been so blasé earlier. 'We need to move up your appointment. Are you free next Friday?'

The mole's heart twisted. 'Friday? I don't know, lemme check –'

'Well, get back to me as soon as possible, please. If not Friday, it can't be any later than the following week.'

'What's the rush? I mean, I'm very busy –'

'You'll have to take that up with the examiner. I'm just a scheduler.' *Click.*

The mole stared blankly at the receiver in his hand, wondering what he'd done to deserve this treatment. He wanted badly to know if they actively suspected him. But asking too many questions about a leak investigation was a very good way to attract the attention of the people running it.

Meanwhile, the tempo in the East Asia unit was picking up. Since September 11, Langley and the White House had paid relatively little attention to China. The agency had focused first on Afghanistan, then Iraq, and now Iran. Along the way, China and the United States had reached a quiet understanding. As long as Beijing helped the United States on terrorism, the White House would stay quiet on economic issues, such as China's trade surplus.

Even China's rapid military buildup, its new submarines and fighter jets and satellites, had gone unchallenged. Some analysts within the agency thought that the United States should confront China aggressively now, while America still had a clear upper hand. But those discussions were largely theoretical. Langley knew that the White House had no appetite for a fight with Beijing at the moment, not with Iraq collapsing.

But in the last few weeks, the unspoken bargain had

broken down, and not because of anything Washington had done. Both publicly and privately, the Chinese seemed to want to force America's hand. The Chinese had moved submarines into the Taiwan Strait, the narrow sea that separated Taiwan from mainland China, and declared that U.S. carriers there would not be welcome without Chinese approval. Washington had simply ignored this provocation, saying that American carriers would travel in any international waters they wanted.

Beijing had also announced the successful test of a missile capable of destroying satellites and said that it didn't intend to allow any nation to have 'hegemony over space.' The words were clearly intended for the United States. Then, a week before, the French intelligence agency had passed along a rumor that China and Iran had struck some kind of grand bargain. No details. Langley had told the White House and State Department, and now the U.S. ambassador to China was trying to get an answer from the Chinese foreign ministry. But the ministry so far had stayed quiet.

An alliance between China and Iran would present the United States with a huge problem. Even if America wanted to avoid quarreling with China, it would have to respond to a deal between Beijing and its sworn enemies in Tehran. What no one understood was why the Chinese had picked this moment to take on Washington.

The mole could see now how effectively he'd betrayed the agency. Over the last five years, his spying had cost the CIA all its top Chinese operatives. As a result, the agency had no access to what was happening at the top levels of the Chinese government. The mole had left the agency blind and deaf. Still, the mole didn't think that either side would push this confrontation too far. Both the United States and China had too much to lose.

It was 3:06 a.m. As Janice sighed softly beside him, the mole felt his mind speeding like a truck whose brakes had failed. He remembered *Insomnia*, an old Stephen King novel. Halfway through, the hero was greeted by demons and devils crawling out of the wall. The mole was expecting to see something similar soon enough. The worst part was that he would actually be relieved to know the monsters were real.

At least now the mole had a good excuse for his inability to sleep. Two mornings before, he'd gotten yet another dose of bad news. He was sitting in his office, wondering if he could find an excuse to push off the poly, when Gleeson called.

'Come by,' Gleeson said. 'Big news.'

When he arrived, Gleeson told him that a Chinese agent had defected in Britain. Wen Shubai. The mole had never met him, but he knew the name. He would bet that Wen knew him too, or at least of him. The mole couldn't imagine what had happened. No senior officer had ever defected from the Second Directorate. The Chinese weren't like Russians or Americans. They stuck together. They always had before, anyway.

'That's fantastic,' he said. 'When did it happen?' *How much time do I have?*

'Don't know,' Joe said. 'I think a couple days ago. But they're keeping it close to the vest.'

'We're sure it's real, it's not bait?'

'He's given up some very solid leads.'

'On what?'

'Wish I could say,' Gleeson said breezily. The mole

253

wondered if Gleeson actually knew what Wen had said. Could Wen have given them enough to find him? Could the agency be tracking his offshore accounts right now? The mole felt his whole body dissolve, as if Gleeson could see through him. He looked down at his hands to be sure he was still real.

'I need you to pull together a report, everything we know about Mr. Wen,' Gleeson said. 'End of the day at the latest.'

'Sure. I was thinking the same thing.' The mole wondered if George Tyson and his counterintel boys were trying to set a trap. This assignment might be intended to provoke him into running, betraying himself.

Well, if that was their goal, they'd failed. The mole went back to his office and called up the thin dossier the agency had on Shubai, putting together the report for Gleeson. On his way home that night, he searched out a pay phone and punched in a Virginia cell-phone number. The call went straight to voicemail.

'You've reached George,' the message said. 'The car is still for sale. If you'd like to buy, please leave your number and the best time to reach you.' All the English lessons that the colonel had taken over the years had paid off, the mole thought. He hardly even sounded Chinese.

'George,' he said, 'that yellow Pinto of yours is just what I've been looking for. I'd like to pick it up as soon as possible. Call me before six a.m.'

The code was simple. Yellow meant he needed an urgent meeting. Pinto meant Wakefield Park, at 6:00 a.m.

While he waited for George to respond, the mole found a TGI Friday's where he could have a beer and watch the idiots on ESPN jaw at each other. He didn't even feel like drinking, but he ordered a beer anyway. When he looked down at his mug, it was empty. He signaled the bartender for another.

'No problem, buddy.'

'What kind of word is "sportscaster," anyway?' the mole said, eyeing the screen. 'I mean, "newscaster" is bad enough, but "sportscaster" makes no sense at all.'

'Got me. That was a Bud Light, right?'

An hour crawled by before the mole slapped a twenty-dollar bill on the bar and walked out. A half-mile down, he found another pay phone. Again the call went to voicemail. 'You've reached George,' the message said. 'Thanks for your inquiry. The yellow Pinto will be ready for pickup on Thursday.'

The mole had to restrain himself from tearing the receiver off the pay phone. *Thursday?* This was Monday. Why were they making him wait two and a half days? He should have demanded a meeting immediately. But now it was too late. Asking for something sooner would make George wonder if he was panicking, and he didn't want to seem panicked. He'd just have to wait.

So he waited, as hatefully as a prisoner counting the days to his execution. But the meeting was still more than a day away. Now, as his clock turned to 3:07 a.m., the mole shuffled out of bed and made his way to the spare bedroom, the room that he had once hoped would become a nursery. He settled in before an episode of *The Hills*, watching the bubbleheads on screen struggle to make it in the high-pressure world of *Teen Vogue*. He'd seen this episode before, but even if he hadn't, nothing in it would have surprised him. These shows were all exactly the same, whispered confidences, manufactured emotion, the tiniest of struggles.

As he watched, the mole wondered what he would do if George warned him that the agency was on him. The sad truth was that he didn't even like China all that much. He certainly didn't want to spend the rest of his life there. And what about Janice? Would George let her come? Would she want to go? He could tell her this was the big foreign adventure she'd always wanted.

Maybe he should just disappear, head for Mexico and points south, with or without Janice. He had enough money hidden away to make a go of it, especially if he wound up someplace like Thailand, where twenty bucks got you a blow job instead of a three-minute dance. But he didn't speak Thai. And wherever he went, he'd spend the rest of his life waiting for the knock on his door that meant the agency – or maybe the Chinese – had found him. He wasn't sure which side scared him more.

Anyway, aside from the polygraph he had no reason to worry. He needed to relax. He'd never even met Wen Shubai. The mole reached into his briefs and massaged himself, watching the lithe California goddesses on MTV, knowing that the whiskey and the wine would keep him from what the Thai bar girls called full release, but feeling halfway decent for the first time in a month. Soon enough, he'd know where he stood. And finally he felt his eyes droop closed.

TWENTY-THREE

'You all right?' Wells said across the Escalade to Exley.

'Fine. Just do what you have to do.'

'Pull the van forward so it's less visible. Then wipe it down. Anything you've touched. The wine cooler bottle too. No DNA.'

'I got it. Now go.'

Now the next step. Wells looked at his watch: 3:07 a.m. Twenty-three minutes left. He would need every one. He dumped Fred the guard onto the driveway and stepped into the Escalade. The German shepherd lay dead in the back, the dog's skull torn in half by two rounds from Wells's Glock, his blood pooling over the floor mats. Wells hadn't wanted to kill the dog, but he had had no choice.

Wells tucked himself in the driver's seat, slipped the Escalade into reverse, eased down on the gas. The big SUV tugged apart from the Sienna with the groan of metal scraping metal. A piece of the Toyota's hood hung from the Cadillac's grille like a battered Christmas ornament. Wells wheeled around, swung up the curving gravel driveway toward the mansion. The Escalade's tinted glass would work in his favor now.

The mansion, a gargantuan version of a rustic Cape Cod beach house, complete with weathered shingles, stood two hundred feet from the gate. As Wells drove toward it, a man ran at the Escalade.

'Jimmy – what the heck –'

Wells twisted the Escalade toward the guard and gunned the gas. The guard's mouth dropped open. He reached into his waistband for his pistol, then gave up on the gun and dove awkwardly out of the way. He landed face-first on the lawn as Wells skidded the Escalade to a stop beside him and jumped out, pistol in hand.

'Down,' Wells said, not too loud. 'Hands behind your back.'

The guard hesitated. Wells fired the silenced Glock, aiming a couple of feet left of the man's head. The round dug into the turf and the guard clasped his hands behind his back. Wells cuffed the man and dragged him up, standing behind him. 'What's your name?'

'Ty.'

'Who else is awake?'

'Nobody.'

Wells jabbed the Glock in his back. 'You already got your warning shot, Ty. Where's Hank?'

Ty hesitated, then: 'Second floor, watching the bedrooms.'

'Any others?'

'They're out with Anna. Takes five guys to watch her.'

A Nextel push-to-talk phone on Ty's waist buzzed. 'Ty?' a man said.

Wells grabbed it. 'Tell him a drunk driver hit the Escalade but nobody got hurt, cops are coming, you'll be right in. Yes?'

Ty nodded. Wells held the Nextel to Ty's mouth and pushed the talk button.

'Hank. Some drunk hit Jimmy, but everyone's okay. Cops are on the way. I'll be back in five.'

'Got it. Keep me posted.'

'Will do.'

Wells tossed the phone away. 'Good boy. One more question. Where's he sleep? Kowalski?'

Ty hesitated. 'Anna's got the master bedroom. He's second floor, left side, in the front.'

Wells pulled a syringe from his pocket and jabbed it in the guard's neck. His eyes widened and he pulled against his cuffs, twisting toward Wells. Then his breathing slackened and he fell like a penitent at Wells's feet.

One to go, Wells thought. He looked at his watch: 3:11.

Wells jogged toward the back of the house, the direction Ty had come from, past an Olympic-sized slate-tiled pool with three diving boards – low, medium, and high. He took the granite back steps of the house two at a time. The patio doors were open. He stepped in and found himself in a gleaming kitchen. Burnished copper pots hung from the ceiling; a Viking stove stood beside a pizza oven. The house was silent. Wells stepped through a corridor lined with hundreds of bottles of wine and up the long back staircase.

Halfway up Wells slowed, pulled the second air pistol from his backpack. He'd brought two, both loaded, so he wouldn't waste precious time on reloading the syringes. He stopped just shy of the top step. The stairs formed the stem of a T with a long corridor that ran left and right along the spine of the mansion. Wells poked his head above the top step. Sure enough, twenty feet down the hall, a man stood before a closed door, a pistol in his waistband.

'Ty,' he said urgently into his phone. 'Come in, Ty . . . Jimmy? Dammit.' He strode toward the staircase. Wells shifted to get a clear shot with the air pistol and fired at the man, ten feet away. *Psst*. The dart smacked into his stomach. The man sighed softly. The phone slipped from his hand as his knees buckled. Wells jumped to catch him before he hit the carpet and laid him down softly.

Wells stepped over him to the white wooden door at the end of the corridor. Locked. He pulled his pistol and took aim at the lock. He fired twice, hearing the grunt of metal as the rounds smashed the lock, and popped the door with his shoulder.

Wells stepped through and down the hall. To his left an open door revealed an empty bedroom. On the other side, a closed door. Wells put an ear to it. Silence. At the end of the hall, another door. Wells heard a steady, heavy snore as he approached.

He opened the door and flipped on the lights. An antique silk rug, its yellows and blues dazzling, reached to the corners of the oversized bedroom. Kowalski, a fat man with little pig eyes, slept alone in the oversized four-poster bed, white silk sheets draped around him like icing on a lumpy cake. He grumbled in his sleep at the lights.

'Pierre,' Wells said.

The snoring stopped mid-breath. Kowalski jerked up his head. His eyes snapped open. With surprising quickness, he rolled toward a little nightstand –

But Wells, even quicker, stepped toward the bed and

covered him with the pistol. Kowalski looked at the gun and stopped.

'Hands up,' Wells said. Kowalski raised his hands tentatively. 'Reach out your arms, grab the posts with each hand.' The fat man hesitated. 'Now.' Wells squeezed the Glock's trigger, put a round in the wall beside the bed.

'Please stay calm,' Kowalski said. He lifted his arms. Wells cuffed him to the bed, one wrist to each post. The sheets sagged off Kowalski, exposing his flabby belly and oversized silk boxers. Still, his face showed no tension. He seemed vaguely bemused, as if he couldn't believe anyone had the audacity to break into his house.

'You must know you're making a terrible mistake.' Kowalski spoke flawless English, with a vaguely British accent. He'd learned it in a Swiss boarding school, according to his dossier. He was half French, half Polish. He'd followed his father into the arms business. 'You must know who I am.'

'Too bad you can't say the same about me,' Wells said. 'For a million and a half, you should have splurged for some security cameras. Answer me five questions and I'll leave.'

'Is this a joke?'

Wells put a hand over Kowalski's mouth, pulled a stun gun from his pack, and jabbed it into Kowalski's neck. The fat man's head jerked sideways and his tongue shuddered obscenely against Wells's gloved palm. Wells counted five before he pulled the gun away. 'Why did you send Spetsnaz to Afghanistan?'

Kowalski didn't hesitate. 'I don't know what you're talking about.'

'Wrong answer.' This time Wells counted ten

261

before he pulled the stun gun from Kowalski's neck. He didn't have time to be subtle and he knew Kowalski was lying.

In the end, Sergei the Russian special forces officer had told Wells his story without much prompting. He had been working security in Moscow for Gazprom, the Russian natural gas company, when the call came. The colonel who had commanded his unit in Chechnya told him he could get $500,000 for six months' work with the Taliban in Afghanistan.

'I said this money seemed to be too good to be true. He promised me it was real, that they needed a hundred of us to go, the best Spetsnaz, and they would pay. He said it was coming from Pierre Kowalski. And then I knew it must be true.'

'You trusted your commander?'

'In Chechnya he saved my life many times. He wouldn't lie about this.' They arranged for special precautions so the money couldn't be traced, he said. Each man got a hundred thousand dollars in cash as a signing bonus. Every month, fifty thousand was wired to a bank account of a family member, with a final hundred-thousand-dollar bonus to be paid at the end of the six months.

'We knew the risks going in,' Sergei said. 'But the money was too good. Everyone agreed.'

'What if the Afghans turned on you?'

'We talked about that. But we knew we'd be here together. We could protect one another. Anyway, we made them better fighters, so they had no reason to hurt us. We were worried about your side.'

'Did you know who Kowalski was working for?'

'No. That was part of the arrangement. When we

arrived, the Talibs told us that it wasn't their money. No surprise.'

'Could Kowalski have been doing it himself?'

'Our commander said no, that he was working for someone else. And taking a rich fee.' Sergei spat. 'That was all we knew. All we wanted to know.'

'And where is your commander? How can I find him?'

'You found him already. In there.' He pointed at the cave.

'Wrong answer,' Wells said now, in the bedroom in the Hamptons. 'Try again. Why were you helping the Talibs?'

'What business is it of yours?'

Wells again covered Kowalski's mouth. Kowalski twisted his head helplessly. 'No one's coming for you, Pierre. It's you and me now.' Kowalski's pig eyes squinted at Wells. 'Yes. I hired them. The Spetsnaz.'

'To fight the United States?'

'Of course.' His voice betrayed no emotion. 'A man called me. A North Korean I'd worked with. He asked me to arrange it. He knew I had contacts with the Talibs and the Russians. He wanted the best fighters, ones who would make a difference.'

'How much did he pay?'

'Five million. No big deal.'

Wells punched Kowalski in the stomach, twice, a quick left-right combination, his fists disappearing into the big man's belly. 'You spent fifty million just on the men.'

Kowalski's mouth flopped open as he struggled for breath.

'How much?' Wells said again.

263

'Calm, my friend.' Kowalski's cultured voice had turned into a thin wheeze. 'It was twenty million a month for six months. For the men and some weapons, SA-7s, RPGs. A good deal, lots of profit. My contact said his side might extend the offer when the six months was over.' A hundred twenty million, Wells thought. No wonder Kowalski had been able to pay $500,000 a man.

'Where was the money from?'

'I didn't ask. My contact was North Korean. I don't know who was behind him. Perhaps the North Koreans, but I don't think so.'

'Why not?'

'Too expensive for them. Anyway, what do they care about Afghanistan?'

'The Saudis? The Iranians?'

Kowalski looked at the stun gun. 'I don't know. Really.'

'You never asked? Considering the risks?'

'I'm paid not to ask. I make the arrangements and I don't ask. Like you.'

'It was safer not to know.'

Kowalski didn't try to hide his contempt. 'What have I been saying?'

'Where did the money come from?'

'Wire transfers from a Macao bank account.'

'Macao? Why there?'

'I didn't ask.'

'Which bank?'

'Banco Delta Asia.'

Wells recognized the name. The bank had gotten into trouble before, accused of laundering dirty money for the North Korean government. 'Account number.'

'I don't have it here. Come to Zurich and I'll look it

up for you. I promise the same hospitality you're showing me.' This time Wells didn't bother with the stun gun but simply locked a hand around Kowalski's neck and squeezed through the fat. To Kowalski's credit, he didn't beg, even as his face grew red and his arms shook against the wooden bedposts. 'I tell you I don't have it here,' he repeated.

Wells choked him long enough to be sure he was telling the truth and then let him go. Kowalski coughed – short, dry puffs.

'Where can I find your contact?'

'His name was Moon. But he won't be talking to you. He died last month. Nothing to do with this. He had a sideline in the heroin business. He ran across some very bad men.'

'But you're still getting paid.'

'Of course.' Kowalski's face was dark pink, the color of medium-rare steak, and his arms hung heavily from the posts, but still he sounded confident. 'Let me tell you something. Whoever you are. Even if you're U.S. government, CIA, Special Forces, whatever. You'll pay for this, what you've done tonight. Even if you think you're safe. I'll break the rules for you.'

More than anyone he'd ever come across, even Omar Khadri, Wells wished he could kill this man. But he couldn't take the chance. And anyway he didn't kill prisoners. He grabbed a roll of duct tape from his backpack and plastered a piece over Kowalski's mouth.

Then, for no reason he could name, Wells began wrapping the silver tape around Kowalski's skull. The fat man tried to twist away, but Wells held him steady. He draped the tape over Kowalski's eyes, over his forehead and his cheeks, loop after loop, until the big man looked like a modern-day mummy, Tuten-Duct, the Egyptian god of electrical tape. He made sure to leave Kowalski's nostrils open so he wouldn't suffocate. Then Wells clapped a hand over Kowalski's nostrils and squeezed them shut. He counted aloud to ten, nice and slow, before letting go.

'Don't forget to breathe.' And with that, Wells ran.

It was 3:29. Exley was sitting in the minivan. 'Got your helmet?'

Exley grabbed her motorcycle helmet from the van and they ran for the bike. Three minutes later, they were at the corner of Newton Lane and Main Street, the Honda purring smoothly beneath them. A police car turned past, its emergency lights flashing, but no siren and not speeding. The chief had kept his word, even given Wells a couple of extra minutes.

Route 27 was empty and quiet, and once he'd picked through the traffic lights of the Hamptons and reached the highway, Wells wound down the throttle of the CB1000 and watched the speedometer creep up and the highway unspool before him. Exley wrapped her arms around him and gripped him tight, from fear or joy or both, and he was as happy as he knew how to be. *Everything dies, baby, that's a fact, but maybe everything that dies someday comes back*, he sang as loudly as he could, knowing that no one, not even Exley, could hear him.

Only when he saw the red-and-blue lights of a police cruiser ahead in the distance did he slow. An hour later, they were on the outskirts of Queens, the traffic on the Long Island Expressway just starting to pick up with the morning's earliest commuters. Wells pulled the Honda off the highway and they found the Paris Hotel, not particularly clean but happy to take cash.

Room 223 of the Paris had a faded gray carpet and a soft moist smell.

'Nice,' Exley said. She poked at the rabbit ears atop the television. 'I haven't seen these in a while.'

'We'll always have Paris,' Wells said.

'We did it. Am I allowed to say it was fun, John? Because it was.'

'Sure it was.'

Exley settled onto the mattress, ignoring the spring poking at her butt. 'I can't believe we're already back in New York City.'

'Told you the moto comes in handy sometimes.'

'You have to slow down, John. Didn't you feel me hitting you?'

'Thought you wanted me to go faster.'

Exley couldn't believe they were fighting about this, after what they'd just pulled off, but they were. 'Such a child. If you're gonna get us killed, do it for a halfway decent reason. You don't have to prove to me you have a big dick.'

'Well, that's comforting.' Wells lay next to Exley, his face almost touching hers. The bed sank under him. 'Think this is one mattress or a bunch stitched together?'

Exley had to laugh. Wells could be impossible, and more than once lately she'd thought that he planned to push his luck until he wound up in a wooden box. But she couldn't pretend she didn't love him. 'So what did he say? Kowalski?'

'Not much.' Wells recounted the conversation. 'But there was one thing. He said he was getting paid out of a bank in Macao. Which doesn't really make sense. Of course, the money could have been coming into that bank from anywhere.'

'Think he was telling the truth?'

Wells propped himself up on an elbow and stroked Exley's hair. Finally, he nodded. 'Yeah. He didn't know who I was, but he knew no matter what, I couldn't use it in court. He wanted me out of there and he didn't know how much I knew. Honesty was his best bet.'

'He's going to come after you. Us. In a way, he was flaunting what he'd done.'

'If he's smart, he'll let it go, be happy I didn't shoot him. He can't track us anyway. And if he does figure out it was us . . .'

Exley understood. They were untouchable. Or so Wells thought.

'Why did you tape him up that way at the end, John? He was angry already.'

'Seemed like a good idea at the time.'

She waited, but Wells was silent, his breathing steady, and she knew he wouldn't say anything more. 'Roll over,' she said.

He turned his big body and Exley snuggled up and ran her hands around him. She pushed up his shirt and touched the raised red scar high on his back. He sighed softly, happily, and reached back for her. She closed her eyes and kissed his back.

'So who do you think was paying for those guys?' he said.

She lifted her mouth from his skin. 'Don't know. And that's real money. A hundred and twenty million.'

'But think on it. We spend a couple billion bucks a month in Afghanistan. For a fraction of that, some-body's making it a lot harder for us. Not a bad investment.'

'Syria. Libya.'

'Iran?'

'Maybe.'

Wells sat up and leaned against the bed's battered headboard. Exley traced her hand over his chest, the muscles solid as iron.

'You close on the mole?' he said.

'We'd be closer if I hadn't come up here. But we'll get him soon. Shubai gave us enough. In a way it doesn't matter, though. He's already done the damage. We don't have one Chinese agent we can trust.'

'Not a good time for it either,' Wells said.

'No. Any day now, China and Iran are about to announce something big. They aren't even denying it. There's all this trouble in Taiwan. And Shubai says there's a power struggle in Beijing. Says the hard-liners want to prove how tough they are, that we have to stand up to them, that showing any weakness will just make them push us harder.' Exley closed her eyes and felt weariness overtake her.

'You think Beijing might have been supporting the Talibs through Kowalski?'

'I wondered too when you said Macao. But why risk a war with us?'

'None of it makes sense,' Wells said. 'The Chinese make this deal with Iran. They betray the Drafter. It's like they want a fight.'

'Yes and no. They're coming at us sideways. They're hoping we overreact.'

'But that's not what Shubai says, right? He says they want us to back down so that the whole world will see how much more powerful they're getting.'

'What would you do, John? If you were running the show? Push back hard on the Chinese or let things simmer?'

He considered. 'I don't know. We can't let them push us around, and it sounds like this guy Shubai knows what he's talking about. But there's something we can't see. Hate to go to war by accident.'

Wells didn't bother to ask what she thought. Without another word, he rolled onto her, his size surprising her, as it always did. He enveloped her, his mouth on hers, wet open-mouthed kisses. He never asked permission, she thought. He never needed to. His big hands gripped her waist, then one was unbuttoning her jeans, the other pulling them off her hips. And as quickly as that, she forgot she was tired.

TWENTY-FOUR

Larry Young, the White House Press Secretary, felt the buzz in the pressroom as he strode to the podium. These afternoon briefings were usually inside baseball, watched by a few thousand political junkies. Not today. Today Young would be live from Los Angeles to Boston, Tokyo to Moscow. The Chinese and the Iranians had certainly gotten the world's attention that morning.

Young waited for the cameras to stop clicking before he read the statement, approved forty-five minutes before by the president himself.

'The United States denounces the action by the People's Republic of China in the strongest possible terms. If China wants the world's respect, it should condemn Iran's nuclear program, not support it. Most important, China must understand that the United States will hold it accountable if Iran deploys a nuclear weapon.'

The statement was short and to the point, as Young had recommended. 'That's all. I'm sure you have questions.' A dozen hands went up. 'Jackson? My hometown favorite.'

Jackson Smith, from the *Washington Post,* stood.

'Any sanctions planned against China? A trade embargo? Will we be recalling our ambassador?'

An easy one, Young thought. Smith was smart but predictable. 'That's three questions, but they all have the same answer. At this time, we're reviewing our options, both economic and diplomatic.'

'But nothing planned at this time?'

'We're not going to be hasty, Jackson. Next.' He pointed to Lia Michaels, from NBC. They'd had a brief fling a few years back, when he was a congressional aide and she was at CNN. They were both married now and never mentioned their history, but he always made sure to call on her and she always smiled at him when he did.

'The Pentagon has announced that the United States is deploying three aircraft carriers to the South China Sea. Why? Do we plan any military action?'

Young took a moment to get the answer exactly right. He'd worked this phrasing out with the president's chief of staff and he didn't want to miss a word. 'The announcement today is only the most recent in a series of provocative actions by the People's Republic. China must be aware that its actions have consequences. Next?'

But Lia wasn't finished yet. 'You said the United States will hold China accountable if Iran uses a nuclear weapon. Does that threat include a nuclear strike against China?'

'It's not a threat. And we never discuss military contingencies. Next?'

Anne Ryuchi, the new CNN correspondent, caught his eye. 'There have been rumors about this agreement for a couple of weeks. Did you try to warn China off?'

'We did attempt to express our concerns. Obviously the Chinese weren't interested in hearing them. Next.'

Dan Spiegel, from the *New York Times,* practically jumped out of his seat. Young didn't much like him. A typical *Times* reporter, smart but not as smart as he thought. 'Mr. Spiegel.'

'You mentioned a series of provocative actions. Does the United States have a theory as to why China is being so aggressive?'

'You'd better ask them.' Young enjoyed snapping Spiegel off.

'To follow up. Aside from their deal with Iran, what other actions have the Chinese taken that the United States classifies as provocative?'

'Their recent missile tests, and their saber-rattling toward Taiwan. Taiwan is a democracy and an ally of the United States.'

'But didn't the Taiwanese start this controversy with their discussion of a possible independence vote?'

Spiegel loved to hear his own voice. Like so many reporters, he believed mistakenly that he was as important as the people he wrote about.

'The people of Taiwan must be allowed to express their opinions without fear of Chinese reprisal,' Young said. Time to give them something new to chew on. 'Also, while I can't provide specifics, we have learned that the Chinese government has damaged a classified program critical to the national security of the United States.'

'Can you tell us more?'

'Unfortunately not.'

The conference went on forty-five minutes more, until almost 3:00 p.m. Eastern. In Beijing, twelve hours ahead, Li Ping watched in his office, sipping tea as a colonel on his staff translated. Cao Se watched alongside him, filling a pad with notes. When the conference ended, Li flicked off the television and dismissed the colonel.

'What did you think?'

Cao flipped through his pad. 'They're very angry, General.'

Li wasn't disturbed. 'Furious words, but no action. As I expected.'

Cao clasped his hands together. He seemed uncomfortable, Li thought. 'I respect you greatly, Li. You're a great leader.'

Li found himself unexpectedly irritated. He was used to having junior officers suck up this way, but he expected more from Cao.

'General,' Li said, emphasizing the word, reminding Cao of his seniority, 'don't waste your breath flattering me. It's very late. Now go on.'

'Sir –' Cao stopped, twisted his hands. 'Fate is a strange beast. Even the most perfect plan can fail.'

Now Li understood. Cao feared the United States. 'The Americans won't fight us, Cao.' Li had studied the flash points of the Cold War – the Cuban Missile Crisis, the Berlin Blockade, the Soviet destruction of KAL 007, a Korean passenger jet that strayed over Russian territory in 1983. Each time, after threats of war, the two sides found a way to defuse the crisis. Nuclear-armed powers didn't fight each other. China and the United States would find a way out too – but only after Li had taken power.

'But what if the Americans miscalculate?'

'There's no reason to worry. We control the situation.' Even Cao didn't know all the levers Li had

274

at his disposal. He hadn't only negotiated the agreement with Iran and given up the Drafter. He was behind the independence crisis in Taiwan as well.

Over the years, the People's Liberation Army had built a huge network of agents in Taiwan, including one of its most senior politicians, Herbert Sen. Now, on Li's orders, Sen had called for the island to declare its independence from China. In doing so, Sen had put the United States in a miserable position. Since 1949, when the Nationalists fled Mainland China and established their new headquarters on Taiwan, the People's Republic had viewed Taiwan as a renegade province. In fact, the island was effectively independent from China, with its own government, currency, and military. America helped guarantee that security. In turn, Taiwan wasn't supposed to rattle China's cage by officially declaring its independence. A Taiwanese move to break that bargain would give China an excuse to invade – and leave the United States with two bad options. Let China attack Taiwan, its democratic ally, or go to war over a crisis that the Taiwanese themselves had started.

Of course, Li didn't want to invade Taiwan. An attack would be worse than messy, even if the United States didn't get involved. Taiwan was extremely well defended. But Li knew better than anyone else that the independence movement wouldn't get far. Soon enough – on his orders – Herbert Sen would have a change of heart. In the meantime, Sen's demand had increased the pressure on the Americans.

'Think of it this way, Cao. We've created a storm the Americans didn't expect. Now they'll try to frighten us. They'll bring up their navy. They'll reach too far. Then all of China will unite against them' – behind me, Li thought – 'and they'll see they have no choice but to ask for peace. When they do, we'll give them what they want. The skies will clear. And America will have a new respect for China.'

'And with your new power, you'll make sure that the peasants are treated fairly.'

'No more riots like the one in Guangzhou. No more stealing at the top of the Party. A new China, where everyone shares in the blessings of the economy. The people have waited too long for honest rulers.'

Li had never before spoken his plan aloud, not even when he was alone. His heart quickened. In a few weeks, the world would see him as he was, Mao's rightful heir.

'The people will thank us, Cao,' he said. 'I'm certain of it.'

The meeting of the Standing Committee began precisely at 2:00 p.m. the next afternoon. The foreign minister discussed the world's reaction to the deal with Iran. Aside from the United States, most countries had hardly blinked. Some had even quietly told Beijing that they supported the Chinese and Iranian efforts to counter American power.

Then Li reviewed America's military maneuvers. As it had promised, the United States was moving three carrier battle groups toward the Chinese coast – a formidable fleet, with hundreds of jets and several dozen ships. In response, China had moved forward its newest submarines and had increased fighter patrols. Already the Chinese pilots were reporting increased contacts with American and Taiwanese jets.

'Our pilots are aware of the delicacy of the situation,' Li said. 'We don't expect any offensive contact, but if the Americans attack we'll respond. Does anyone have questions?'

For a moment, the room was silent. Then Zhang spoke. 'Defense Minister, the American reaction to our announcement concerns me. Didn't you promise that the United States wouldn't act against us?'

'So far they've done nothing but talk,' Li said, as he had that morning to Cao.

'But what if that changes? The Americans have discovered that we betrayed them to North Korea. They said so at their meeting with the reporters.' Zhang was almost shouting across the table at Li, a bit of theater to show his anger. 'You told us they wouldn't find out about that. Obviously they have, thanks to that traitor Wen Shubai. One of your men, Minister Li.'

In turn, Li spoke quietly, without raising his voice. Let Zhang yell, he thought.

'Minister Zhang, I fear you're correct. I curse Wen. He's a treacherous snake. But the Americans can't prove anything. Anyway, they aren't children. They know we've used North Korea against them for many years. They won't go to war over this.'

'Not this alone, but in combination with what we've announced with Iran –'

Li turned to Xu, the committee's nominal leader, subtly cutting Zhang out of the discussion. 'General Secretary, what do you think?'

Li knew that in asking Xu, he was taking a chance. Xu might cut him down, say that he too was worried by the American response. But Xu had smiled and nodded throughout his presentation. Li thought the old man wanted a little excitement. And maybe Xu was tired of having Zhang order him around.

Now Xu nodded. 'I think . . . Comrade Li is correct.

So far the American hegemonists have done nothing but talk. And I think it's time we taught the Americans a lesson. It's no longer up to them to control who has the special weapons.'

'Are you certain, General Secretary?' Zhang said. 'At our breakfast this morning, you expressed concerns about whether a fight with the Americans might hurt our economy.'

Zhang had just blundered, Li thought. Like all old lions, Xu hated to be embarrassed publicly. Sure enough, Xu swiped Zhang down.

'I've expressed my opinion. Comrade Li has done a fine job. And trade isn't the only measure of national pride, Comrade Zhang.'

'Thank you, General Secretary,' Li said. 'Now, there's something else. Besides help with the special weapons, the Iranians have asked us to provide delivery systems.'

'Missiles? No.' Zhang sat up in his chair. 'This is madness. We have too many problems at home to invite more anger from America. Our economy is too uncertain.'

'How strange, Minister Zhang,' Li said. 'All these months you've told us our economy is a glorious and strong wall. Did the wall fall down while none of us were looking?'

'Of course not. But –' Zhang stopped, trying to figure out how to explain the contradiction in a way that wouldn't sound foolish.

'We don't have to do anything. It's enough that the Americans know that we're considering the request, that they haven't frightened us.'

Xu stepped in. 'Minister Li, please continue your discussions with the Iranians. Let's make sure the

American hegemonists know that their ships won't stop us from acting in the interest of the Chinese people.'

'Thank you, General Secretary.' Li smiled. Across the table, Zhang's black eyes flashed with anger, and something else. He knew he was losing control, Li thought. Of course, desperation could make Zhang more dangerous. But it might also lead him to make mistakes, like his effort to browbeat Xu. Either way, the fear in Zhang's eyes told Li that he was on the verge of success.

TWENTY-FIVE

The mole set his alarm for 5:15, wanting to be sure he'd make his meeting with George in plenty of time. But when he opened his eyes in the blackness, Janice snoring lightly beside him, the radio's display told him it was 3:47 a.m. Insomnia had its advantages. Tonight he'd woken like a spring uncoiling, immediately clearheaded, though he'd been asleep three hours at most.

He ran his hand down Janice's back, resting his fingers on her soft, fleshy ass. She turned sideways, shifted one leg forward and the other back, an unconscious invitation. Before he could wake her, he pulled his hand away. His marital duties would have to wait. She grumbled softly but didn't wake.

In the basement he collected his Smith & Wesson, slipping the revolver into a little shoulder holster. Fortunately the morning was cool, so he could wear a windbreaker without attracting attention. He'd never fully trusted the Chinese, and part of him worried that they would shuck him now that the heat was on.

He shaved in the basement bathroom, nicking himself under his chin. The cut didn't hurt, but blood covered his neck, matching his bloodshot eyes. He dabbed at the cut with toilet paper until finally the blood stopped flowing. Then he lifted the bathroom mirror off the wall and spun the dials on the black safe behind it until the heavy steel door clicked open.

For the last couple of weeks, he'd pulled cash out of his bank accounts, $2,000 or so a day. Now he had $45,000 in the safe, neatly organized into blocks of hundreds and twenties, along with two Rolex watches and loose diamonds in a little Tupperware box. He riffed through the cash, then stacked it in two plastic Priority Mail envelopes.

In another envelope were two passports, one American, one Canadian, both very good quality. He'd picked them up in Panama a couple of years ago. Ten thousand dollars went a long way down there. Now he flipped through them carefully, checking the laminated photographs, examining the tiny hexagonal holographs on the American passport. For the Canadian, he'd dyed his hair black and worn glasses. The dye and glasses were in the safe too.

Real as they looked, the passports wouldn't get him into the United States, not anymore, not with the new scanners that the Department of Homeland Security was using. But they'd be good enough to get him out, to Mexico or Jamaica or some other third-world hothouse with soft borders and no visa rules. And getting out was what counted. If he left, he wouldn't be back anytime soon.

The moon was still glowing in the sky when the mole reached Wakefield Park. As far as he could tell, he was the only creature moving. Even the deer and the raccoons were asleep. It was 4:45 a.m. The sun wouldn't rise for another hour. Under his windbreaker, his .357

itched in its holster and he had a mad urge to pop off a couple of rounds in the dark.

He sat on a stump by the granite outcropping where he would meet George. Then he reconsidered and walked up the hill behind the rock to a stand of beech trees. He pushed between the trees and settled himself behind a low hummock of dirt. From here he could glimpse the outcropping without being seen by anyone below. If everything looked fine when George showed up, he would brush himself off, stroll down the hill, and say hi. If not . . . well, they'd have to find him.

As he waited, his consciousness drifted. Suddenly he was in the Washington Hilton with Evie, the stripper. She smirked at him as she propped herself upside down against the hotel room's door, naked, spreading her legs –

He bit his lip to stay awake. 5:25. Dammit. He'd been snoozing for half an hour. Ironic that after these months of insomnia he was overwhelmingly tired, just when he most needed to be awake. He heard birds waking, the first faint chirps of the morning.

Then something else. Footsteps moving north from the park's main entrance. He waited. The footsteps crackled closer. Then he spotted the men. Two, both Chinese. He'd never seen either one. The first was small, wearing binoculars around his neck, like some kind of birdwatcher. The second man was tall and thick, a bodyguard type, wearing a sweatshirt and jeans. The mole was suddenly conscious of his pulse thumping through his head, *whoosh-whoosh, whoosh-whoosh.* Who were these men? Where was George?

The men reached the big granite outcropping. The first man raised his hands to his eyes – the park was still too dark for the binoculars to be useful – and slowly scanned the hill where the mole was hidden. He seemed to be talking to the other man, though from this distance the mole couldn't make out what he was saying. Then he pointed up the hill.

Step by step, the big Chinese closed in on the beech stand where the mole was hiding. The mole wished he could burrow into the dirt. Then the big man turned right, cutting over the hill, disappearing. The mole waited to be sure he was gone, then reached across his body to draw his S&W out of his shoulder holster. With the gun free, he lay down again and waited.

The man below leaned against a rock, pulled a pack of cigarettes from his breast pocket, and lit one up. He smoked quietly, the tip of his cigarette glowing in the darkness. When he was done, he stubbed the cigarette onto the sole of his shoe and dropped the burned-out butt back into the pack he carried. Trying not to leave evidence of his presence, the mole thought.

The minutes ticked by. As 6:00 a.m. approached, the man stood up. 'Mr. T?' he said. He whistled into the darkness. 'Mr. T?'

From his spot in the trees, the mole wondered if the Chinese planned to shoot him this morning. They had to know that if they killed him they would never be able to recruit anyone else. The CIA would broadcast this story to the world, so that any potential agent would know how the Chinese treated their spies. But then where was George this morning? And why bring two men? Nothing made sense.

At 6:10, the temperature was rising, the black sky turning blue. The mole covered the S&W with his hand so its metal glint wouldn't give him away. In a few minutes more the sun would be fully up, exposing his position. Still he waited. At this point he had no choice. Under his windbreaker, sweat pricked down his back.

Crunch-crunch-crunch. The mole held his head steady but twisted his eyes right. The big Chink was coming back over the hill, looking toward the beeches where the mole lay. The mole's fingers tightened around his gun. Then the man's narrow eyes slid past and he walked down the hill. When he reached the granite outcropping, he said something the mole couldn't hear. The little guy shook his head. He tapped out two cigarettes. The men stood there silently until they were finished smoking. Then the little guy tapped his watch and they walked back to the main entrance. The mole waited ten minutes more, tucked his S&W away, and headed home on shaky legs.

Three hours later he sat in his Acura in the parking lot of a 7-Eleven, fumbling with the clamshell packaging that surrounded a disposable cell phone he'd bought at a Radio Shack. The thick plastic cut his fingers, and as his frustration grew he felt like throwing the phone into the traffic. Finally he managed to rip the phone from its packaging. He breathed deep, tried to relax, powered up the phone, and punched in a 718 number, to be used only in absolute emergencies. He let the phone ring three times and hung up. He stared at his watch, allowing three minutes to pass, then repeated the drill. Three minutes later, he called for a third time. This time the phone was answered on the first ring.

'Washington Zoo. George here.'

'Do you still have the giant pandas?' An idiotic but necessary code.

Pause. 'Has something happened? Where were you today?'

'Where were you? Who were those guys?'

'It was for security. They would have brought you to me.' Pause. 'Since what happened in England, we are concerned.'

'*You're* concerned? Worst case, they give you a one-way ticket home.'

'It isn't smart to talk anymore on this phone.'

'Okay. Let's meet in person. Somewhere nice and public, George.'

'Public?'

'Like Union Station. I'll figure it out, let you know.'

'Please don't panic. We've worked together a long time. I'm your partner.'

'Then you should have come this morning.' *Click.*

Twin flower beds lined the driveway, an explosion of roses, daffodils, and tulips in red and yellow. The house itself was brick, big but nondescript. A two-car garage and white painted shutters. Exley walked up the driveway without much hope. It was the last of the five on her original list. Of the others she'd visited, one had been empty when she arrived, which proved only that both parents worked. The other three had been typical suburban homes, with typical suburban moms. Exley worried that she was wasting her time. What had she expected to find? A Post-It on the refrigerator that said, 'Meeting w/ Chinese handler Tuesday night – don't be late!' On the other hand, Tyson's team hadn't nailed anything down either. Even with only a few suspects to check, this kind of work was seriously time-intensive.

This place looked like another bust. The driveway was empty and the curtains shut. Exley mounted the front steps, and to her surprise heard a soap opera blaring from a television inside. A dog barked madly as

Exley pushed the bell. She'd heard a couch creak as she rang. Then nothing. Whoever it was seemed to be hoping she'd go away. She rang again, feeling vaguely nauseated and headachy. Too much coffee and too little sleep.

'Coming,' a woman said irritably. Janice Robinson, wife of Keith, according to the agency's dossier. Janice pulled open the door and peered heavy-lidded into the afternoon Virginia sun. The house behind her was dark, though a television flickered in a room off the front hall. A fat golden retriever poked its snout at the door, barking angrily while wagging its tail to prove it wasn't serious.

'Can I help you?' Janice said, in a solid southern drawl. She wore a faded red T-shirt with 'Roll Tide' printed in white across the chest. Her face was pretty but chubby, her hair a dirty-blond mess, her eyeliner thick and sloppy. The scent of white wine radiated off her, decaying and sweet as a bouquet of week-old flowers.

'I'm looking at that ranch on the corner and I was hoping you maybe could tell me about the neighborhood,' Exley said. 'My husband and I have an apartment in the District, but we're looking to move. My name's Joanne, by the way.'

Confusion flicked across Janice's face, as if Exley had tried to explain the theory of relativity and not her house-buying plans. 'You want to hear about the neighborhood?'

'Nobody knows it like the neighbors, right?' Exley smiled.

'Hard to argue with that,' Janice said. Exley couldn't tell if she was being sarcastic. Maybe she wasn't as ditzy as she seemed. 'I have to take my car into the shop, but I guess I can spare a minute.' Janice opened the door and waved Exley inside.

'Do you do those?' Exley indicated the flower bed. 'They're so beautiful.'

'My babies.' She patted the retriever's head. 'Lenny tries to eat them, but I don't let him. My name's Janice. Come in.'

Janice led Exley through the dark house to the kitchen, where more flowers awaited, fresh-cut this time. A ceiling fan mopped the air. Exley couldn't remember the last time she'd been in a room so stifling. Probably twenty years ago, some airless fraternity basement in college, getting drunk and looking for what she thought was a good time.

'I don't like air-conditioning,' Janice said. 'It breeds colds.' Lenny plopped down heavily, his tongue flopping out. Even with the flowers and dog, the house seemed sterile to Exley. The darkness. The television blaring. The bottles lined up by the sink. If this were a movie, a serial killer would be hiding in the basement. Or Janice would have her grandmother chained to a bed upstairs.

'Would you like a glass of water? You seem peaked.'

'That'd be great,' Exley said.

'Maybe some wine. I find a glass in the afternoon keeps away the colds.'

'Just water, thanks.' Exley worried she seemed snappish. 'I'd love a drink, but I have to get back to the office.'

'Of course.' Janice poured a glass of water from a pitcher in the refrigerator and set it on the table. Exley had a brief paranoid fantasy that the water was laced with something. She'd take a sip. The world would go black. When she came to, she'd be locked in the basement next to a fat guy in a leather mask. No. That was *Pulp Fiction*. She ought to stop this nonsense. She, not Janice, was the one in here under false pretenses. She did feel light-headed, though. She dabbed a few drops of water on her face. Janice sipped from her wine.

'Your place is nice,' Exley said.

'So you wanted to hear about the neighborhood? It's all right, I guess.'

'Have you lived here awhile?'

Janice paused. 'Seven years or so, I guess. We're thinking about moving.'

'Oh.'

'But it's nothing to do with the neighbors. My husband might be getting moved overseas. It's something we've wanted to do for a while.'

Keith Robinson was in line for an overseas assignment? Exley hadn't seen that possibility in his file. But then, he wouldn't be the first man to fib to his wife about his job prospects.

'Seems like a real nice place, though.'

'The neighbors are friendly enough. We kind of keep to ourselves.' She indicated a flyer stuck to the refrigerator. 'There's a block barbecue next week.'

'How about the schools? We've got two little ones.'

Janice flinched and Exley saw that she'd touched the source of the strange melancholy in the house.

'Can't help you there. We don't have kids.'

'Oh.' Exley never knew how to respond when a woman said she was childless, especially in the tone that Janice had used, equal parts anger and disbelief. 'Sorry?' 'There's always adoption?' 'They're over-rated?' Every answer sounded patronizing and futile. 'My mistake,' she finally said.

Janice ostentatiously looked at her watch. 'Sorry to

rush you, but I have to get to the dealership. I'm probably not the right person to talk to anyway. What with having no kids.' She pulled back her lips in an ugly smile, like a viper about to unleash a mouthful of venom.

'No problem. Thanks for your time.' Exley sipped her water and stood.

'By the way, what did you say you did, Jill?'

'Joanne. I'm a consultant. Market research. Guess that's why I'm always trying to find out about neighborhoods and stuff.'

'Do you have a card?'

'Sure.' Exley poked into her purse for a card as Janice finished off her wine.

'Never understood what you consultants do anyway.' Janice looked at Exley's card fishily.

Exley hadn't felt so disliked in a long time. 'Thanks for all your help, Mrs. –'

'Robinson.'

'Robinson. I'm embarrassed to ask, but can I use your toilet?' Exley was hoping for an excuse to get a quick look around the first floor.

'Right through the living room. I'll show you.'

The bathroom and the living room were unexceptional, though both hinted at hidden wealth – an expensive Persian rug in the living room and fancy granite fixtures in the bath. In five minutes, Exley was back in her car. Maybe Keith Robinson wasn't the mole, but he was *something*, Exley thought, as she put the Caravan in gear and drove off, mopping sweat from her forehead. His house stank of secrets.

Exley went back to the office in Tysons Corner and spent the rest of the afternoon poring over Robinson's work history. She already knew that his biographical details fit what Wen Shubai had given them. She was looking for smaller, subtler signs. Sure enough, she found one. Beginning eight years earlier – the time when the mole had approached the Chinese, according to Wen – Robinson's performance evaluations had steadily improved. After being lazy and unmotivated for years, he'd shown new interest in his work, his bosses said. As a result, he'd wound up with new responsibilities – and new access to information.

When she was sure she'd seen every scrap of information they had on Robinson, she poked her head into Shafer's office. He'd spent the last several days casting a wide net, asking vague questions about possible suspects to officers in and around the East Asia Division. Exley thought he was being too cautious. Legwork wasn't his strong suit; he was much better thinking through threads that other people had gathered. All his jujitsu wasted time, and time was suddenly in short supply.

Since Shubai's defection five days earlier, Langley's top two agents in the People's Republic had gone dark. One spy, the logistics chief at the giant naval base at Lushun, had simply disappeared. He'd requested an urgent meeting with his case officer, then hadn't shown up. Now his cell phone was turned off and his e-mail shut down.

The other agent, a deputy mayor in Beijing, was the highest-ranking political source the agency had inside Zhongnanhai. At least he had been until Tuesday, when he'd been arrested on what China's official news agency referred to as 'corruption charges.'

Of course, the arrest and disappearance might have been coincidences. But no one at Langley believed that.

The odds were higher that Osama bin Laden would quit al Qaeda to become a pro surfer. Chinese counter-intelligence officers had surely tracked both men for years, allowing them to remain free to provide false information to the CIA. Effectively, the men had been tripled up – used by China against the United States, even as the United States believed that it had doubled them back against China.

But Wen's defection had ended that game, and so the spymasters in Beijing had arrested the men. And now the United States was flying blind at the worst possible time. Did the PRC want open war with Taiwan and the United States, or was it bluffing? Was its leadership unified, or was its belligerence the product of an invisible power struggle inside Zhongnanhai? The president, the Pentagon, and the National Security Council were desperate for answers. Too bad the CIA had none to give.

'I think I have something.' She recounted her meeting with Janice Robinson, as well as Keith Robinson's strange personnel evaluations. When she was done, Shafer looked down at his notes.

'She didn't specifically mention children, then?'

'I'm telling you the whole house was *off*.'

'Jennifer. I don't doubt it. I'm only trying to figure out where to go next. Remember, Robinson's only on the list because he failed a poly. He doesn't meet Shubai's criteria for a personal problem. He hasn't had a heart attack, gotten divorced, sued, anything like that –'

And then Exley knew. 'We should have figured it from the beginning, Ellis. What's the worst personal crisis you can have? Not getting sick, not an accident –'

'You think he lost a kid.'

Exley nodded.

'Well, that we can find out. If you're right, it'll be time to tell Tyson.'

The mole was surprised by the silence that greeted him when he opened his front door. Janice always left the downstairs television on while she made dinner. And where was Lenny? 'Janice? Jan?'

No answer. Then he heard her in the kitchen, crying softly.

She sat at the kitchen table, fat tears rolling down her cheeks. Lenny lay at her feet, looking up hopelessly. An empty pan sat on the stove. A shrink-wrapped plastic tray of chicken breasts sat unopened in the sink, alongside uncut tomatoes and peppers.

Janice looked up as he walked into the dark room. For a moment she didn't seem to know who he was. Then she covered her face in her hands and offered a high-pitched moan, *Ooooooooooooo*, a soft dirge that sounded like a distant tornado. He went to her and rubbed her neck. More than anything, he wanted the moan to stop.

'I'm a failure, Eddie.' The words emerged in a damp, stuttery blubber. 'Such a failure.'

The mole – Keith Edward Robinson, known as Eddie only to his wife – pulled up a chair. 'Sweetie. Did something happen?'

'This woman, she and her husband are looking at the Healy place, on the corner, and she asked me about the neighborhood and the schools and I just, I just snapped –'

The cabinet where the mole kept his whiskey was within arm's reach. He grabbed a bottle of Dewar's and took a long slug, not bothering with a glass.

'Woman? What woman?'

'She came by the house. She wanted to know about the schools, Eddie. Look at us. What's happened to us?'

The mole put the bottle on the table. No more whiskey. He needed to think clearly now, and quickly. The strange part was that he really did want to comfort Janice. But first he had to figure how close they were. 'This woman, honey, who did she say she was?'

Janice lowered her hands. She seemed perplexed at the turn the conversation had taken. 'Said her name was Joanne.' She pulled a crumpled business card out of a dish on the table and handed it to him. 'Said she was a consultant.'

The mole examined it as though it were a tarot card holding the secret to his future. Which in a way it was. Ender Consulting, a Professional Corporation. Joanne Ender, MBA. Beneath the name a phone number and an e-mail address. The mole wanted to call, but whether or not Ender Consulting was real, the number would go to a professional-sounding voicemail. And if it was a trap, they'd have a pen register on the line and they'd know he called. He tucked the card into his shirt pocket. He'd check later. 'Did she ask anything about me, Jan?'

'What? No.'

'Please. I know it seems like a strange question, but think on it.'

Janice twisted her hands. 'I told you we didn't talk long. She mentioned her kids and I started to get upset, so I made her go.'

'Did she look around the house? The basement?'

'Of course not. Why?'

'Did you ask the Healys about her? If she actually went to their house?'

'She was just some lady asking about the neighborhood. What are you so worried about? Is she your girlfriend?'

'What are you talking about?'

'I'm not stupid, Eddie. Don't make things worse than they already are.'

'Sweetie. I promise I'm not having an affair with this woman.'

'Swear.'

'I swear on Mark's grave.' He'd never said anything like that before.

'Do you love me?'

'Do I love you? What kind of question is that? Yes. Of course I do.' The mole surprised himself with the words. But as he said them, he knew they were true. For too long he'd forgotten that Janice was a real person. 'Do you love me?'

As an answer, she put her arms around him and sobbed into his shoulder. 'Can we just start again, Eddie? Can't we?'

Strange to hear the question asked so baldly, the mole thought. Like they could dunk themselves in a river and wash away not just their sins but their whole messy lives. Stranger still that the answer was yes. He had the means and the motive to leave all this behind. Because maybe he was panicking, but he didn't think so.

The polygraph. Wen's defection. George not showing up this morning. Now this woman visiting. Too many coincidences too soon. Nothing definitive, but if he waited for definitive he'd wind up in a cell or a wooden box. Both Ames and Hanssen had known the walls were closing in. They just hadn't had the guts to run. Now they were spending their lives in prison.

'Jan. What if I said yes? What if we could start again?'

'I think I'd like that.'

'We'd have to change our names. Leave the country.' He couldn't believe what he was saying.

She didn't freak out. She giggled.

'I'm not kidding. We'd have to do it now.'

'What are you talking about?'

'Do you want a new life or not?' Sailing around the Caribbean, fishing, hanging out. Maybe buying a cabin somewhere, trying again to have a baby. It would be a long shot, but what wasn't?

'Yes, but –' She stopped, stood up, looked around the kitchen. 'Could we take Lenny? And where would you work? Your job is so important.'

The mole's visions of beachfront paradise faded. This wouldn't work, he saw. When she said start over, she meant that they should take a vacation, be sweeter to each other. The things normal people meant. Not dropping everything and moving to Indonesia. Anyway, he didn't have a fake passport for her, or any way to get one. And what would she think when she saw his face on TV? *The FBI has named Keith Edward Robinson, a veteran CIA employee, as a person of interest in an ongoing espionage investigation. . . . Keith Robinson, who disappeared two weeks ago, is suspected of the greatest intelligence breach in more than twenty years. . . . Authorities now say they believe fugitives Keith and Janice Robinson have fled the country. . . .*

'Got that right, sweetie.' He made himself laugh. 'And we can't leave Lenny. Guess we'll make do here.'

That night he lay beside her, listening to the suburban night, sprinklers rattling on and off to keep the lawns green. He was afraid, he couldn't pretend he wasn't, but excited too. His last night in this bed, this house, this life. He supposed he'd known all along that the path he'd taken would end this way.

He'd had sex that night with Janice, not once but twice, the first time in years. Ironic. But not surprising. Part of her knew he wasn't joking about leaving. Part of her wouldn't be surprised when she woke up and found him gone.

He rolled out of bed, quietly, sure not to wake her. He padded out of the bedroom, down the stairs, into the basement. And there he unlocked his safe and filled a canvas bag with everything he needed.

TWENTY-SIX

EAST CHINA SEA, NEAR SHANGHAI

Every day Henry Williams thanked God he'd been given the chance to command the USS *Decatur*. He knew it sounded like a cliché, but it was true. Nothing was better than controlling a five-hundred-foot-long destroyer armed with enough cruise missiles to level a city, or steaming into Bangkok or Sydney beside a carrier loaded with F-18s. The oceans were the world's last frontier, and the United States Navy ruled them, full stop.

Plus Williams found life aboard the *Decatur* satisfying in a way he would never have imagined growing up as a landlubber in Dallas. He didn't come from a Navy family. He'd chosen Annapolis mainly because the academy's basketball coach had offered him the chance to start his freshman year. But after twenty-two years in the service, Henry Williams had fallen in love with the ocean – or more precisely, with the ships that plied its waves.

The sea was unpredictable, but the *Decatur*'s rhythm was steady as a heartbeat. Its floors were scrubbed each day. Its bells chimed every half-hour. In the wardroom, the tablecloths were spotless, the silverware polished. Williams could no longer accept the chaos of real life, life on land. So his wife, Esther, had told him three years ago, when she filed for divorce. She still loved him, but she no longer understood him, she said. Williams didn't try to change her mind. In his heart he knew she was right.

Within the *Decatur*, Williams's word was law. He could call a general-quarters drill at noon or midnight. Demand that the laundry room be scrubbed until it shined – then scrubbed again for good measure. The 330 sailors and officers aboard the *Decatur* obeyed his orders without question. Nowhere in the world was the chain of command followed more closely than aboard ship.

And that discipline was vitally important now, with the *Decatur* in hostile waters, at the forward edge of the *Ronald Reagan* carrier strike group, almost in sight of the Chinese coast. Even the dimmest of the *Decatur*'s crew knew that the United States was close to war with China. The tension aboard the ship was palpable from the engine room to the bridge, and nowhere more than among the sonar operators, who had the job of listening to the ship's SQR-19 towed array. The biggest threat to the *Decatur* came from the Chinese submarines that lurked in the shallow waters off the coast.

Now Williams sat in his stateroom, poring over the classified report that contained the Navy's new estimate of the capabilities of China's subs. The Chinese had made progress, but their fish still couldn't hope to compete with the Navy's nuclear attack subs, it seemed.

A knock on his cabin door interrupted him. 'Yes?'

'Captain. Lieutenant Frederick requests permission to enter.'

'Come in, Lieutenant.'

Frederick stepped in and saluted Williams crisply. 'I'm sorry to bother you, sir. It's about the reporter.'

'What's she gotten into now?'

As a rule, the Navy was the most publicity-friendly of the services. With the War on Terror having become the focus of U.S. foreign policy, the admirals in the Pentagon felt constant pressure to demonstrate the Navy's relevance – and protect its $150 billion annual budget. After all, al Qaeda didn't exactly present a major naval threat. The clash with China had given the service its chance for a close-up, and the Navy didn't intend to miss the opportunity. Reporters and camera crews were thick as roaches aboard the *Reagan*, the *Abraham Lincoln*, and the *John C. Stennis*, the giant nuclear-powered flattops steaming toward the China coast. The *Decatur* had a reporter of its own, Jackie Wheeler. With her long dark hair and deep brown eyes, Wheeler could have been a TV babe, though she actually worked for the *Los Angeles Times*.

Williams generally disdained the media, but he didn't mind Wheeler. Pretty women were good for the crew's morale, and the *Decatur* was controlled too rigorously for her to get into much trouble. And Williams knew that being chosen to host a reporter from a national paper was something of an honor. He also knew that he hadn't been picked to host Wheeler solely because of the *Decatur*'s spotless record. He was one of only a handful of black captains in the service. But he didn't mind being trotted out this way. Like his commanders, Henry Williams knew the value of good press.

'She's been asking again about the CIC.' The Combat Information Center was the windowless room deep in the *Decatur*'s hull that functioned as the destroyer's brain. 'Says she can't write a proper profile without spending a few hours inside.'

Williams sighed. He'd already given Wheeler a tour of the CIC a few days before, and he didn't want her in there with the *Decatur* on combat footing. But he supposed he'd have to compromise to get the glowing profile he wanted.

'Okay, Lieutenant. Tell her to come over here at 2100.'

'Yes, sir.'

'Dismissed.'

An hour later, a knock roused him. 'Captain?'

2058. Wheeler had learned something about naval etiquette during her week on board. 'Ms. Wheeler? Come in.'

She stepped in tentatively. Until now Williams had been polite to Wheeler, but nothing more. He'd been busy. He'd also figured that keeping her at a distance, then slowly opening up, would make for the best profile. Up close she was younger than he had expected, barely thirty. Prettier too. 'Sit.' He indicated the couch. 'So you want another look at the CIC.'

'I won't describe anything classified, Captain. I know the rules.'

'You bored with this skimmer?'

She laughed nervously. 'Skimmer?'

'Some of us oldsters use that term to refer to any boat that floats.'

'Don't they all float?'

'Not the submarines.'

'Oh, right.' She smiled, and Williams wished for a half-second that he were twenty years younger and meeting her in a bar instead of this cabin.

'Be honest. Wish you were over on the *Reagan* with the flyboys?'

'No, the crew's treating me great.'

'Not the question I asked, but okay. Has Lieutenant Frederick told you about the man the *Decatur* is named for?' He flicked a thumb at the painting behind his desk, of a dark-haired dandy in a crimson jacket and fringed white shirt.

'No.'

Williams smiled with real pleasure. Telling this story reminded him that the Navy was different from the other services, more connected to its past. The men who had crewed the first ships in the fleet would recognize the way the *Decatur* was run – though they might not enjoy having a black man give them orders.

'You're fortunate to be aboard a ship named for a famous American captain.'

'Aren't they all?'

'I wish I could say yes, but we don't have enough famous captains to go around. Some destroyers are christened after real second-raters. Or worse, Marines.'

'Tragic,' Wheeler said, playing along.

'Behind me is Commodore Stephen Decatur. During the War of 1812, he destroyed two British vessels. We won't mention the third battle, the one he lost. After the war, he sailed to North Africa and shook down the Libyans. Along the way, he got famous for a line Machiavelli would have appreciated. "In her intercourse with foreign nations, may she always be in the right; but our country, right or wrong!" Sort of a "Better dead than red" for the nineteenth century.'

'I hope you don't throw me overboard, but I'd say that kind of thinking has gotten us in a lot of trouble the last few years. We need more questioning of authority, not less.'

'You reporters have that luxury. Not us. Once the order comes, we follow it.'

'So what happened to Decatur?'

'He died in 1820. A duel.'

'I can't say I'm surprised. Who was on the other side?'

'A retired captain named James Barron. Thing is, Barron couldn't see all that well – the contemporary accounts say that Decatur could have killed him easily. But the good commodore wanted to be sporting. He limited the duel to eight paces and said he wouldn't shoot to kill. So Barron blew out Decatur's stomach, and he died a few hours later. You know the lesson I take from that story?'

'Duels are dumb. And dangerous.'

'War's no game. Ships like this are deceiving. We're so big that maybe we seem unsinkable. But put a deep enough hole in the hull and we'll go down fast. I don't intend to let that happen to my crew.'

'Can I quote you on that?'

'Of course. And be at the CIC at 1100 tomorrow. You can stay all day.'

'Thanks, Captain.'

Just then Williams's phone rang. 'Yes?'

'Skipper, you might want to get down here.' The *Decatur*'s TAO, tactical action officer, was calling from the Combat Information Center. 'We have a situation.'

'Be there in five.' Williams cradled the receiver.

'What was that?' Jackie said.

'Looks like we may get some action sooner than I thought.'

'Can I –'

Williams shook his head. 'Sorry, Ms. Wheeler. No tour tonight.'

If the *Decatur*'s four giant turbine engines, capable of 100,000 horsepower at full throttle, were its heart, the Combat Information Center was its brain. The CIC was a well-lit room, fifty feet long, forty wide, in the center of the ship, equally protected from missiles and torpedoes. The windowless space looked like an air traffic control center at rush hour. Dozens of pasty-faced men and women huddled over blinking consoles that pulled in information from the *Decatur*'s radar and sonar systems, as well as the E-2 Hawkeye overhead. Williams sat near the front of the room, facing away from the chaos and toward the big, bright blue flat-panel screens that offered an integrated view of the threats facing the *Decatur* from sea, air, and land.

As an Arleigh Burke-class destroyer, the *Decatur* came equipped with an Aegis combat system, which linked the ship's radar and sonar systems with its missile batteries. The Aegis could simultaneously track scores of planes and ships, labeling each as hostile, friendly, or unknown. In case of open war, the system could be put on full automatic mode, taking control of all the ship's weapons. Besides its cruise missiles, the *Decatur* carried surface-to-air missiles, antiship missiles, antisubmarine rockets and torpedoes, an artillery launcher, and a pair of 20-millimeter heavy machine guns for close-in defense, should all else fail. With the Aegis on full automatic, the *Decatur* could probably blockade Shanghai all by itself.

But the Aegis wasn't on full automatic. This wasn't open war. And Williams didn't want to overreact to provocations and bluffs aimed at tricking him into firing the first shot. Under the rules of engagement governing this mission, Willams didn't have to wait until he'd been acted upon before firing. He could launch first if he believed the Chinese were about to attack. 'The commanding officer is responsible for defending his ship from attack or the *imminent threat* of attack,' the rules read.

Williams almost wished the orders were stricter. Under these rules, if the Chinese hit the *Decatur* with a first strike, he'd face terrible second-guessing about his decision not to launch first. And the Chinese had turned increasingly aggressive as the *Decatur* closed on their coast.

For a day, two Chinese frigates had shadowed the ship. Now, with the *Decatur* barely thirty miles from Shanghai, two more frigates had moved in. They were Jianwei-class, among the more modern ships in the Chinese fleet. Still, they were only one-quarter the size of the *Decatur*. Williams could destroy them easily, especially with the help of the F/A-18s from the *Reagan* circling overhead, as the Chinese surely knew.

In other words, the frigates weren't there to fight. Still, Williams didn't want to give them an excuse. Over the last few hours, he had turned south and slowed to fifteen knots. The *Decatur* was now heading roughly parallel to the coast, not closing on it. Still, the Chinese boats had ignored repeated warnings from the *Decatur* to back off.

Making matters worse, the *Decatur* was close to the Shanghai shipping lanes, forcing it to navigate around freighters and oil tankers. And in the last few hours, civilian Chinese boats had shown up. Motorboats, fishing vessels, even a couple of sailboats, all flying the

Chinese flag and carrying signs in Chinese and English: 'Hegemonists out of East China Sea!' 'Taiwan and China! One people, one nation!' 'US Navy go home!'

Williams thought that being ordered this close to the coast was unnecessarily provocative. But provocation seemed to be the point. Two days before, Rear Admiral Jason Lee, the commander of the *Reagan*, had told Williams and the other captains in the carrier's battle group that the White House wanted to send the Chinese government a stern message about the risks a deal with Iran would bring.

'We're not backing down this time. Up close and personal, that's what the big man wants. Make them blink. Our intel says that's the right move. And if that's what the big man wants, that's what he gets. Now, I don't want you to do anything rash, but if you need to protect your ships, no one's going to second-guess you. We've got three flattops out here, we can turn their navy into scrap in about twenty minutes, and we're not backing down. Understood?'

No one said anything when Lee was finished.

But there were good tactical reasons to stay farther offshore, Williams thought. Carrier battle groups were lethal on the open ocean, so-called blue-water combat. The *Reagan*'s jets could destroy enemy aircraft and ships long before the hostile boats got close, and the nuclear attack subs that served as its escorts were faster and had sonar superior to that of the diesel subs most other fleets used.

But this close to shore, the carrier group's advantages shrank. First off, the *Reagan*'s jets no longer completely controlled the air. Land-based aircraft could take off from Chinese bases and be on top of the

Decatur in minutes. Making matters worse, with hundreds of civilian planes taking off from Shanghai's airports every day, even the Aegis system had a hard time tracking all the traffic in the air.

China's submarines were also a serious threat in these shallow waters. The diesel-electric subs that made up the Chinese fleet could operate almost silently, and they didn't have to worry about being outrun by the faster U.S. subs so close to shore. They hardly needed to move at all – the American fleet was coming to them.

Add the tactical problems to the strategic uncertainty, and Williams knew he'd been given a difficult job. Now the Chinese seemed to want to bring matters to a head, much sooner than Williams had expected.

Williams took his seat at the center console, beside Lieutenant (j.g.) Stan Umsle, his tactical action officer, a bespectacled man with a Ph.D. in engineering from Purdue. 'Lieutenant, talk to me.'

'Didn't want to bother you, sir, but we have two issues. First off, there's one fishing boat aft and three starboard running steadily closer to us. Looks like they're coordinating their movements with the frigates. In the last half-hour they've gone from two thousand yards to eleven hundred' – just over a half-mile away.

'Any weapons?'

'None we can see. We've signaled and radioed them to leave, sir. Told them they're subject to imminent defensive action if they come any closer.'

'In English.'

'Yes, sir.' Umsle didn't have to tell Williams that no one on the *Decatur* spoke Chinese. Another reason the destroyer ought to back off a little, Williams thought.

'All right. If they get to five hundred yards, splash

them with the Phalanx for five seconds. Warning shots only. No contact. And let's don't hit the frigates by mistake.' Williams hoped the *Decatur* could scare off the fishing boats with its machine guns, which fired depleted-uranium shells that could cut the trawlers apart.

'Yes, sir.'

'Also let's throttle up to thirty knots, get some distance from those frigates.'

'That's the second problem, sir. There's a red' – enemy – 'destroyer in our path.' Umsle pointed to the Aegis display, where a red blip was moving toward the *Decatur*. 'Twenty NMs' – nautical miles – 'to our south, closing at twenty-five knots. It's painted us twice already.' Meaning that the enemy destroyer had hit the *Decatur* with radar, possibly in preparation for a missile launch.

'Do we have positive identification?'

'Believe it's one of their Luhas, sir. And the Hawkeye just picked up emissions from another hostile. Seventy NMs south.' The radar plane overhead could track a far larger area than the *Decatur*'s radar. 'The Hawkeye believes it may be a Sovremenny-class boat.'

'We need visual confirmation on that ASAP. Tell the *Reagan*.'

'Yes, sir.'

Since the late 1990s, China had bought four Sovremenny-class destroyers from Russia. The Sovremennys were the only surface ship in China's fleet that posed a serious threat to the *Decatur*. They carried supersonic antiship missiles with a range of a hundred miles and a nasty radar guidance system. Though the missiles could be detected by infrared sensors because of the massive heat they generated, they were nearly impossible to intercept, because of their speed and the fact that they flew less than fifty feet above the water's surface. Worse, they carried a 660-pound warhead, big enough to cripple the *Decatur*.

Williams turned to his communications officer. 'Get me Admiral Lee.' If he was going to war, he wanted his boss to know. Meanwhile, backing off seemed prudent. He looked at Umsle. 'Take us to twenty knots and a heading of one-fifty' – a southeast heading, away from the Chinese coast.

'What about the trawlers? We'll be on top of them.'

'Then they better get out of our way.' Williams preferred to pick a fight with an unarmed trawler rather than a Chinese destroyer. 'Get ready to splash them with the Phalanxes. I want them to know we're serious.'

'Captain,' his coms officer said, 'I have the *Reagan*.' Williams picked up.

'Captain Williams.' The admiral spoke softly but with absolute authority, as befitted the commander of a 102,000-ton aircraft carrier. 'Looks like the Chinese don't want to grant you shore leave.'

'I could use more air support, Admiral.'

'It's already happening.'

'Sir, request permission to pull back to the *Lake Champlain*.' The *Lake Champlain*, a guided-missile cruiser, was fifty miles northeast, seventy-five miles offshore.

'Understand your concerns, but that would send the wrong signal, Captain. Our intel's clear on this.'

Easy for you to say in your floating castle, Williams thought. 'Yes, sir,' he said aloud. 'In that case, I'm going to lose these boats on top of me, open up some space, come back around for another look.'

'Sir, Captain, we've just fired warning shots at the trawlers –' This was Umsle, his voice rising. Williams waved a hand. *Not now.*

'Affirmative, Captain,' the admiral said in his ear. 'We'll have four more eighteens' – F/A-18 Super Hornet attack jets – 'in the air for you by 2130.'

'Thank you, sir.' *Click.* At least he'd gotten approval, in a backhanded way, to pull back a few miles, buy some time.

'Lieutenant, I want us at twenty-five knots, heading of sixty.' A sixty-degree heading was northeast, a hard left turn from the *Decatur*'s current path.

'Sir, the trawlers –'

Williams didn't want to hear about the fishing boats anymore. He had bigger worries.

'We've warned them, Lieutenant. Every way we know how. It's time for them to make way. Now! Hard over.'

The collision came thirty seconds later.

In the Combat Information Center, men skidded sideways. Manuals and pens and anything else not nailed down spilled to the floor. On the bridge, Wheeler, the *Los Angeles Times* reporter, banged her knee hard enough to leave it black-and-blue, but she hardly cared. She'd have the lead story in tomorrow's paper, she knew.

The sailors and officers on the bridge of the *Decatur* insisted afterward that the trawler refused to move out of the *Decatur*'s way, as if daring the destroyer to run it down. The Chinese disagreed vehemently, saying that the *Decatur* had deliberately hit the little trawler, which weighed eighty tons, compared with the *Decatur*'s eight thousand. Jackie, who was as close to a neutral observer as anyone who saw the collision, wasn't entirely sure what had happened. Both boats seemed to expect the other to turn away.

But neither did, and so the destroyer's prow tore the little fishing boat nearly in half, slicing neatly through a banner that read 'China Will Not Bow to America!' Besides its usual crew of ten, the boat contained another twenty-four passengers, mostly college students who had come out to protest – and snap some souvenir photographs of the destroyer. Only five people died in the collision, but most of the students couldn't swim. Seventeen drowned afterward.

The *Decatur* slowed down after the collison, but before it could put any rescue boats in the water, one of the Chinese frigates fired warning shots at it. After consulting with Admiral Lee, Williams decided to sail away. The Chinese boats were moving quickly to the trawler, and staying around might inflame the situation. Later, the *Decatur*'s decision not to stop would add to the controversy.

Aside from a few bumps and bruises, no one aboard the *Decatur* was hurt. But in the days that followed, no one would say the United States escaped the collision unscathed.

TWENTY-SEVEN

Even with Tyson's help and the written approval of the agency's general counsel, Exley needed almost a full day to get the agency's health insurance records for Keith Robinson. Those showed that Robinson's wife, Janice, had given birth to a boy, Mark, a decade before. Cross-checking Mark's date of birth against Social Security death records revealed the boy had died eight years earlier, about the time the mole first contacted the Chinese, according to Wen Shubai's timetable.

And so Exley and Shafer decided it was time to talk to Robinson. 'We don't have to ask about the dead kid,' Shafer said. 'He might get upset.'

'Mr. Tact. Thank God you're here to help. Of course we're not mentioning his son. That failed poly gives us plenty of reason to interview him.'

But when Exley called Robinson's office early Friday evening, he didn't answer. His voicemail said he was out sick. With a couple of calls, Exley tracked down an admin on the China desk who told Exley that Robinson had seemed fine the day before.

In the next office over, Wells was catching up on the mole investigation, poring over the transcripts of

Shubai's interview. He had put aside for now his efforts to find out who was paying Pierre Kowalski to support the Taliban. Without account numbers, the Treasury Department couldn't trace the payments from Macao that Kowalski had admitted getting. And the CIA's dossier on Kowalski offered no clues to the mysterious North Korean that Kowalski had mentioned – though the file had enough detail about Kowalski to infuriate Wells.

Kowalski has brokered weapons sales of $100 million or more for dozens of sovereign nations and paramilitary organizations, including Angola, Armenia, China, Congo, FARC (Revolutionary Armed Forces of Colombia), Indonesia, Libya, Nigeria, Poland, Russia, Saudi Arabia, and Yemen.

This list should not be considered conclusive. Kowalski often operates through intermediaries in cases where he hopes to sell weapons to both sides in a conflict (i.e., Chad and Sudan). His commission ranges from 2 percent, in cases where he is merely negotiating a price and package of weapons, to 25 percent when he acts as a third-party dealer. Kowalski has earned about $1 billion since 2000, although the exact amount is unknown.

One billion. A thousand million. Maybe on Wall Street or in Congress that number was just another day at the office. But Wells couldn't get his head around it. In Pakistan, he'd seen kids die from cholera because their parents couldn't afford antibiotics that cost a few bucks.

The rest of the dossier detailed Kowalski's personal history. Not surprisingly, he had never served in the military. As far as Wells could tell, he had never been near a battlefield, never seen what his mines and AK-47s and mortars did to the human body. He preferred the bodies in his vicinity to be young and blonde, and he could afford what he liked. Twice divorced, he'd acquired a taste for second-tier Russian models, who cost more up front than a wife but didn't rate alimony on their way out. More than ever, Wells regretted not having put a bullet between Kowalski's eyes back in the Hamptons.

After reading the dossier, Wells had paid a visit to the analyst who'd written it, Sam Tarks, a career officer in the agency's arms control/nonproliferation unit.

'Pierre Kowalski? Nasty man.'

'I'm looking for anything that might have been too juicy to make it into the dossier,' Wells said. 'Personal or business.'

'His personal life is about what you'd expect. He's got a yacht called the *Ares*. Lots of coke, lots of Eurotrash. Good times had by all.'

'Ares like the Greek god of war?'

'The one and only. But he doesn't have any serious glitches as far as we know. I mean he's not a pedophile or a sadist or anything. He likes to party is all.'

'How about the business side? Is there any country he's especially close to? The Russians, say?' Wells still didn't think the Russians would have helped the Taliban, but anything was possible.

'Not particularly. He sells mostly Russian stuff, but he keeps them at arm's length. Smart man. And he makes sure to keep his business far from Zurich. Also smart. Pays enough in taxes to keep the Swiss happy and keeps his money in local banks, mainly UBS.'

'Did he ever work for U.S. companies?'

Tarks nodded. 'Lots of folks wish he still would. The Indian Air Force is looking at a huge order, close to a hundred thirty planes, and the French have hired him to convince the Indians to go with the Mirage' – a French-made fighter jet – 'and not the F-16. That would be a very big sale. North of five billion. If we don't get it, some Lockheed lobbyists' – Lockheed Martin manu-factured the F-16 – 'will tell the Armed Services Committee it's because we don't have guys like Kowalski on our team. They'll say it quietly, but they'll say it.'

'Wonderful world,' Wells said. 'Could you see him selling weapons to the Taliban?'

'That'd be pushing it, even for him. He'd know we wouldn't be happy if we found out. To put it mildly.'

'But if the money was right, and he thought he could get away with it?'

'Under those circumstances? I'd say there's nothing he wouldn't do.'

Wells's last conversation with Ed Graften, the East Hampton police chief, had been more gratifying. After the East Hampton police freed Kowalski, he refused to answer any questions. He had no idea who had attacked him and his guards, he said.

'Boys will be boys. Why don't you ask them? I was in my bedroom.'

'What about the tape, the handcuffs?' the lead cop on the scene said.

'A new weight-loss method recommended by my physician. With my mouth taped shut, I cannot eat.'

'Sounds like you need a new doctor.'

'I have already lost five pounds,' Kowalski said, sucking in his gut in a show of dignity. 'Now, I appreciate your leaving my property so I can return to bed.'

The unconscious guards were taken to Southampton Hospital. By morning, they were stirring. All four claimed they had no memory of what had happened. They refused to answer questions and demanded to speak to Kowalski's lawyers. Since they appeared to be victims, not perpetrators, the cops had no choice but to let them go. They were asked to return for interviews later.

But they never showed up. And when the police went to Two Mile Hollow Road to find them, they discovered the mansion was empty. Flight records showed that Kowalski's Gulfstream had flown out of the East Hampton airport less than eight hours after Wells's courtesy call. According to the flight plan they'd filed before takeoff, the jet was bound for Miami – which probably meant it had wound up in the Dominican Republic or Barbados or Venezuela. In any case, Kowalski and his men were gone.

'Just thought you might like to know he'd flown the coop. My guys said he was a very cool customer,' the chief said. 'Hardly complained when that tape came off him.'

'He is smooth.'

'A weight-loss program. Have to give him credit for coming up with that.' Graften chuckled. 'Did you get what you needed?'

'Thanks for the help, chief. If you hear anything more, let me know.'

'Will do.' *Click.*

Wells hoped he was only temporarily stalled on
Kowalski, although in truth he wasn't sure where to
look next. The trail seemed to have dead-ended. So
he'd decided to catch up on the mole investigation. But
as he read over the personnel reports that Exley and
Shafer had put together, Wells wasn't convinced that
Exley's hunch about Keith Robinson made sense. Then
again, he hadn't seen the guy's house or his wife.

A rap on his door startled him. Exley. 'Want to go for
a drive?'

When they got to the Robinson house, Exley was glad
she'd asked Wells to come. The lights in the house were
off, but through the windows Exley saw the television
in the den flashing.

'Sure she's home?' Wells said. He was standing
beside the door, hidden against the wall of the house.

'She's home.' Exley knocked again. Finally she
heard footsteps. Janice pulled open the door, glassy-
eyed, a steak knife wavering in her hand.

'You,' she said. She jabbed the knife in Exley's
direction. She seemed more likely to drop it on her foot
than do any serious damage, Exley thought. Janice took
a tiny step forward, and Wells reached out his big right
arm and twisted her wrist until the knife clattered down.
Janice's mouth opened and closed in wordless drunken
confusion as Wells tossed the knife aside.

Exley knew Wells was just making sure they
wouldn't get hurt, but somehow she was angry at the
almost robotic ease with which he'd disarmed this
pathetic woman. Forget breaking a sweat. Wells hadn't
even blinked. She realized something about him then,
something she should have known all along. For all the

316

emotional weight Wells carried, the thought of death hardly scared him. On some unconscious level he must feel immortal, Exley thought. He probably couldn't imagine losing a fight, couldn't imagine anyone was stronger or faster than he was. Exley had seen firsthand what he could do in close combat. She wondered what it would be like to have such physical confidence. She'd never know. Women never got to feel that way. No wonder Wells was addicted to action.

Janice staggered forward, tripping over her feet. Wells put a hand on her arm and held her up. Her eyes flicked helplessly between Wells and Exley.

'You can't –' she said softly.

'Ma'am,' Wells said. 'We're sorry, but can we talk to you inside? Please.'

Janice's face crumpled on itself like a leaky balloon. She didn't answer, just stepped into the yard and stared at the sky. The golden retriever stood behind her in the doorway, tail down.

Finally she waved them inside. 'What difference does it make anyway?' she said. 'Wait in the kitchen.' She wandered upstairs as Wells watched, a hand near the Makarov he had tucked into his shoulder holster before they left the office. But they had nothing to worry about, Exley thought. Janice was harmless now. Sure enough, her hands were empty when she reappeared. She seemed to have gone upstairs mainly to fix herself up. She'd pulled her hair back into a ponytail and fixed her makeup.

'I thought maybe when you showed up again that you were his girlfriend. But you're not.'

'Your husband's girlfriend? No, I'm not.'

'Because I know he's got a girlfriend, and he got all nervous when I told him you came by. He wanted to know what you wanted. Then when I woke up this morning, he was gone.'

'You know where?'

'Haven't seen him or that Acura of his since last night. He hasn't called neither, and his phone's turned off.' Janice focused her wobbly attention on Exley. 'But anyway I see you're not his girlfriend. He likes 'em younger than you. And prettier. You from the agency?'

'Yes, ma'am,' Wells said. 'We are.' He passed her his identification card, the one with his real name. Janice held it close to her face, her eyes flicking between the identification and Wells.

'I don't believe it, but I guess I do,' she said. 'Is Keith in trouble?'

'We're trying to find out,' Exley said. 'He tell you where he was going?'

'As I just recounted' – Janice sat up straight as she used the half-dollar word – 'he didn't even say he was leaving, much less where. He was just gone when I woke up, and his favorite clothes too.'

'Did he take anything else?'

'I don't rightly know. Maybe some stuff from the basement. He spends a lot of time down there. Last night he was saying strange stuff, like what would I think if we left the country and started over somewhere else.'

'Do you mind if we take a look?' Wells said. 'In the basement?'

'I guess not. It's locked, though. And I can't find the key. I don't know if he took it or what.'

'I can take care of that.' Wells reached into his jacket for his pistol.

Janice followed them downstairs, chattering. She'd turned from self-pitying to wheedling, actively seeking

318

their approval, an alcohol-fueled mood swing. Exley was not surprised to see that she was devoting her attention to Wells. For his part, Wells was hardly listening as he looked around the basement. The place was littered with bottles of bourbon and empty cigarette packs and stank like the morning after a weeklong party. Wells popped open the DVD player and extracted a disk titled *Girl-n-Girl 3: The Experiment*.

Janice wiggled her eyebrows at Wells when she saw the disk. 'He never tried that with me.'

Exley wanted to slap this drunk woman and tell her to stop embarrassing herself. Instead, she smiled. 'Before he left, did Keith say where the two of you might end up?'

Janice plumped down on the couch and put a finger in her mouth like a misbehaving four-year-old. 'Not that I recall. No.'

'Anything about Asia? China?'

'He didn't like the Chinese much. Called them slant-eyes and Chinkydinks and said they couldn't be trusted.'

'Did he ever bring anyone over to the house? I mean, anyone unusual, somebody he didn't identify?'

Janice reached for an open bottle of wine on the table. She poured the contents into a dirty glass and took a long swallow. 'No. We don't have too many friends, not since we moved here, not since our son died.'

'Your son –'

But then Wells called out from the bathroom. 'Jenny. You need to see this.'

Janice followed, and they crowded into the bathroom, staring at the black safe.

'Any idea of the combination?' Wells said to Janice.

'I didn't even know it was there,' Janice said. 'I swear.'

'We can call Tyson, get someone over here to get it open,' Wells said. 'Not that it matters, because it's gonna be empty.'

Janice pursed her lips, a look Exley recognized. She'd be crying again soon. All this was too much for her.

'Come on, let's go in the other room.' Exley led Janice back to the couch. 'Did Keith keep money around? Did it seem like you were spending more than his salary?'

'He never said much about our finances. Gave me a couple thousand a month for expenses. If I ever wanted a dress or something, he was generous. We had an old-fashioned marriage, I guess you'd say. He made the money, I kept the house.'

'Did you ever see any mail from banks you didn't recognize? Anything from outside the United States?'

'Once or twice. A few years ago. Then it stopped. I think he had a post office box. He was so secretive.' Janice tipped the wine bottle to her mouth. 'I just attributed it to his having a girlfriend. He liked strippers. I pretended I didn't know, but of course I did.'

'Men are pigs.' Exley patted her hand. A mistake. Janice flinched.

'What would you know about it? You lied to me yesterday. You're not even married.' She began to cry, her tears cutting through the mascara she'd just applied, sending black streaks down her cheeks. She grabbed a dirty paper towel and dabbed at her face.

'I was. Married.' Exley didn't know why she felt the need to defend herself.

'Divorced, huh? Just like I'm gonna be.' Janice stood. 'God. Look at this place. Look at my life.' She stumbled toward the stairs. 'You do what you have to do. You're going to anyway. But leave me alone.'

As Janice pulled herself up the stairs, Exley put her head in her hands. They had to get moving, get the word out to the FBI and Homeland Security, add Robinson's Acura to police watch lists, check his name against passenger manifests, review airport security cameras to see if they could match his face with whatever name he was using these days, maybe even get the media involved. But it wouldn't matter. With an eighteen-hour head start and a few thousand bucks, Keith Robinson could be anywhere. He could have driven to Atlanta and then flown to Panama City, New York, and then Istanbul, Chicago, and then Bangkok. They'd find him eventually, but eventually would be too late.

She felt Wells's hand on her shoulder. 'What's wrong, Jenny?'

'It's my fault. I flushed him.'

Wells pulled her up. 'That's crap and you know it. He was all set to run. You're the reason we might find him. Let's get Janice to give us something in writing –'

'She doesn't want to talk anymore.'

'A couple sentences, so no one can say later we didn't have permission to be here. And then let's start making calls.'

Seven hours later, Exley, Shafer, Tyson, and Wells sat in the library of Tyson's house in Falls Church, a windowless square room that Tyson had assured them was as secure as any at Langley. Books about spying, fiction and non-, filled the shelves, from classics like *The Secret Agent* and *The Thirty-nine Steps* to Tom

321

Clancy's massive hardcovers. Wells and Exley shared a love seat, and Exley allowed her hand to rest companionably on Wells's leg. Two silky Persian cats slept in the corner. Tyson just needed a cigar and a glass of whiskey to complete the picture of the gentleman at ease, Wells thought. But the calm in the room was deceptive.

A few miles east, in Langley, an FBI/CIA task force was tearing up Keith Robinson's office, trying to figure out exactly what he'd stolen over the years, what databases he'd accessed, what files he'd copied, what operations and spies he'd destroyed. Of course, if Robinson showed up the next morning, the agents in his office would have some explaining to do. But everyone agreed the chances of that happening were approximately zero.

'Guess we found our mole,' Tyson said. 'Or rather, he found us.' He didn't smile. 'This is as bad as it gets. He had almost total access to our East Asian ops. Everyone in China is blown. North Korea too, and maybe even Japan and India. The only place that's really insulated is the GWOT' – the global War on Terror, the U.S. fight against al Qaeda. 'China's peripheral to that, so people might have wondered if he asked too many questions.'

'Anyway, I don't think that his friends in Beijing care much about Osama bin Laden,' Shafer said.

'We don't know *what* they care about,' Tyson said. 'We've got no sources left. Aside from our friend Wen Shubai, whose advice has been less than perfect. Anyway what happened yesterday' – the collision between the *Decatur* and the fishing trawler – 'has changed things so much that I'm not sure anyone on the other side of the river' – in the White House – 'cares anymore what Wen thinks. Confrontation hasn't worked so far.'

'So what now?' Wells said.

Tyson tapped on his desk, disturbing the cats. They blinked sleepily, rearranged themselves, and then lay back down. 'What do the Chinese want? Why did they sign that deal with Iran? Why provoke us? It's never made sense from the beginning. That's what we have to know.'

Wells slumped in a love seat. He was sick of Tyson's grandstanding. 'And how do you propose that we four get the answer, George? Last I checked, our collective experience in China added up to a big fat zero.'

'And now I need to come clean with you. I believe, I hope, we have one live source left in the People's Republic.'

In the silence that followed, Wells glanced at Exley and Shafer. They looked as surprised as he felt.

'A couple years after Tiananmen, a PLA colonel reached out to us. He was an evangelical Christian, a silent convert. They're some of our best sources. He gave us good stuff during the nineties. But he went dark when Robinson approached the Chinese. Completely dark. At the time, we couldn't understand why. Now it seems obvious. He was keeping his head down so Robinson couldn't out him.'

'Any idea why he didn't just tell us about Robinson?'

'Maybe he didn't know enough about Robinson's identity to give him up. Or maybe it was the other way. Maybe so few people knew about Robinson that our guy figured he'd compromise himself if he gave Robinson up. Anyway, one day he missed a meeting. After that, we never saw him again. Didn't respond to any of our signals.'

'But he wasn't arrested,' Exley said.

'No. He's still around. In fact, he's senior enough that he gets into the papers over there every so often. His name's Cao Se.'

'Still. He could be doubled. Robinson could have given him up along the way.'

'We ran him out of Australia rather than China. Not for any great reason. Just that he initially found us at a military conference in Sydney. Then later he wouldn't do business with any other office.'

'You really think he's protected himself?' Shafer said.

'It's possible. By luck or design.' Tyson huffed and settled back down in his chair. 'I think if they'd doubled him he would have reached out a few years back. He would have been another thread in the web they spun for us. Instead he just disappeared.'

'So he's been gone ten years?'

'Until last week. A visa applicant in Beijing dropped off a letter with the right codes. Amazing but true, the consular officers recognized it and passed it to our head of station. Cao wants a meeting. He says that he would, quote, "prefer an officer who has never worked in East Asia." Hard to argue with that.'

Shafer jumped to his feet. 'I know where you're going with this, George. And I want to say for the record it stinks.'

'Where's he going?' Wells said.

'He wants you to go over there, make contact with this general.'

Tyson nodded.

'Why don't you send somebody two years out of school, somebody who's not in their files?' Wells said.

324

'At this point we have no idea who's in their files,' Tyson said. 'Like Ellis said, the Chinese don't care about bin Laden. What you did in Times Square was a sideshow as far as they're concerned. And Cao needs to know we care enough to send somebody important. Like it or not, you're in that category.'

'Let me add another reason,' Shafer said. 'Vinny Duto can't stand you and wouldn't mind you spending the rest of your life in a Chinese jail. This is his big chance to get rid of you. If it works, great. If not, bye-bye.' Shafer looked to Tyson. '*Et tu*, Georgie? Still embarrassed you were on the wrong side last year? Or just looking for new and exciting ways to kiss Vinny's ass?'

'That's nonsense, Ellis. This is up to John. If he doesn't want to go, there'll be no hard feelings –'

'I'm not finished, George.' Shafer turned toward Wells. 'He knows you're too hardheaded to turn this down, even though we can't save you if this is a trap. You know that, John. They may not even lock you up. Considering the way things are right now, they may just shoot you.'

Tyson pushed himself to his feet. 'Ellis, the PLA has no reason to set up such an elaborate sting at this moment. They're more worried whether we're going to bomb Shanghai. I think this approach is genuine, and I want John to go because he gives us the best chance of reaching Cao. No other reason.'

'Yeah, he's a great choice, considering *he doesn't even speak Chinese.*' Shafer stepped toward the desk and leaned over Tyson. He looked like a terrier about to launch himself at a bulldog. 'What exactly do you think Cao's going to tell us? You think he's gonna give us their launch codes so we can nuke Shanghai and not worry about them retaliating? What we ought to do is pull the Navy back to Hawaii and let things settle down.'

'Maybe. And maybe then the PLA will think they have carte blanche to invade Taiwan. The point is we don't know what they want, what they're thinking. Now somebody on their side, somebody who *knows*, wants to tell us.'

'Let him defect, then, if he's so damn important.'

'He's making the rules, Ellis, not us. And what he wants is a meeting, his terms, his turf. If John doesn't want to go, that's fine. I'll find someone else.'

'One last question, George. Did you and Duto discuss this little plan?'

'Why wouldn't we?'

'I rest my case.'

'I'd like to say something,' Wells said.

Exley folded her hands together in an unconscious prayer.

'I'll go.'

Exley and Shafer spoke simultaneously.

Shafer: 'Don't do this –'

Exley: 'No, John –'

'I'll go.'

Part 4

TWENTY-EIGHT

Every morning more protesters showed up in Tiananmen Square: peasants stooped by age and work, university students, factory hands, even office workers. They came on bicycles and buses that dropped them by the McDonald's at the south end of the square. They carried bags of fruit and dumplings so they could stay all day. Each evening they emptied out, as thousands of police officers watched. And all day, under the hazy sky, they sang and chanted and waved banners:

'The will of the people is strong!'

'One people, one China!'

'Hegemonists apologize! No more American war crimes!'

'U.S. out of China Sea! China will never forget the twenty-two murdered martyrs!'

A few of the sloganeers even showed sly humor:

'1.5 billion Chinese can't be wrong.'

'The American century is over! The Chinese millennium begins today!'

The first morning after the *Decatur* sank the fishing trawler, 50,000 people came to Tiananmen. Two days later, the Beijing police estimated the crowd at 150,000. Similar crowds filled People's Park in Shanghai,

329

Yuexiu Park in Guangzhou, and the central squares in the rest of China's metropolises.

On the fifth day, with the Beijing police estimating the crowd in Tiananmen at a quarter-million, Li Ping took a helicopter over the square and looked down on the people, his people. They weren't yet close to filling the square – Tiananmen could hold a million or more – but even so Li's heart swelled at the sight.

What a change from 1989, the last time Tiananmen had been so full, Li thought. Then the people had been angry at their leaders. Not this time. The peasants were glad to have an officially sanctioned outlet for their fury at being left behind. The middle class wanted to show the world that China could no longer be cowed. The sinking of the trawler had brought them together. *Li* had brought them together. This outpouring was the living emblem of his will. Soon he would replace Zhang as the unofficial leader of the Standing Committee. Two of the liberals on the committee had already reached out to him, hinting they would support him if he promised not to push them off the committee when he took charge.

Then, at the next Party Congress, he'd take over from Xu as the Party's general secretary. It was time for the old man to retire. Li would be the head of the army *and* the Party, the most powerful leader since Mao. He would remake China, making sure ordinary people shared in its prosperity, while building up the armed forces. No longer would the United States be the world's only superpower. This was China's destiny, and his own. Around him the great city rose in every direction, Beijing's apartment buildings and office towers stretching through the haze, traffic thick on the ring roads and boulevards, and Li thought: *Mine.* All this. *Mine.*

But first he needed to press his advantage. The people filling the square beneath him were crucial to his next step toward power. Zhang, that weakling, wouldn't like his new proposal. But Li believed that old man Xu saw the situation the same way that he did, though the general secretary was too canny to promise his support explicitly. Li waved to the crowds below – not that they could recognize him – and checked his watch. 11:18. Good. A lucky time. He tapped his pilot on the shoulder and they swung back to the landing pad inside Zhongnanhai.

The meeting began two hours later, in the banquet hall in Huairentang, the Palace Steeped in Compassion. The foreign minister spoke first, discussing the international reaction to the sinking. The world had sided with China. The United Nations had voted to condemn the United States for its 'unprovoked aggression against a civilian boat.' Even America's closest allies, like Britain and Poland, agreed that the United States had overstepped its bounds and provoked the confrontation.

'We must remember, if a Chinese warship rammed an American boat near New York, the American anger would be unsurpassed,' the French prime minister said. The United States had refused to apologize for the collision, arguing that it had happened in international waters and the *Decatur* had warned the trawlers away. In the days since the accident, the *Decatur* had pulled back two hundred miles off the coast, but other American warships had taken its place.

'The world has seen the violence of the Americans,' the foreign minister said. 'Our position is secure. Of course, if we act rashly, we may lose support.'

'Thank you, Foreign Minister,' Xu said. 'Now, Minister Li.'

'The People's Liberation Army is prepared to carry out the will of the Standing Committee, General Secretary. Whatever we decide.'

'And what is your view of the correct action?'

'We must punish the hegemonist aggression.'

'But what about the risks?' This from Zhang. Li looked around the room, as if the interruption were hardly worth answering.

'Do you know why the Mongols burst through our walls eight hundred years ago, Comrade Zhang?'

'I'm not a general, Comrade Li. I imagine their troops were strong, like the Americans.'

'Wrong. They defeated us because we let them. And then we blamed them for being stronger than we were. The people want us to show our strength. They remember what the Americans did in Yugoslavia.' In 1999, American jets had bombed the Chinese embassy in Belgrade, killing three Chinese. The United States had always insisted the bombing was accidental, but many Chinese didn't accept that explanation. 'The people are tired of excuses from the hegemonists. They want us to act.'

'And when the Americans counterattack, when they destroy our navy, what will the people say then?'

'The Americans won't attack us, Comrade Zhang. The world won't allow it.'

'Perhaps the world won't stop it.'

'We will push them once more, just once, and then give them a way out.'

'What do you mean, push them? Speak clearly now.'

The moment he'd been working toward for all these

months had arrived, Li knew. He explained his plan. When he was finished, the room was silent.

'And you think the Americans won't respond.'

'As long as they understand that we don't intend to invade Taiwan, they'll accept our response as justified. They know they've overstepped their bounds even if they won't admit it. Besides, our action will give them a new respect for our capabilities.'

Zhang pounded a fist against the table. 'Comrade Li, go back to your tanks and leave strategy to wiser men. We've gone up the mountain twice now, first with the agreement with Iran and then with our missile tests. Now you want us to go up a third time. We will surely encounter the tiger.'

'The Americans aren't the tiger. Our people are the tiger, Minister Zhang. If we don't defend the honor of the Chinese nation, they won't forgive us.'

'The honor of the Chinese nation?'

'Perhaps you've forgotten what those words mean.'

'Because I'm not a warmonger?'

Xu pushed himself to his feet. 'Ministers. We are all servants of the people. There is no need for this. Now. I have decided.'

'*You* have decided?' Zhang couldn't hide his astonishment at the old man's tone.

'I have, Economics Minister. Am I not the general secretary?'

Xu paused. And Li realized that the old lion was enjoying himself. For years, Zhang had usurped Xu's power, leaving Xu as a figurehead. Now Li's challenge to Zhang had given Xu a taste of his lost power. So Xu's next words didn't surprise Li.

'General Li. Please use our forces to carry out the plan you've outlined.'

'Thank you, General Secretary.' This time, Li didn't even bother to look at Zhang as he walked out of the room.

Outside the hall, Li's limousine waited to ferry him to his offices. As he trotted toward it, another limousine pulled up. General Baije Chen, head of the PLA's intelligence directorate, jumped out.

'Minister. I'm sorry to disturb you. There's something you need to see. May we speak alone?'

'As you wish.' Li followed Baije into the parking lot beside the hall. Whatever Baije wanted, it must be important. He lived on pots of green tea and rarely left his office. When they were well away from the entrance, Baije handed Li two sheets of paper, one in English, the other in Chinese.

'As you can see, it's from our contact at the American embassy –'

Li raised a finger to his lips. He'd read the note for himself. When he was done, he had to call on all his discipline to keep from shouting curses at the sky. All his work, all his planning, and now *this*? A traitor among them?

'When did this come in?'

'This morning.'

'And it's reliable?'

'Yes, General.'

Nearly a year before, Matt Kahn, a Marine guard at the American embassy, had fallen hard for Hua, a waitress in Sanlitun, a northeast Beijing neighborhood where expats gathered to drink cheap beer and watch day-old football and soccer. Only after they had been together for three months did the unfortunate Marine discover that his girl Hua was actually a boy named Hu. By the time the Beijing police arrived at Hu's

334

apartment, Kahn had gouged out one of Hu's eyes and both of his testicles. The officers called in their captain, who saw the situation's potential as soon as he learned where Kahn worked. Within an hour, the police had sent the case to the Second Directorate, who offered Kahn a choice. He could face a court-martial and public humiliation on two continents. Or he could give the Chinese a peek at the embassy's intelligence files, whatever he could get in a quick one-time sweep.

'It will take only a few minutes,' the Second Directorate colonel told Kahn. 'And then all this' – he gestured to the slim, hairless man in the bloody dress in the corner – 'will be over.' For Kahn, the choice was no choice at all.

But Kahn realized too late that spying was easier to get into than out of. The colonel came back to him a month later, and a month after that, each time demanding more information. Now Kahn wished he'd taken his punishment at the beginning instead of stepping into this pit. Three times, he put his pistol into his mouth and wished he had the guts to pull the trigger. But he didn't. Meanwhile, he needed to keep the Chinese happy. And so twice a month he filled a flash drive with all the files he could get and passed them to the Second Directorate.

This time, the files included Cao Se's note to the agency asking for a meeting. Of course, he hadn't used his name in the note. Still, its importance was obvious as soon as it was translated. It reached Baije in hours.

Li reread the note, to be sure he understood. A Chinese spy, code-named Ghost, was asking for an immediate meeting with a CIA operative, someone who had never worked in China. 'How?' Li said, under his breath, more to himself than to Baije. He had been sure that his American mole had rooted out all of the CIA's spies inside China. But he'd been wrong.

Yet this spy, whoever he was, obviously didn't know that the Second Directorate had penetrated the embassy. The note explicitly set out the time and place of the meeting.

'Of course, the Americans may not respond,' Baije said. 'They know we've penetrated them. They may think this Ghost of theirs has been doubled too.'

'General Baije.' Li put a finger into the smaller man's chest. 'Don't tell me what the Americans may or may not do. Tell me that our men are tracking every American who comes into Beijing this week. Tell me that we are going to catch this agent, and the traitor who's helping him. Those are the only words I want to hear.'

TWENTY-NINE

Even before he reached the center of Beijing, Wells felt the electricity of approaching war on the avenues of the giant city. Enormous banners in Chinese and English dangled from overpasses: 'China stands as one!' 'America will be sorry!' A torn American flag fluttered off the skeleton of a half-finished office tower, while the flag of the People's Republic, five yellow stars against a blood-red background, waved off every car and truck.

As his cab swung from the airport expressway onto the third of the ring roads that surrounded Beijing, Wells saw a dozen mobile antiaircraft missile batteries, their green-painted rockets pointing in every direction. Hundreds of Chinese surrounded the launchers, taking pictures, saluting the PLA soldiers in their crisp uniforms. Their excitement was palpable. They were standing up to the United States, and the show was about to start. The First Battle of Bull Run must have felt this way, Wells thought, the crowds turning up to watch the Rebs and the Union boys fight, shocked when the pageantry ended and blood began to flow.

Indeed, aside from the flags and banners, life in Beijing seemed to be proceeding fairly smoothly. The

337

immigration officers at Beijing airport hadn't been overly hostile to Wells or the other Americans who'd come in from San Francisco. The cabbie outside the terminal had shown no irritation when Wells told him to head to the St. Regis, a five-star hotel close to the United States embassy and favored by Americans. Workers were hammering away everywhere on new buildings. And the traffic was the worst Wells had ever seen, making Washington's supposedly busy roadways look like racetracks in comparison.

As the cab again stopped dead, the driver glanced at Wells in his rearview mirror.

'Where from?'

'California.' So his passport said, anyway. Wells waited for the driver to explode in anti-American slurs, or throw him out of the cab and make him walk the rest of the way. Instead the driver turned to Wells and smiled, revealing a mouthful of broken yellow teeth.

'Ca-li-fornia. My cousin – Los Angeles.'

'I'm from Palo Alto,' Wells said. His cover story. 'Northern California. Near San Francisco.'

But the cabbie wasn't interested in Palo Alto. 'Los Angeles,' he said again. 'Hollywood. Hungry.' The cabbie offered a thumbs-up.

'Hungry?'

'Gong-ri.' The cabbie held up a glossy magazine, a Chinese tabloid that featured a beautiful woman on the cover. Amid the Chinese characters were the English words 'Gong Li.'

'Gong Li. She's an actress, right? I don't see too many movies.'

'Gong-ri. Holly-wood.'

'Got it. I guess we'll save the serious discussion for next time. You have no idea what I'm saying, do you?

338

I mean, I could be offering to sell you my sister for all you know. If I had a sister.' Wells felt a pang of guilt. He hadn't talked to Evan, his son, in weeks. When he got back, he was taking the boy fishing in the Bitterroots – the mountain range on the Montana–Idaho border, just outside his hometown of Hamilton. Maybe hunting too, if Heather, his ex, would let him. But fishing for sure. *When* he got back. Not if.

The cabbie grinned and gave Wells another big thumbs-up, then reached back through the cab's plastic barrier with a crumpled pack of 555s, Japanese-brand cigarettes. 'You like cigarette?'

'No, thanks.'

'You like China?'

'Sure.'

And with that, the cabbie seemed to have exhausted his English. He popped a 555 in his mouth and smoked silently until they reached the hotel a half-hour later.

But outside the St. Regis, the mood turned grim. Four jeeps and a dozen soldiers formed a makeshift barricade that blocked the driveway. As the taxi stopped, a young officer rapped on Wells's window.

'Passport,' he said. The passport, sent by courier to the Chinese consulate in San Francisco for an expedited visa application, identified Wells as James Wilson, a thirty-seven-year-old from Palo Alto. If anyone asked, Wilson was the founder of Prunetime.com, an Internet start-up that specialized in small-business software. The business was real, at least on paper – one of the dozens of ghost companies that the agency had created over the years. Prunetime had a bank account, a Dun & Bradstreet credit report, a record of incorporation with the California secretary of state, even an office in San

Francisco. Wilson was real too. Besides his passport, he had a California driver's license, a working Social Security number, and a wallet full of credit cards.

Of course, none of those records could answer the red-flag question: Why was James Wilson so anxious to get to Beijing at this moment, with China and America close to war? Why had he applied for a visa on such short notice? But Wells had a plausible cover, a three-day trade fair for software and Internet companies. And despite the rising tensions, he was hardly the only American in China. His 747 from San Francisco had been half full, mostly Chinese but a couple of dozen Americans too, joking nervously that they hoped the bombs would wait until they got home.

'Passport,' the Chinese officer said again. Wells reached into his bag and handed it over. The officer flipped through it nonchalantly. 'Out.' As Wells unfolded himself from the cab, the officer walked off, passport in hand, disappearing into a windowless black van behind the jeeps. Wells leaned against the cab and waited. A few minutes later, an older officer in a pressed green uniform stepped out of the van and waved him over.

'You speak Chinese?' He looked up at Wells, his chin jutting out, his face square and unfriendly.

'No, sir.'

'Of course not. First trip to China?'

'Yes.'

'Why you come now?'

'There's a computer conference starting tomorrow. I'm looking to hire some programmers –'

The officer held up his hand. *Enough.* 'How long you staying?'

'Five days.'

'You doing anything for United States this trip?'

'I don't understand.'

'You don't understand? I'm asking you if anyone in America told you to report back on what you see here,' the officer said. 'Military preparations.'

Wells raised his hands defensively. 'No, no. I'm a businessman.'

'If someone did, it's better to tell now. We put you on a plane, send you home.'

'Nothing like that.'

'This bad time for Americans in China,' the colonel said to him. 'Be careful. If we catch you by military base –' He left the threat unfinished, handed Wells back his passport, and waved the cab through.

A minute later Wells walked through the hotel's big glass doors and felt whipsawed again. A giant pot of fresh-cut orchids and tulips sat on a marble table near the front door, filling the lobby with fragrance. The air was cool and calm, the doormen brisk and efficient. At the front desk, a smiling concierge upgraded him to a suite, telling him that cancellations had left the hotel empty.

And finally, Wells lay on his bed, hands folded behind his head, watching CNN International play silently on the flat-panel television, constant updates on 'The China Crisis' scrolling across the bottom of the screen, accompanied by stock footage of F-14s soaring off an aircraft carrier. The correspondents were doing their best to manufacture news, though not much had changed since Wells took off from San Francisco.

Following the sinking of the fishing boat by the *Decatur*, China had ordered the United States to pull all its vessels at least 1,000 kilometers – 620 miles – from the Chinese coast. The Chinese had also threatened to blockade Taiwan, and even made noise about dumping their trillion-dollar foreign reserve, a move that would send the dollar's value plunging and put the United States into recession. In response, the United States insisted that China needed to end its support for Iran and stop threatening Taiwan before it would even consider pulling back. America also warned China not to 'play games with the world economy.' The sinking was an accident and shouldn't impact the broader crisis, the White House said.

Wells closed his eyes and heard the hotel's thick windows rattle as fighter jets rumbled in the distance. He supposed Exley and Shafer were right. He shouldn't have come. He was meeting a man he'd never seen or even spoken with, a man who might already have been doubled. He was here on a contingency plan that was a decade old and that no one had ever expected to use. At best, this trip was the equivalent of heading out for a three-day backcountry hike in March without a backpack or even a compass. If nothing went wrong, he might get home with a touch of frostbite and an empty stomach. But he had no margin for error. And, of course, if Cao Se had been doubled and the Chinese knew he was coming, he was as good as dead already.

His actual instructions for the meeting were simple. Since Cao didn't know how to recognize or reach him, he was using what the agency called a 2-F protocol. Fixed location, fixed time. Essentially, Wells would show up at the meeting point and follow the instructions of whoever met him. Ideally, Cao Se would be waiting. More likely he would be greeted by a courier, by the police, or no one at all. If nobody showed up, Wells had no backup spot. He was simply supposed to return to the meeting point an hour later, then once more the following day. If Cao didn't show by the third meeting, Wells would leave – assuming the flights between China and the United States were still running. The embassy and station chief had no idea he was here, of course. The agency assumed that the mole had compromised all its networks in China. Wells had to come in alone to have any chance of staying clandestine.

Wells flicked off the television and lay on the floor. The opulence of the suite made him uncomfortable. He didn't like having his bags carried, or fancy soap and shampoo in the marble bathroom. Strange but true: he'd rather be on a cot in Afghanistan. The room's luxury made the danger of the mission seem less real. What could possibly go wrong inside a five-star hotel? Would he choke to death on an undercooked steak?

Wells supposed his uneasiness here proved he was a less than perfect spy. A true master could fit in everywhere, from a Siberian prison camp to a Des Moines mall to a Brazilian beach. That was the theory, anyway. Wells had his doubts such an animal existed in real life. A spy who could infiltrate an Iraqi insurgent network probably didn't have much in common with one who could talk his way into a private casino in Moscow.

Wells shucked his clothes, padded into the bathroom, turned on the shower. No low-flow showerheads here, and no waiting for the water to heat up. He had to admit that staying at a five-star hotel had some advantages.

At the height of China's tensions with the Soviet Union in the 1960s, Mao had ordered the building of a bunker under Zhongnanhai capable of surviving a direct hit from a nuclear warhead. The vault had been expanded over the years. It was now a miniature background city, sprawling across six acres, with its own electrical supply, food stocks, even a seven-room hospital.

But the bunker's newest and most technically advanced room was the strategic-operations center that the People's Liberation Army had opened just six months before. A room 150 feet square, the operations center was more advanced than the White House Situation Room or the Air Force's NORAD facility inside Cheyenne Mountain in Colorado. Video feeds allowed the PLA's generals to watch takeoffs and landings at China's air bases in real time. Secure fiber-optic links connected them with the silos that housed China's nuclear arsenal. One wall was devoted to a giant digital map of the eastern Pacific that offered an integrated view of the positions of the Chinese and enemy fleets.

The room was crowded but not claustrophobic, thanks to its twenty-foot-high ceilings, and surprisingly quiet. Its humming hard drives and clicking keyboards provided background music that was as soothing in its own way as ocean waves, and as unceasing. All the while, information moved up the chain of command, orders back down. They met at a raised platform in the center of the room, where Li stood, reading a message from the *Xian*.

When he was done, Li turned to the wall-sized map of the Pacific.

'Highlight the *Xian* and the target,' he said to Captain Juo, the commander of the center's Eastern Pacific Defense Unit.

'Yes, sir.' Juo tapped his keyboard, and suddenly two lights began to blink on the screen, a red circle indicating the *Xian*, and a green square for the target.

'How accurate are these positions?'

'For the *Xian*, we're estimating based on its last known position forty-five minutes ago. For the target, we're accurate to fifty meters. We're watching it in real time with the *Yao 2*' – a new recon satellite that the PLA had named after the Houston Rockets center.

'So we know the enemy's location better than our own ship.'

'That's correct, General.'

The paradox of submarine warfare. The *Xian* could communicate only irregularly with its commanders, lest it betray itself to the Americans. But China's satellites could track enemy ships with ease.

'And when does the *Xian* next report?'

'At 0100, sir.'

'How confident are you in your identification of the target?'

'I've looked at the photographs personally, General.'

'And you're certain.' Li wanted to hear the captain say the words.

'I'm certain, sir.'

Li put a hand on Cao's elbow and guided him out of the captain's earshot. 'What do you think, Cao?'

Cao's lips barely moved. He spoke so quietly that Li had to bend in to hear him. 'I think we should wait. I also think that what I think doesn't matter. You've decided.'

'And you're right.' Li turned to Juo. 'Captain, I won't be here when the *Xian* reports in next. But here's the message that I'd like you to send.'

The pen spun over the sketch pad, leaving behind a tiny blurred city of palaces and cathedrals. Cao had never

345

visited Paris, but he'd seen pictures. Sketching cleared his mind, helped him think. He threw in a couple of gargoyles atop a cathedral that might have been Notre Dame and eyed what he'd done. Not his best work.

He shoved the pad aside and stared out at the Beijing sky, tapping his pen on the plastic stump of his lower left leg. Midnight had come and gone, but the sky was more white than black, the lights of the city reflecting off clouds and smog, turning night into a perpetual half-dawn.

Cao lived in a four-room apartment in an Army compound near Zhongnanhai. His place was simple and spare, decorated in traditional Chinese style. Scrolls hung from the walls, long rice paper sheets covered with stylized characters in thick black ink. As a senior officer, Cao could have had a much bigger apartment if he'd wanted. But he preferred this space. With no family, he'd be lonely in anything bigger. Besides, he spent most of his time visiting bases and traveling with Li.

Normally, the apartment was calm and quiet, protected by the compound's high walls, an oasis in the center of Beijing's tumult. But today Cao heard the rumbling of helicopters over Tiananmen. The last time the square had been this crowded had been 1989. Back then, Cao wondered if the Party's leaders would survive. But he'd underestimated their ability to hold power. This time the masses had filled Tiananmen to challenge America. But what would they do if they discovered they were being used in a power struggle?

'The choice of heaven is shown in the conduct of men.' The proverb dated from the fourth century B.C., from Mencius, a follower of Confucius. But what was heaven's choice now? Cao clasped his hands, closed his eyes, and asked God to help him understand. In 1991, on a trip to Singapore for a regional defense conference, Cao had overheard singing from a blocky concrete building that turned out to be a church.

He'd never even seen the inside of a church before, but the joy in the voices he heard drew him in. Cao was hooked immediately. To this day he couldn't explain why, not even to himself. On his next trip to the church, he secretly converted, dunking himself in a bathtub and accepting that he'd been born again. His Christian name was Luke.

Cao was hardly alone in his faith. Protestant and Catholic missionaries had been active in China since the nineteenth century, and millions of Christians were scattered across China. They were tolerated, but not encouraged. The government saw Christianity as a source of trouble, a possible rival to its power. As far as the men of Zhongnanhai were concerned, Communism and nationalism were the only acceptable faiths in the People's Republic. Cao could never have become a senior PLA officer if he'd declared his faith openly. Even Li wouldn't have stood by him.

So Cao had hidden his faith. Every couple of months, he found his way to a restaurant in southeast Beijing owned by Wei Po, a heavyset man in his late fifties. Wei had been a Christian even longer than Cao, since the mid-1980s. But most of the time, Cao prayed at home. As a senior officer, he didn't have to worry that his quarters would be searched. Even so, he locked his cross and Bible in a drawer in his desk. He took them out now, running his fingers around the cross, trying to think his way out of the dilemma he faced.

Cao had been stunned when Li told him that the Second Directorate had discovered a traitor's message to the embassy. He hadn't imagined the Americans could be so corrupt. The meeting he'd asked for was supposed to take place in just a few hours, not far from here. And he knew that Li's men would be watching. The army's internal security force was tracking every American who'd come to Beijing in the last week, especially anyone traveling alone who had requested an expedited visa. Only about forty-five people fit that profile in all of Beijing, Cao knew. Of course, the CIA could have turned instead to a foreign service, but Cao thought that the Americans wouldn't take that chance on a mission this sensitive. No, whoever showed up at the meeting would be an American, and he'd be under surveillance.

But if Cao didn't show, he'd miss his only chance for contact. The Americans couldn't reach him. And with the embassy compromised, he effectively had no way to reach them either. After a decade underground, he no longer had active dead drops or signal sites, which was the reason that he'd been forced to send his coded message directly to the embassy.

Cao could also try to get inside the American embassy and ask for asylum. But Li had anticipated that possibility. Chinese police had surrounded the embassy grounds, claiming their cordon was necessary to protect the Americans inside 'from the passions of the Chinese people.'

Even if Cao did get inside, he'd have forfeited his chance to stop Li. There had to be a way to break Li's hold on the Standing Committee, but Cao hadn't figured it out yet.

Since the war in Vietnam, Cao had considered Li his closest friend. He knew the relationship had been one-sided. Li was tall, handsome, smart. The picture of an officer. Cao was short, his leg a stump, a plodder rather than a philosopher. As they'd risen through the ranks together, other officers had called Li and Cao the 'Big and Little Brothers,' as well as other, less friendly names.

But Cao had never cared. He'd been proud to call Li his friend. 'A man should choose a friend who is better than himself,' the proverb went. Cao had never forgotten how Li saved his life in Vietnam. And Li didn't steal or take bribes, unlike so many officers.

Yet the Devil knew every man's weakness, Cao thought. Li lusted for power the way lesser men chased money. Now that hunger had eaten him up. Perhaps Cao should have tried to stop him sooner. But at first he hadn't understood what Li planned. Later he'd figured that Li couldn't possibly succeed, that the others on the Standing Committee would block him.

But Li had proven them all wrong. He'd manipulated the Iranians, the Americans, even the protesters who filled Beijing's wide avenues. The confrontation between Beijing and Washington was nearly out of control. The liberals inside Zhongnanhai wanted to back off, but they couldn't, not without seeming weak, not after the way the American destroyer had sunk the Chinese trawler. China needed revenge. But whatever Li had told the committee, the Chinese retaliation wouldn't end the confrontation, Cao thought. The Americans would want their own retribution. At best, tit-for-tat provocations would go on for months. The Americans would blockade Shanghai. China would dump its dollar reserves or fire missiles over Taiwan. Finally both sides would tire of the phony war and turn to the United Nations as cover for a deal.

And at worst? At worst, the two sides would

miscalculate each other's seriousness. The attacks would get more and more deadly, until nuclear-tipped missiles went soaring over the Pacific. 'A sea of glass mingled with fire,' John had written in Revelation 15. Nuclear war. The ultimate sin, Cao thought. Man choosing to bring the end of days, a choice that was God's alone.

Even assassinating Li – something Cao knew he could never do anyway – wouldn't defuse the crisis. Others within the government would take up the fight, seeing, as Li had, that confrontation with the United States was a path to power. Only by finding a way to discredit Li totally could Cao turn back the clock.

And so, in desperation, Cao had reached out to his old allies at the CIA. He didn't expect they would have any answers. But at least he wanted them to understand that not everyone in Zhongnanhai wanted confrontation. And he thought they should understand exactly what had happened with the mole and with Wen Shubai, the defector.

Yet he wondered if he would be able to betray Li when the moment came, or if in the end his nerve would fail and he'd stay silent. In the last two weeks, he had suffered the same nightmare a dozen times. He marched next to Li on a muddy Vietnamese road as snipers decimated their company. The screams of the wounded raced inside his head. Step by step he neared the mine that he knew would tear off his leg. He tried to turn away but couldn't. But when the explosion came, he felt no pain. He looked down and saw his body was undamaged. Instead it was Li who writhed helplessly on the dirt beside him, his leg torn in half. Li opened his mouth to speak. And though Cao always woke before

Li said a word, he knew that Li meant to call him Judas, to accuse him of the ultimate betrayal.

He was actually relieved each night when he touched his withered leg and found that nothing had changed.

But he couldn't allow his friendship with Li to stop him from doing what he had to do. He wasn't Judas, and Li . . . Li wasn't Jesus. He needed to focus, to figure out how to meet the American agent without betraying himself. He flipped open his Bible, then shut it irritably. The answer wouldn't be found in there.

Then he looked at the book again.

Unless it would.

As the plan filled his mind, Cao slid the Bible back into his desk. The idea was a long shot, and he would have to trust in the endurance of this American, this American he'd never met. But he had no other options.

Ten minutes later Cao was in his jeep, navigating through the night, heading east. Armored jeeps and paddy wagons blocked the entrance to Tiananmen, but when the soldiers manning the blockade saw the stars on Cao's uniform, their scowls turned to salutes and they waved him through.

To the east of Tiananmen, the traffic picked up again, and the city turned bright and shiny. This stretch of road was Beijing's answer to Fifth Avenue, chockablock with stores that sold thousand-dollar handbags to China's elite. Cao passed a Ferrari dealership, low-slung yellow cars glowing under the lights. *A Ferrari dealership.* Less than a mile from Tiananmen. While all over China farmers and factory workers scrambled to eat. Perhaps Li was right after all. Perhaps China needed him in charge.

No. Even if Li was right, he couldn't be allowed to

take such insane risks. Cao pushed the pedal to the floor. He didn't have much time.

Wells dialed a number he'd never called before, a 415 area code. Exley answered on the first ring. 'Hello?'

'Jennifer?'

'Jim.' His cover name sounded strange in her mouth. She kept her voice steady, but still he could hear the tension. 'Was your flight okay?' In the background he heard CNN.

'Everything's fine. The hotel's great. Might as well be Paris.' Wells wanted to keep this conversation as banal as possible. No doubt the Chinese were monitoring every phone call into and out of the St. Regis tonight.

'What time is it there?'

'Two a.m. But I'm wide awake. Jet lag. Is anything happening? Anything I should know about?' This would be her only chance to tell him if his cover was blown.

'No. The kids are fine. Everyone misses you.' An all-clear, or as close as he would get.

'Tell them I miss them too. How's my niece?'

'Still hasn't called. Your brother's worried sick.' So the mole was still gone.

'Well, tell him not to worry. Listen, honey, this call's costing a fortune, so . . . I just wanted to check in, say I love you.'

'I love you too, honey. Stay safe, huh? You're on your own this time.' A reference to the way she'd saved him in New York. Her voice cracked, and before he could say anything else, she hung up.

THIRTY

'Sir.' The concierge, a small man in a three-button suit, waved frantically as Wells strode toward the St. Regis's front door. 'Good morning, sir. A moment, please. We are asked to give this to our American guests.'

The concierge handed Wells a paper embossed with the State Department's logo and headlined 'Notice to Americans.'

'*Last night the U.S. consulate in Guangzhou was informed that an American couple visiting China for an adoption had been attacked. The incident was apparently motivated by anger at deteriorating American–Chinese relations.*' Bureaucrats and diplomats loved the word *incident*, Wells thought. It avoided touchy issues, like what had really happened and who was to blame.

'*So far this incident appears isolated. However, U.S. citizens should keep a low profile and avoid anti-American demonstrations*' – good call – '*and large groups of Chinese.*' With 1.5 billion people in the country, that might be tough. '*The situation is fluid and updates will be issued as conditions warrant.*'

'Maybe you stay in the hotel today, sir,' the concierge said.

'And miss my chance to see Beijing?'

'Where to, sir?'

'Tiananmen Square.'

The St. Regis doorman looked unhappy. 'No cars in Tiananmen today, sir.'

'Just have him get as close as he can. I want to see the Forbidden City' – the former Chinese imperial palace, north of Tiananmen. 'Forbidden City is open, right?' It better be, Wells thought. He was supposed to meet Cao Se there.

'Yes.' The doorman waved a taxi forward, but his frown didn't disappear, not even after he palmed Wells's tip.

Wells wasn't surprised to see that the cabbie had a soldier's close-cropped hair. Everyone who left the St. Regis today would be watched. He'd have to assume that Cao had planned for the surveillance. Trying too hard to ditch his watchers would only draw more attention. Though if he could lose them without seeming to work at it, he would.

'So what do you think about this mess?' Wells said to the cabbie. 'I think we'll work it out. In two years it'll be like it never happened.' Jim Wilson was an optimist. Wells wasn't so sure.

'No English.'

'Oh. Not that many Chinese speak English, I'm noticing. Course, I don't speak any Chinese, so there it is. The language of the future, everyone says.' The driver just shrugged.

As they moved west toward Tiananmen, the traffic slowed to a standstill. Ahead the road was blocked and police were diverting cars off the avenue. Around them a steady flow of Chinese walked west. Wells saw his chance. He handed a hundred-yuan note to the driver and popped out, ignoring the cabbie's sputtering.

Wells picked his way through the soot-belching trucks, packed minibuses, and shiny black Mercedes limousines jammed together on the wide avenue. The sweet smell of benzene mixed with the stink of unburned diesel. He joined the Chinese heading west on the sidewalk, following the human current toward Tiananmen, and peeked back at the cab. The driver had a radio to his mouth, no doubt warning other agents to watch for Wells. Which wouldn't be easy in this crowd. Mostly men, they had the same buoyant mood he'd sensed the day before. They waved Chinese flags and didn't seem to mind having Wells among them. Two men traded a camera back and forth, snapping pictures, holding their hands high in a V-for-victory salute. Though Wells knew from his years in Afghanistan that under the wrong circumstances a crowd like this could become a mob in seconds.

He felt a tug on his elbow. 'American?' A tall man in a fraying blue sweatshirt pointed an angry finger at him.

'Canada,' Wells said. No need to start a riot. He was taking enough risks today. His questioner pushed by and was swallowed in the crowd. After the next intersection the road was clear. Men surged onto the pavement. Police clustered around cruisers and paddy wagons, watching for trouble but not interfering with the flow.

Farther on, a herd of television trucks sat close together, Chinese channels that Wells didn't recognize, along with CNN, Fox, BBC, NHK. *The whole world is*

355

watching. A company-sized detachment of soldiers massed near the trucks, to protect the reporters, or maybe to intimidate them.

For ordinary Chinese – and their rulers – this moment had to be thrilling and frightening, Wells thought. Every person in this crowd was both a spectator and a participant in the action. They wanted to remind the world, and themselves, of that most easily forgotten fact: that they existed. Wells half expected to see Gadsden flags – the yellow banners flown by colonists during the Revolutionary War, emblazoned with a coiled rattlesnake and the words 'Don't Tread on Me.' The crowd was delivering that message to America. But their rulers in Zhongnanhai would have to hear it too.

And yet . . . after the Tiananmen massacre of 1989, ordinary Chinese had given up politics and focused on the economy. Maybe this demonstration, big as it was, would be forgotten in a few weeks. Or maybe –

'Maybe I don't know what I'm talking about,' Wells murmured. He'd been in China not even twenty-four hours, didn't speak the language, and now was forecasting the country's future. Classic American arrogance. He ought to spend less time making predictions, more time figuring out if anyone was watching him.

Past the television trucks, the crowd quickened. They were close now. Just ahead the avenue opened into Tiananmen like a river pouring into a lake, and Wells saw the astonishing breadth of the square. He'd expected something like the Washington Mall. A manicured space, carefully maintained. Instead Tiananmen was a fixer-upper, a hole in the middle of a giant city, all the more powerful for its rawness.

356

From its northeast corner, where Wells had walked in, Tiananmen stretched south a half-mile, west a quarter-mile. The thick red walls of the Forbidden City marked its north side. The hall housing Mao's body sat in the southern half of the square, behind a tall granite obelisk, a smaller version of the Washington Monument.

As Wells oriented himself, protesters flooded by, joining the hundreds of thousands of people already huddled in the center of Tiananmen. Shouts came in bursts from the loudspeakers around the square. Warnings or exhortations to the crowd? Wells didn't know. There was so much he didn't know today. All his life he'd felt privileged, and sometimes cursed, by what he'd been allowed to see. But he had never, not even on his first day in Afghanistan, been so much of an outsider. He was in the eye of a human hurricane, watching a maelstrom whose physics were beyond his understanding, a force of nature uninterested in him, yet with the power to tear him apart.

The security forces had left the center of Tiananmen to the protesters. But at the northwest corner, where an avenue led toward the Zhongnanhai leadership compound, a green wall of soldiers stood shoulder to shoulder before a phalanx of armored personnel carriers. Hundreds more soldiers blocked the entrance to the Forbidden City, where a giant banner of Mao hung from the outer wall of the palace.

Wells turned right, toward the banner, where the police had opened a path for any tourists brave or dumb enough to come to the Forbidden City today. An archway cut through the outer palace wall, directly under the portrait of Mao. This was the Gate of

Heavenly Peace, the southern entrance to the palace complex.

And as Wells walked through the gate, it lived up to its name. The crackle of the Tiananmen loudspeakers faded away. 'Open?' Wells asked the sweet-faced girl inside the ticket booth. He still couldn't quite believe it. But she nodded.

As she handed him a ticket, a man grabbed his elbow. 'You American? I student. Beijing University. Name is Sun.'

'Sure you are,' Wells said. Cops looked the same everywhere. This guy could have been the brother of the cabbie Wells had ditched two hours before. His shoes – black lace-up boots – were polished. Had any student anywhere ever polished his shoes?

'I take you,' Sun said. 'Practice my English. Free.'

'I'll pass. I'm kind of antisocial.' Wells held up the audio guide, which, weirdly, was narrated by Roger Moore. 'Besides, I got the tour and everything.'

Wells handed over his ticket to the guard and walked through the front entrance. When he looked back, he wasn't surprised to see Sun about a hundred feet behind, conspicuously tailing him. What would Jim Wilson do? Wells turned around.

'This is my only day sightseeing and I don't know why you're bothering me.'

'Not bothering,' Sun said. 'Just watching out. Not good day for American here.'

'So I'm told.'

But Wells decided not to argue further. It was only 9:45 a.m., and the meet was supposed to be at noon, so he had two hours to lose this guy. He wandered through the palace, doing his best impression of a half-bored, half-awed American tourist. Which wasn't difficult.

The Forbidden City wasn't a European-style palace like Versailles, a mansion filled with decorated rooms. Instead, the complex consisted of empty courtyards divided by ceremonial halls. The Hall of Complete Harmony. The Hall of Preserving Harmony. The Hall of Supreme Harmony. The emperors had been big on harmony. They wouldn't have been happy today, Wells thought.

To the north, the inner palace held the emperor's living quarters, elaborately carved wooden pavilions, painted deep red to symbolize the emperor's power. The average Chinese had been barred from the complex on pain of death – hence the palace's name. But over the years, the palace had been ransacked so many times that today its buildings were mostly empty. Without Roger Moore to guide him, Wells wouldn't have known what he was seeing.

Besides the audio tour, he'd brought his own pocket-sized guide to the Forbidden City. He thumbed through it as Sun trailed behind, the world's slowest chase. Wells shooed him off a couple times, to no effect. The complex got slightly busier as the morning went on. At 11:00, a dozen nervous-looking American tourists walked past, watched by two bored police officers. Wells guessed they'd come through the palace's northern gate, not the Tiananmen entrance. He wondered what they were making of this. Joe and Phyllis from Sacramento probably hadn't expected war when they signed up for seven nights in China.

Finally, at 11:45, in the northwestern corner of the palace complex, where narrow cobblestone corridors connected irregularly shaped courtyards, Wells found a way to lose Sun. He reminded himself not to run.

Wells ducked through a group of Japanese sightseers

and into a wooden pavilion housing a display of court costumes. As the Japanese clustered at the entrance, blocking Sun for a precious few seconds, Wells jogged through the pavilion and hopped over a railing into an alley, then sprinted along the side of the building. Thirty yards down, the building ended and the alley formed a T-intersection with another pathway. Wells swung right, ran a few feet along the pavilion, then hopped over another railing and back inside the building.

He flattened himself against a display case and peeked out. Sun reached the intersection, panting. He twisted left and right, looking for Wells. Finally he trotted left, toward the center of the complex. Perfect. Wells waited a few seconds more, then walked out the pavilion's front entrance. He felt as though he'd rid himself of a piece of gum stuck to his shoe. Losing Sun wouldn't matter if the cops were watching the meeting site, but Wells was glad to be rid of the guy anyway.

He made his way into the palace's northeast corner, a quiet area filled with narrow pavilions and gardens. Over the years, emperors had competed to build the most beautiful spaces, adding narrow cypress trees whose bodies twisted like flames and the Buddhist rock gardens more common in Japan. The meeting with Cao was supposed to happen in a garden famous for a sculpted piece of rock known as 'The Stone That Looks Like Wood.' All morning Wells had wondered if he'd recognize it. But when he stepped into the garden where the stone stood, he knew he was in the right place.

Unfortunately, the stone wasn't the reason.

Until now, Wells had seen no Chinese tourists in the palace today. Understandable, considering the protests in Tiananmen. But this garden was the exception. Five

Chinese had decided it was a perfect place to relax. A young couple sat side by side on a bench, holding hands. Three men in their early twenties sketched a cypress tree, their hands flying over their pads.

Why here? Why now? Wells knew. The agents were good, nonchalant, and yet their nonchalance was a tip-off as obvious as Sun's polished shoes. Two hours before, when he'd walked through the Gate of Heavenly Peace, he'd stepped into the open maw of the People's Republic, and yard by yard he'd slipped into its gullet. The game he'd played with Sun seemed absurdly childish now.

Maybe Cao had been set up too. Or maybe Shafer and Exley had been right all along, and Cao was part of the trap. But the bad guys knew about the meeting for sure. Somewhere nearby a squad of secret police was waiting to arrest him.

Wells kept walking. Turning and running wouldn't help. He had nowhere to go. He might as well see who showed up. He stopped beside the stone that looked like wood. It did, too, like a piece of flotsam sculpted smooth by waves. Wells checked his watch – 12:00. In a minute, or two, he would walk on, casually, leave the garden. Then –

'Hey, mister!' A kid scuffled into the garden, waving at him. *A kid?*

Per Cao's instructions, Wells was wearing a green T-shirt, the contact signal. The kid, also wearing a green shirt, walked over. 'Mr. Green,' he said.

'Is this a joke?' Wells couldn't help himself. Was this part of the setup? Why didn't they just arrest him?

'You Mr. Green, right? I meet you at stone like wood.' The kid seemed to be enjoying himself. 'I know code word,' he said.

Somewhere over the walls of the courtyard, a man shouted in Chinese. The students dropped their sketch pads and walked toward him.

'Tell me,' Wells said.

'Ghost.'

'You're crazy, kid.'

'For you.' The kid reached into his pocket for a package hardly bigger than a pack of Juicy Fruit. A flash drive. He handed it to Wells and ran away. He didn't get far. The students grabbed him roughly. Then footsteps clattered behind Wells.

He turned to see two men, the biggest Chinese he'd ever seen, as tall and muscular as NBA power forwards. They reached for him, wrapped their meaty hands around him. He didn't try to fight. Another man followed. And as the power forwards twisted Wells's arms behind his back, the third man reached into his pocket for a black canvas hood.

'Wait –' Wells said. But the world went black, and around his neck the string drew tight.

THIRTY-ONE

The dark blue buoy, about the size of a basketball, popped to the surface of the East China Sea and fired an electronic burst into the atmosphere. A fraction of a second later, the *Bei*, a satellite 22,000 miles overhead, registered the buoy's electronic signature and responded with an encrypted transmission of its own.

Just that quickly, the *Xian*, the newest submarine in China's fleet, was in contact with its masters onshore – all the while remaining five hundred feet below the surface of the ocean, connected to the buoy by a fiber-optic cable. The technology was the most advanced in the world, a generation ahead of similar systems on American submarines. The *Xian* could even get real-time video imagery of ships all over the western Pacific, thanks to a network of Chinese satellites in low earth orbit that were connected to the *Bei* through a control center near Beijing.

Of course, the *Xian* had to be careful not to stay connected for too long. The United States monitored Chinese satellites, and after a few seconds, American signals-intelligence equipment on Guam, Okinawa, and Alaska could begin to target the buoy's location.

To protect itself, the *Xian* made contact with the *Bei* only twice a day.

Still, the satellite link had proven extraordinarily useful, Captain Tong Pei thought. Especially now, with American ships searching for Chinese subs. Thanks to the link, the *Xian* could get orders while staying hidden at the bottom of the thermocline – a layer of water where the ocean's temperature dropped quickly, distorting sound waves and making the *Xian* much harder to find.

Before taking over the *Xian*, Tong had commanded attack submarines for almost two decades. He was the most experienced commander in China's fleet. But he had never commanded a boat remotely like the *Xian*. And he had never been on a mission like this one.

Twelve hours before, at 0100, Tong had received his initial orders for this operation. He expected that the transmission they'd just received would include the final confirmation. He was glad to have the fail-safe of two separate orders. He wasn't nervous, not exactly, but what he was about to do would echo around the world, and he wanted to be sure he wasn't making a mistake.

The *Xian* was the third of China's new Shanghai-class subs, by far the most advanced submarines that China had ever built. Until a few years before, China's armed forces had relied on leaky ships, rusting submarines, and fighter jets whose design dated from the Korean War. China had refused to show its weapons to visiting American generals, for fear that they would sneer at the country's weakness.

These days, China still kept its ships and jets secret. But now the country wanted to hide its strength.

Chinese students studied engineering and software and fluid dynamics at the top universities in the United States. Some stayed in America and made fortunes in Silicon Valley. But most came home, and more than a few were working for China's navy – whose top priority was building a submarine that could challenge the American fleet.

China's focus on undersea warfare was pragmatic. Building surface ships capable of challenging the United States would cost hundreds of billions of dollars, more than China could afford, at least for now. Even a single nuclear-powered aircraft carrier was a massively expensive proposition. No country, not even the Soviet Union at the height of the Cold War, had tried to compete with the United States in aircraft carriers.

But submarines were much cheaper, billions of dollars instead of hundreds of billions. And a lone sub could wreak havoc on an opposing fleet. In World War II, a single German submarine had sunk forty-seven boats in less than two years. Of course, the *Xian* wouldn't sink forty-seven American ships, but if it scuttled even one it would change the balance of power in the western Pacific, forcing the Americans to back off China's coast.

Taking out an American boat wouldn't be easy. The American navy had not been seriously challenged since the Battle of Midway in World War II, when it decimated the Japanese fleet and started the United States on the path to victory in the Pacific. The collapse of the Soviet Union had only lengthened its lead. Its aircraft carriers, destroyers, and nuclear attack submarines were the best in the world.

But if any submarine could successfully break

through the American defenses, it was the *Xian*. Put into the water just last fall, the *Xian* was the most advanced diesel-electric submarine ever built – in China or anywhere else. Noise-reducing anechoic tiles coated its hull. A seven-blade skewed propeller enabled it to slice through the water almost silently. Advanced electric batteries powered it, allowing it to stay underwater for weeks.

Further, the PLA's engineers had greatly improved the *Xian*'s secondary power source. Besides its batteries, the sub had an 'air-independent propulsion' system of hydrogen fuel cells. When the batteries and fuel cells ran together, they could push the *Xian* to thirty knots in short bursts, almost as fast as American nuclear subs.

The Chinese had also nearly closed the gap with the electronics and sonar systems that the U.S. Navy used. The *Xian*'s computers ran noise-filtering and noise-recognition software that made the *Xian*'s sonar operators, for the first time, competitive with those on American submarines. And the *Xian*'s satellite link meant that it could get regular updates on ships far outside its sonar range. The combination meant that the *Xian* could avoid the submarines and frigates that formed the outer cordon of American battle groups and get within torpedo range of the big prizes, the destroyers and cruisers and carriers that were the heart of the United States fleet.

And at that point the *Xian* had an even more unpleasant surprise for the American navy.

Inside the *Xian*, Tong read over the order one final time and tucked it into his pocket. 'Retract the buoy,' he murmured to his communications officer. Then, to his operations officer, 'Any change in the target's direction?'

'No, sir. Still one-eighty at twenty knots' – directly south, toward the *Xian*, which was cruising north – 'at fifteen knots. Range now seventy kilometers' – about forty miles.

'Take us to sixty meters' – two hundred feet, in the middle of the thermocline.

'Yes, sir.' The ops officer tapped the touch screen in front of him a few times and the *Xian* began to ascend, so gracefully that Tong could hardly feel it rise.

'Set us on combat status.'

'Yes, sir.' The officer tapped his screen three more times. All over the submarine, LCD panels turned from a steady green to a flashing yellow, warning the *Xian*'s crew that an attack might be imminent and that silence – always important on a submarine – was more crucial than ever.

'And ready the Typhoons for launch.'

Tong felt the surprise in the room as he spoke. The ops officer paused, only for a second, before he answered.

'The Typhoons. Yes, sir.'

The control room was nearly silent now. On his control monitor Tong saw the *Xian* slowly rise toward the surface: 150 meters . . . 140 . . . 130 . . . The officers and crew moved precisely, no wasted motion, not even wasted breath, yet the anticipation in the cramped room was palpable. These men all knew now what they were about to do. And they were ready.

Twenty minutes later Tong's monitor briefly flashed red, alerting him that they were now twenty kilometers – about twelve miles – from the target, within range of

367

the Typhoons. The *Xian* carried two of them, Chinese versions of the Russian VA-111 Shkval.

Though they were called torpedoes, Shkvals were basically short-range cruise missiles that targeted ships, and the Russians had never been able to make them work properly. They often outran their guidance systems and badly missed their targets. They also had an unnerving habit of swinging back on the subs that launched them. When the *Kursk*, a Russian nuclear sub, sank in the Barents Sea in 2000, there were rumors, never proven, that a malfunctioning Shkval had caused the accident. For whatever reason, after the *Kursk* went down, the Russians stopped trying to build Shkvals.

Despite those problems, China's admirals had seen the Shkval's potential as they searched for a weapon that might overcome the American fleet. At a secret lab outside Shanghai, their naval scientists had spent five years redesigning the missile's guidance systems and engine. And they'd succeeded. In tests off Hong Kong in the last two years, the Typhoon had proven capable of successful launches from as far as twenty-five kilometers out – about fifteen miles.

But those targets were obsolete oil tankers, not American destroyers with the most advanced counter-torpedo systems in the world. No one in the Chinese navy really knew how the Typhoon would perform in combat.

They were about to find out, Tong thought.

'Reduce speed to ten knots,' he said.

'Yes, sir.'

'Do we have final visual confirmation?'

The operations officer tapped his screen again, and there it was, a recon photo straight from the satellite overhead, time-stamped 12:55, the big gray boat cutting sturdily through the waves, the photograph's resolution good enough to reveal the big '73' painted in white on its side.

The DDG-73. The USS *Decatur*.

Tong admired the precision with which his commanders had calculated this mission. Despite all China's progress, America still thought that China was a poor backward nation unworthy of respect. The *Decatur* had killed twenty-two Chinese, and the United States had not even apologized.

Today China would have its revenge. The *Xian* would fire one Typhoon, enough to cripple the destroyer but not sink it. An eye for an eye, as the Americans said. And the Americans would learn what they should have already known, that they needed to treat the People's Republic as an equal.

'Reduce speed to three knots.' The Typhoons had one great weakness. They could be launched only when the *Xian* was nearly stopped. But since the *Decatur* had no idea that the *Xian* was in the vicinity, the submarine's speed hardly mattered.

'Yes, sir.' The *Xian* slowed perceptibly.

'Prepare to dive to two hundred meters on my command.' Hit or miss, Tong didn't plan to hang around once he launched. The Americans would expect him to flee west, to the Chinese coast. Instead he planned to take the *Xian* southeast, into the open ocean, and depend on the sub's ability to stay silent.

The combat center was hushed now, every man looking at Lieutenant Han, the sub's weapons control officer. Tong nodded to Han. 'Fire.'

'Away,' Han said quietly.

The *Xian* shifted slightly as the Typhoon left its hull. Tong heard – or maybe just felt – the hum as the underwater missile accelerated away. A couple of his men gave each other tentative thumbs-up signals, but Tong didn't even smile. 'Now dive,' he said. They would have time later to savor what they'd done. If they survived.

Two hundred feet above the *Xian*, and ten miles north, Captain Henry Williams sat in the *Decatur*'s combat information center. He was glad to be well off the coast, out of range of Chinese captains who might want to avenge the previous week's accident by trying to ram his ship.

The Navy had finished its preliminary inquiry into the crash. As Williams had expected, it had found he'd done nothing wrong. Still, the days since the accident had been difficult. Willams couldn't understand why a bunch of college students had thought that playing games with an American destroyer would be a good idea.

So now the *Decatur* was cruising loops in the East China Sea, and Williams was splitting his time between his ship and the *Reagan*, where he'd met three times with the Navy's internal investigators. He'd even lost the pretty *L.A. Times* reporter, Jackie, who'd gotten bored after a couple days sailing laps and headed back to the *Reagan*. Probably for the best, Williams thought glumly. Neither he nor his men believed they had caused the accident, but killing twenty-two civilians didn't do wonders for morale. Even in the combat center, his officers seemed to be moving at three-quarters speed. Maybe he ought to call a meeting, make sure his men knew they'd done nothing wrong.

The torpedo alarm blared, jolting Williams to full attention. Had to be false, he thought. No way could a

Chinese sub get close enough to launch on them without being picked up by his sonar operators.

Next to Williams, Lieutenant Umsle, the *Decatur*'s tactical action officer, was already on his phone. 'Sonar's confirming a launch, sir.'

In an instant, the ship's morale became the least of Williams's problems. 'General quarters!' he said. 'Immediately!'

A siren rang across the ship. 'General quarters! All hands to battle stations! This is not a drill!'

Umsle listened for a few seconds more before hanging up. 'The good news is we should have plenty of time. It's way out. Twenty thousand meters.'

Even a fast torpedo covered only forty-five knots an hour, about 1,300 meters a minute. The *Decatur* would have at least fifteen minutes for evasive action, and the fish would probably run out of fuel before it reached the *Decatur*. Obviously, the Chinese captain had been so worried that he would be spotted that he had been afraid to launch from close in.

'Full power to the turbines and hard left,' Williams said. Preserving his ship was the first priority. Then the Navy could bring its attack subs into the area and take out the Chinese sub that had been foolish enough to make this hopeless swipe.

'Yes, sir.' A jolt of power ran through the ship as the engines began to produce peak power.

Umsle's phone rang again. He listened, then handed Williams the black handset. 'You need to hear this, sir.'

'Sir.' It was Terry Cyrus, the *Decatur*'s sonar chief. 'We're getting an unusual read. The bogey looks like it's running at two hundred fifty knots.'

'That can't be right.'

'I know. But it is.'

A Shkval? Those were Russian, and anyway they didn't work.

'You're certain?'

'Certain, sir. The arrays are running perfectly. It's unmistakable.'

'Is it on us?'

'Unclear. It may be a two-stager.' In other words, the missile would slow once it got close to the *Decatur* and become a conventional acoustic wake-homing torpedo.

'Okay. Assuming it's on us, how many minutes to impact?'

'Three.'

Three minutes. 'Thank you, chief.' Williams turned to Umsle. 'Hail the XO' – the executive officer, the *Decatur*'s second-in-command, currently on the bridge – 'and tell him to get the damage teams ready for impact in three minutes. We're not outrunning this thing.'

The next minutes seemed to pass in a single breath. The torpedo-missile, whatever it was, closed steadily. It seemed to be running blind, not changing course to track the *Decatur*, but that didn't comfort Williams. It surely would deploy a second guidance system once it got close. Indeed, two miles from the *Decatur*, the torpedo surfaced briefly and corrected its course, turning toward the destroyer.

What Williams didn't know was that the Typhoon had a GPS system and a satellite transceiver that linked it to the *Bei* overhead, enabling it to home in on the *Decatur* effortlessly. The *Decatur*'s towed array, which created a noisy 'wake' capable of confusing a conventional acoustic homing torpedo, had no chance of stopping the Typhoon.

Once the torpedo corrected its course, Williams accepted the inevitable. Time to focus on saving his men. 'Clear the turbine room,' he said to Umsle. The engine rooms were close to the waterline and filled with heavy equipment – among the most vulnerable spaces on the ship. 'And tell everyone else to buckle down for impact.'

For just a second, Williams let himself pray. Please, God, make it a dud.

It wasn't.

The explosion cut through the destroyer's half-inch-thick steel hull, tearing a twelve-foot hole just above the waterline. For a few moments, chaos ruled. The 8,000-ton warship shuddered with the impact, then began to list. Water roared through the hole in the armored plates, flooding the turbine room. Eleven sailors died in the explosion, and six others were swept into the ocean, their bodies never recovered. Fuel poured out of a line burst by the explosion, setting off two small fires.

Still, Williams was proud of the way his crew and his ship responded after the explosion. The years of emergency training had paid off. Within three minutes, the *Decatur*'s firefighting squads had put out the fires, the most serious threat to the integrity of the ship. Within seven minutes, the bulkheads were sealed and Williams had his first damage report. And five minutes after that, the most seriously injured sailors had been evacuated and were receiving medical attention in the infirmary, awaiting helicopter transfer to the *Reagan*.

At that point Williams allowed himself to think for the first time of what the Chinese had done. The sub was gone. The explosion had damaged the *Decatur*'s sonar gear, and even if he could find the sub, Williams was in no position to chase it. Not with his boat crippled, not facing this silent submarine and mysterious supertorpedo. Already the Navy had begun to search for the sub, moving a half-dozen surface ships and three attack submarines toward its last known location. Williams wondered if they'd find it. It had sure sneaked up on his sonar operators, and they graded above average every time the Navy tested them. The Chinese had obviously improved their technology in the last couple of years. The fleet was going to have to be much more careful out here, Williams knew that much.

He knew something else too. New torpedoes, new sub, new whatever, the Chinese had made a big mistake today. Did they really think that the United States wouldn't punish them for what they'd done?

THIRTY-TWO

Wells snapped awake.

And wished he hadn't. Lava burned through his right shoulder, the one he'd dislocated in Afghanistan. He twisted his head, looking around, trying to get his bearings. He seemed to be . . . he was . . . hanging off the ground, trussed like a pig in a slaughterhouse. His wrists were handcuffed over his head, dangling from a steel chain attached to the wall behind him. His ankles were pulled up behind so they were at waist height and attached to shackles mounted directly to the wall. His knees and shoulders bore all his weight, and his body tilted forward, over the cement floor. If his arms were cut loose, he'd slam his head on it before he could get his hands down to break his fall. He tried to hold himself still; the slightest twitch caused the pain in his shoulder to spike, tendons catching fire one by one.

Wells looked around the room. His pants, shirt, and shoes and socks sat neatly in a corner. But they hadn't taken off his black, Halloween-themed boxers. Exley had tried to switch him to boxer-briefs, promising that they'd flatter him, her only effort to upgrade his wardrobe. Now he was glad he'd refused. Though even formfitting shorts might be less ridiculous than smiling jack-o'-lanterns. Trick or treat indeed. What underwear went best with torture, anyway? Wells supposed the question was unanswerable. Black might be a good choice. Hide the blood.

A tiny part of him admired the precision of the setup. His captors could get at his face, his legs, his neck, his everything, without repositioning him. Escape was a fantasy. The shackles were so tight he could hardly feel his hands and feet. He would be up here until they let him out. Or he died.

The cell around him wasn't reassuring. Twenty feet square, with only a couple of battered wooden chairs for furniture. Windowless, of course. White-tiled walls. The floor stained with dark whorls, remembrance of agonies past. A drain set in the middle of the floor, to ease the disposal of blood and vomit. A sour smell, half locker room, half slaughterhouse. The only comforting item was the security camera mounted in a corner, its black-rimmed lens making slow circuits of the room.

At the end of the cell, a wide steel door with a tiny peephole. But Wells couldn't hear anything of the world outside. The walls were soundproofed, he supposed. He had no idea where he was, or even if it was day or night, though he didn't feel as though much time had passed since his arrest. As soon as they'd gotten him out of the courtyard, they'd knocked him out with some kind of fast-acting anesthetic. Maybe the same stuff he'd used on Kowalski's men.

Wells's stomach tightened. Shafer had been right. Cao Se was a treacherous bastard. Or maybe the mole had given Wells up somehow. Either way the Chinese had known he was coming. Now he would just have to take his punishment, and stick to his story.

James Wilson. Thirty-seven. His first trip to China. Prunetime.com. Here to recruit engineers. A three-bedroom split level. Palo Alto. A wife. Jennifer, a doctor. Two kids, in grade school. Amanda and Jim Jr. Button-down blue shirts and pressed khakis. Marathons in his spare time. A comp sci degree from the University of Illinois. The biggest mistake of his life: passing on a job offer from Google in 2001. Until now, anyway. He didn't know what he'd done, but this was all a misunderstanding. They had to let him go.

Would they believe him? No chance, Wells thought. But maybe he could make them doubt themselves, slow them down. At least notify the embassy, get the diplomats involved.

Wells knew he didn't deserve what was about to happen. And yet he wondered if he did. Primordial justice for the killing he'd done over the years. Or maybe for something more: For the way his country had walked away from the Geneva Conventions. For Abu Ghraib and the ghost prisoners whose names the CIA had never given to the Red Cross. For water-boarding and stun guns and the torture that the lawyers had decided wasn't torture at all. For the madness that had descended on Iraq since the invasion, the uncounted men and women and children who'd died because the fools in the White House told themselves the mission was accomplished back in May 2003. And the soldiers who'd been blown to bits because armchair generals in the Pentagon thought armored Humvees were a luxury, not a necessity. For everything that had happened in the lost days since 9/11.

Judge not, lest ye be judged. A stupid, stupid way to think. He wasn't America, and the agony he was about to face would be real, not metaphorical. And yet Wells

377

clung to the idea that he was due for this, for whatever happened next.

He didn't know how else to endure it.

The door at the far end of the cell slid open, and the two power forwards who'd grabbed him at Tiananmen walked in. They were dressed for a workout, wearing T-shirts and sweatpants. They wore latex gloves and cheap rubber galoshes and carried identical zippered canvas bags. Metal batons dangled from belts on their hips.

Three more men followed. Wells recognized them all. The first was the man who'd put the black hood over his head. He'd seen the other two only in photographs. They wore PLA uniforms with stars on their collars.

Cao Se. And Li Ping.

Li and Cao stood at the back of the room silently as the third man rummaged through a bag he held. Wells tried to understand why Cao was here. Did he want to see the fool he'd duped? Was his presence intended to signal Wells that he ought to confess, that the Chinese already knew everything and it would be pointless not to? But then why not just say that? Why play this brutal game? Or did Cao want to let Wells know that he wasn't alone, that Cao was still on the American side and had come to save him?

Maybe, though the odds were long. Anyway, he couldn't possibly find out unless Li and the others left him and Cao alone. Meanwhile, Wells had to keep playing the role of terrified American tourist, an act that shouldn't be too difficult.

'I don't know who you guys think I am, but you're making a mistake,' Wells said.

378

No one responded. The third man pulled a black box, slightly bigger than an eyeglass case, from his bag. He stepped toward Wells and held the box open so Wells could see what was inside.

A small set of pliers, and three scalpels. The steel blades gleamed under the lights. Wells's stomach clenched. Use the fear, he thought. Any civilian in your position would be terrified. 'Please don't do this.'

Again the man reached inside his bag. This time he pulled out a red-painted metal canister that looked like an oversized beer can with a nozzle attached to the top. He pushed a button on the side of the can. A blue flame spurted out with a tiny *whoosh*. A miniature acetylene torch, the kind welders used for close-in work. The man twisted the nozzle until the flame glowed a bright blue, three inches long. He clicked off the canister and put it and the scalpel case on the folding chair.

'I'm telling you. This is a mistake.'

The man reached into the bag once more. This time he held up the flash drive that the boy had given Wells in Tiananmen. Li Ping stepped quickly across the cell and in a single fluid motion hit Wells under the ribs, in the solar plexus once, twice, three times – and then three times more.

Considering his age, Li hit hard, Wells thought. Wells had a boxer's abs, flat and tough, and the punches themselves didn't hurt all that much. But every one rolled him side to side in his shackles, sending shots of pain through his damaged shoulder. Li and the men around him watched him without a word. They were on another planet, in another universe, one where pain didn't exist.

Li took the flash drive from the man who'd been holding it. 'Who gave this?' he said in broken English.

379

'A boy. In Tiananmen. This is all a mistake. Please, sir, I don't know who you are, but you have to help me.'

Li spoke in Chinese. 'He says, you know very well who he is,' the man who'd been holding the flash drive said to Wells in English. He spoke with a heavy Russian accent. 'He is head of the People's Liberation Army. He wants you to know, he doesn't speak much English. So he's going to leave you now. But he wanted to see you for himself. The American spy who was so foolish as to come to the Forbidden City on this day.'

Li said something more. 'And he says it is nothing to him if you live or die. This is your last chance to tell the truth. If you do, maybe the Chinese people will show some mercy. If not –' The interrogator shook his head.

'Tell him, I promise, he's making a mistake –'

The interrogator said a few words to Li. 'Okay,' Li said in English. 'Your choice.' He stepped away. At the door, he turned to Wells and made a throat-cutting motion. Then he walked out. Cao followed wordlessly.

As soon as the door closed, the power forward stepped up, but the interrogator waved him back and reached into the bag. Despite himself, despite everything he'd seen and done, Wells was afraid. He pulled himself back. *Think.* Stay calm. They want you to imagine your tortures, to hurt yourself before they hurt you.

The interrogator lifted a piece of paper from the bag.

'What is your name?'

'Jim Wilson. James Wilson –'

The man shook his head. 'Your real name. Please.' The interrogator held up the paper for Wells. 'The reason you're here. The letter your embassy received last week. The instructions are quite specific. You are to come to the Forbidden City today. As you did. To wait at the stone that looks like wood at noon. As you did. And finally, you are to wear a green shirt.' The man pointed at the corner where Wells's shirt lay.

'Coincidence. I swear.'

'Coincidences don't exist in our world. Listen to me. *Please*. You will save yourself much torment. You must know we examined the Forbidden City very' – with his Russian accent, the word sounded like 'wery' – 'thoroughly today, Mr. Wilson. Twenty-two other Americans. None with green shirts.' He held up two fingers. 'Only two visited the stone. Gerry and Tim Metz. From New York.' He held up a Polaroid of a smiling couple, both in their sixties. 'Do they look like spies to you?'

'I don't know what spies look like.'

'Do you know who I am?'

'No, sir.'

'My name is Feng Jianguo. I specialize in these . . . discussions. I wish we could talk like men, solve bit by bit this puzzle of who you are. But General Li told me I don't have time.'

Feng walked to Wells, leaned in, locked his eyes onto Wells.

'Do you understand? I don't have time. And I must know three things. First, your name. Second, what you were expecting to receive. Third, most important, the name of the man who you meant to meet.'

'I wish I could help.' Again Wells wondered. Was it possible they didn't know he was here to meet Cao Se? Or were they setting up some larger trap, something he couldn't see?

'If you are honest. I cannot promise you'll live. Only Li can do that. But I won't hurt you unnecessarily.' He paused. He seemed to sense that he was losing Wells.

381

'This way, once we start . . . even after you beg us to stop. As you will. We won't stop. Once we start, we must be sure we've broken you. *Do you understand, Mr. Wilson?*'

'Your English is very good. You give this speech a lot?' Wells said nothing more.

Feng's face never changed. The silence stretched on. Wells focused on the heat in his shoulder. He had an insane impulse to twist in his shackles, amp up the agony for himself before these men did it for him. He restrained himself. Plenty of pain coming. No need to rush.

Feng shook his head, walked away, shuffled the papers back in the bag.

'A quiet American,' he said. 'One of the few. And all the worse for you.'

Feng pulled a black towel from his bag and stepped onto a chair. He reached up, draped the towel over the closed-circuit camera, making sure the lens was covered.

The power forwards reached into their pockets and slipped on brass knuckles, the kind that bridged four fingers at once. They stepped forward and set themselves on either side of Wells. Feng sat down, pulled a Coke from his bag. He sipped quietly as he waited for the show to start.

'*Ave, Caesar, morituri te salutant,*' Wells said under his breath. A bit of Latin said by the gladiators before they entered the ring: *Hail, Caesar, we who are about to die salute you.*

And the torture began.

The power forwards took turns. The one on the left began, punching quickly, hard jabs, right-left-right-left.

382

When he tired, the other took over, swinging more slowly but more powerfully, long hooks that crashed into Wells's stomach and ribs. They stayed off his face.

Wells had a tiny advantage at first from the adrenaline he'd mustered when Feng was talking. He kept his stomach tight as long as he could, sneaking in breaths when they weren't hitting him. But then his body twisted in the shackles, and his shoulder popped out. He lost focus for just a second and a jab caught him unready and his abs loosened and the punches crashed through and then he couldn't breathe –

Black spots filled the room and the demon-men kept punching and he couldn't breathe God he had never hurt like this too bad he wasn't going to tell them anything –

Then the severed head of the guerrilla he'd blown apart in Afghanistan showed up, rolling around like a soccer ball with a face, smirking and chattering nonsense –

And just as the darkness closed in to give his oxygen-starved brain relief from its delusions, they stopped hitting him. Cruelty in the guise of kindness. They stepped back and watched him flail, their flat square faces impassive, like they were watching a lab experiment.

Wells couldn't breathe, couldn't get his diaphragm steady, and then finally he remembered. The trick was to relax, let the voluntary muscles go soft and the diaphragm work on its own. He sucked in the room's stale air and pushed suffocation away. But the agony in his shoulder intensified as he returned to full consciousness. Wells wondered how long they'd been hitting him. Five minutes? At most. Five minutes down, an eternity to go.

They reached side by side into their canvas bags, pulled out water bottles, took a couple of sips each. Bert and Ernie, Wells thought. Or maybe Ernie and Bert. Just as his breath evened out, Bert nodded at Ernie and they stepped toward him.

'Round two,'Wells said aloud. 'The beatings will continue until morale improves.'

Round three followed, and round four. The beatings didn't get harder to take, but they didn't get easier either. The brass knuckles shredded his skin, exposing his twitching abdominal muscles. Blood dripped from his stomach, blackening the concrete beneath him.

By round five, Bert and Ernie had tired and were cheating. One of Bert's punches slipped low, catching Wells full in the testicles. Wells screamed, an inhuman howl, and thrashed against the shackles. Bert and Ernie stepped back as a pure white light filled Wells's mind –

Bismillah rahmani rahim al hamdulillah –

Forgive us our trespasses as we forgive those who trespass against us –

English and Arabic, the Quran and the Bible, mixing inside him –

And tears dripping from his eyes, joining the blood on the floor.

Still they didn't stop.

After the fifth round they stepped back, wringing their hands, giving Wells a momentary, pointless flash of pleasure. He'd made them work a little, at least. They'd cracked two, maybe three, of his ribs somewhere along the way, he wasn't sure when.

They stowed the brass knuckles in their canvas bag,

dabbed at their foreheads with a little towel that Ernie had brought – an oddly dainty gesture – and took a long drink of water.

'Snack break, gentlemen?' Wells nearly delirious now. 'Like Rodney King said, can't we all just get along?' They ignored him. He wasn't even sure they could hear him, wasn't sure he was speaking aloud. 'Can I ask you boys something? Are you partners? Not like Starsky and Hutch, but *partners*. Okay, Starsky and Hutch is a bad example, but you see what I'm saying.'

As an answer, Bert and Ernie pulled out their batons.

The change of weapon seemed to suit them. They worked his legs for a while, mainly his thighs, bringing the steel batons down with gusto. Then Ernie slammed the baton on Wells's damaged left shoulder, a quick chop. Wells couldn't help himself. He moaned. Ernie said something in Chinese to Bert and started to work the shoulder hard. The pain doubled and redoubled and redoubled again, all the way to infinity.

Drink this and you'll grow wings on your feet.

'God,' Wells mumbled. 'Please.' He sagged against the shackles. The worst part was that they probably knew already. Most likely Cao Se had set him up. He was enduring all this for nothing.

Then the door slid open and Cao walked in.

THIRTY-THREE

As Cao closed the door, Ernie took one last shot, bringing his baton down so hard that Wells's shoulder popped out again and didn't slide back in. A whole new level of hell. *Don't scream.* The room whirled, faster and faster. The severed head of the guerrilla stared at him, not on the floor this time but directly in front of him. Wells felt his stomach clench and the room-service eggs he'd eaten that morning at the St. Regis spill out of his mouth and land in a stinking pile at his feet.

The vomit tasted sour and acrid in his throat, but it brought him back to reality. Feng moved behind him and unshackled his legs so he could stand, though his arms remained locked over his head. Ernie and Bert popped his shoulder back in. The pain eased. A little.

Feng turned to him. 'You see now, Mr. Wilson?' He looked at his watch. 'You've been here three-quarters of an hour. Imagine weeks. Months.'

But Wells was no longer listening. He was looking at Cao, trying to understand if this was the final act in his betrayal. Was Cao working with Li, or against him?

Cao trotted forward, hobbling a bit on his artificial

left leg. He looked impassively at Wells's flayed stomach and bruised legs.

'Name?' he said in English, heavily accented but recognizable.

Wells closed his eyes. He could hardly stay upright, but if he sagged the pressure on his shoulder became unbearable.

A finger poked at his abs. 'Name?'

'Wilson. Jim Wilson.' Wells coughed, twisted his head, spat a clot of phlegm, thick and streaked with blood, onto the cell's concrete floor beside Cao Se's shiny black boots.

'My name Cao Se.' Cao paused. 'You understand?'

Wells felt a glimmer of hope. 'Yes,' he said. 'Maybe.'

'What you tell them?'

'That I'm here on business –' The effort of speaking left Wells exhausted.

'Nothing. You tell nothing.'

'That's right. Nothing.' Cao and Wells speaking their own language now, one that Feng the interrogator couldn't understand no matter how closely he listened. So Wells wanted to believe. Feng said something to Cao, but Cao cut him off and turned back to Wells. A thick scar ran down the left side of his neck, an old jagged wound. Shrapnel, Wells thought.

'You American spy. Arrested in Forbidden City.'

'I'm not a spy.'

Cao twisted Wells's head in his strong little hands. Wells met his stare.

'*Who?* Who you meet there?'

'Nobody.' Wells snapped his head out of Cao's hands, looked at the men standing behind him. Time to jump. Time to find out which side Cao was on. 'What

387

do you want me to say? I came to meet Chairman Mao. Only he's dead. I came to meet *you*. You. Cao Se. Happy?'

Cao pulled a pistol from his bag, a long black silencer already screwed onto the barrel. 'You confess? You spy?'

'Sure. I confess.'

Cao stepped forward and put the silencer barrel to Wells's temple. Wells wasn't even afraid, just angry at himself for miscalculating, letting Cao trap him a second time. They'd played him so perfectly. He'd thought –

But what he thought no longer mattered. He closed his eyes, saw his head exploding, brains splattering the floor. Exley came to him then, and Evan –

And Cao fired, three times, the silencer muffling the shots, three quick quiet pops, *pfft pfft pfft*, a surprised yelp, then two more shots. Wells heard it all and knew he was still alive. Again.

He opened his eyes. Three men lay on the floor, Bert and Ernie dead, shot pinpoint between the eyes, Feng still alive, a hole in his face and two in his chest. He'd gotten a hand up. He moaned, low and tired. But even as Cao raised the pistol to finish him, a soft death rattle fluttered from his mouth, the hopeless sound of a balloon deflating, and his chest stilled.

Cao dropped the gun into his bag. He knelt down, careful to keep his boots clear of the blood pooling on the floor, grabbed a set of keys from Feng's jacket, unlocked Wells's arms. Wells could hardly stand. He leaned against a wall, fighting for balance.

'You my prisoner now,' Cao said. 'Stay quiet. Understand?'

Wells nodded. Already he was pulling on his pants. Even the lightest touch of the cloth set his bruised and swollen legs afire. He tried to put on the green T-shirt but couldn't get his arms over his head. Coursing under the sharp pain of his broken ribs was a deep throbbing bruising that was getting worse by the minute. He wondered if he was bleeding internally.

Cao gently pulled Wells's T-shirt over his head. Then he cuffed Wells's hands behind his back and nudged him forward. They picked their way through the blood and brains on the floor as carefully as children stepping over sidewalk cracks. And not for the first time Wells wondered why he'd been allowed to live, and what price he would pay.

Cao slid the cell door open. Behind it a short corridor ended in another steel door. Cao punched numbers on a digital keypad until the second door snapped open. They walked down a concrete hallway to a double set of gates where a guard sat in civilian clothes. Cao said a few words. The guard nodded and the gates slid open. As they walked through, Cao pointed to the cell where Wells had been held, pointed at his watch, said something sharp. Wells imagined he was warning the guard against entering the cell. He probably didn't need to explain much. Generals rarely did.

And then they were out, into the Beijing haze. Wells had the strange sense of being on a movie studio back lot, rounding a corner and traveling from New York to Paris in a second. He'd figured they were in the belly of a military base outside the city. Instead they were in the middle of Beijing, and the nondescript building behind them could have been a cheaply built elementary school, two stories high and concrete. In fact Wells could hear children shouting not far away. Only the guardhouse at the front gate and the razor wire atop the property's outer walls offered a clue to the building's real purpose.

Cao helped Wells into a jeep. They rolled up to the thick black gate at the front entrance, and a uniformed soldier jumped out of the guardhouse and trotted over. He pointed at Wells, but before he could say a word Cao began to shout. Without understanding a word, Wells knew that Cao was reaming out the soldier for daring to question him. The soldier turned tail and pulled the gate open with almost comic speed.

Five minutes later Cao turned into an alley and unlocked Wells's cuffs.

'What about the kid who gave me the flash drive?' Before anything else happened, Wells needed to hear the kid was okay.

'The kid?'

'The boy. In the Forbidden City.'

'Nothing happen. He not know. I give him fifty yuan, tell him he playing game,' Cao said. Wells bowed his head. He wanted to rest but feared what he would see if he closed his eyes. 'No other way,' Cao said. 'We have spy in your embassy. Know you coming.'

Wells understood. Cao had known that the PLA had intercepted his message to the embassy. He'd known that whoever the CIA sent would be arrested at the meeting point. He had no way to warn his contact off or change the meeting place. But no one would question his presence at the prison afterward with Li.

Still, Wells couldn't see how he and Cao could possibly escape. As soon as someone found the bodies in the interrogation room, all of China would be searching for them. 'Why didn't you just defect?' Wells thinking out loud. He figured his broken ribs gave him the right to ask.

'Didn't know about spy in embassy. Wanted to stay in China.'

'When will they find the men you shot?'

'Two, three hours. I warned the guards, don't go to the room.' Smart. Cao had bought them some time, Wells thought. But soon enough another officer would come along with different orders. 'Anyway, things very bad now with America,' Cao said. 'We torpedo *Decatur*.'

'You really must want war.'

'America not understand what happening,' Cao said.

'So tell me.'

In his strained English, Cao explained to Wells what Li had done. How he'd betrayed the Drafter to the North Koreans, made the deal with the Iranians, and maneuvered the United States and China closer to war. When Cao was finished, Wells felt like a treasure hunter who'd drilled through a mountain to find an empty tomb. But not quite empty. In a corner, a single, tiny gold figurine. *One man?* One man had brought the world's two most powerful nations to the brink of war?

'Why doesn't anyone stop him?' Wells said when Cao was done. 'On the Standing Committee.'

'They afraid they look weak. And also, they don't like America telling China what to do. America should be quiet when China make agreement with Iran.'

'But the defector, Wen Shubai, he said –'

For the first time, Cao raised his voice. 'Wen Shubai not real defector! Li Ping send Wen Shubai to fool you.'

'But the mole – Wen gave us enough to catch our mole –' Wells sputtered silent. Of course. Keith Robinson had been the bait that Wen had used to prove his bona fides. Li had known that Robinson's most useful days as a mole were behind him. He'd told Wen to sacrifice Robinson. That way, Wen's defection would seem credible.

Then, after Wen had proven his reliability by giving up Keith, he'd encouraged the United States to confront China – exactly the wrong strategy, one that gave Li Ping the leverage he needed internally to take control. Give up a pawn to position your forces for a wider attack. The gambit had worked perfectly. No wonder the agency and the White House hadn't been able to understand why confronting China had backfired so badly. Li's foes on the Standing Committee were probably equally bewildered that the situation had deteriorated so fast. Li had played the United States against his internal enemies, and vice versa. For the biggest prize in history, the chance to rule the most populous nation in the world.

'Li want to be Mao,' Cao said.

'To save China.'

'Yes. But China not need saving.' Cao gestured at the prosperous street behind them. 'Li good man, but he not see all this.'

Good man? Wells wasn't so sure, not after the casual way in which Li had waved a hand across his throat and ordered Wells dead. *He says it is nothing to him whether you live or die.* The casual cruelty of a man who had risked billions of lives in his quest to rule. But they could save that discussion for later.

'Then what?' he said to Cao. 'When he takes over? Does he want war?'

'No war. He think once he take over, he make everything okay.'

'Nice of him.' Wells laughed. A mistake. The agony in his ribs surged and he bit his tongue to keep from filling the jeep with vomit. He closed his eyes and tried to be still. Cao squeezed his shoulder until the pain faded.

'So . . . General . . .' Wells fought to stay focused, keep the fog away. 'How do we stop him? Can you tell the Standing Committee?'

'Say what to committee? That Li wants power? That I spy for America?'

Wells saw Cao's point. 'Then why did you bring me here if you didn't have anything?'

Cao was silent. Then: 'I don't know. I thought –'

Wells fought down his anger. He couldn't spare the energy. He rested a hand against his wounded ribs and tried to think things through. 'The committee wants to stop Li. Some of them, anyway.'

'Yes. Minister Zhang hate him. But he afraid.'

'I understand.' Cao might have stars on his collar, but he wasn't meant to lead, Wells saw already. He was a born subordinate. Smart and tough. But unimaginative. 'We need proof he's planned this all along. Something they can see. What did he hide from the committee?'

'Never told them about Wen.'

Wells felt a flash of hope, but it faded. The agency would need time to prove Wen's defection was fake, and time was just what they didn't have. 'What else?'

The jeep was silent. Wells waited, meanwhile wondering if Cao had an escape route planned or if they'd be reduced to making a desperate break for the embassy.

'What else. Li had one other operation. Top secret. Started last year. I set up the money.'

'The funding.'

'Yes. Funding. Said United States would be angry if it knew. Was in Afghanistan.'

Just like that, Wells knew. 'You were helping the Taliban.'

'He never told me, but I think so. But no Chinese soldiers.'

'No. Russian special forces.' Wells wondered if Pierre Kowalski had known all along where his money had come from.

'The account was in Banco Delta Asia,' Wells said. 'In Macao. Yes?'

Cao didn't hide his surprise. 'How you know this?'

'Did he tell you what this was for, Cao?'

'For Iran. All he said.'

Of course. Wells saw the logic of the scheme. The Iranians had worried that China might walk away from the nukes-for-oil deal. By supporting the Taliban, Li had convinced Iran he was serious about standing up to America.

'Cao, those records prove Li has been planning war against America since last year. And he never told the Standing Committee. If you get them, we can stop him.'

If we live long enough to get them out of China, Wells didn't say. If my guess is right, and they prove the money went to Kowalski. If the White House can get them back to Beijing, and to Zhang. And if Zhang can use them to get control of the committee back from Li.

But first they had to get the records, and get out.

'No war?' Cao said.

'No war.' Maybe.

'Then I get them.'

Cao reversed the jeep onto the road, looking sidelong at Wells as he did. 'What your name? Real name.'

Crazy but true. Cao had saved his life, killed three of his own countrymen to do so, and didn't even know his name. Wells wiped his hand against his mouth and came away with a pungent coating of dried blood and vomit. 'John Wells.'

'Time Square Wells?'

'Time Square Wells.' Wells wondered if Cao was ready to move to Florida, live in a witness protection program. No matter what happened next, this would be his last day in China. 'But if we get out, you can call me Tiananmen Square Wells. When we go to Disney World.'

'Disney World? Don't understand.' The jeep hit a bump and Wells moaned a little.

'Me neither, Cao.'

Fifteen minutes later Cao honked his way across four lanes of traffic and swung into an alley cluttered with wooden crates. A cloud of flies hovered around a pile of rotten vegetables. Normally the trash would hardly have bothered Wells, but the beating had left him weak and queasy. His green T-shirt was black with his blood. His heart was randomly speeding and slowing – *thump*, pause, *thump*, pause, *thump-thump-thump-thump*. He figured he was coming down off the adrenaline rush that had carried him through the immediate aftermath of the beating. Or maybe they'd done more damage to him than he first thought.

Cao stopped behind a low concrete building with a heavy steel door. The words 'Dumping Home' were painted, in black and in English, on a splintered wooden sign. Dumping Home? Wells wondered if he was delirious, but when he looked again, the sign hadn't changed.

Cao pointed at the building. 'Friends inside. Christians.'

Wells wondered if he should mention his own confused beliefs. Probably not the time.

Cao honked. The back door creaked open and a man in a dirty chef's apron jogged over. He and Cao spoke briefly before he nodded and ran back inside. Cao tapped his watch. Four p.m.

'One hour. If I not back, you go with them. To Yantai –'

'Yantai?' Wells was struck again by how little he knew about this country.

'Port. Five hundred kilometers from here. Shandong Province.'

Now Wells understood, or thought he did. Shandong Province – the name literally meant 'east of the mountains' – extended into the Yellow Sea toward the Korean Peninsula. They were going to make a run for South Korea.

'They take you to boat.'

'To Korea?'

'Yes. Korea.' Cao's lips twisted in what could have been a smile. 'Make sure not North Korea.' Cao reached into his bag and handed Wells a little pistol, a .22 snub.

Wells pulled back the slide. It was loaded all right. It was too small and inaccurate to be useful at more than thirty feet. Still, better than nothing.

Two men emerged from the Dumping Home and trotted to the jeep.

'Rest,' Cao said.

'Good luck, Cao. *Vaya con Dios.*' Wells extended a hand and Cao shook it awkwardly. Cao reached across Wells and opened his door. The men helped lift him out, staggering under his weight. Wells could hardly feel the ground under his feet, as if his legs were encased in ski boots that ran from ankle to hip. The men guided him to the door, as Cao put the jeep in reverse and rolled out of the alley.

Inside, Wells found himself in a busy kitchen. Two women and two teenage boys were making dumplings, their hands flickering over the balls of dough, shaping and smoothing each one before moving to the next. Wells understood now. The Dumping Home was a dumpling restaurant.

The men started to let Wells go, but as they did his legs buckled. One of the women squawked and the men grabbed him and guided him to a storeroom off the kitchen. They sat him down and left. Wells tried to rest, but if he closed his eyes for too long the dizziness took him. He focused on the room around him, looking from shelf to shelf, examining the baskets of vegetables and spices, the glass jars of green tea.

A couple of minutes later, he wasn't sure how long, the women came in, carrying a pot of bubbling water, a soup bowl, and a big shopping bag. Wells watched mutely as they extracted the tools for minor surgery from the bag: two quart-sized brown plastic bottles, a water bottle, scissors, a knife, a tube of something that looked like antibacterial cream, a roll of surgical tape, and a half-dozen clean white cloths. One of the women, tall and thin, her hair streaked with gray, put a soft hand on his shoulder.

Meanwhile, the other woman, the shorter and stockier of the two, lifted the bowl of soup to Wells's mouth. He sipped, a few drops at a time. Chicken stock, with a few mushy carrots. Liquid kindness. His stomach clenched, but he held it down. He drank as much as he could, maybe a half-cup, and then shook his head. She nodded and set the bowl aside. Now the gray-haired woman was cutting off his shirt, careful not to touch the flayed skin underneath. When she was done, she gasped, one quick breath. Wells looked down and wished he hadn't. His chest and abs were skinned raw, and blood was oozing from the wounds. No wonder he couldn't close his eyes without getting the spins. He had to make sure he stayed hydrated. If he wasn't careful, the blood loss would put him into shock.

The gray-haired woman dipped a cloth into the pot of boiling water. Then she unscrewed the plastic bottles and poured their contents over the cloth. She held the cloth to his face, giving him a whiff of rubbing alcohol and hydrogen peroxide. Wells understood. She wanted him to know what she was about to do. He nodded. She pressed the cloth to his chest.

After the beating he'd endured, the burn of alcohol and peroxide was barely a pinprick. Wells nodded. The woman seemed to understand. She pulled away the cloth and poured the rubbing alcohol directly onto his chest. She wiped him down with a fresh cloth, then rubbed the antibacterial ointment across his chest. She said something to the other woman. They leaned him forward and slowly they wrapped a long white bandage around his torso, compressing it tightly. Apparently the gray-haired woman had decided Wells had a high pain tolerance.

When they were done, his chest and abs were bound

in white. Despite the pressure of the cloth against his broken ribs, Wells felt stronger than he had just a few minutes before. He reached for the soup and slowly sipped it until the bowl was empty.

'Good as new,' he said.

For the first time since the beatings started, Wells could think clearly enough to see his next move. He reached into his pockets. There it was. His new phone, bought five days before and registered to Jim Wilson of Palo Alto. Still in his pants. He'd debated carrying it today before deciding that there was no reason an American businessman wouldn't have a phone with him. Now he was glad he had. Extremely.

He removed the slim Motorola from his pocket, turned it on, saw he had full service. Thank God for technology. Wells wondered whether the Chinese had put a bug in the phone, before deciding they probably hadn't. They'd had no reason to imagine that he would escape.

Anyway, he had to reach Exley now, before the Chinese cut off all communication to the United States. He'd be as quick as he could. Wells called her cell phone, not the 415 number but her real one, the one she always carried. Three rings. And then –

'Hello. Hello?' Washington was twelve hours behind, Wells remembered. She must have been asleep, or wishing she were.

'Jennifer.'

'Yes. John.' She'd blown his cover, but he didn't much care. In his name, he heard all her questions: Where are you? Are you okay?

'Remember where Ted Beck went down, Jenny?' In the Yellow Sea, southwest of Incheon.

'Sure.'

'I need a pickup. In that vicinity. Or west. As far west as possible.' Even if the Chinese were monitoring this call, Wells didn't think they would understand what he meant.

'When?'

Five hundred kilometers to Yantai, then a boat ride. 'Eight to twenty-four hours. Any longer, I'm in trouble.'

'Can you help us find you?' Exley was wondering if he had a transponder or any other equipment to aid the search.

'No. But Red Team' – the standard American military description of the enemy – 'will be looking. Hard.'

'Figured.'

'One more thing. Whatever they're planning, make them wait. *No counterattacks.* I know why it happened, all of it. And we can stop it.'

'I'll tell them.'

'I love you, Jenny.'

'Love you too, John.' Exley sighed. Even from 6,000 miles away, Wells knew her tone, sad and prideful at once. 'Try not to die.'

Wells hung up and turned off the phone. Now it was up to Exley to find a way to make the White House and the Pentagon back off for a day or two, long enough for him and Cao to get out.

The clock on the wall of the storeroom said 4:45. Cao didn't have long. The guards at the interrogation center would soon defy his orders and break into the room where Wells had been held. Then he and Cao would be the most wanted men in China. Before that happened, he and Cao had better be on their way to Yantai. Though Wells still didn't know how Cao planned to get them there.

Wells flexed his legs and tried to stand. Nope. He sat down heavily and the jolt set his ribs on fire. His gray-haired nurse shook a finger at him and clucked in Chinese. Wells could guess her meaning: *Rest*. Then the two women left him, turning off the lights and shutting the door. In the warm darkness the tang of potatoes and onions surrounded him.

He closed his eyes. His head drooped. But before he slept, he made sure the .22 was curled in his hand. If Li's men came through the door, he planned to take as many of them with him as he could.

THIRTY-FOUR

Twelve time zones behind Wells, Exley pulled on sweatpants and a mostly clean blouse and walked downstairs to Thirteenth Street, where her security guards waited in their black Lincolns under the dark predawn sky. The doors of the front Lincoln opened as she approached, and the guards stepped out.

'Ms. Exley.'

'I need a ride.'

The Lincolns screamed off, a two-car convoy with sirens and flashing lights. Fifteen minutes later she was knocking on Shafer's door. She hoped he had some ideas. On the ride over, the reality of the odds that they faced had hit her. Wells had no transponder, no way to reach them. He hadn't even told her what kind of ship he'd be on, much less its name. The Yellow Sea was practically Chinese territory, especially under these circumstances. How would they possibly find him and get him out?

Shafer opened the door, bleary-eyed. He motioned her inside, down to his basement, into the laundry room. 'Ellis –'

'Wait. I get the house swept every other month but

just in case.' He flicked on the washer and dryer. 'Now,' Shafer said.

'John called.'

'Where from?'

'Beijing.' She explained what Wells had told her.

When she was done, Shafer shook his head. 'No hint of what he's got?'

'No. Just that he could stop it. We have to talk to Duto.'

'And tell him we need to pull out the stops to save John Wells. This'll be fun.' He motioned her upstairs. 'Go home, get dressed. I'll see you in two hours at Langley.'

'Two hours.'

'Nothing we can do before then. He won't get off the coast for several hours. Besides, no one's going to take us seriously dressed like this.' He was wearing Redskins pajamas, a fact she'd chosen to ignore until now.

'Point taken.'

Exley and Shafer sat in a windowless, soundproofed conference room at Langley, across from Tyson and Vinny Duto. The stress of being director seemed to be getting to Duto. He was fatter than she remembered, and his hair – always his pride – had receded, offering hints of scalp. But his eyes were as hard as ever.

He listened silently as Exley told him and Tyson what Wells had said. No one spoke when she finished, and for a few seconds the only sound in the room was the drumming of Duto's fingers against the wooden table.

'So you understand: In the last hour, our satellites have picked up a major mobilization of Chinese forces.

403

Regular army and paramilitary. Increasing by the minute. The White House knows.' Duto opened a black-bordered folder. 'They're putting roadblocks on the highways and main secondary roads in and out of Beijing. Military units at the entrances to every civilian airport. The Friendship Bridge, between China and North Korea, has been shut.'

'Sounds like they haven't found him yet.'

'Unfortunately, we haven't found him either,' Tyson said. 'And unless you and he are connected telepathically, I'm not sure how we're going to. Since he has no transponder and didn't see fit to give us coordinates. Perhaps he should have asked for an airlift out of Tiananmen. It might have been easier.'

Exley's ears burned. Wells might be dead and Tyson was *cracking jokes*? Her face must have shown her anger, because Tyson quickly backed off. 'I am only saying that the attack on the *Decatur* proves the Chinese are acting recklessly, Ms. Exley. If we move our ships deep into the Yellow Sea, they may think that we're intentionally provoking them.'

'They've got ten thousand miles of coast. They can't watch it all,' Shafer said. 'He gets twelve miles offshore, he's not in territorial waters anymore. And there's still heavy traffic in the Yellow Sea. I checked.' He held up a two-page printout filled with ship names and registry numbers. 'All due at Incheon today.'

'Let me point out something you may not wish to hear,' Tyson said. 'Mr. Wells told you we should wait, not do anything stupid.'

'Right, he said he had something –'

Tyson knocked her down. 'But he didn't say what.'

'It was an unsecured line.'

404

'At the same time, he wants us to take an incredibly aggressive action. Bit of a contradiction there, wouldn't you say?'

'He wants us to save his life,' Exley said.

'Or perhaps the call was a setup arranged by the Chinese.'

'It was him. I know his voice.'

'What if he's been turned and they're using him to get at us? To move our ships into a vulnerable position.'

'He wouldn't. He'd die first.'

'People do strange things when they're in pain.'

This couldn't be happening, Exley thought. They weren't seriously arguing about whether to let Wells die out there. 'Then why are they mobilizing their army and all the rest?'

'Part of the setup.'

'You don't really think that,' she said. 'Save me the mirrors within mirrors nonsense.' Her voice rose, and she reminded herself to stay in control, not to give them any excuse to marginalize her. 'This was your idea, George. If not for you he wouldn't be in this mess.'

'Jennifer,' Duto said. 'I don't think we can risk putting our assets that far forward. Let Wells get to Incheon. At least into Korean territorial waters.'

Shafer laughed, a thin angry laugh.

'Something to say, Ellis?'

Shafer waited until they were all looking at him. Normally, he was a jumble of tics and wasted motion. Not now. Exley had never seen him so still.

'Never thought I'd have to play this card, Vinny. I underestimated you. You sent him there and you'd rather let him die than lift a finger. The craziest part is, he might actually get us out of this mess.'

'We don't know what he has, Ellis, that's the point.

I'm not going to recommend that we put thousands of sailors in harm's way. Maybe push the Chinese over the edge. To save one man.'

'To stop a war.'

'What if he's been turned?'

'Where have I heard this song before? It's not his fault he saved New York while you tried to arrest him. Get over it.' Shafer stood. 'Jenny, come on. Over the river and through the woods. To the president's house we go.'

'Ellis –' Duto said.

'Herr Director. This is so simple, even you can understand it. You tell the president we have a chance to stop this war. You tell him we're going to go get Wells. Or I will.'

'And what do we tell the Chinese when they ask why half our fleet is twenty miles off their coast?'

'We'll burn that bridge when we come to it.'

'You've forgotten the biggest problem, Ellis,' Tyson said. 'We have no idea how to find Mr. Wells. Are you suggesting we sail in circles and hope he paddles up on his wooden raft or whatever he'll be on? I assure you the Navy will dislike that plan, especially with that Chinese supersub still on the loose.'

'I have an idea,' Exley said.

'Do share,' Tyson said.

'You're right. We can't find him. So we're going to have to make it easy for him to find us.'

Exley outlined her plan. Duto was shaking his head before she was half done. 'No way,' he said. 'The Air Force will never –'

'They will if the big man tells them to,' Shafer said.

'How do you know Wells is even going to understand what we're doing?'

'He'll understand,' Exley said.

And suddenly Duto smiled at her, the easy smile of a poker player watching his opponent make a bluff that was doomed to fail. 'You, me, Ellis. We'll ride over there together. You and Ellis can tell the big man whatever you like. I don't mind. As long as he knows it's from you.'

THIRTY-FIVE

Asleep –

Then awake –

And Wells had the .22 up before he knew where he was. The storeroom. Cao stood in the doorway. He raised his hands as Wells lowered the pistol.

'You okay, Time Square Wells?'

'Perfect.' Wells coughed. His bandage was still white, at least on the outside.

Cao tossed Wells a blue zip-up sweatsuit, and Wells tugged it on. His shoulder was loose in its socket, maybe permanently damaged from the torture. He took a long drink of lukewarm water to soothe his parched throat.

'Ready?'

Wells tucked the pistol in his waistband and struggled up. He took a few steps and sagged. Cao's men helped him out of the restaurant. A dirty white panel truck waited, its engine running. Wooden crates and furniture were stacked high inside the twenty-five-foot-long cargo compartment.

'You need piss?' Cao waved a fist in front of his crotch. 'Go now.'

'I'm okay.'

'Then we go.' Cao stepped into the truck and offered a hand to Wells. At the forward end of the cargo compartment, behind a big wooden bookcase, was a space maybe three feet wide. Just big enough for two men to sit, if they didn't mind a little incidental contact. A blanket covered the compartment's wooden floor, along with provisions: water bottles, a flashlight, blankets. A handful of airholes ensured they wouldn't suffocate.

Wells and Cao settled themselves, close enough for Wells to smell the green tea on Cao's breath. As Cao's men rearranged boxes and furniture to hide the space, Cao reached into his jacket and handed Wells a manila envelope.

Wells opened it. Three pages of Banco Delta Asia bank records, showing transfers to UBS accounts in Zurich and Monte Carlo, $20 million a month. A fourth page covered with Chinese characters and topped with an official-looking letterhead. Wells wondered if these four pieces of paper could really stop a war.

Cao pointed to the fourth page. 'This from Army.'

'Authorizing the transfers?'

'Authorizing, yes. Says money for special operation.' Cao pointed to a raised emblem near the bottom. 'Li's stamp.'

'I'll take your word for it.'

Wells didn't plan to ask how Cao had gotten the papers. Presumably he'd just made his final trip inside Zhongnanhai. If Wells hadn't just seen Cao shoot three of his own soldiers, he might have wondered whether this was all some superelaborate sting operation designed to prove Wells was a spy. But the Chinese had no need for an operation that elaborate. The torture had been working well enough on its own. Cao was a genuine defector.

Wells tried to give Cao back the papers, but Cao shook his head.

One of Cao's men shouted something. The back panel came down and they were locked in the dark. Wells hardly minded. After the cave, this truck was easy. At least they were above ground.

The truck grumbled into gear and reversed down the alley. A few seconds later horns honked, and they were in Beijing's traffic.

'Now we run.' In the dark Cao laughed humorlessly.

'Yeah, tramps like us,' Wells said. He liked Cao very much. Probably because the man had saved his life. 'What about roadblocks?'

'Roadblock?'

Wells couldn't figure out how to explain. 'Are they looking for us?'

'Very soon.' Cao lit his watch – 6:10. 'Maybe twenty minutes. New officer come, open door. See bodies.'

Wells thought he understood. There would be a shift change at the interrogation center where Wells had been held. The new commander would insist on seeing the torture room. And once he discovered the bodies, the hunt would be on.

'But isn't Li Ping wondering where you are?'

'When we leave, I say to Li, let me take care of spy. He trust me. Anyway, he busy. Special meeting with Standing Committee.'

'Must be hard fighting two wars at once.' Wells closed his eyes and tried to settle himself in the darkness. But he had too many questions. 'Cao, who are these people helping us?'

Cao said nothing for a minute. Then, finally: 'Don't know.'

Don't know? Wells waited.

'I tell my pastor last night. About you. He send me these people from his church. They help when Christians get in trouble, need hiding.'

A Christian underground railroad, Wells thought. 'Do they know who we are, the risk they're taking?'

'Yes.'

'But you trust them?'

Again Cao laughed, low and hard. 'You have other idea?'

Minutes later the truck turned, accelerated. 'Third Ring Road now,' Cao said.

'We're making good time.'

'Many people stay home now. Scared what America will do.'

And without warning –

The truck scissored down into a pothole. Wells's broken ribs jumped under the bandage, stabbing from the inside out. The pain in his lungs and stomach was enormous and didn't fade. Wells bit his lip to keep from screaming.

Thump! Thump! More potholes. Wells braced himself against the side of the truck, feeling his ribs rattle like pencils in a coffee cup. If he wasn't bleeding internally already, he would be soon.

To distract himself, he thought of Exley, and their little apartment on Thirteenth Street, NW. In the utility closet in the front hall, Wells had hung the letters the president had sent them after they'd stopped the attack on New York. '*You have earned the respect and gratitude of an entire nation . . .*' et cetera, et cetera. No one had ever understood him like Exley, Wells thought. He never had to tell her why the flowery words embarrassed him. Yes, he was proud of what they had

411

done. But he hated being called a hero, especially by men who had never shed blood. Let the president save his soupy words and send his own children off to a battle zone for even one day.

Wells wondered if he could claim to understand Exley nearly as well as she understood him. She rarely talked to him about marriage or having kids. Did she think that having more children would be selfish when she hardly saw the two she already had? Or was it that she couldn't imagine a future with *him*? Maybe she decided that as much as they loved each other, they weren't going to get over the finish line.

When he got home, he would ask her to marry him.

If it wasn't too late.

THUMP! The truck bounced again, the hardest jolt yet. Wells couldn't help himself. He screamed. The blackness around him merged with the void in his head and down he went.

Later – he had no idea how long it was – his eyes opened. His stomach was throbbing and uncomfortably tight. He was bleeding internally now, he was sure. He raised the water bottle to his lips and sipped, trying to force the liquid down.

The truck had stopped, its engine silent. Wells heard voices and footsteps on gravel. The compartment was totally dark, no light coming through the airholes. Night had fallen. How long had he been out?

The footsteps crunched to the back of the truck and –

The back panel opened. Cao gripped Wells's leg, a warning to stay silent.

A flashlight shined in, making slow loops around the compartment.

A man's harsh voice, shouting questions.

The replies, soft and deferential.

Then the truck's springs creaked as someone stepped onto the back bumper.

Wells pulled his snubnose pistol from his waistband, silently dropped the safety.

The light shined around, closer now.

But not finding their compartment.

And the truck came up on its springs as the man stepped down.

The back panel closed. The doors to the truck's cab opened, slammed shut. The engine groaned and they were off, slowly at first, then more quickly.

Only after they reached highway speed did Cao finally speak. 'Close.'

'No kidding,' Wells said. 'What time is it?'

Cao flicked on his little digital watch and showed it to Wells – 9:15. He'd been asleep at least two hours.

'How much longer?'

Cao shined his flashlight over Wells. 'Five hours, maybe. Okay?'

'I'll get by.' Wells coughed a little black clot of blood and phlegm into his hand. 'General, what made you –' Wells stopped, wondering if he was overreaching. He settled on a more neutral formulation. 'Why did you decide to leave? After all these years.'

Cao turned the flashlight to his own face, as if interrogating himself. 'Why I betray General Li, you mean?' Wells was silent. 'I tried to say once.'

'What you thought.'

'What I thought. He never listen.' Cao tapped the flashlight against the stump of his leg. 'Li forget what war is like. I don't forget.'

'Some wars you have to fight,' Wells said.
'Not this one.'
'Not this one.'

The truck rolled on. The road turned smooth, a blessing, and the compartment cooled as the night air rushed in. They were probably taking a chance on an expressway now, Cao said. The danger had lessened now that they'd reached Shandong Province.

'But why doesn't Li just shut everything down?' Wells asked. 'Put in a countrywide curfew.'

Cao's explanation stretched the limits of his English, but eventually Wells understood: Li was afraid to tell the Standing Committee that Cao had defected. Cao was Li's closest aide, so Cao's treachery would reflect badly on him. Li's opponents might use it to undo Li's grip on power, which was still tenuous.

But without the approval of the Standing Committee, Li couldn't simply shut all of China down. So the roads were still open. Li was depending on roadblocks to catch them, and the Navy if they somehow got to the Yellow Sea.

'So there's a window.'

'Yes. Window.'

And with that, Wells closed his eyes uneasily. He tried to imagine what would happen after he handed the papers over and explained what they meant. Treasury would connect the Banco Delta Asia accounts with Kowalski's accounts in Zurich and Monte Carlo. The Pentagon would give the State Department the confession from Sergei, the Russian Spetsnaz that Wells had captured in the cave.

Then the American ambassador would ask Li's enemies on the Standing Committee for a secret

414

meeting. There he'd give Minister Zhang the proof of what Li had done.

Zhang and the rest of the committee would know they had to act. They'd know that if the United States publicized China's support for the Taliban, world opinion would turn in America's favor. After all, American soldiers weren't the only ones fighting the Talibs in Afghanistan. By supporting the guerrillas, China had committed an act of war against all of NATO.

Zhang wouldn't need much convincing, anyway. He and Li's other enemies on the committee were looking for any excuse to stop Li. This was a good one. They wouldn't care that it had come from the United States.

For the first time, Wells allowed himself to believe that they might actually get out of this mess. He pressed his hands together in front of his face. *Here's the church and here's the steeple. Open the door and there's the people.* He and Exley wouldn't have a church wedding, though. Not a mosque wedding either. They'd go down to city hall and do it quick and dirty. Exley liked it quick and dirty. . . .

He knew he was drifting and didn't mind. Drifting made the shooting pains in his belly easier to take. And so he drifted, dozed, woke, drifted again. All the while, the truck rolled on. Eventually they left the highway and passed along a series of narrow switchbacks, rising and falling, not mountains exactly but certainly good-sized hills. Wells snapped awake as the truck took a turn too hard, its left rear wheels briefly leaving the pavement.

'Shandong,' Cao said. 'Back roads.'

'How long?'

Cao lit his watch – 12:45. 'One hour, maybe two. No more.'

It was 12:45 p.m. in Washington, Wells thought. The attack on the *Decatur* had happened about twelve hours before. He wondered whether Exley had persuaded Duto and the White House to hold off. Surely the president would be speaking to the country tonight, and politicians on both sides would be pushing for action. God. Until now he hadn't even considered the possibility that they'd make it to South Korea and still be too late.

Then the truck slowed, hard, pushing forward on its shocks –

And stopped.

Again the engine went quiet. Again voices shouting in Chinese. Again the back panel slid up.

But this time two men stepped into the truck. This time the flashlight searched the compartment much more thoroughly than it had before.

This time the cops smelled something wrong, Wells thought. Maybe the fact that the truck had two drivers. Maybe the route they were taking, running back roads in the middle of nowhere at 1:00 a.m. Maybe the cops were just having a little fun, looking for a television or something to steal. Whatever it was, these guys weren't giving up until they turned the compartment inside out.

Wells wondered how many there were. How many he'd have to kill. A country roadblock in the middle of the night. Two cops, maybe? Two in the truck, two out? Four at most.

Now the cops were shouting and throwing furniture out of the back of the truck as the drivers yelled. Cao leaned forward and whispered to Wells.

'They say, "You four have no right." Four. Understand?'

'Four.'

Crash! A couch landed on the ground. The flashlight closed in. Wells drew his .22, dropped the safety, pulled himself to a squat, braced himself against the side wall. The empty bookcase scraped sideways and started to tip. The compartment echoed with shouts in Chinese. Not so long ago, Wells had told Exley the secret to surviving these moments: *Shoot first. Don't wait.* He was about to follow his own advice.

He pushed himself up, ignoring the agony in his stomach. As the bookcase tipped, Wells saw the cops, five feet away, tugging at the case. They reached for their guns as they saw him. Too late. He squeezed the pistol's trigger, twice.

And then they were dead.

The bookcase fell. Wells dropped behind it. The other two cops stood at the back of the truck. They should have gone for cover. Instead, they were shooting, but wildly, high. A mistake, the last they would ever make. Wells focused and fired, hearing the *pfft* of Cao's silenced pistol beside him. One of the cops twisted, his head turned at an unnatural angle, and dropped. The other doubled over, his hand on his stomach, beginning to yell. Wells moved his pistol a fraction of an inch and fired again. This time the shot caught the cop in the shoulder. He dropped his gun and fell, still yelling.

Wells staggered out of the cargo compartment. He took aim at the moaning cop at his feet and then lowered his .22 without firing. Let Cao do it. Let someone else. Anyone.

Then he raised his gun again, took aim. He was what he was. No point in pretending otherwise. No point in making someone else do his dirty work. He fired. The cop's body twitched and went still.

417

The roadblock had been in front of a bridge over a narrow canal. A police car and a jeep sat at the edge of the road, their emergency lights still flashing. Wells leaned against the truck, looked around. The hills behind them were forested and seemed empty, but a couple of miles ahead Wells saw the beginnings of a town, red smokestack lights blinking in the night. Fortunately, the two-lane road was silent. For now.

Cao jumped down from the truck, yelling at the men who'd driven them. Wells understood his frustration, but there wasn't time. They couldn't hide this. They had only one choice.

'Cao.' Wells grabbed the smaller man's shoulder. 'Tell them, put the cops in the truck. Leave everything else. Let's go. Now.'

Cao looked around, nodded. He said something to the men and they threw the bodies in the truck as casually as if they were slinging sacks of rice. Wells stumbled over one of the corpses as he stepped back into the truck. The body was still warm. Practically still alive. Except it wasn't.

The truck rolled off. Wells slumped against the floor of the cargo compartment and tried to think through what would happen next. Assuming the Chinese had any command-and-control at all, they'd discover the missing police well before daybreak. Two hours, say.

Li wouldn't know exactly what had happened, but he would be able to make a very good guess. He would assume that Cao and Wells were trying to escape by boat. He would blanket the eastern half of the province, and the sea around it, with every soldier and ship he could muster. He'd declare a state of emergency covering the province and the coast, order all civilian boats to stay docked for the day. All China would be hunting them. They had to get off the mainland as soon as possible. Even if they could stay hidden somehow, Wells didn't think he could last another day unless he got to a hospital. He felt flushed and weak, and his stomach was dangerously tender from the blood he'd leaked. A surgeon could fix him easily, he had no doubt. But with no surgeon he'd bleed to death, or die of an internal infection when the bacteria in his gut crossed into his bloodstream.

'Cao.'

'Time Square Wells.' Cao flicked on a lighter and touched the dim yellow flame to a stubby cigarette clenched in his teeth. He held out the pack. Wells shook his head, realizing that Cao hadn't smoked before because he hadn't wanted to give away their presence in the compartment. But now being discreet was pointless. Their hiding place had become a slaughterhouse.

'How far?'

Cao flicked on his watch. 'One hour maybe. Hundred ten kilometers' – seventy miles. 'No more back road.'

As if to prove his words, the truck accelerated, throwing Wells against the side of the cargo compartment. He groaned and caught his breath. 'The highway goes all the way to Yantai?'

'Yes. Then east, twenty kilometers, Chucun. Boat there.'

'And the boat, what kind is it?'

The tip of Cao's cigarette glowed brightly. 'We see.'

Wells laughed. It was all he could do.

It was 2:20 a.m. They'd made good time. The cove was a pleasant surprise, a narrow semicircular strip of white sand protected by thick trees. The boat was another

419

story, not much more than an oversized rowboat, maybe twenty feet long, with a big outboard engine. It sat low in the water, its black paint peeling, fishing nets hanging off its hull, four red plastic canisters of gasoline tucked under the wide wooden slats that served as seats. A Chinese man, sixty-five or so, sat on its side.

Wells knew the Yellow Sea was flat, but still he couldn't believe this bathtub with an engine could reach Incheon, three hundred miles away across open water. And even if it could, they would need twelve hours or more, with the Chinese navy chasing them. Suddenly their odds seemed worse than hopeless.

'No way,' Wells said.

'No choice.' Cao hugged the men who'd driven them, spoke a few words in Chinese to the old man beside the boat. Wells wondered what their helpers would do next. Probably ditch the truck as best they could and disappear.

Cao stepped inside, his plastic leg thunking on the side of the boat. Wells followed, nearly falling over as he did. Cao was right. They didn't have a choice. In the distance he heard a helicopter. He sat down heavily on the wooden bench and rubbed the bandage that covered his broken chest. He felt light-headed and feverish despite the cool night air. He wondered if he could last even twelve hours.

The drivers and the fisherman stepped forward and pushed the boat off the sand. It slid forward easily, lolling on the flat waves. Cao jabbed at a red button on the side of the outboard and the engine grumbled to life. He turned the tiller sideways and they cruised into the cove. The men on shore waved.

'Cao, do we even have a compass?'
Cao handed Wells a compass. 'Straight east. Easy.'
'Incheon or bust.'

THIRTY-SIX

OSAN AIR BASE, SOUTH KOREA

The C-130J Hercules lumbered down the runways, slowly accelerating as it bounced over the tarmac. Not far from the grass overrun at the end of the 9,000-foot strip, its nose finally lifted. Inside the cockpit Lieutenant Colonel Paul Bosarelli exhaled. The C-130 was a sturdy beast, but he wouldn't have wanted to skid off in this particular plane.

Nobody joined the Air Force to fly C-130s. But during eighteen years as a Herc pilot, Bosarelli had grown fond of the ugly old birds, the four-propeller workhorses of the Air Force. They weren't as sexy as F-22s or B-2s, but they were far more useful most of the time. They could endure massive damage and still take off or land just about anywhere. Besides hauling cargo and airdropping special-ops units, they worked as fuel tankers, firefighters, even gunships.

But Bosarelli guessed that in the five decades since the first C-130 joined the Air Force fleet, none had ever carried a load like this one.

And that was probably for the best.

*

The tactical operations center at Osan had received the first reports of the attack on the *Decatur* three minutes after the Chinese torpedo smashed the destroyer's hull. With no way to know whether the attack was a one-off or part of a larger Chinese assault, the center's director, Brigadier General Tom Rygel, had put the base on Force Protection Condition Charlie-Plus, the second-highest alert level – just short of Delta, which signaled imminent attack. Rygel's decision was understandable, for Osan was the closest American base to China. The PRC's border with North Korea was just three hundred miles to the north, a distance that China's newest J-10 fighters could cover in fifteen minutes on afterburner.

Within an hour of the *Decatur* attack, Osan's 51st Fighter Wing had put six F-16s in the air to join the two already on patrol. Eight more jets waited on standby. Of course, the sixteen fighters were vastly outnumbered by the hundreds of Chinese jets waiting over the border. But the American planes were so much more capable than even the most advanced J-10s that the Chinese would be insane to challenge them. Though the skipper of the *Decatur* had probably made the same assumption, Bosarelli thought.

While the fighters soared off, Bosarelli had nothing to do except drink coffee in the ready room and try to ignore the acid biting at his stomach. Ninety percent of the time – heck, ninety-five – he had more to do than the fancy boys. But at moments like this, he felt like a fraud. Against a fighter jet, *any* fighter jet, his C-130 was nothing but a flying bull's-eye.

Then the door to the ready room opened. A lieutenant looked around and headed straight for the table where Bosarelli sat. 'Colonel Bosarelli.'

'Yes.' Bosarelli knew the guy's face, though not his

name. He was one of Hansell's runners. Lieutenant General Peter Hansell, the commander of the 7th Air Force, the top officer at Osan.

'Colonel, General Hansell would like to see you.'

Hansell's office was in the Theater Air Control Center, a squat building that everyone at Osan called Cheyenne Mountain East because of its ten-foot-thick concrete walls. As he trotted through the center's narrow corridors, Bosarelli wondered what he'd done wrong. Or right.

Before Bosarelli could figure it out, they reached Hansell's office. 'This is where I get off,' the lieutenant said. 'Go right in. He's expecting you.'

Bosarelli wished he had a minute or two to shine his shoes and make sure his uniform was squared away. But he wasn't about to keep Hansell waiting. He threw back his shoulders, stepped inside, and gave the general the crispest salute that he'd offered anyone since his first year as a cadet in Colorado Springs.

'Sir.'

'Colonel. Please sit. You've been flying the Herc for eighteen years, is that right?' It wasn't a question. Bosarelli nodded. 'Your record's spotless. Two years ago, you landed in Bagram on one engine.'

Bosarelli was thoroughly nervous now. Three-stars didn't butter up lieutenant colonels this way unless they wanted something.

'And you requalified on the chutes just last year.'

'That's correct, sir.'

'I have a mission to discuss with you, Colonel. An unusual mission. You're the first Herc pilot I'm offering it to. But I want you to understand. This is a request. Not an order. No hard feelings if you say no.'

'Yes, sir. I accept, sir.'

'Thank you,' Hansell said. 'But first I need to know if it's even possible.'

For the next five minutes, Bosarelli sat silent as Hansell outlined what he wanted.

'So? Can we do it?' Hansell said when he was done. 'I'd rather use a Predator' – a lightweight unmanned drone – 'but they just don't have the payload to make it work.'

Bosarelli wished he could ask who'd okayed this insane idea, and why. On second thought, he didn't even want to know. Somebody up the chain, that was for sure. Way high up. Maybe all the way. He looked at the ceiling, avoiding Hansell's ice-blue eyes, visualizing the steps he'd take.

'And we'd be doing this –'

'Tonight. The goal is four a.m.'

'No time like the present.' *Craziest thing I've ever heard*, Bosarelli didn't say. He'd always wanted to be in the middle of the action. Now he was. *Be careful what you wish for.* 'I think it's possible, sir. In a way it's a throwback, a big dumb bomb. I'll need one other officer. Jim Keough ought to be game.' Bosarelli paused. 'So assuming he's in, obviously we'll want altitude fuses. The JPFs, the new programmable ones. And, ah –' Bosarelli stopped, not sure how much the general wanted to hear.

'Go on, Colonel.'

'I assume we've got the smart boys at JPL and AFRL' – the engineers at NASA's Jet Propulsion Laboratory in California and the Air Force Research Laboratory in Ohio – 'running sims to figure our trajectory after we flip the switches.'

'We'll have projections within an hour.'

425

'Then, yeah, if they sign off. We can do it. And you'll damn sure be able to see it a long way off.'

'So. Now you know. Are you still game? Take a minute, think it over.'

Bosarelli couldn't pretend he wasn't nervous. Any sane man would be. The risks were off the charts. But in Iraq and Afghanistan, soldiers and Marines took chances just as big every day. No way was he turning this down. He got the words out fast, before he could change his mind. 'I'd be honored. As long as you promise to come get us quick.'

'Understood. You have my word on that.' This time Hansell was the first to salute. 'Thank you, Colonel.'

Four hours later, and Bosarelli and Major Jim Keough, his flight engineer, were at 22,000 feet, flying slowly east-southeast over the Pacific, giving Keough time to arm the fuses that would turn the C-130 into a sixty-five-ton bomb.

What they were planning wasn't so different from what Mohamed Atta had done on September 11, Bosarelli thought. Though there was one very big difference.

Instead of its usual load of Humvees, Bosarelli's C-130 carried twenty GBU-29 bombs, upgraded versions of the old MK-82. Each of the bombs held its standard load, 150 pounds of high explosive. They were scattered among forty-gallon drums that held roughly equal amounts of gasoline, benzene, and polystyrene plastic – the basic ingredients of napalm.

Officially, the United States had destroyed all its napalm bombs by 2001. The increasing lethality of conventional bombs eliminated the need for napalm, a jellied gasoline that burned as hot as 5,000 degrees. The

426

stuff had been a public relations nightmare since Vietnam, when an Associated Press photographer had caught on camera the agony of a nine-year-old girl overtaken by a napalm bomb.

But though the premixed bombs were gone, the Air Force still stockpiled the raw ingredients necessary to make napalm. Despite napalm's terrible reputation, there was nothing magical about it. The polystyrene simply made it a lot stickier than ordinary gasoline, so it was hard to scrape off. Once it touched something – an enemy soldier's uniform, a little girl's face – it burned until it was gone. Even more important for this mission, it burned much more slowly than gasoline.

Keough stepped into the cockpit. 'Good to go.'

Bosarelli swung the C-130 to the right, tracing a long slow semicircle over the Pacific until they were heading west, back toward South Korea. It was just after 3:00 a.m. locally – 3:00 p.m. in Washington – and the civilian flights into Seoul had ended for the night. The only other planes within thirty miles were friendlies. Without being too obvious about it, the Air Force had put Bosarelli's plane inside a bubble of fighter jets. Four F-16s were running interference along the North Korean border, with four more to the west, over the Yellow Sea, though they were being careful to give plenty of room to the Chinese jets patrolling to their west.

Meanwhile, the South Korean navy had been asked to send every ship it had into the Yellow Sea. A flotilla of cutters and frigates had fanned out from Incheon, heading west toward the Shandong Peninsula. Every boat was carrying loudspeakers, and at least one American military observer. But the boats had been

427

absolutely prohibited from coming within eighty miles of the peninsula's tip. At the same time, every available rescue helicopter, both South Korean and American, had been prepped for takeoff, though none was in the air as yet.

Back in the C-130, Bosarelli permitted himself a brief look through the wispy clouds at the sleeping countries below. The difference was literally white and black. South Korea glowed prosperously; North Korea lay in darkness. Somehow the view reassured Bosarelli. He might never know the point of this mission. But he believed, had to believe, that he was fighting for the right side.

At Langley, Exley and Shafer were getting hourly updates. So far, the mission was on track – though so far, nothing had really happened. Exley still couldn't quite believe the president had agreed to her proposal.

After the confrontation with Duto, the meeting in the White House had been oddly anticlimactic. They'd helicoptered onto the White House lawn and been ushered straight into the Oval Office, where the president and the national security adviser were waiting. Exley had again recounted her conversation with Wells, and told them of her plan to rescue him.

Then Duto had made plain what he thought.

'Not to sugarcoat this, sir. There's almost no chance of success. If it weren't for what Ms. Exley and Mr. Wells did in New York, I wouldn't even have bothered you with it.'

The president murmured something to his national security adviser, who nodded. Exley didn't like either of them, but she had to admire their composure. She couldn't tell what they thought of the idea.

The president turned to Duto. 'If it doesn't work? What's our downside?'

'Well, sir, given the current tensions, the ultimate downside is that the Chinese could view it as an act of war.'

'That's possible,' Shafer said. 'But it won't be on Chinese territory.'

'Sir,' Duto said.

'It won't be on Chinese territory, *sir*,' Shafer said. 'We don't know what Wells has, sir. But I trust him. If he says it's important, it is.'

'Because tonight I'm going to have to stand up and tell the American people' – Exley winced privately as she heard the words; she hated when politicians talked about the American people – 'I'm going to tell the people what we're going to do about this attack. And you all know the pressure we're under to come back hard.'

'Sir. Nothing about this locks you into further action. All your options are still open. I agree it's a long shot, but if the odds are even one percent –'

At that, the president nodded. 'All right. Get me a finding' – the official written authorization needed for this kind of black operation. 'I'll sign it.'

'Sir –' Duto said.

'Director Duto. Your objections are noted. For the record. But let's try not to go to war if we can help it. We've all learned a few things since 2003.'

Now everything was in place, or so they'd been told. They didn't have much time. The sun would rise over the Yellow Sea in barely three hours, and Exley and Shafer knew that if Wells wasn't in friendly hands by then, he probably wouldn't make it. The Chinese didn't have great night-vision equipment – it was one area where they were still a couple of generations behind the United States – but by tomorrow morning, they would have covered the Yellow Sea with their navy. Any civilian boat still on the water would be searched from stem to stern, or simply blown to bits.

Left unsaid was the fact that the plan depended on Wells getting off the mainland in time. If he was still stuck in Beijing, then all they were doing was wasting a planeful of gasoline – and putting a couple of brave pilots at risk.

Shafer's phone rang. He picked up, listened for a moment. 'Good,' he said, and hung up. 'Still on track. Our boats are nearing the exclusion zone. They're projecting another hour or so.'

'I wish the sun would just stop,' Exley said. 'Let it stay afternoon here, night over there, until we find him.'

'Do you –' Shafer stopped, cleared his throat. Exley waited.

Finally she couldn't wait anymore. 'What?'

'You wish you were there, Jennifer? With him? I mean, knowing the odds right now . . .' Shafer trailed off. 'I didn't mean that the way it sounded.'

Exley smiled, a thin, sad smile. Let Shafer wonder. She didn't plan to satisfy his curiosity. But she knew the answer: Yes. In an instant.

THIRTY-SEVEN

The waves were low and flat and the boat skimmed over them without too much trouble. Still, Wells felt his ribs rattle every time the sea caught the boat sideways. He sat on the front bench gripping the wood so hard that his hands felt welded to it. There was probably a better way to hold on, but he didn't know it.

They'd run along the coast for more than an hour, maybe a half-mile from land, Cao handling the tiller. Wells didn't have much to do. They'd heard helicopters overhead and seen the lights of a boat in the distance, but so far no one had been within hailing distance. They were running the engine full-out, and despite its peeling paint and rusty engine, the boat seemed seaworthy. It wasn't leaking, anyway, which was the only way Wells could judge. His naval experience was limited to the occasional bath with Exley.

To the south, the coast grew rockier. During the day, the development was probably obvious. But tonight, under the weak light of a quarter-moon, the land looked surprisingly unspoiled. Wells supposed that even China had a few places that hadn't been overrun.

The lights of the coast grew sparser and sparser, then faded entirely.

'Tianjintou,' Cao said. He pointed south. In the distance, the land ended in a rocky spit, waves kicking up narrow white flumes around it. 'Tianjintou?' 'Means "end of the world." Farthest east place in Shandong. Only water now.'

'Let's hope we don't have to swim.'

A half-hour later, Wells's line looked more like a prophecy than a joke. Two helicopters shined their spotlights along the coast behind them. And in the distance to the west, Wells saw the lights of three boats. At least one was a destroyer or a frigate, something big. The boats were heading east, into the open water. Chasing Wells and Cao, even if they didn't know it yet.

Then, to the south. Two boats. Small and fast. Wells couldn't hear them, not yet, but he could see their spotlights. He tapped Cao's shoulder, pointed. Cao just shrugged.

They weren't going to make it, Wells thought. With the cloud cover helping them, they would last until sunrise. But once the sun came up, they wouldn't be able to hide. They'd be caught far before Incheon.

Wells focused on the rolling dark water ahead of them, stale and brackish. In college, he had been a decent swimmer. Not his favorite sport, but he'd liked it in the winter, as a way to rebuild his muscles after the pounding of football. But even if he hadn't had a chestful of broken ribs, swimming two hundred miles to Korea would have been a hopeless fantasy. Like the rest of this mission, Wells thought. But he didn't regret taking the chance. He knew the secret now, the reason for this war. If only he and Cao could survive, they could stop it.

Anyway, he'd been playing with house money ever

432

since Exley had saved him in New York. He didn't want to die, not like this, but some part of him had accepted the fact that he would. If not today, soon enough. He would push his luck until it snapped. He could excuse himself for risking this mission, because it meant so much. But what was his excuse for screaming down I-95 at 125 miles an hour? How could he ask Exley to trust him?

He remembered an old joke from an intro philosophy class in college: *I'm an optimist, not a fatalist. Anyway, if I were a fatalist, what could I do about it?* Or in the words of that great philosopher Bruce Springsteen, *Everything dies, baby, that's a fact.* Wells was drifting again. Tianjintou. End of the world. He sagged down and the curtains closed on him.

At 22,000 feet the night air was smooth, though the clouds were thickening quickly beneath the C-130. Bosarelli eased back on the engines, slowing the plane to 180 knots. Osan had asked him to slow down, give the flotilla on the water beneath him a chance to get a few miles farther west.

'Ninety-five hundred rpm,' Keough said. 'One hundred eighty knots, heading two-seventy.' Straight west.

'Taking us down to sixteen thousand.' Bosarelli extended the wing flaps to fifty percent to begin the descent. As he did, an alarm briefly sounded and the flat-panel display before Bosarelli flashed red before returning to its normal black background. The Chinese J-10s were now within a hundred nautical miles – five minutes on afterburner.

For now Bosarelli wasn't too worried about them. He was over international waters and flying slow and straight – hardly signs of hostile intent. He looked down through the cockpit's glazed windows, and through the clouds he saw the lights of a ship beneath him, heading west. A friendly, he hoped. 'Everything set back there?'

'Sure hope so,' Keough said.

Bosarelli leveled them out when they got to 16,000 feet, and for another fifteen minutes the plane cruised steadily. Bosarelli and Keough hardly spoke. After thousands of hours in these C-130s, Bosarelli could fly them, almost literally, in his sleep. And there wasn't much to say anyway. Beneath them the clouds became an unbroken white mass, glowing under the moon and the stars like a little girl's dream. Under other circumstances, Bosarelli would have considered the clouds beautiful. Tonight he would rather have seen the water. A crosswind kicked up, lightly rocking the plane.

'One hundred NM west of Incheon,' Keough said. 'Two minutes to centerline.' Incheon was about 210 nautical miles west of the tip of the Shandong Peninsula. In two minutes, the plane would be closer to China than Korea, a fact that would set off alarms for the Chinese jets.

'Two minutes to centerline, twelve minutes to Z point.' Bosarelli throttled back again, to 150 knots, not much above the plane's stall speed.

Their last F-16 escorts peeled off, one turning north, the other south, looping back toward Osan. Now Bosarelli and Keough had no cover at all, though for the moment the sky ahead was clear. For some reason – maybe the same reason that they were on this mission – the Chinese J-10s had swung back west, toward the Shandong coastline, and dropped to about 4,000 feet.

But Bosarelli knew the Chinese fighters could easily

434

reverse course again and tag the C-130, which wouldn't have a chance, especially with this payload. Herc pilots liked to joke that the plane's antimissile system consisted mainly of an alarm to let them know that their ride was about to explode.

Bosarelli hadn't been this scared since his first roller-coaster ride, at the Six Flags in Arlington, Texas. He was seven. His older brother had spent a whole week telling him how great it was. Bosarelli had pleaded to go until his dad finally took him. But when the coaster had clanked slowly up over the flat Texas plains, getting ready for that first drop, Bosarelli had wanted to puke his guts out. He hadn't, though. And once they'd finally gotten over the hill, he'd had a blast – though that probably wasn't the best choice of words right now.

'Five minutes,' Keough said.

'Five minutes.' Again Bosarelli extended the flaps. 'Taking us to twelve thousand.'

At 12,000 feet, Bosarelli again leveled out. 'Chutes and helmets on.'

Bosarelli reached for his parachute and pulled it onto his shoulders. Keough did the same. They'd packed their chutes themselves at Osan, watched over by a Special Forces major who had completed 250 jumps. Now Bosarelli had to stand over the control panel, since he couldn't fit in his seat anymore. The designers of the C-130 hadn't expected that the plane's pilots would be wearing parachutes.

'Check your transponder.' They were both carrying emergency beacons, black plastic boxes attached to their waists.

'Check.'

'One twenty-five NM from Incheon,' Bosarelli said. 'Twenty NM west of the centerline.'

'Two minutes,'Keough said. His screen flashed red and an alarm beeped loud and fast in his headset. Just in the last fifteen minutes the Chinese had a half-dozen more fighters in the air. Two of them had now decided to check out the C-130.

Now another alarm went off, higher-pitched and more urgent than the first. One of the Chinese fighters had painted the Herc with its targeting radar, a wordless warning that if it broke into Chinese airspace it could expect to be hit with an air-to-air missile.

'One minute to Z point,' Keough said.

'One minute.' Bosarelli flicked the Herc's transponder to 7700, the signal for an aircraft emergency.

'Ready, Jim?'

'Ready.'

The radar warning alarm sounded again, for a full fifteen seconds this time. 'I'll get it,' Bosarelli said. He flipped the Herc's radio to the Military Air Distress band, 243.0 MHz. The warning, in heavily accented English, was what he expected: 'You are approaching Chinese airspace. Turn back or face immediate action.' Pause. 'You are approaching Chinese airspace. Turn back . . .'

'I'll take that under advisement,' Bosarelli murmured. He flipped off the radio.

'Thirty seconds to Z.'

'Thirty seconds. Flaps fifty.' Again, Bosarelli extended the plane wing's flaps. 'Now, Jim. Go.'

Keough stepped out of the cockpit. Bosarelli heard a loud *whoosh* as he popped open the crew entry door a few feet behind the cockpit. The plane began to shake. Again the radar alarm rang in his headset.

Now. Bosarelli pushed the power levers past flight idle to turn off the engines. Then he reached over to Keough's station and flipped off the fuel pumps.

Just like that, the C-130 turned into a sixty-five-ton glider. Alarms began screaming, both in his headset and in the cabin, as the engines lost power. The propellers still had some leftover momentum, so the plane didn't dive immediately, but Bosarelli knew he didn't have long. Time to get out. He stepped out of the cockpit. Keough was standing in the open door of the plane, waiting. When he saw Bosarelli, he nodded and stepped out of the plane, hands at his sides. In an instant, he was gone.

Bosarelli flipped on his goggles and stepped to the open hatch. Instead of the normal noise of the turboprops, he heard only the klaxons in the cockpit and the rush of the wind. He looked into the night sky, and for a moment his nerve failed him. He thought of running back to the cockpit and trying to restart the engines. But he knew better. Down was the only way out.

And before he could change his mind again, he pushed himself forward and stepped into the cool night air.

With arms and legs extended, the human body falls at a maximum speed of about 125 miles an hour – a thousand feet every five seconds. Bosarelli was holding his arms tight to his chest and extending his legs straight down, hoping to top out closer to two hundred. He wanted to separate from the Herc quickly to lessen the chances he'd be caught in the plane's blast wave.

Then a wind gust ripped Bosarelli sideways, twisting his back and throwing his shoulders outward. He raised his arms for balance and instead began to spin, bouncing through the air like a pebble caught in a wave. Suddenly he was in no position to pull his chute. He breathed deeply and tried to remember his training as the seconds ticked by. And then he reached the cloud layer and the air around him turned white and suffocating.

Relax. He extended his arms and legs as far as he could and arched his back to create maximum drag. He emerged from the clouds. He was no longer spinning, but the sea was close beneath him, a couple of thousand feet at most, the water dark and featureless. He could already see two boats chugging west. They'd find him. If he could just get to his chute. Bosarelli reached across his body and grabbed the cord, praying it would open smoothly. He wasn't sure he had time to get to the reserve.

Then –

His body jerked upward as the chute snatched him from gravity's grasp. He looked up to see an open canopy, spreading above him like an angel's wings.

A mile ahead, the empty C-130 plunged toward the Yellow Sea, its nose tipped nearly straight down, klaxons sounding uselessly in its cockpit. Four thousand feet. The bombs and barrels of gasoline strained against the netting securing them to the floor of the cargo bay, but the thick nylon held.

Three thousand feet. The C-130 was approaching the speed of sound, six hundred miles an hour, a thousand feet a second. As the plane accelerated, the massive g-forces generated by the dive began to shear the left wing from the hull –

Two thousand feet –

The ghost plane began to break apart, but by then its

structural failure no longer mattered. The Herc had done its job.

One thousand feet –

Five hundred –

The altitude fuses on the GBU-29s blew, setting off 3,000 pounds of high explosive. In a fraction of a second, the cargo compartment turned into an inferno, and the jellied gasoline in the oil barrels blew up.

Bosarelli saw the explosion before he felt it. The night came alive with a second sun, a yellow-gold cloud that exploded up and out, forming a classic mushroom cloud, like a miniature nuclear bomb. So bright, so beautiful. A couple of seconds later the blast wave hit him, hotter than he'd expected, rich with gasoline and benzene vapor, but by then he was close enough to the water that he knew he'd survive.

He only hoped the bomb had done its job.

THIRTY-EIGHT

Wells thought he was dreaming when the sky turned white. Then he heard Cao shouting and knew he wasn't. He started counting, one one-thousand, two one-thousand, three one-thousand, waiting for the sound of the explosion to reach them, trying to calculate how far off they were. On his twelfth 'Mississippi,' the blast filled his ears. Maybe fifteen seconds – fifteen to twenty miles, give or take.

In the last hour the Chinese had put more and more helicopters in the air, and he'd had a bad moment a few minutes before when a helicopter swung by them, its searchlight missing them by no more than a few hundred yards. Now this explosion, which couldn't possibly be a coincidence. Had a Chinese jet or copter exploded? No, this fire was far too large. It looked to be slightly southeast of them, burning in the night like a beacon.

Like a beacon.

Cao was steering the boat north, away from the blast. Wells tapped his shoulder. He pointed to the white fireball, already losing its shape, melding into the clouds, but still burning brightly. 'Go toward it.'

'Toward?'
'It's for us.'

Unfortunately, the Chinese seemed to have come to the same conclusion. Helicopters were buzzing toward the crash site, their spotlights shining over the waves. Jets too. Wells couldn't see them, but he could hear the whine of their engines. As they made their way west, the sky lightened, the giant fire producing a muddy yellow glare. No way could a helicopter cause such a big explosion. Maybe a 747 had been shot down by accident. Or maybe it wasn't a plane at all. Maybe it was some kind of oil tanker.

The good news was that the Chinese didn't seem to have any boats in front of them. And the heat of the blast would make it hard for the helos to get too close.

Not that Wells wanted to get too close either. As they moved toward the site of the explosion, the air grew heavy with the stench of burning gasoline and something else too, some kind of plastic, though Wells couldn't figure out exactly what. Farther on, the air was alive with burning embers that looked like sparks from a backyard barbecue. The strange part was that they kept burning when they landed on the water. As Wells shielded his eyes and looked toward the fireball, he saw patches where the sea itself seemed to have caught fire.

'Napalm,' he said aloud.

Cao swung the boat hard left, north. Wells braced himself against the side of the hull and gritted his teeth as his ribs reminded him they were still broken.

Then a huge secondary explosion, maybe a fuel tank, lit the night. The boat rocked in the blast wave and Wells covered his mouth against the fumes. In the sudden glow Wells knew they were obscenely visible.

441

Even as the firelight faded, a jet swooped toward them, hard and low, its running lights blinking red, the wash from its engines kicking up waves and rattling the boat.

'Close,' Cao said.

The fighter screamed off.

Three minutes later it came back for another pass. This time red flares popped off the wings, not directly on top of them but close, too close, dimly visible through the thick black smoke that was flooding the air. Two helicopters – one from the north, the other from the south – began to converge on the flares, closing like scissor blades.

And then Wells saw the lights of a ship, barely visible through the smoke. Toward the east, not the west. Toward South Korea.

'Cao.' Wells pointed at the lights.

'Could be Chinese.' Nonetheless, Cao swung the tiller, turning the boat east, into the depths of the filthy black soot. The helicopters closed, but they couldn't fly blind. Wells closed his eyes and tried not to breathe. Then the wind shifted. The smoke lightened and the helicopters closed again. The spotlights swung at them, and one caught the hull of the boat in its glare. Behind them, a heavy machine gun opened up, kicking up flumes on the right side of the boat and then on the left. Cao swung the boat hard right, toward the center of the inferno, the heaviest smoke, and Wells ducked down, all he could do.

The spotlights swung over them and again the machine gun raked the waves around them, an angry hard rattle that blocked out every other sound, until Cao screamed, a short sharp cry. He collapsed, his body slumped over the outboard.

The engine lifted out of the water and the boat

442

slowed to a creep. A lucky break, since the helos were now ahead of the boat and the wind was shifting direction again, catching the helicopters in the smoke. Wells crawled across the boat to Cao. The general was dead, his neck and chest torn open. 'Damn you,' Wells said to nothing and no one, knowing that he'd be joining Cao soon enough, as soon as the wind turned enough to give the helos a clear shot. He pushed Cao aside and dropped the engine into the water. He couldn't see where he was headed and he supposed it no longer mattered.

Then, from above, the grinding sound of metal on metal. Followed almost instantly by an enormous explosion, two hundred yards ahead, and a second even closer. Wells bowed his head as sizzling bits of metal crashed around him.

They'd collided. The wind shift had left the helicopters blind. In their eagerness to get the kill, they'd come too close. They had crashed into each other in the dark and gone down, both of them. This filthy cloud had saved his life. Wells lifted the engine out of the water and looked around, trying to orient himself in the dark, thick air. Distant helicopters behind him. Somewhere overhead, a jet.

And ahead, a voice. Amplified. American.

Calling his name.

He closed his eyes and lowered the engine into the water and steered for it.

EPILOGUE

ONE MONTH LATER

'*Cerveza, por favor*. No, make it two. *Dos*.' Keith Robinson held up two fingers, watching them float in the bar's murky air as if they weren't connected to his body. Keith Edward Robinson, late of the Central Intelligence Agency. Now at liberty and seeking other employment.

'Anybody need an expert in counter-counter-intelligence?' he murmured to the empty room. A soccer match played on a television high in one corner, two local teams kicking the ball around halfheartedly.

The bartender, heavy and dark-skinned with a long white scar down his right arm, plunked down two Polars. They joined the half-dozen other bottles – all empty now – in front of Robinson. 'Ten dollars,' he said in English.

'Ten dollars? Last time it was two bolivars' – a bit less than one dollar.

'Ten dollars.'

'Okay, okay. I'm a lover, not a fighter.' More than anything, Robinson wanted to relieve the pressure on his bladder. Drain the main vein, as they said in the

445

trade. What trade? The room swam as he extracted a crumpled twenty-dollar bill from the dollars and pesos stuffed in his wallet. Robinson wished he hadn't brought so much money. The sight of the cash had undoubtedly provoked the sudden price increase. The bartender plucked the bill out of Robinson's wavering fingers and turned away.

'Don't forget my change.' Robinson tapped the bar. 'Hey, I'm serious.' But the little brown man was gone. 'I don't like your attitude,' he mumbled. 'Don't cry for me, Venezuela.'

He tipped the beer to his mouth and took a long swallow. Better. He was drunk, drunk as the drunkest skunk. At this point he didn't even know why he was drinking. More alcohol wouldn't make him any more intoxicated. Intoxicated. A good word, from the Latin for wasted. But he was awake, and these days, consciousness seemed to be reason enough.

He wasn't even having fun anymore. Getting this drunk was work. Every morning he felt as though someone had taken a hammer to his skull. Soon enough the feeling would be more than metaphorical, he knew. He'd pick the wrong bar, the wrong whore, the wrong hotel. Wind up with a knife between the ribs. Like he cared. He was a wanted man. Even down here he'd been in the papers. A few days ago, he'd felt the shock of seeing his picture on television. A celebrity at last. He'd rather die in a hotel room in Caracas than rot in solitary in the Supermax.

Of course, somewhere in his mind he had a plan. Not so much a plan as a single word: Cuba. The Cubans would love him. Anything to piss off the American government. Heck, even the Venezuelans might refuse to extradite him. They hated America too. But making his presence officially known would turn him into a bargaining chip, to be traded in the moment his hosts wanted better relations with Washington. For now he'd decided to lie low.

And with that thought, he lost his balance and toppled sideways, knocking his beers over in the process. A golden river of beer ran down the bar.

'*¡Puta!*' the bartender said. 'Out!'

'Show a little mercy, hombre,' Robinson said. 'I just wanted a cocktail.'

But the bartender said nothing more, only pointed at Robinson, then the door, like God evicting Adam from Eden. Robinson shuffled onto the narrow street. He checked his watch – 9:40. How could it be only 9:40? He had hours to drink away before he'd be exhausted enough to pass out.

A hand touched his shoulder. To his right stood a brown woman in a denim miniskirt. She had legs like a linebacker's. A fading shiner poked through the makeup under her tired eyes. The girl of his dreams.

'Date, mister?' Her breath stank of pisco, a grape brandy that burned like turpentine. Even Robinson avoided it.

'You had me at hello.' He took her arm and away they went.

The stylist brushed a hand over Pierre Kowalski's head. 'You see, Monsieur Kowalski,' he said. 'I promised the blemish was only temporary. *Et voilà*. Use the ointment and all will be well.'

Indeed, Kowalski's hair was growing back, sparsely and cautiously, like grass after a long winter. As a boy, he'd been handsome. He still thought of himself that way, despite his triple chin, C-cup breasts, and size 50

447

waist. But no one could convince him his skull looked good at the moment. When the duct tape had come off, it had taken most of his hair with it. He looked like a chemotherapy patient, only fatter and less sympathetic.

'Fine, J.P.,' Kowalski said. He waved a hand. The stylist flounced out of Kowalski's office, a square wood-paneled room decorated with famous weapons. Rommel's personal Luger. A saber that Napoleon had carried.

Alone now, Kowalski stared out at Lake Zurich and the mountains behind it. Peace at last.

But not for long. Steps outside his office. Fast young steps in high heels. Natalia, his current favorite. 'Not now,' he said, not bothering to turn around, as she walked in.

'Pierre –'

'Not now. If you need a check, tell Jacques.'

She walked off.

Kowalski had nearly gone into hiding after the Chinese announced that they'd arrested Li Ping for unspecified 'crimes against the state.' He'd guessed, correctly, that the United States had discovered how Li had used him to help the Taliban and passed the evidence to Li's enemies on the Standing Committee.

For two anxious days Kowalski wondered whether the United States would come after him too. Then he heard from friends at Langley and the Pentagon that he was safe. Both America and China wanted to pretend that their confrontation had never happened. China apologized for torpedoing the *Decatur* – Beijing called the attack a 'tragic and unnecessary accident' – and agreed to pay $1 billion in reparations to the United States and sailors on the ship. The Chinese also ended their nuclear aid to Iran, and – in a move that offered ironic proof of China's new military prowess – gave the American navy a fully functioning Typhoon torpedo to reverse-engineer. In turn, the United States was paying millions of dollars to the families of the students who had drowned when the *Decatur* rammed the fishing trawler. Neither side wanted to dredge up Kowalski's involvement and admit that Li had funded the Taliban. After all, Li had manipulated the United States as badly as his own government. More disclosure would only mean more embarrassment for both sides.

Kowalski knew he ought to let the matter rest there. He'd escaped retribution. As a rule, he prided himself on staying above the fray. His vainglorious clients fought the wars. He sold tools, nothing more. But this time reason failed him. Presidents and generals begged him for the weapons they needed. He was no one's servant, no one's whore. No one touched him without his permission.

Yet when he closed his eyes each night he felt thick silver tape across his face, hands squeezing his neck tight. Insolence. Beyond insolence. A stone in his shoe, irritating him with every step. He couldn't allow it. He needed to know the name of the man and the woman who'd done this to him.

Of course, they worked for the United States. The arrest of Li Ping proved it. But even his best sources, two former CIA agents who now ran a boutique lobbying firm in Reston, hadn't been able to crack the secrecy surrounding the China case. Every morning the question gnawed at Kowalski. Then Anatoly Tarasov, a former KGB agent who ran his security, found the answer.

'We want to know who attacked you in East

Hampton. Why are we asking in Washington? Let us ask the police in East Hampton.'

Kowalski knew Tarasov was right. They should have realized before. *Of course* the police had known all along. That was why they'd taken so long to get to the mansion that night. Why they hadn't pushed harder to keep him and his men inside the country.

'I don't mean ask them directly –'

'I understand, Anatoly.'

And after two days of drinking beers with off-duty East Hampton cops, a Long Island private detective found the answer that had eluded Kowalski's expensive informants in Washington.

The detective passed the name to the lawyer in Queens who'd hired him. From Queens it jumped over the East River to a white-shoe law firm in Manhattan, made a U-turn, and crossed the Atlantic, landing at the offices of an investigator in Geneva. Only then, properly washed, did John Wells's name arrive at Kowalski's Zurich château.

Kowalski heard soft steps approaching. He turned as Tarasov walked in. The Russian was under six feet, close to two hundred pounds, with a cruiserweight's broken nose and solid chest, which he showed off under tightly tailored white shirts. He had a nasty temper, especially when he was drunk. Kowalski had seen him beat a bouncer in a Moscow club nearly to death after the bouncer stared too long at his girlfriend. He was a very good head of security, and Kowalski paid him enough to assure his loyalty.

'John Wells,' Tarasov said. 'I'm very sorry I didn't get to meet him.' Tarasov had stayed in Zurich to mind the estate when Kowalski went to the Hamptons.

'As am I, Anatoly.'

'So what would you like me to do?'

Kowalski shook his head. He couldn't possibly go after John Wells. And yet. No. It was madness.

Tarasov stood next to Kowalski. Side by side they looked at the placid lake. Tarasov tilted his head forward and wrinkled his smashed-up nose like a pit bull that wanted off his leash. 'John Wells,' he said again.

'And the woman? Who was she?'

'I don't know yet. Another from the agency, no doubt. We'll find out.'

'Would you say I'm a man of my word, Anatoly?'

'Of course,' Tarasov said.

Kowalski opened the drawer desk where he kept his personal pistol, a Glock 19. Simple, effective, not too expensive, nothing like the fancy toys he sold the Africans. He hefted the gun, pointed it out over the lake, then slipped it away.

'I told the man who attacked me that I would make him pay. No matter who he was. And I think . . . I must keep my promise.'

At the sound of footsteps in the corridor, Li Ping dragged himself off his cot and stood before the heavy steel door that covered his cell. A panel slid open and a plastic tray popped into Li's hands.

'Thank you.'

As an answer the little slot clanged shut. Li looked at his lunch. A cup of lukewarm tea, an overripe orange, a bowl of rice soup. And the pills, of course.

Li was in isolation in a concrete cell in a maximum-security military prison just outside Beijing. The jailers had laughed when he'd asked to see his wife. But for the last few days, they'd given him copies of *China Daily,* the official Party paper, as well as a couple of the semi-independent Beijing dailies.

Showing him the papers wasn't an act of charity. Zhang and the Standing Committee wanted him to know his position was hopeless. They had united to portray him as a rogue general who had brought China to the brink of war for his own benefit. During the last days of the crisis Li had illegally ordered the attack on the *Decatur,* they said. They had even hinted that Li might have acted on behalf of Russia to weaken China. Of course, they were lying. They'd approved the *Decatur* attack, and they knew he wasn't working for Russia or anyone else.

But no matter. Zhang had won. Li would never forget the moment when Zhang showed the Standing Committee the papers that proved Li had used army money to help the Taliban. Zhang's triumphant look. The anger of the committee members, the shock on the faces of men who hated being surprised more than anything. Soon enough they found their voices. They ranted and raved, accusing him of treason, telling him he'd nearly destroyed all China's progress. Zhang merely smiled as they denounced him. Li didn't bother to deny what he'd done. He'd been trying to save China. If these cowards wanted to punish him, so be it.

Zang had come to his cell a few days earlier, just after the newspapers started to arrive. With Li's lunch that day were three oversized pills, two white and the third blue. They were unmarked, but Li understood their purpose. He left them untouched, finished his lunch, and handed back the tray.

A few minutes later his cell door opened. Zhang stepped inside. 'General.'

'Minister. Did you come for the pills? You're welcome to them.'

'You've always been generous.'

'And you've always been a thief.'

'If you weren't such a fool you'd be dangerous, Li. Don't you see you almost caused a war? Bones turned to ashes for your fame.'

'The Americans would have backed off. Now, thanks to you, they've humiliated the Chinese nation.'

'Do you really think so? Has anything changed? Every day they buy our steel and televisions and computers. Every day they send us more money. Every day our economy grows faster than theirs.'

'And every day you steal more from the people. Every day peasants die from hunger because of your crimes. Don't judge a hero by victory or defeat.'

'Hero?' Zhang laughed. 'You're a deluded old ox we should have ground up years ago. Why do you think the people didn't riot when we announced your arrest? Why do you think they went home from Tiananmen quietly when we told them to?'

'Because they were afraid.'

'Because they're satisfied with their lives. With the economy.'

'The economy is shrinking.'

Zhang shook his head. 'Growth is rising again, Li. The people are smarter than you. They respect the Party. They know that soon enough China will be even more powerful than America. We'll sell them cars, airplanes, everything. And then we'll rule. There was no need for what you did.'

'One day the people will storm the gates of Zhongnanhai and you'll see.'

Zhang smiled, the tolerant smile of a man who'd heard a crazy uncle's crazy arguments and wasn't listening anymore. 'General. The world won't end if a few migrants go hungry. Not everyone can be rich. Now. If you don't want to take the pills, don't. The choice is yours. But don't forget your family. For now, the Party doesn't believe Jiafeng' – Li's wife – 'knew of your treasonous acts. But if this situation persists, we may reach another conclusion.'

Zhang stepped out of the cell, into the concrete corridor. Li was silent. He wouldn't plead for his life. He wouldn't give Zhang the satisfaction. He should have known these cowardly bastards would use his family against him.

'Be sure to take the blue pill first, General.' Zhang walked away as the cell door slammed shut.

Zhang hadn't been back since. But today's *China Daily* proved that he hadn't been bluffing. A front-page story explained that the Standing Committee had opened a 'wider corruption investigation' into Li's affairs. They wanted him gone, without a messy public trial, and they would destroy his family if he resisted.

Li finished his tepid tea, drank the last of his watery soup. He'd been so close to success. Even now he was sure that the Americans would have backed off, pulled their ships out of the East China Sea. He would have ruled China.

How could Cao have betrayed him? Bitterness upon bitterness.

Li wanted to talk to his wife and sons again, explain what he'd done. He wanted to see Tiananmen one last time, go for one more run along the lakes of Zhongnanhai. But he'd lost the chance to choose his fate. None of his wishes would come true. Only the pills were true. He gathered them off the tray. They were almost weightless. Hard to believe they could destroy the body that he had spent so many years building, this body that had survived war unscathed.

The blue pill first. Li popped it into his mouth and took it down in one clean swallow. He closed his eyes and counted to thirty, seeing Mao in his tomb in Tiananmen. When he opened his eyes again, the concrete walls of the cell seemed to be melting. Now, before his brain melted too. He slipped the other two pills into his mouth and choked them down. And then he could do nothing except wait.

The black CB1000 rolled up Memorial Drive, its engine burbling, and stopped beside three Harleys festooned with POW/MIA stickers. Two riders hopped off. Wells and Exley. They picked up a map at the visitors' center and made their way to Section 60, among the newest parts of Arlington National Cemetery.

Inside the gates the green, rolling hills glowed in the sunlight with an unearthly beauty. Clean white headstones rose from the earth like dragon's teeth. Oak trees offered pockets of shade. The sweet smell of fresh-cut grass filled the air. A city of the dead, 300,000 graves in all. The ugliness of war turned splendid, as politicians – and civilians in general – preferred, Wells thought.

Every day, fifteen to thirty funerals were held at Arlington, mostly veterans of World War II, Korea, and Vietnam, but some soldiers killed in action in Iraq as well. Wells and Exley walked over a rise and came on mourners waiting for a ceremony to begin. Six people sat under a canopy, five women and one man, all in their eighties, the man painfully thin, his forearms narrow as chewed-up corncobs. World War II, Wells assumed.

Over a rise, they came upon another tent. This time the crowd overflowed the canopy. In the front row, two children clung to a woman in a long black dress. The woman stared at the coffin before her, her body rigid with grief. Iraq? Afghanistan? How many children would come to Arlington this year? Wells wondered. And the next? And the next? And how would history judge the leaders who'd sent their parents to die?

Finally they found the plot. Greg Hackett. The young sergeant who'd bled to death in Afghanistan. Gregory Adam Hackett. He had died honestly, doing his duty. More than most men could say.

More than Pierre Kowalski could say, Wells thought. As his ribs had knitted together these last four weeks, he'd found himself thinking about the arms dealer. Part of him hoped that one day he'd have a chance to see Kowalski again, end the man's dirty business once and for all. Though there'd just be another Kowalski, and another, as long as men wanted land or money or power.

Forever.

Anyway, he hadn't come here to think about Kowalski. He wanted to remember Hackett. Instead his mind slid sideways, to the Talib whose brains he'd blasted on the night that Hackett died. He could see, actually see, the man's skull shattering, as if he were in Afghanistan instead of Virginia, as if he were living the night over again. He closed his eyes and sagged down.

He had destroyed that Talib as easily as the average person swatted a fly. He'd killed so much that killing had become automatic, a reflex. Only after the action ended could he realize the horror of what he'd done. Only now.

Wells wished he could cry. But he never cried. Instead he put his head to the soft turf and closed his eyes and watched a movie of the men he'd killed playing on the screen in his mind. Forgive us, for we know not what we do.

'John.' He felt Exley's thin arms around him. He lifted his head and forced his eyes open.

'I don't know if I can do it anymore.'

'You don't have to, John. You can always quit.'

But even before Exley's words rose out of the cemetery and floated south over the Pentagon and into the past, even before they joined everything that had ever happened and everyone who'd ever lived in the place that never was –

Wells knew she was wrong.

He would never quit.

ACKNOWLEDGMENTS

While in Boston on book tour for *The Faithful Spy,* the predecessor to this novel, I was fortunate enough to meet the lovely and talented Dr. Jacqueline Basha, a wonderful woman and a wonderful reader. Without Jackie, John Wells – and his creator – would be a lot more tortured.

Thanks also to:

David, my brother, who was present at the creation.

Neil Nyren, whose suggestions are always on point.

Heather Schroder, who is never afraid to fight for her writers.

Deirdre Silver, a careful and thoughtful reader.

Doug Ollivant, who knows the difference between an LZ and a DZ.

Mark Tavani and Jon Karp, who knew John Wells when he had a different name.

Larry Ingrassia and Tim Race, my editors at the *New York Times,* who gave me more days off than I deserved.

And last but certainly not least, to all the readers who e-mailed me (alexberenson@gmail.com) to say how much they liked (or in a few cases didn't) *The Faithful Spy.* Writing a book isn't easy, but knowing that people are actually reading it – and care enough to respond – makes the work worthwhile.